Unable to sit still without reading, **Bella Frances** first found romantic fiction at the age of twelve, in between the deadly dull knitting patterns and recipes in the pages of her grandmother's magazines. An obsession was born! But it wasn't until one long, hot summer, after completing her first degree in English Literature, that she fell upon the legends that are Mills & Boon books. She has occasionally lifted her head out of them since to do a range of jobs, including barmaid, financial adviser and teacher, as well as to practise—but never perfect— the art of motherhood to two now almost grown-up cherubs. Bella lives a very energetic life in the UK, but tries desperately to travel for pleasure at least once a month—strictly in the interests of research! Catch up with her on her website at www.bellafrancesauthor.com.

Growing up near the beach, **Annie West** spent lots of time observing tall, burnished lifeguards—early research! Now she spends her days fantasising about gorgeous men and their love lives. Annie has been a reader all her life. She also loves travel, long walks, good company and great food. You can contact her at annie@annie-west.com or via PO Box 1041, Warners Bay, NSW 2282, Australia.

REDEEMED BY HER INNOCENCE

BELLA FRANCES

SHEIKH'S ROYAL BABY REVELATION

ANNIE WEST

MILLS & BOON

First Published in Great Britain 2019
by Mills & Boon, an imprint of HarperCollins*Publishers*
1 London Bridge Street, London, SE1 9GF

Redeemed by Her Innocence © 2019 by Bella Frances

Sheikh's Royal Baby Revelation © 2019 by Annie West

ISBN: 978-0-263-27358-8

Printed and bound in Spain
by CPI, Barcelona

REDEEMED BY
HER INNOCENCE

BELLA FRANCES

For Graham Frize,
redeeming innocence wherever he goes.
Beautiful, sinful and wonderful friend.

Acknowledgements

With grateful thanks to Joyce Young,
By Storm, Glasgow and London, for her insights
into the world of wedding dress design.

CHAPTER ONE

Nikos Karellis walked straight into the bridal suite of Maybury Hall, Wedding Venue of the Year, and slung his suit carrier down on the four-poster bed. *So this is romance*, he thought, frowning at the frills and flowers and buckets of girly fizz. He lifted a bottle, checked the vintage and slipped it back into the watery ice. He was a long way off celebrating yet. He'd travelled through eight time zones and three continents, and he needed something a bit harder to take the edge off.

Finally he saw what he wanted, tucked underneath a gilt mirror featuring chuckling cherubs—a tray with decanter, glasses and water jug. Perfect. He poured a generous measure, then he added a little more, skipped the water, and sank it, the burn and peaty fumes soothing as they slid down his throat.

Cheers, Martin, he thought, tipping his glass at the chandelier. At least his former brother-in-law's taste in whisky was better than his taste in décor.

The bridal suite.

Of all the rooms in his flagship luxury hotel, Martin had chosen to put him up here. Maybe it was his idea of a joke, but it wasn't a very funny one. Pretty much nothing about being married to Maria made him laugh any more.

Nikos reached for the decanter, pausing in the act of pouring a second. The temptation was strong, but clear-headed was the only way to be tonight, because tonight was the beginning of the end, the face-to-face to get it all out in the open. Whatever it was that Martin thought had been hidden away in Maria's legacy, this was the night when they'd sort it out, because it was draining—and not just financially.

Despite what Martin's lawyers and the Inland Revenue seemed to think, there were no hidden assets, no secret stash of cash, no offshore investments. She had drunk them all, or snorted them all. And that was that. It would be a hard story to tell her doting brother, but Nikos was damned sure he wasn't going to leave anything out, because he'd had enough.

The tit-for-tat legal wrangling had gone on for too long so he'd done it the old-fashioned way; lifted the phone, and asked for a meeting. When Martin suggested this black-tie event in one of his chain of luxury hotels, Nikos didn't hesitate. It was that or wait another six weeks until they'd even be on the same continent.

He could barely wait six more minutes now that he finally had the end in sight. Five years since Maria's death—but it was only his wedding ring he'd tossed into the cool, blue Aegean; the pain and the memories had been much harder to shift.

Too late to stop himself, he touched his ring finger. Empty space, smooth skin. Even though House, his high-end chain of department stores, was now in the *Forbes 100*, with turnover almost hitting the four billion mark, that feeling of bare skin felt better than anything. It was the feeling of freedom. More than that, it was the cast-iron knowledge that he was on his own now. On his own, forging his path, no wife hanging off his arm, or around his neck, no damage to clean up after—just these final few crumbs and then he really was home free.

He filled up a fresh glass with water and walked to the window. The estate was impressive, immense, expanding off into horizons of oak trees and lawns, and willow-draped lakes. He could just see the roof of the lodge house he'd passed and the huge iron gates at the end of the road, where a car had just pulled up. Something about it made him strain forward to see better...

But just then a knock sounded on the door, and he turned.

'I heard you'd arrived.'

Martin Lopez stood in the door and for a second they looked at each other. The same dark hair, dark eyes, sallow skin and high cheekbones as Maria—a look that he'd once found ravishing, irresistible, forging a love so strong he'd moved from delinquent eighteen-year-old biker to husband, in three years.

Looking back, which he had done all too often in the ten years they'd been together, it had been a predictable car crash of wrong place, wrong time. The minute he'd rescued her from the Bentley she'd wrapped around a lamp post on the side of the Sydney highway, they'd been inseparable—he was tennis coach, swimming coach, personal trainer, anything she could do to keep him in her life, and, after where he'd been, it had felt like arriving at the Promised Land.

Unfortunately some promises were very hard for Maria to keep.

'Martin. Good to see you.'

He walked towards him, stretching out a hand, reading in the light press of Martin's palm and the shifting of his gaze that he was on edge.

'Nikos. I'm glad you came. It's been a long time.'

'Too long,' said Nikos, holding the handshake a second longer, reassuring him that they were friends, no matter what had gone before.

'Yes, and I wanted to get in touch, but it's not been easy since Maria died.'

'I guess not. Our lives have taken different directions.'

'But we'll always have her in common.'

'I can't deny that,' said Nikos, staring hard at Martin, wondering what was really going on in his mind. He had done everything for the Lopez family; they were all set up for life. He had nothing left to give.

But something was eating the other man up. Martin dropped his gaze and turned back to the door.

'Shall I show you around, before the guests start to arrive?' he said, over his shoulder.

'Absolutely,' Nikos said, strolling out to the grand hallway, where the faces of various English rose aristocrats in grand gilt frames hung around the walls, no doubt wondering what the hell had happened to the old house now that the Lopez Hotel Group had transformed it.

'Yes, it's great to see you,' Martin said, stepping alongside him now like a best buddy. 'And I'm really grateful that you've agreed to present an award. We sold an extra fifty seats when it was announced yesterday.'

Nikos shrugged. 'It's no problem. I was on the way back from Sydney when I got the call.'

'Visiting your mother? How is she?'

They were at the top of a wide sweep of carpeted stairs, no doubt a prime photo opportunity for the hundreds of brides who used Maybury Hall.

'Ah, she's OK. Thanks for asking. She doesn't know

me any more but she seems quite happy, and they look after her well.'

His monthly visits to Sydney were the one fixed item in his calendar. He knew they wouldn't last for ever...

'So how's business?' he asked, keen to change the subject.

They walked down the stairs, as staff carrying huge displays of flowers and cakes criss-crossed over the black-and-white floor beneath them.

'I'm getting out soon,' said Martin, with a mirthless laugh. 'This is the last sponsorship I'm doing. I want to end on a high. The hotels are doing well, but the wedding industry's being choked to death by overseas competition.'

'China?'

Martin nodded. 'It's hitting the dress side worst of all. With the volume they can produce overseas, there's just no profit margin for the little guy. Unless it's high-end, bespoke, but even then it's tough.'

'People will always want to get married,' said Nikos. People other than himself.

'Yes, but it's not what it was. Even the ones that have been on the go for years are feeling it. Another one of them is just about to hit the buffers, and it's one of my old pals who once owned it. It's his daughter's now.'

They rounded the corner of the staircase and fell into step walking on through the lobby. All around, the paraphernalia of an industry built on hormones and fiction—love and marriage. A sham that left Nikos stone cold.

'It's a pity, because she is a lovely girl—at least she was last time I saw her. But she's out of her depth.'

'As in overinvested, or out of her depth because she doesn't have the skill?'

'A bit of both probably. Which makes it awkward. She'll be here tonight and I've got a feeling she's going to make a pitch. And I don't have the heart to tell her she's the problem.'

'Yes, that's a tough one,' said Nikos, who had his own tough message to deliver to Martin, as soon as they got the chance to talk in private.

They turned the corner of the hall and stood on the threshold. Tables, heavy in white linen, spread off in all directions; the band at the side of the stage was tuning up a series of mismatched sounds.

Soon the movers and shakers of the wedding world would all be here to congratulate themselves on their achievements in this phony industry, and he, the man least likely to marry ever again, would be presenting one of them with a cube of etched Perspex that would wind up displayed on a shelf somewhere. The irony wasn't lost on him.

Suddenly screens at either side of the stage flickered to life with images of Titian-haired brides in long flowing dresses running through fields of corn. That was it—he'd had enough.

'So what's the schedule?' he asked, folding his arms and facing Martin. 'Because we've got our own difficult conversation to have. And I want to make sure we've got enough time.'

'As soon as this is over. I promise you.'

'I'll wait until ten. We talk from then until this thing is finished. And then I'm leaving, Martin. And I won't be back.'

A shadow fell across Martin's face. His eyes darted furtively down and back up.

'I hear you,' he said, stepping closer. 'But it's not just me who's trying to get to the bottom of this. There are some people Maria was involved with that are very unhappy, Nikos. People that you know well.'

As if he'd felt a blow, Nikos flinched. Hair stood up on the back of his neck. Someone did a microphone check and a short burst of static screeched through the space.

'People that you know well.'

He'd thought this was all dead. Buried, with his wife. But it wasn't. It was still there, always there. Shadows that didn't fade in the warm afternoon sunshine or fresh summer mornings. Dreadful, dark shadows that never went away, no matter where he went or what he did.

'OK, Martin,' he said, dredging up his words, like hauling on armour. He stood tall, he breathed deep, he squared his shoulders. There was no option; there was never any option. But his mother was safe, so nothing else mattered.

He looked at the other man. It wasn't his fault. There was no one to blame but himself.

'We'll talk later,' he said. 'We'll get this sorted. They won't bother you.'

He patted Martin's shoulder as he passed, and made his way through the tables, scattered like giant confetti on the ground.

Two miles east of Maybury Hall, in the pretty market town of Lower Linton, Jacquelyn Jones, owner of Ariana Bridal, was also getting ready to attend the Wedding Awards, and with almost the same mix of dread and trepidation.

As designer-in-chief of the bridalwear boutique that had occupied the same spot on the main street for the past fifty years, she *could* have been going to collect an award. Her father had managed to do just that, scooping five top awards in the past two decades, but that was before she had taken over from him, and before the business had stopped turning such healthy profits.

No, she was going there tonight to get money. Or she was going to die trying. Because if she didn't, the whole thing was going to fall apart, one stitch at a time.

But first she had to get rid of Barbara, who had just slipped in through the courtyard garden as Jacquelyn had been closing up for the evening. With five husbands in the bag, she was the boutique's best, but also nosiest, customer. No doubt she had scented blood, or at least the high anxiety that Jacquelyn was trying to conquer as she arranged a vase of white arum lilies.

'So you're definitely going to the Wedding Awards at Maybury Hall tonight? Even though that snake-in-the-grass Tim Brinley will be there? Good for you! You go and show them all. It's disgraceful. He should be struck off, not getting a blooming award!'

'You can't be struck off for being unfaithful, Barbara,' said Jacquelyn, though goodness knew she would have done a lot worse to her ex-fiancé. 'And he deserves the award. He's a good photographer.'

'Tsk. You say that. But he owes everything to you and your connections. And it's not going to be easy on you though, no matter how hard you try to put on a brave face. After what he did! The thought of everyone whispering behind your back...'

'No one will be giving me a second's thought. Nikos Karellis is going to be there so they'll all be star-struck and googly-eyed over him.'

'What? Nikos Karellis, owner of all those House department stores? The billionaire Greek god who is now conveniently unattached?'

'I believe he's Greek Australian, actually, though I

really don't see the big attraction. He's not my cup of tea at all.'

'Oh, Jacquelyn,' said Barbara. 'You mustn't judge all men badly. Tim was cruel but there are plenty more fish in the sea and it's time you started looking.'

'This is an awards dinner, Barbara, not a singles bar.' She twisted a lily to the side, stood back to examine it.

'But Nikos Karellis—you might never get another chance! Think of the doors he could open for you! And you could do with some cheering up. You've not been yourself at all since Tim jilted you. It's affecting the business. Everything's got a bit shabby, if you don't mind me saying.'

Jacquelyn kept her face fixed on the lilies even though she couldn't see them, her eyes crushed closed in frustration and anger.

Barbara was right. She was completely right. And that it was so obvious was even worse. There was barely enough money to pay the machinists' wages let alone invest in a refresh of the boutique. And all avenues to borrow money had closed. The bank wanted the previous loan repaid and capturing the interest of a financier had seemed impossible.

She knew they cast her as a silly girl playing at shops, not as a serious businesswoman. She was caught in a vicious circle of stiff competition, poor profits and higher costs, and she couldn't seem to break free.

'I don't know what your parents were thinking disappearing off to the south of Spain, leaving you in charge here, after what happened. No wonder the place has run into difficulties.'

'Mum's rheumatics are what's taken them to Spain,' said Jacquelyn, 'and the last thing they need is worrying that they need to come back here. If you'll excuse me a moment...'

She stood up, scooped up the debris from the flowers and tossed it into the bin, then kept walking through into her studio, standing in the vale of light that flooded the space, desperate for a moment of calm.

But there was no escape, because right in front of her, spread out on her work desk, were the sketches she'd been poring over for the past two days. She swept them up, bundled them into a pile and bashed them off the top of the desk. They were rubbish. She knew they were, but she had lost all feel for designing fairy-tale dresses. She had lost her feel for fairy tales too. She needed practical things—like money—to hire someone who did.

'Oh, don't worry on that account,' called Barbara from the kitchen. 'I never mention a word about Ariana when I call. We keep it strictly social now. So much goes on in Lower Linton for such a tiny little town.'

And is regurgitated every Sunday on calls to Mum, thought Jacquelyn. Nothing went unnoticed or unreported. Nothing.

She looked up and saw Barbara position herself at the doorway.

'Barbara, it was lovely of you to drop by, but don't let me keep you. I'm sure you've got loads to do tonight.'

'Yes, I am rather busy,' said Barbara, narrowing her critical eyes as she wandered round the studio, like a detective in some third-rate TV show.

Jacquelyn wondered what clues she had left out and too late saw the piles of dirty teacups and balled-up handkerchiefs. Clues that might even find their way muttered into the hors-d'oeuvres of wherever Barbara dined tonight.

'Well, I hope you show that Tim Brinley what he's missing.'

Jacquelyn did her best to smile and tidied the scattered sketches into a pile. The inky sharp-limbed figure on top seemed to flinch as she was set down and Jacquelyn cursed the stress that was flowing through her, stress that was making it harder and harder to get these sketches right. And she had to get them right. She absolutely had to.

'I bet Nikos Karellis would happily help out. He's definitely got an eye for the ladies. If all else fails…' Barbara's voice trailed off as she raised a pencilled eyebrow and stared directly at Jacquelyn's figure.

'If "all else fails" what, Barbara? What are you trying to suggest? That I throw myself at a total stranger? Do you really think that's my style?'

Behind her, the row of mannequins looked on like a jury of headless Greek goddesses. She'd been baited and caught, exposing herself as easily as if she'd taken out an ad in the front page of the *Lower Linton Chronicle*.

'Darling, if it was your style you wouldn't be in this mess,' said Barbara as she lifted her clutch and re-formed her perfectly engineered face. 'And if I were you I'd start getting ready now. You're looking a bit puffy around the eyes. I'll see myself out.'

And she did, sailing past in a haze of sickly sweet scent, on through the studio to the hallway, heels clicking on the stone steps and then out into the courtyard where they faded and were finally silenced by the dull thud of the wooden door.

Jacquelyn stood tight and tense until she finally heard the car roar off, then she let out a huge sigh and felt her eyes burn—again.

'Stop it, stop it. Pull yourself together!' she hissed through the hot self-pitying tears that had formed.

You knew this moment would come. Five years in charge and you let it all trickle through your fingers. Well, now it's happened. And you've got one chance left to stop this before it's too late.

She'd taken the once thriving family business and run it into the ground and had no one but herself to blame. She'd taken her eye off the ball, worried herself sick about things that turned out not to have been worth worrying about at all. Like a man. Like that stupid, stupid break-up, with that stupid, weak-willed man.

She sat down again, propped her elbows on the table and bowed her head.

Before her, the blank-faced sketches said nothing. She spread them out and stared at them. Any fool could see that there was something missing, something wrong. But she just didn't seem to know how to get them right. She'd whittled it down from twenty to twelve to this final bundle of six.

When she'd showed them to Victor, the pattern cutter, he'd been gracious and complimentary, but she'd known he'd been faking it. She'd seen the confusion in his eyes. Another dud collection. Again?

Around the studio, light was sinking into a pale mauve sunset. Through the window she could see traffic on the main road out of town that led to London. Just two miles east sat Maybury Hall, where the Wedding Awards were being held tonight.

She was running out of time. She had to get going. Everyone else could gush over Nikos Karellis, but it was Dad's friend Martin Lopez and his millions that she needed to see. She was going to approach him tonight and ask him to finance the business. She'd offer five per cent. Twenty per cent. Whatever it took.

Outside she heard a car prowl along the lane. Surely Barbara wasn't back again…?

She jumped up and ran out through the studio and down the stairs, then burst out into the courtyard. She slid the bolt across the wooden door and leaned back against it, breathing a deep sigh. But there was no knock, no screeching voice, just the quiet sounds and sights of a summer evening: water bubbling over the giggling cherubs in the fountain and the sun-dappled flower beds, sleepy and still.

Peace. If only she could stand still and enjoy it—but that was half her problem. Instead of busying herself out in the world, she had shut herself away, hiding in the familiar silks and satins, and beads and crystals that hung in the boutique.

She looked through the French doors of the shop.

Fairy tales were made real in there. Women were made into princesses. Dreams came true.

Once upon a time she'd believed that. She absolutely had. Happy ever after was the only ever after there was.

How wrong she'd been. Happy ever after didn't exist.

CHAPTER TWO

JACQUELYN STRETCHED HER SMILE and lifted a glass of champagne. She wouldn't drink it but it was the perfect accessory, and gave her something to do with her hands.

She might be feeling as if she were dying but she knew how to put on a show. Her dress was a fairy tale. How could it possibly be anything else? Her blonde hair was tousled, in a knot held up with beads of fine crystals, silken and soft and sparkling.

Her gown was cerulean-blue satin. The chiffon bodice crossed over her chest and the skirt billowed out in the signature 'Jones' cut that flattered and flowed to the floor. Her long neck and elegant shoulders were shown to perfection with a single pearl droplet on a fine chain. Her make-up was just the perfect blend of colours and tones to hide and highlight, and her lips were glossily, naturally, plump and soft.

All in all she was a walking miracle, she thought to herself. It was amazing what a few tricks of the trade could do. But if she, with her know-how and connections, couldn't make a silk purse out of a sow's ear tonight, who could?

She pulled her lips into a superhappy smile as a camera flashed a photo of the table, and all the while she surreptitiously scanned the crowd. She would not crack an inch in front of anyone, in case it got back to Mum and Dad. She was on show, wearing the most flattering cut and colour of dress.

'The best model you have is yourself,' as Dad always said.

'Don't you get too big for your boots,' said Mum.

Jacquelyn tried to straighten her shoulders, but they didn't need straightening. She twisted her head a tiny bit to the left, to see if Martin was here yet, but not so much as to be too obvious. Not that it mattered. They'd all think she was showing off to Tim Brinley or, worse, pitching for Nikos Karellis. As if.

She had been flippant, blasé, when Dad had phoned her about the awards.

Of course she'd be fine with Tim being there. Life moved on. And she would have a chat with Nikos Karellis if she got the chance, and, yes, she remembered his friend Martin Lopez. She promised she'd make a point of saying hello to him. She could give him a cast-iron guarantee on that front.

She felt the smile slip from her face and tension creep across her brow, and checked herself, taking a tiny sip of champagne and putting the glass down as if she were having the most marvellous evening, chatting and gossiping with the people at her table.

'I hear Nikos Karellis has arrived.'

'Made quite a splash already. In the bridal suite but with no bride, of course.'

'Ha-ha. I wonder who'll be the second Mrs Karellis.'

'I only just found out he was married to Maria Lopez. She was old enough to be his mother!'

'I don't think he's looking for a mother now!'

'I'd never heard of her before…'

'Where have you been? I thought everyone knew that story!'

Jacquelyn knew. She'd known the story for years, since the morning at breakfast her father had put the newspaper down with a, 'Good grief, you'll never guess who's died,' and then proceeded to tell them the story of his friend Martin Lopez and his beautiful sister, who'd married a man fifteen years younger. Photographs of him carrying her coffin, grief painted onto such a handsome face, had filled the nation's need for gossip for a day or so.

'Poor man,' her mother sighed, lifting the paper from her father's hands.

'Poor man, nothing. Rich man. He's worth a fortune now,' said her father.

'He's just lost his wife,' her mother chided. 'Money can't take away that pain, no matter what you say. He must have really loved her. Just look at him.'

Jacquelyn sipped her tea. She knew what love was. Every fibre of her being pulsed with it for Tim, her childhood sweetheart. Love was going to school with him, listening to music. He was her best friend, boyfriend and soon-to-be husband.

Love was them agreeing to save themselves for their wedding night, no matter how tempting, because there was nothing more important than that. Their secret pact, their complicit agreement. Their bond of trust.

There was no other option. Because that was what good girls did. Although it was never shown in public, Nonna Ariana was sniffy about the girls who wore white when they should be wearing ivory.

'If this is the most important day of their life, then they should act like it. It isn't just a fancy dress, it's

real. They should know better, bringing shame on their families!'

So Jacquelyn was steadfast. She was determined. And Tim was too, because it was all going to be worth it. It was all leading to a rosy future. It was the rest of their lives. What did a few more months matter?

So no, Nikos Karellis had meant nothing to her then.

And unlike every other woman here, he meant nothing to her now. She wouldn't waste a moment talking to someone whose interest in women was superficial.

It was Martin Lopez she needed to find, and fast. She couldn't bear it if this whole night passed without a chance to give him her pitch.

'It's him. Here he is.'

She started, like a deer at the burst of a gun, but it was just the hotshot Australian that had entered.

'Wow, isn't he amazing?'

Despite herself, her head swivelled to the front of the stage to see.

Well, physically—there was no doubt about that. Was it the height of him, the breadth of his shoulders, or the gleaming white shirt and midnight-blue tux? Was it the short-cropped dark hair and dark stubble, the trademark tattoo that snaked from below his left ear and disappeared under the shirt collar?

Whatever, he was devilishly dark and handsome, and like every other woman in the room she found herself unable to stop staring. One by one, people crossed over to say hello, gushing and scraping before him—people that Jacquelyn knew to be supremely confident in business, acting star-struck and silly.

'Are you coming over to meet him?' said the woman next to her.

'No, thank you. I don't want to be caught in the crush of groupies,' she said, a little unkindly.

'Suit yourself,' said her companion, and stood up.

Jacquelyn turned to watch her shimmy her way across the floor, still trying desperately to catch a glimpse of Martin, but the crowd around Nikos Karellis was thick now and totally obscured the table.

And then she saw him seated beside Nikos. He was older than she remembered. Streaks of silver in his dark hair, but still a handsome man, and, she hoped, still a gentleman.

Her stomach turned a somersault and her hands dampened. She tried to wipe them on the tablecloth discreetly as she stood up.

Please, please, please *remember me*, she thought, and began to make her way across the floor towards him.

Nikos's patience had almost completely run dry. His smile was still fixed in place but he'd chatted and shaken hands with people all evening, in the bar and now here at the table. He hated the side effects of fame. The people who wanted to say hello were nice enough but they had no idea who he was—or where he'd come from. They were only seeing some airbrushed version of reality, as fake as the whole wedding industry itself.

He glanced down at Martin with a raised brow.

'How much more of this?' he said, leaning over.

Martin shrugged and smiled.

'The awards start in five minutes. After that we'll disappear off to my suite and talk properly.'

Nikos nodded and straightened up, trying to remember the name of the woman to his right who'd just introduced herself, but when he turned around, it wasn't a plump old lady who was right in front of him, it was a beautiful young woman.

She was tall, toned and blonde, and with a practised sweep he took her all in—from the stunning cerulean-blue floor-length gown that held her feminine curves to perfection, and all the way up past the graceful curve of her shoulders, to the top of her elegant topknot.

She wasn't overtly sexual, but something about the shape of her hips and the neat swell of her breasts made his body react violently. And he noted with some pleasure that he hadn't felt such a reaction for a long time.

Suddenly the night was looking up, and even as he reached out his hand to shake hers, he made a mental calculation of how long he would be occupied with Martin before he could properly get to know her.

But she didn't take his hand.

She didn't even look in his direction. Instead she sailed right past him and stopped, as Martin looked up and got to his feet.

'Jacquelyn. It is you! I saw you coming across the floor and I wondered if it was. I thought I might see you tonight.'

Jacquelyn? Nikos quickly noted her name and watched, wondering how this exchange was going to play out. By the warmth in the way Martin was leaning towards her, lingering as he kissed each proffered cheek, he was clearly fond of her. But he had to be at least twice her age...

And the way she was holding herself was interesting: she was transmitting anxiety, with her spine so rigid, shoulders tense; and that smile, beaming a bit too bright.

'And this is my brother-in-law, Nikos Karellis. Nikos, Jacquelyn Jones—owner of Ariana Bridal. Her father Joseph and I were at school together.'

So, Martin really was old enough to be her father. That was helpful.

She turned her flawless face and keen blue eyes to Nikos. The smile she'd given Martin slipped slightly, he noted, and her spine tightened a notch more too. She blinked and with a long stretch of her arm she permitted her hand to be shaken.

Which he did and he read in that tense-fingered, quickly retracted handshake that he'd just been judged and dismissed. She didn't like him.

Well, it did happen. Not often, but he wasn't every woman's cup of tea. Particularly the ones who thought they were a bit above him. Even with all his money, he never forgot where he'd come from. And nor, it seemed, did they.

He knew the type. They saw his tattoos, his *warpaint* as his mother called it. The sensual ones saw brutality and found it fascinating. The repressed ones didn't get him. They saw brutality and found it disgusting.

The truth, of course, was that he had left brutal back in Sydney at the side of the road. Bikers were brutal; his dad was brutal. His entire childhood had been brutalised beyond what any of these lovely people could understand. They had no idea that his mother suffered brain injury as a result of a beating from his father. Or that he had run drugs for him as an after-school chore.

The fact was that he'd made it his life's work to be free of every trace of violence and aggression. He'd severed ties with everyone except his mother, and poured millions into projects for delinquent kids.

So to be judged as 'less than' pressed his buttons, just a little.

He stood tall, squared his shoulders, one hand on his hip, in a gesture that called out her condescension.

'Former brother-in-law. My wife passed away five years ago.'

She dropped her gaze completely, and when she swept her perfectly oval lids open again there was a tiny flash of recognition.

'I'm sorry for your loss. I never met her but my father spoke about Maria. And you.'

Did he now? thought Nikos, his mind conjuring up an image of her baby blues widening over some story or other. Maria's high jinks were always being reported on some media space. And the look on her face told him that she was remembering something of that sort right now.

'Thank you,' he said. 'I appreciate your kind words. And I'm very pleased to meet you. Are you up for an award tonight?'

The dart of her eyes down to her feet and the blush of pink that bloomed over her face told him all he needed to know on that front. He was beginning to remember the earlier conversation. Was this the woman who was bad in business?

'No, I'm afraid not.'

'Someone else's turn, this year. But Ariana has won awards in the past, Jacquelyn, haven't you?' cut in Martin, gallantly.

'Oh, yes, one or two. We've won Wedding Dress of the Year and been runners-up a few times.'

'That's quite an achievement,' said Nikos. So the business was once at the top of its game. 'And is this one of your own designs?'

Despite her slightly dismissive glance he stood back to view.

He had a practised eye. He was a retail giant, for heaven's sake. House was the 'stylish woman's department store of choice', built on his keen eye, and in one of the most rapid, successful expansions in retail in recent years, he'd taken on concessions in all other departments. So he had every professional right to cast his critical eye over the very seductive shape of Ms Ariana Bridal, even as she tried to shield herself with her long slim arms, twisting to the side, speaking the least subtle body language he'd ever witnessed.

Then she started staring over his shoulder, as if looking for someone better to talk to, even more clearly communicating, *I'm not interested.*

Didn't she know that being not interested made her uniquely the most interesting person here?

'Sorry, did you say you designed this yourself?' he repeated quietly.

She turned, with a slightly irritated look on her face, which he found curiously seductive.

'Not me, but this is our original design.'

'Isn't this the Jones cut?' said Martin, whom Nikos was beginning to find more than mildly irritating himself.

'Nonna Ariana's, yes. Martin, I wonder if we might have a word,' she said, lowering her voice as she turned to him now and took a step away from the table. Martin mirrored her and moved away too. She was clearly trying to cut Nikos out of the conversation. 'Later on this evening? Would that be all right?'

Music started to play, people were taking their seats, Martin hesitated and Nikos raised his eyebrow, reminding him that he had a prior engagement.

'Tonight? Oh, I'm not sure. It's not ideal.'

'Please, Martin. There's something I want to discuss.'

The floor was emptying, people were taking their

seats. They were beginning to look very conspicuous as the only three people still standing.

Jacquelyn knotted her fingers together as if she was praying. She looked truly anguished.

Martin looked at Nikos with a *what can I do?*

Nikos felt a tiny twinge of regret on her behalf but he had bigger things to worry about than a buttoned-up Englishwoman, no matter how attractive.

'Ah, this could be tricky. I've got Nikos here as my guest.'

She turned to look at Nikos as if he was even more of a pariah than she'd first thought, as if he were personally responsible for the fact that her business was dying on its feet.

'We'd better take our seats now. See you later, sweetheart,' he said, with a wink.

Jacquelyn walked back to her table as if she were entirely made of wood and tried to take her seat with grace that seemed to have completely deserted her.

Had she blown it already? She reached for her glass, something to hold as she quickly replayed the meeting in her head. Martin seemed to have been friendly enough but he'd been totally eclipsed by Nikos Karellis. And no wonder. The man was completely unnerving. She'd never met anyone so—*intense*. So physical. He'd made her self-conscious, tongue-tied and totally put her off her stride.

She slipped a glance to the side to look at him as the band struck up and was met with him staring right back at her. The hairs on the back of her neck stood up in an instant and she looked away.

All through the starter she could feel him staring and she absolutely would not look at him. Maybe he thought that she had gone over there to meet him? He probably thought that every woman was in love with him. He was so off the mark. She'd never let herself fall for a man like him. Anyway, she had one single mission here tonight, and it had nothing to do with love.

She turned again to tell him that with her eyes but he was talking intensely with the woman on his left. She watched as he listened to her, tilting his head towards her and smiling as the woman started flirting, throwing her head back when she laughed, playing with her hair, touching her chest and batting her eyelashes, all while Martin looked miserably at his salad.

She felt more and more desperate and in a haze of self-pity she began to cast around the room, looking for Tim. At the back of the hall she found him, his once boyish good looks now paunchy, his blonde hair thin.

He could have been her husband. They could have been sitting together at that table, waiting to collect awards, gossiping about how everyone was fawning over Nikos Karellis. At one point any other future would have been completely unimaginable.

Jacquelyn Jones not married to Tim Brinley? Don't be ridiculous—it's written in the stars...

But strangely enough she didn't feel wistful. And she didn't blame him for the mess of Ariana. She blamed herself. Funny how a crisis could put everything into perspective. And this was a crisis. For all she played it down with everyone, especially her parents, she was in a full-blown state of emergency.

She pushed the food about on her plate, unable to eat, and words seemed to stick in her mouth like cardboard. All she could focus on were the minutes ticking by and the location of Martin Lopez.

She sat through the tables being cleared, the lights

being dimmed, and then the award hosts, two TV pre-senters she recognised from a breakfast show, arrived on stage to start the ceremony.

And then in a never-ending series of announcements and applause she sat through the awards, from Best Florist to Best Accessories, Best Cake to Best Make-Up, Best Venues to Best Stylist. When the Best Photographer names were called out, she prepared herself.

Suddenly there was the image of the winning photograph. A bride and groom on a horse. It was Tim's—it had to be. He loved to ride and he loved to use the riding motif in his photographs. It looked so phoney to her now.

The compère boomed out his name.

As the crowd burst with applause, she lifted her hands from her lap and tapped them together briefly. Most people wouldn't know what he'd done to her, but some of them would, and she couldn't let herself down by acting so childishly.

She forced herself to watch him accept his award, and she realised then that there was nothing there now other than the memory of a man she'd once loved, an outline of something once vivid. A bare-branched tree in winter, once so full of leaves.

She had so much more to worry about now.

The final award was Best Wedding Dress, and to announce it Nikos Karellis bounded athletically to the stage.

'He was her tennis coach,' she heard the woman beside her whisper.

'Ooh, he could coach me in anything he wanted,' said someone else, and giggled.

Jacquelyn tried not to roll her eyes, but she couldn't help looking closer, measuring his stature with her own

innate sense of proportion. He was quite physically perfect. Exceptionally physically perfect. In the pit of her
stomach something awoke, a swirl of longing, a primal
feeling that tugged and shocked her, and she squirmed
and moved in her seat. She looked around to see if anyone had noticed, but everyone's face was turned to the
stage, eyes wide with interest.

The finalists were announced. The winning dress
displayed on the screen and then the flushed and jubi-
lant face of the designer, a pretty brunette. Nikos delivered the glass trophy, kissed her warmly on each cheek
and gave her an affectionate squeeze.

Nice, thought Jacquelyn.

She had barely had a peck on the cheek in the three
years since Tim. She was never the most physical person, but she liked affection, as much as everyone else.
She liked being held close; she liked her hair being
stroked and all the intimacy that came with being with
someone you cared for.

Another wave of self-pity washed over her.

Was she destined to be single her whole life? Would
she ever meet someone else?

She looked around the room. She might not be the
youngest person here, but she was almost certainly the
only one who was still a virgin.

She wondered if anyone knew. Sometimes she felt
as if she were wearing a sign. And sometimes, there
were moments she wished she could just go out and find
someone and have sex and be done with it.

Those months after Tim left she'd tortured herself
thinking she'd been wrong, stupid, blindly falling in
with Nonna's views, not thinking for herself. She'd *almost* considered tracking him down to tell him she'd

changed her mind. But he'd gone. And that was that. And now she was glad. She really was.

The ceremony was over. The audience was applauding. The final comments were being made. Some people had already started to move. The lights came up. She spun back round to see if Martin was still there, but he'd gone.

She threw down her napkin and pushed back her chair. It caught on the carpet. She struggled to right it as she looked up. Where on earth had he gone? Everyone was heading off to the bar, but where was Martin?

Panic gripped her. What if she lost sight of him? What if he disappeared and she couldn't find him?

Then she saw him, heading off in the opposite direction. She picked up speed, almost stumbling over the parquet dance floor in her heels, desperate not to lose sight of him. But then suddenly from nowhere Tim appeared!

'Jacquelyn, wait,' he called, and he reached a hand around her arm.

She turned, confused, wondering what on earth to say.

The days she'd spent longing for the tiniest glimpse of him, five seconds of his time so that they could 'work it out'. Yearning to see his face, feel his hands, just be in the same room as him, again.

Now all she felt was embarrassment. All she could think was that he was holding her back from the one thing she had come here to do.

'I've got nothing to say to you,' she said, tugging her arm away. His face, the one she had once thought handsome, twisted as if she had slapped him.

'I know this isn't the right time,' he said, grabbing for her arm again, 'but you have to know that I'm really sorry about the way I treated you. I've grown up, I've moved on...'

'Look, I'm not interested.'

People were crowding at the opposite doors; thankfully no one seemed to be looking this direction. But he was right in front of her, blocking her view of the door to the hallway where Martin had disappeared.

'I thought I could do it but what you wanted was unnatural, Jacquelyn,' he whispered. 'I'm a man. I have needs and you wouldn't listen.'

'We made a promise!' she hissed. 'You never once said that you couldn't do it. Instead you just vanished! So you'll have to live with that. Now let me go, I'm in a hurry.'

'*You* made the promise for both of us. Your martyrdom is wasted, you know. That whole "pure as the driven snow" act is so last century.'

'Look, get out of my way. I couldn't care less what you think.'

She tried to step past him, but someone else was there.

'Is everything OK here?'

A deep Australian drawl, a strong unflinching presence.

'I'm trying to find Martin. Is he still here?' she asked desperately, smoothing her hair. The last thing she wanted was *him* to hear any of this.

Nikos's eyebrows were raised over dark eyes that flashed concern.

'I need to see him.'

'Yes, he's here,' he said, and he came towards her, reading the situation with a frown. Then he turned to Tim, bearing down on him with his six-foot stature.

'Don't you know any better than to crowd a woman?'

he said, stepping further into the space, his body tele-
graphing masculinity, strength, power, the like of which
she'd never experienced before.

Tim's face blanched and he took a step back.

'Now look here. I'm a friend of Jacquelyn's and I'm
only trying to have a conversation.'

She looked at the two of them and a moment of clar-
ity struck like a thunderbolt. Tim looked so short and
plump and silly next to this man. What on earth had she
seen in him? She had wasted so much time and tears,
and now she was reduced to begging for crumbs from
some rich man's table when she should have been taking Ariana on to the next level?

She shook her head in despair. Where had she gone
so badly wrong?

'Tim, the only reason you're here right now is because there are people here tonight who remember what
you did, and you want me to say it's OK. Well, it's not
OK. Nothing about it is OK. So why don't you take your
half-baked little excuse for an apology and your stupid
plastic award and get out of my way?'

She turned to Nikos, whose eyes were wide. She'd
shocked him too. Good.

'I want to see Martin. Now. Where is he?' she said.

A grin broke out across his face and he stepped to
the side.

'Come with me, I'll take you to him.'

CHAPTER THREE

MARTIN'S SUITE WAS in the Duchess Wing, about a mile of plush velvet carpet to the east of the grand ballroom. They walked in complete silence along its length until the ornate double doors came into sight.

Nikos had the good sense not to say a word until they got there but he was weighing up what he'd just heard and it sounded nasty. Whatever the guy had done, breaking a promise sounded like the least of it. And accusing her of being a martyr. Nikos had met more than a few of those, but in his experience they tended to be the nice ones.

Maria had never played the martyr. Maria took what she wanted and what other people wanted too...

'You all right?' he asked, his hand on the doorknob. 'Is there anything I can do?'

Jacquelyn looked up at him with eyes that told him she was still feeling some pain.

'I'm fine,' she replied. 'Thank you.'

Nikos nodded and opened the door of Martin's suite, ushering her in.

'I found your friend Jacquelyn. She wants a word.'

Martin looked up, surprised. He was sitting at a fireplace filled with yet another giant arrangement of flowers.

'Of course. If that's OK with you, Nikos?'

Nikos stood back and watched her sail right past him and perch on the sofa opposite Martin. Her back was ramrod straight and she turned, flashing Nikos a look that might have said, *thank you*, but might as easily have said, *beat it*.

'Yeah, sure. I was on my way to get my phone. I'll be back in five. That long enough, do you think?'

Martin nodded vigorously. Jacquelyn didn't move a muscle.

Nikos closed the door and walked back to his suite.

She was a force of nature, that one. The Ice Queen, but the way she'd blasted that guy was pure fire. It was impressive. And if she pitched like that to Martin he didn't stand a chance.

Maybe he'd been too harsh on her. She was clearly passionate about her business, and good for her. If he'd been in tough times, the last thing he'd want to do was waste his precious time on small talk with a stranger.

He collected his phone and checked for messages and emails, frowning when he saw yet another one from his accountant, Mark, about the investigation into Maria's missing assets. He had better get answers from Martin. This whole thing was getting more and more out of hand.

He rounded the corner of the hallway and paused. He put an ear to the door to see if they were still talking.

Martin's deep voice was making reassuring noises; Jacquelyn seemed to be silent. He knocked on the door and walked in.

'OK? All wrapped up?'

He didn't have time to worry if it wasn't. He had his own issues to deal with now.

'Nikos. Great timing.'

Martin was facing Jacquelyn. They were both standing, but now Martin was the one who looked imploringly at him, and Jacquelyn's eyes were bright with—hope?

'I was just explaining to Jacquelyn that I'm retiring. She's looking for an investor and I was trying to think of someone else who'd be a good fit. I don't know if I mentioned but Ariana Bridal goes back quite a long way. They need to modernise, perhaps? Would that be right, Jacquelyn? And so maybe you or your connections would be a...better fit...?'

Nikos shook his head.

'I'm not looking to invest in anything, Martin. I'm here to sort a problem.'

He held up his phone.

'A problem that's giving me a headache. While we were giving out awards, I've been getting more messages.'

'I won't take up much of your time, Mr Karellis.'

On a heartbeat Jacquelyn turned and walked towards him. She was breathtaking and he realised he was still standing holding his phone in the air. Quickly he pulled his arm down.

'Time is what I don't have. Martin?' he said, meaning, *Martin, what the hell are you thinking?*

'Maybe you could squeeze in five minutes with Jacquelyn before you go?'

'I promise it won't take longer than five minutes. Ten at the most. Martin understands. This is a business that has so much to offer. We go back decades and we've got great plans. We just need a break.'

Nikos looked at Martin, who raised his eyebrows and shrugged his shoulders as if to say *wouldn't hurt.*

With a sigh that he didn't even know he was going to make, he breathed out an, 'OK.'

'Five minutes. *If* we get this sorted,' he said to Martin. Then turning to Jacquelyn, 'Wait in the bar and I'll send someone.'

She nodded and smiled, and as she breezed past she stopped suddenly and grabbed his hand in both of hers. 'Thank you,' she whispered. 'I guarantee you won't regret it.'

He nodded gruffly, but the sensation of his coarse hand in her delicate fingers was sweet and soft and he was happy to linger there for a moment. He smiled, and she smiled back. Light seemed to sparkle in her eyes and her features lit up. The face of an angel.

She squeezed his hand and then let go and headed for the door, trailing behind her delicate scent.

He waited until she had gone and then closed the door. 'What the hell's going on, Martin?' he said. 'You know I'm under pressure here.'

'You could have said no,' said Martin, eyebrows raised.

'Garbage. You set me up. There's no way anyone could say no to that.'

'She's quite something, isn't she?'

'Hmmm,' said Nikos, 'but you do know that I won't be giving her anything other than some hard home truths? I'm not getting mixed up in anything. Especially with a woman who just needs to stand in a corner and whistle and she'll have men lying at her feet.'

'She's not like that at all. She's from a very good family.'

'That counts for nothing. Anyway, let's get on with this. What's going down? Why the year-long battle with your lawyers? Just what are you trying to prove?'

Martin stood with his back to the fireplace of flowers. The top of his greying head was visible in the ornate mirror. His face was cast in a sickly pallor, and he frowned and clasped his fingers. He was clearly agitated.

'I'm not trying to prove or disprove anything. My back's against the wall. All I know is that Maria had some investments. She was involved in something just before she died. I think it was illegal.'

Nikos nodded. No shocks so far...

'I see. Do we have any clue as to what it was?'

He noticed Martin wringing his hands again.

'Not exactly. She never confided in me—apart from the garbled message she left the night she died. And I think that's what the police are following up too.'

Nikos turned away. The night she died...almost the worst night of his life.

He'd turned up at his villa in Greece and found his wife topless in the hot tub with his old man. The night her drug-taking and his old man's drug-selling had combined in one fatal party. The night Nikos had walked away and never looked back, not even when she ran screaming after him.

No, he didn't ever want to think about that night again, but it didn't seem he had any choice.

'That stuff about the drugs?' he said quietly. 'We both know she bought them from my dad.'

'I think it's more than that. I think he's the one behind the other investments. At least, that's what he's telling me...'

Nikos looked up sharply.

'What do you mean?'

'I've had some communication from him.'

Suddenly Martin's sickly pallor and wringing hands

made sense. Communicating with Arthur was never pleasant and Nikos had studiously avoided it for nearly twenty years. He blocked calls, emails, and every security guard knew his father's face on sight. He'd left Australia to get away from him, and he was damned if he was going to let him into his life in any way, shape or form ever again.

'OK. Out with it. What does he want?'

Martin cleared his throat.

'He wants forty million dollars. He says that that night they both went fifty-fifty on some investment she'd bought into in Cayman. He transferred five million dollars and then she… Well, you know what happened.'

'You don't really believe that, do you?'

Martin turned and leaned his hands on the fireplace.

'I don't know what to believe. He says he gave her the money and the company has quadrupled in value. He says she invested it—and he works it out to be forty million that he says he's owed.'

'Owed?'

'By you as her beneficiary. And if you won't pay up—me.'

'He's insane. Did you tell him that she left nothing? Zero? That there is no estate—only trails of debt that lead in a hundred different directions. All I have is what I built myself and, trust me, I don't have a spare forty million lying around. I'd have noticed if I did. What evidence does he have for any of this?'

Martin shrugged.

'That's all I know. But I'm guessing you'll find out one way or another.'

Nikos laughed mirthlessly.

'I wouldn't give him forty cents, never mind forty million dollars. After what he did?'

He'd had enough of all this. He walked to the door, was there in three strides.

'Is that all you've got to say?' said Martin, still hooked around the fireplace.

Nikos turned. 'What else is there? He's a lowlife blackmailing piece of scum and if he thinks this is going to result in anything other than me hating him even more, he's mistaken.'

He opened the door and then closed it again.

'And I suggest you get yourself some better company to keep, Martin.'

He pulled the door closed and stood in the plush silent hallway, his heart thundering in his ears and his body primed for fight. He had to get a hold of himself or he'd rip someone's head off. He had to throw everything he had at it. But the fact that it was his old man who had stoked it all to life wasn't wasted on him. Everything he touched turned poisonous. Every goddamned time.

There would be some grain of truth in that cock-and-bull story because it was too crazy for there not to be. But he wasn't leaving it up to chance. He was going to go back to the villa and go through the vault. The one place he'd avoided for years might be the one place he'd find what he was looking for.

He speed-dialled his accountant.

'Mark,' he said, 'as soon as you get this I want you to check out every transfer that went into or out of Maria's accounts around the time she died. I'm looking for an investment in a company registered in the Cayman Islands. It's probably something that she'll have buried so it might be hard to find. That's all I have for now but

I think this could be what's behind the investigation and the letters from Martin Lopez's solicitors.'

He clicked off the phone as a waiter walked past with a tray of drinks. Parties were still kicking off but he was in no mood to party. What he needed now was silence. And sleep.

He was jet-lagged and pumped with adrenalin, and there wasn't enough whisky in the whole place to knock him under. He needed to stand in a hot shower and hit the sack.

He pushed open the door of his suite, stepping out of his trousers, removing his jacket, heaving at his tie and unbuttoning his shirt with fingers that even now still shook with rage.

In the shower he stood, water from all angles pummelling his back and legs and head. He had to cool it. *Be cool. Rein it in, Nikos. Calm it.*

He thought of his mother lying in her bed in the nursing home. He thought of her sweet smile in the photograph of them at the beach, and then he thought of the blank, unseeing eyes that had looked at him the day before.

Every step he took was for her. To make her proud, to make all her own suffering worthwhile. He wasn't going to go under because of his father. He wasn't going to let Arthur ruin his reputation or his fortune. He was going to fight back.

He turned off the jets of water and dried himself. There was a noise outside. He opened the bathroom door a crack and listened. Someone was battering on the door. Martin?

He walked through the room, kicking up his suit trousers and catching them in his right hand as he opened the door with his left.

But it wasn't Martin. It was the blonde in the blue dress.

'Hi,' he said, confused. Then he slapped his forehead. 'Damn. Sorry. You've been waiting in the bar to see me. I said I'd send for you.'

Her eyes opened like starbursts, falling from his face to his chest and the towel knotted at his hips.

'Sorry, I was taking a shower.'

She stared at her feet, then down the hall, then at her feet. 'I am so sorry. I really did not mean to disturb you. It was getting so late… I'll go back and wait downstairs.'

'What time is it?' he said, trying to bury his impatience. This he could do without.

'Um…' she said. 'I'm sorry, I don't know. My phone ran out of power.'

'And I clearly don't have a watch on,' he said with a cynical chuckle.

She blushed furiously. She was very, very pretty when she blushed. She was very pretty, full stop. He could be in the mood to spend some time with her. That would be better than whisky at taking the edge off, for sure.

'Come in. I'll get some clothes on. We can chat now.'

He threw the door back and walked inside, tossing the trousers over a chair in the passing.

'If you don't mind, I'd rather not.'

He turned around, couldn't hide his surprise, but she was staring at her feet, her hands clasped in front of her.

'Much as I want to have a meeting with you, it wouldn't be appropriate for me to come in while you're undressed.'

He walked to the wardrobe and helped himself to a large white fluffy bathrobe, tied it at his waist.

'Suit yourself,' he said.

She looked up. Further along the hallway, noise bubbled out as a door opened. After-parties were probably taking place all over the hotel and she was too prudish to step over the threshold of his room?

'I hope you understand,' she said, taking another step back from the doorway. 'I want to talk about my business—that's all.'

He almost laughed out loud but when her face didn't break into a smile, he realised she was completely serious. How about that? She'd secured a meeting with him, but only on her terms. And those terms were…refreshing.

'Well, that's fine by me—but I won't be around for much longer if you still want that five minutes.'

'Maybe I could come by tomorrow morning before you leave?'

That would be a no, he thought.

With his flight scheduled for ten thirty, he'd be out of here an hour earlier, and the thought of cramming anything else into his head right now was not appealing at all.

But she looked so young, so full of hope. Like a flower opening its petals at the first burst of sunshine. He didn't really want to crush her, did he?

He nodded.

'OK. Come for breakfast. Nine.'

The sweet joy that spread across her face was beautiful, like a child's, and it was amazing how good that made him feel—for a second.

'Thank you so much. I promise not to waste your time.'

'We'll see,' he said.

But as he put his hand on the door and began to close it, his phone lit up. Mark. More bad news.

CHAPTER FOUR

A SLEEPLESS NIGHT, anxiety and a heatwave. What a killer combo. But at least she had a reason, and a fast-approaching deadline.

Jacquelyn flew around the studio tidying up the mess she'd made over the previous four hours. She was exhausted but she was getting ready to meet Nikos Karellis and for the first time in ages she felt hopeful, optimistic—happy?

It wasn't what she'd set out to do, but it was even better than finance from Martin Lopez. This was a chance with House, for goodness' sake! It was the retail sensation that had expanded when everyone else was shutting up shop and disappearing down online rabbit holes.

Just those four brief meetings with Nikos Karellis had lit something up inside her, ignited some hunger that she'd never possessed before. Something had rubbed off and made her want to be part of that world. It was as if he'd sprinkled some of his magic dust and she'd breathed it in, and from the moment she'd closed the door to his suite, she'd been unable to get him out of her mind.

Who are you trying to kid? she thought fleetingly. *You saw him nearly naked and you're as hooked as every other woman. The only difference is that you were*

*afraid to step through the doors to see where it might
lead. But you could have...*

No. This drive to get it right had nothing to do with
any attraction to him as a *man*. She would never dream
of having a business meeting in his suite. This was all
about Ariana. It was so important to get it right!

And she would. She'd tossed and turned for a couple
of hours, got up at three and then started work. By six
she had completely reworked the strategy. She'd created
four personas of Ariana Bridal clients. She'd sketched
out a cost-benefit analysis, which presupposed cash injection from House. And then she'd gone the extra mile
and thrown in some figures based on the concession opportunities that she'd gain linked to the brand. It was
all pure speculation and she could be way, way off, but
it showed imagination. It showed that she'd done some
homework at least.

So she still hadn't fixed the designs. But that part
would come. With cash they could hire a designer again,
someone who could really capture what it meant to be
an Ariana bride...

She practised her pitch out loud as she poured her
fourth coffee and walked with it through to her bedroom to start getting ready. She would show him what
she was capable of. She wasn't some airhead under-
achiever; she was the heart and soul of this business,
and with his cash injection Ariana could be a great little
addition to his portfolio.

But first she'd need to make a start on her appearance.

The clock showed seven. Just under two hours should
be fine. She'd have time for a quick face masque and
then some brightening cream. Then she'd plaster on the
concealer and some coral lipstick.

She heard the door and tried to peer outside. There was a huge black car in the lane. Barbara, in one of her current husband's limousines. She'd be 'on her way to the gym', which really meant she'd been scouring social media since she woke and couldn't wait to get the details. She probably already knew about her breakfast meeting with Nikos.

'Hello, Barbara,' Jacquelyn said, as brightly as she could, as she pulled back the bolt on the door. 'This is an early call today.'

'Hello, Jacquelyn.'

Nikos!

He looked fresh and vital in a crisp white shirt and dark jeans, but with that solar intensity that made her take a step back. Her hands flew up to her hair in a defensive motion as she did a mental checklist. Three hours' sleep, four hours' staring at a screen, four coffees, no make-up, hair everywhere. She stared down— a skimpy camisole and pyjama shorts.

'What are you doing here? How did you know where I lived?'

'I looked it up,' he said simply.

'But I thought I was to come to Maybury Hall at nine. Isn't that what you said? Oh, no, I've not messed this up completely, have I? I've been working on a presentation all morning. I've personalised it just for you. And House.'

'No, it's not nine,' he said with a wry laugh. 'It's only seven. And I've come by here on my way to the airport. Something's come up and I've got business to attend to I can't put off.'

He was solemn, sullen and serious. He was going and taking with him the air that she needed to breathe. She felt bereft—as if the ray of hope, the hot air balloon that she had finally found to take her over this rocky ground had just been punctured. All those hours she'd spent she'd completely convinced herself that there was no way forward now other than with concessions in the House stores.

'We can reschedule?'

Reschedule? She knew a brush-off when she heard one.

'Oh. I see.'

She knew by the slight surprise in his eyes that she hadn't hidden her disappointment at all well. But this was awful. This was the pacifier that Martin Lopez had passed her. There was nothing else.

'I'm sorry—I realise that you are a very busy man. I hope everything is OK.'

'Everything will be OK, thanks. And I'm perfectly serious about another time. My assistant will be in touch in a couple of days to sort out a date…'

She hesitated, the words of despair held back in her mouth. *When?* she wanted to whine. *Because in six days we could be closed down…gone…forgotten.*

'Oh, that would be wonderful. If you have the time.'

'Of course. It would be my pleasure.'

He looked so sincere, and seemed to hesitate when she extended her hand, put on her smile.

'Well, thank you anyway. It was lovely to meet you last night, and I'm very grateful for your time. I do realise how busy you are.'

He looked away. 'I'm a man of my word, Jacquelyn. I said I would listen to your pitch and I will.'

She heard the words but her disappointment seemed to know no bounds. It was the light going out. It was exhaustion. It was being up all night and so full of adrenalin.

'Please, don't worry about it,' she said, on a sigh.

'Look, I'm heading to Greece. Why don't you come along on the flight—make the pitch then? I often have meetings as I travel; if you're OK with that, I'd be happy to accommodate it.'

Travel with him on his plane? Alone? To talk about Ariana and House. That was intense. Insane. That was the offer of a lifetime.

'Why yes, that would be super,' she said, her mind running ahead, but then... 'When do you fly?'

'I'm on my way to the airport now.'

'Now? As in right now?'

She looked down again at her skimpy clothes and then up into his face, which seemed to have softened slightly.

'Don't worry. I won't ask you to pitch in your pyjamas. The flight will take a few hours. I'm going to be busy for a while—you can finish your presentation, if that's what you want to do. There should still be plenty of time for the pitch. If there's not enough time, do it after lunch. You can come to the villa. Fly home later this evening. You'll be back at work tomorrow.'

He stepped out into the street and seemed to look over his shoulder.

'OK? It's the best I can do.'

'I'll take it,' she said, knowing that this was in fact a better offer than she could ever have imagined. Travelling with Nikos to his villa in Greece. Lunch and then making her pitch. Surely this indicated that he was really interested in what she had to offer?

'Could you give me ten minutes?'

He checked his watch; he raised his eyebrows.

'Five?' she said.

He nodded and stepped inside.

'I'll be right back.'

With an energy she didn't know she possessed Jacquelyn flew upstairs to the flat, ran a shower and was in and out of it in under a minute. She dragged a brush through her damp hair and tied it into a braid. She lathered cream on her face, hands and arms and threw her favourite cornflower-blue sundress over her head. With a minute to spare she applied deep pink lipstick, slid on gold jewellery and leather sandals.

Never in her life had she gotten ready so fast. She looked flushed and desperate, but the light golden tan and blue of the dress picking out the blue of her eyes made the whole appearance somehow alive.

Let that be a lesson, Jacquelyn Jones, she thought.

She tossed a jersey dress into her bag and clean underwear, just in case, then grabbed her laptop, the folio of designs and looked around the studio. Coffee cups, handkerchiefs and the half-eaten slice of toast she had started and then discarded.

She ran downstairs, pulled the door closed and went out into the courtyard where Nikos was waiting. He stood in profile, staring at the fountain, lost in thought.

She beamed at him, carried away by her own enthusiasm and energy, but when he turned to look it was with a face etched deep with concern.

'Is everything OK?' she asked, suddenly stalling on the steps.

He focused on her, swept her with his eyes and then his face seemed to brighten.

He put his phone in his pocket.

'Yeah,' he said. 'Sure. All good. You look beautiful, Jacquelyn.'

'Thanks,' she said, astonished. Because getting a compliment from a man like him seemed to be worth more than getting a compliment from anyone else. It didn't make her flesh crawl or make her feel patronised. And she wanted him to think she was beautiful.

How odd that she should care…

He smiled.

'Let's go to Greece,' he said.

CHAPTER FIVE

So HE DIDN'T always make the right decisions, and extending a pity invitation to Jacquelyn Jones was definitely not one of his best. As soon as he'd taken the second call from Mark, he should have followed his first instincts and sent her a message.

But when he'd found out that Ariana Bridal was only two miles from Maybury Hall he didn't have the heart to drive by. And all he was going to do was offer her another place, another time, and, if he was completely honest, hopefully another agenda—one not related to business.

With every passing minute he had regretted this gut reaction to those blue eyes. He owed her nothing but somehow he'd found himself agreeing to meeting her not once but twice. This was getting way out of hand.

They'd had no time to talk on the flight—he could have predicted that—and the time of this pitch had dragged on now, to some post-lunch rendezvous, every minute heightening her optimism and dimming his.

But in a way it had been a salvation having her chatting away and oohing and ah-ing about the scenery on this first journey back from the airstrip to the villa. He doubted she'd noticed him turn his head away when they neared the hairpin bend that dropped to the steep olive grove where Maria's car had taken its tragic turn.

The skid marks were still on the road, twin black lines, baked into the cement. On through the village of Agios Stephanos they drove—it was almost exactly as he remembered, the bakers, the store, the old men who stared, and dogs tied up in pockets of shade, barking at the cars as they passed.

He pointed out the tiny old white church clinging to the side of the steep cliff, roughened with centuries of hot sun and windswept winters. His great-grandparents had been married there, and their parents and grand-parents before them, but he kept those facts to himself.

Further on, faded signs sent far-travelling tourists to sacred wells, and a stream trickled down to the level of the sea, where his private shingle beach presented itself to crystal-clear aquamarine waters, and where once upon a time he'd moored his boat.

Once upon a time this had been the one place on earth he'd felt truly alive, and truly alone. It was in his DNA and it was a thousand miles from Sydney.

Maria hadn't particularly liked it here—too basic, too boring—and he'd seen no reason to try to change her mind. He'd kept it private and personal, loving his times alone here. Occasionally he'd entertained like-minded clients who'd turned into friends, but never, it had to be said, anyone who was still at the stage of pitching a proposal.

He stood now in the library, sheaves of papers strewn all over the table. Beyond them, through the window, he looked out over the old familiar gardens and tennis courts, down to the pool house to where, with another apology, he'd sent word for her to wait for him.

The hour he'd asked her to wait had become three, as he'd rummaged through Maria's unfiled documents, with calls back and forth to Mark. He'd sent more apologies and the offer of anything his guest's heart desired, including food and drink, spa treatments from his private masseuse and her choice of clothes from the vast wardrobes in the villa.

Finally, he closed the door of the safe, clutching the bundle of papers that he'd been searching for. They were a mess but they showed Maria's ownership of a company listed in Cayman. He connected by video phone to Mark and his lawyer and together they went through them word by word. It seemed that she'd bought a shadow company, but that it had ceased trading six months later.

There was no sign of any money ever changing hands between her and his father. And there was no sign of any profits, which meant that neither his father nor Martin nor the Inland Revenue were due anything at all.

Finally even the calm, unflappable Mark breathed out a sigh of relief. And that said something.

'That was a close call. I don't think we're out of the woods yet, but at least we know there was stuff happening that you weren't party to. This is good news.'

Good news. He nodded as the knowledge sank in. His wife had deceived him in new and even more dangerous ways. It shouldn't really have been a surprise, but it was still painful. And what else was he going to find out?

'I take it you'll be out of commission for the next few hours in some kind of post-apocalyptic celebration?'

'For your information, I'm going straight into another meeting. I've got someone waiting to pitch a new concession for House.'

'A pitch? On Sunday. After what you've just been through?'

'It's no big deal. I don't think it'll come to anything.

It's a favour to a friend—it's bridalwear, bespoke—
not something I see working for us. It's not the right
brand, but I might be able to give her some feedback
that'll help.'

'Sounds like just the way to unwind after averting an
unaffordable tax bill, a rush on your stock and a media
storm. But hey, who am I to judge?'

Nikos raised his eyebrow at Mark's attempt at humour. He was emotionally wrung out, stressed out and
jet-lagged. And now he had this to do. Mark was right.
He wouldn't be able to focus on a word she was saying.
He had to just chill for a couple of hours.

'Incidentally, I've doubled your security in the short
term. Until all this blows over. I think it's best to be on
the safe side.'

'Is there anyone here in Greece?'

'Not since after the break-in. Your last-minute
change of plans caught us off guard but I can get a
couple of guys there if you want.'

'It's OK, I'll be heading back soon. Thanks,' said
Nikos, then clicked off the phone and pocketed it. The
break-in six months earlier had taken him by surprise,
but it was just some opportunistic petty criminal.
They'd been disturbed before they could take anything.

Still, he was glad Mark had the sense to step things
up. He'd felt uneasy leaving Manhattan, but then, these
days he felt uneasy everywhere. Leaving Maybury Hall
he'd felt something wasn't right, that strange car, parked
too long, that just happened to stop off at Lower Linton when he did…?

He was probably getting paranoid.

He tripped down the steps to the pool, just as he
caught sight of Jacquelyn, sitting under a parasol in the
shade, her laptop in front of her, staring intently at the

screen. Her brow was furrowed and her eyes intense, her lips moving, her hands gesticulating—she was practising her pitch to him.

Oh, man. She was all geared up and he was gearing down.

He took the last flight of steps, slowing his pace, trying to think of the best words to begin his own pitch to her. He knew his own body—he was buzzed up and he needed release. It was either sex or exercise. It wasn't politely listening to a friend of a friend telling him about her plans to bring more fishtail wedding dresses to market.

He strode past the drained hot tub, ignoring it, and right up to the pool house, just as she noticed him. She looked up, startled, touched her hand to her chest in an endearing way. In her simple blue sundress, with broad straps over sleek shoulders, she looked good. She looked great. That was all he could think.

'I'm so sorry!' she said. 'I didn't see you there. I would have been ready for you up at the house if I'd known.'

'I'm the one who needs to apologise, dragging you all this way and then leaving you here to fend for yourself all afternoon. Have you been OK? Got everything you need?'

'Yes. Totally,' she said. 'I've had a lovely afternoon sitting out here. It's the best waiting room I've ever been in. It's beautiful. You're so lucky.'

He looked around, nodding. The Aegean was particularly calm, particularly blue. Behind him sparrows were flying in and out of the bushes and hedges that screened the pool, just as they'd always done. The sun was beginning its late afternoon slide, the light that perfect hot, bright dazzle that made everything look at its best. And the pure, cool twenty metres of water right beside him looked as inviting as he'd ever seen it. It was pretty near as perfect as anywhere could be.

Jacquelyn stood up and smoothed her dress, catching his eye. He forced his gaze to remain on her face.

'So where do you want to do this?' she said brightly. 'Up in the house? It's only me and the laptop. I can fall in with whatever suits.'

He ran his hands through his hair, biting down on the adrenalin that was building in him. He didn't want to go back in there. He didn't want to sit down politely and listen to anything she had to say. He wanted to be out here, in the sunshine, living life, remembering Greece the way it used to be for him. He wanted to shake off the cobwebs of Maria's death once and for all, and he couldn't think of a more engaging woman to do it with.

'To tell you the truth, the thing that would suit me most now is just to chill for a while. I've been on the go for hours and I need to unwind.'

He glanced at the pool house and her eyes followed his, widening when she looked back at him.

'How about we shelve the business talks for a bit? I don't think that tagging on a pitch right now is going to be the best idea—we both need to be clear-headed. What do you say?'

He winced as the words came out of his mouth. She was going to be more and more convinced that there was a crock of gold at the end of this rainbow when, really, it was much more likely to be a crock of something else.

'Well, yes. Of course. I don't want to get in the way. I'll fall in with your plans. You were good enough to invite me here in the first place—I'm just happy to get the chance.'

Why did that irritate him slightly? That she was glad only to be here for her five-minute pitch? He wanted her to want to be here because he was Nikos Karellis the man, not the CEO of House. He opened a bottle of water and splashed some into two glasses, handing her one.

'You need to stop apologising for yourself. Would be my first piece of business advice. If what you've got to offer is worthwhile, people will be prepared to wait for it.'

Her lips formed a surprised 'oh' and he was sure she was about to start with another apology but she clamped her mouth closed.

'Thanks for the advice, then,' she said, taking the glass and putting it straight down on the table.

'You're welcome. Always better to say thanks for your patience than to apologise for holding someone up. It's assertive. Someone in your position needs to be very assertive.'

'I've never had any complaints before,' she said, and he noted as she drew herself up. He noted because the slight movement drew his eyes to the curves under her dress, the way it creased and hugged and flattered.

'I'm sure you haven't had many complaints at all,' he said, and he meant it innocently enough, but in the pause that extended now between them, in the moment in which they each regarded the other, the unmistakeable heat of sexual tension began to bloom. He felt the physical rush and saw it reflected in the widening of her eyes, the slight parting of her lips.

'If any,' he finished, underlining the point, unnecessarily.

'I meant,' she said, clearing her throat, 'I haven't had any complaints about being assertive. Though that doesn't seem to get me anywhere. In the business world.'

He drained his glass and reached for more. In the quiet afternoon, the only sounds were the slosh of water in his glass, and the bursts of cicadas through the heavy heat. The sun beat down on his back, warmth spread and seemed to soothe his tense shoulders. The world was beginning to slow and right itself. Greece was seeping under his skin again.

'Maybe you've been talking to the wrong people. I guess some people, some men, are threatened by an assertive woman.'

'Well, I can't seem to be any other way,' she said, walking to the edge of the terrace. She placed her hands lightly on the top of the barrier and stared out to sea. Sunlight glinted on her golden hair and bathed the edges of her shoulders; the skirt of her dress floated up in the warm summer's breeze.

'Be yourself,' he said. 'It's working well from where I'm standing.'

She cast a glance back over her shoulder.

'With all due respect, it's easy for you to say. You don't have to ask anyone to finance your company. You've got everything you could ever need.'

Everything he could ever need? People thought that having the cars and houses and planes was everything. Easy mistake to make but they were so wrong. He wanted peace. He wanted trust. He wanted to be able to wake up in the morning to birdsong; he wanted to roll over in his bed and hold the warm body of the woman he loved, not slide into cold space, wondering where she was and who she was with, and what she'd done.

But he doubted he would ever find it, if it even existed.

'I'm sorry,' she said, and he looked up from his self-pity. 'I overstepped the mark there. I had no right to say that. It was unprofessional. I just want you to know that I'm really grateful for this chance—I don't want to do anything to ruin it.'

'Oh, come on, Jacquelyn. Give yourself a break. Maybe you should try being a bit less professional for a while. All I'm saying is that I'd be grateful for your company for the next few hours. As one human being to another, the real Nikos and the real Jacquelyn.'

She was on the back foot. He could see tension in her eyes and the nervous way she clasped her hands. She walked over to where her laptop sat and moved it out of the wedge of sunlight that had crept onto the table. Then she closed the lid halfway.

'Well, the thought of spending time here... Who wouldn't want to do that? I mean, it's gorgeous, and I haven't had a holiday in four years, but...'

'There's a "but"?'

'But can I get your word that the pitch will definitely go ahead?' she said, her hands clasped in front of her chest.

'The pitch will definitely go ahead,' he repeated, nodding. 'Come hell or high water, you'll get your chance to talk about your business. I'm only talking a walk, a swim, then an early dinner. You could stay here tonight—there's plenty of space,' he said quickly, when he saw a look of surprise and shock sweep over her face. 'Get an early night and then you'll be fresh for the morning. Pitch at nine and I'll have the jet ready for ten-thirty. I'm heading back to New York via London tomorrow too. I think that would work—yeah?'

'You mean stay all night? I don't think so. I wasn't really counting on that. I'm not really prepared.'

'I wasn't counting on it either,' he said, with an honesty that he didn't expect. 'This is the first time I've been back here in years. I thought I'd hate it, I thought I'd want to get away the minute I…found what I was looking for in the vault, but I don't. I really want to hang out, relax.'

He looked round again at the terrace, the pool, the bushes popping with colour and even the empty hot tub that shimmered in the baking heat. The olive groves behind him on the hillside, the goats roaming free. This was home, and he'd had no idea how much he'd missed it.

'Come on. If you won't do it for me, do it for the staff who're slaving in that kitchen preparing dinner for us tonight. You can't let them down.'

'That's not fair. That's blackmail,' she said, but a smile was tugging at her lips.

'I never said it was fair. But if you want that on your conscience…'

'OK. I'll stay. As long as I can get an early night in the guest bedroom…'

'Of course. That's a given. So on that basis we have a deal?' He laughed, and extended his hand.

'Deal,' she said, and as she slid her hand into his, and looked up with those cool blue eyes, he knew there was a fire that burned there, and he was even more sure that there was nothing he wanted more on this earth than to light it.

CHAPTER SIX

THE BRIGHT AFTERNOON sparkled and finally faded as the lilac clouds of dusk slipped through purples and mauves and came to settle over the low hills. Night wrapped warm arms around the vast lands of the villa, snuffing out everything except the sconces on the walls, the lamps dotted on paths and the fiery glow of the man himself.

Jacquelyn, freshly showered, hair long and loose, slipped into her silk jersey maxi dress and stepped out on the terrace to watch.

Her hands curled round the cool metal barrier and she breathed, deeply. What a day. From the moment the plane had touched down on the soil she'd been swept up in love for this place. The light, the scents and sounds, every fabulous aspect of this fabulous villa. And then spending the last part of the afternoon walking through shady olive groves, visiting the fabled Well of Agamemnon and sitting on Nikos's private beach.

She could hardly believe she was the same person who had been so dismissive of Nikos Karellis only one day earlier. Now her heart raced and her stomach fluttered at the thought of his face breaking into a smile, as he took her hand to guide her down the worn sandstone steps onto the baking sand.

She'd been right not to strip off and swim though, tempted as she was. But that would have been a step too far. Instead she'd kept her sundress on and her dignity intact, and watched happily from the tiny terrace as he'd emerged from the pool house in a pair of swim shorts and jogged past her into the sea.

He was magnificent. All that she'd denied herself in that flash as he'd opened the door to his suite, she'd then feasted on from the safety of her deck chair. She'd gorged herself on the rippling muscles of his back, his firm calves and thighs as he'd pounded past her to the waves. The sight of his fabled tattoos winding from his neck over his back and his chest, tracing their silky path over strong, hard, perfect muscles.

He'd pounded the waves, swimming out some fifty metres and back, making her feel stupidly, ridiculously nervous when he'd almost seemed to disappear in the foaming white horses.

And then finally he'd emerged and walked towards her, dragging a towel this way and that, mesmerising her, like a magnificent godlike hypnotist. She'd been powerless to stop herself. And that was OK. Because all she'd been doing was looking. And as long as she remembered that, she was in no danger.

But even now as she stood watching him on the terrace below, she knew that every single thing about Nikos Karellis eclipsed every single thing about every other man she'd ever met. Back and forward he paced, like a general pacing in front of his army. In the calm, silent night his voice carried to where she stood, switching from the Greek she barely recognised, to Italian and then back to his deep, drawling Australian English—he was orator, statesman and king all in one.

She knew she should be thinking about her presentation, but she simply couldn't make her mind focus. Yet. As long as she had an early night, she'd be up at dawn and get back into the zone.

'Hey up there! Juliet! Coming to join me?' said Nikos. He had walked to the end of the terrace and was almost underneath her.

'Yes, Romeo, just coming,' she laughed. She lifted her fingers to her lips to blow him a kiss, and then stopped—what was she thinking? She drew her hand back as if she had been intending to tuck her hair behind her ear.

But the look in his eyes told her he knew. He knew she was attracted to him. She was useless at hiding it. From the way she'd drooled as he'd dried himself down, to the way she'd been caught, open-mouthed, watching him just now.

Of course she was attracted; who wouldn't be? The question was, what was she going to do about it?

She slipped silently along the hallway, her feet slipping on the marble, her silver bracelets jangling. She caught sight of herself in the mirrored doors that led out to the terrace.

You'd better be careful, Jacquelyn, she told herself. *You're almost out of your depth. Don't spoil it all now...*

She walked across the lamp-lit terrace. Nikos walked towards her, and her heart leaped in her chest. She breathed, she smiled. She took the cheek he offered, right, then left, and she kissed him quickly, ignoring the swirl of musky male scent and the smooth warmth of his skin.

'You look very beautiful,' he said. 'That coral colour suits you. The cut of the dress—really nice.'

She knew it did. The soft jersey draped over her figure, hugging her curves, the coral pink toned with her skin. She was lucky.

'Thank you,' she replied as he showed her to her seat at a round table, tucked in the corner of the trailing rose arbour, lit by candles and strings of little lamps.

'Are you hungry?' he asked as he settled himself beside her and speared a bit of melon, watching her carefully.

'Oh, yes,' she said, looking at the plates of appetisers. But she wasn't. She wasn't hungry in the slightest.

He nodded, still watching, and she lifted some food to her plate.

'Your room OK?'

'Oh, yes. Thanks. Very comfortable.'

He nodded. 'I've been busy, but that swim did me the world of good. Unfortunately it was all waiting for me when we got back from the beach.'

'I guess you're always on call.'

'Aren't you? As head of a business, there never seems to be a moment when someone doesn't want an instant solution to some problem or other.'

'I'm not quite in your league. My issues are more around being taken seriously.'

He raised a sharp eyebrow.

'Not by my staff. But by men. Bank managers usually.'

'You feel objectified in the business world?'

'Objectified. Patronised. Demoralised. Take your pick. I'm sorry if I sound bitter, but the number of times I've heard *"Oh, isn't your father coming?"* Honestly. It would never happen if I were a man.'

'People make judgements in less than a second. It takes a lot to change a preconceived idea, but I bet you can do it if you want to.'

It was the thing that upset her more than anything else. Taking over from her father, and feeling that sense of disappointment every time it was she alone who walked into meetings. It was fine when she was just there as window dressing, but as soon as she was running the whole show she knew she'd been judged and filed before some of them had even read past the first line of her accounts.

'I don't imagine anyone has ever told you you're far too handsome to be getting all mixed up in business before?'

'No,' he said, scathingly. 'And I honestly can't believe in this day and age that anyone would doubt your credentials because you're a woman.'

'It happens,' she said, taking a sip of wine, feeling it slide warmly into her stomach.

'If it's any consolation, you wouldn't begin to imagine what's been said to me. The question is, do we let what other people think affect our decisions?'

'Is this about to turn into my second piece of business advice?' she asked, smiling as she took another little sip of the very delicious wine.

'Life advice,' he countered.

'So why exactly does Mister Seventy-Sixth-on-the-*Forbes*-List feel so maligned?'

'I don't. But what I'm trying to get across is that people paint pictures in business. And in life. The perfect world you think you see here…'

He jerked his fork around the space. Lamps were now glowing softly right along the lines of the terrace, highlighting clumps of sleeping flowers nestled in their bushy beds. Further on, the blue glimmer of the pool and the solid lines of pale loungers stretched out expectantly under the watchful hillside, and the bright-faced moon above.

'This paradise and every other paradise like it will be hiding all sorts of cracks and holes and heartache.'

As she stared up at him lazily spearing watermelon and letting it slide down his throat, she recalled another article she had read, about his early childhood and humble beginnings.

'You had it tough at one point in time, didn't you?'

He raised an eyebrow, continued to munch melon and she watched in a hazy trance now as his muscled forearms flexed with each movement of his fork, and the thick column of his throat constricted with each swallow. It was poetry in motion, dark and male and utterly magnetic.

'No tougher than any other kid growing up in an abusive, dysfunctional family. All things considered, I had it pretty easy.'

'I'm sure you could take care of yourself,' she said, a trifle dismissively. He might have had humble beginnings but he had it all laid out at his feet now. He had no idea how she'd had to struggle.

'Well, you see, that's where you're wrong, Jacquelyn. I couldn't. So that's how I ended up here.'

He sounded so different, so quiet. He glanced down at the plate where a few glistening pink cubes of melon remained, but then he put his fork down, stared at it for a moment.

'I ran away. I met my wife at the side of the road when she was still someone else's wife. I knew what she was doing was wrong but I was eighteen. I was in so much trouble, with the police, with the gangs, with my father. I knew if I stayed in Sydney I'd be dead within a year. And then along comes Maria. And she wanted to be my wife and so I married her, I "reinvented myself" and now here I am. And here you are.'

As he spoke she felt the ghosts of his past swirl around. She saw him look at her, really look at her. He wasn't looking at her like a boss, he was looking at her like a man.

'Here we are indeed,' she said, and she glanced around with a nervousness that she wasn't sure was real.

'So, you see, I've bought the T-shirt with the whole marriage crap. It doesn't really do it for me now that I've grown up. No offence,' he said.

'None taken. For the record, I may work at one end of the marriage production line, but I'm well aware of how it can end up.'

'Things didn't work out for you either, did they?'

She flushed. She hated bringing all that up again. Not here, not now.

'Things worked out,' she said, but she couldn't meet his eye.

'Still hurts, huh? You're not alone. Men can tend to have the upper hand in relationships. Things seem a bit less complicated for us.'

'That's just an excuse for dishonourable people to act in a dishonourable way,' she said, and there was the bitterness in her voice, still there because she really didn't buy the argument that men were different from women. There were people who were good and there were people who weren't. There *were* good men in the world, like her father. The trouble was, they all appeared to be taken...

'OK. I hear you. But relationships come in many forms. I'm not saying it's OK to lie, but if everyone is clear about the boundaries, who are you to judge?'

'Not everyone is as clear about the boundaries as you think they are,' she said.

Nikos looked at her with understanding painted in his eyes.

'That Tim guy,' he said, quietly. 'What did he do to you?'

She'd told no one apart from her mother the facts of that night, but somehow the whole story had made it around town before she'd even taken her ring off and flushed it down the toilet.

'It's no secret. We were going out for four years, engaged for two and he left me five weeks before we were due to get married.'

He nodded. He reached over and squeezed her hand, but she drew it back again quickly. 'I'm sorry, but people split up, all the time. It happens. Better that it happened before you got married than after.'

'I know that. And believe me, I thank my lucky stars every day now. But it was how he did it. We were out for dinner. He ordered fillet steak, medium rare—he even said that—and then he just excused himself to go to the bathroom and never came back.'

She'd sipped her gin and tonic, watching the light dance off the self-same engagement ring, and feeling so proud and pleased that she would soon have a golden band there beside it. And she'd sipped some more as she'd waited on Tim, and then some more until she'd finished her drink. And then she'd realised, he was away too long. Far too long.

The shame, the humiliation. How long she had sat there, calling for help. *My fiancé is stuck in the toilet... something must have happened to him. Please call the police...he's been abducted...*

All the silly nonsense she'd convinced herself was

true until, gently but firmly, the police officer had told her he had driven away in his own car—and had shown it to her there on the CCTV.

'That's pretty tough. You mean you didn't actually split up—he just split? Was there someone else?'

Nikos poured a little more wine, the gentle slosh of liquid in the glass a mesmeric accompaniment to his words.

'I think so. I heard he went abroad, met someone else, a woman with children of her own. He's only been back in the country a few months.'

She wasn't going to tell him about the email he'd finally sent a month later. Saying it was all her fault, that she wouldn't listen. She'd driven him away.

'Rubbish,' her mother had said.

'I'll kill him if I get my hands on him,' her father had said.

'And yet you're "pure as the driven snow". Wasn't that what he called you?'

So he'd heard that. She wondered what else he'd heard. She swallowed and looked away.

'I might not have had the same experiences as some other people.'

'Experiences?' he asked. 'What kind of experiences are we talking about?'

How could he lace a simple word with such meaning? The hairs on the back of her neck stood up, a shiver ran through her and she forced herself to stare at her wine glass. She was hardly going to tell him about her sexual experiences, or lack of.

'I don't really care for the things other people care for.'

He watched her as he poured her another glass of wine. His eyes sparkled wickedly in the candlelight.

He was as intoxicating as the wine. One more lingering stare and she'd be drunk. She reached for the water.

'You've been a good girl your whole life long.'

And look where it's got me, she thought, but sipped her water, said nothing. Being good was the only way she knew how to be. She didn't ask for it to be this way; she simply couldn't imagine any other way.

Her teenaged years with Tim had been innocent. They'd had their fun, but she'd been told by her mum and Nonna what wearing white meant. It had been drummed into her, like her date of birth, her address, her vital statistics.

All she'd wanted was to wait until they were married. What was so wrong with that? Why couldn't Tim do the same?

'Have you ever stepped onto the dark side, Jacquelyn?'

She swallowed, looked at him hard.

'I've never been tempted,' she said.

He smiled then and all over his face was temptation. In every hard line of his jaw, every brooding inch of his eyes, in the devilish swirl of his tattoo, she could see now, clearly, the other side of Nikos Karellis. The profit-driven retail mogul was gone and in his place was the Sydney Hell's Angel, and there was nothing remotely gentlemanly about him.

No more polite tolerance, no more board-meeting manners, now she was picking up something else entirely. Now he was seeing her as a woman, and nothing else.

Her heart thundered in her ears. Her body was swirling, she felt drunk, out of control, exhilarated, afraid.

'Never been tempted?'

He pushed away his plate and sat back, one hand

resting on the white linen cloth. She shook her head. Things were shifting, the ground moving from under her, the world reforming into another place entirely. She was suddenly conscious of her legs, bare, her arms resting on the chair, her spine erect, the bodice of her dress with its revealing view of cleavage.

She pushed herself back from the table and the silk jersey of the dress slid over her bare legs as she crossed them, leaving her thigh exposed. He looked right there, at her leg, and she knew he liked what he saw.

'Not even a little?' he said, his fingers drumming a slow tattoo on the white linen.

Prickles of awareness swept over her arms, her legs and right to the tips of her breasts. She felt a tingling at the nape of her neck. Her body was waking up from a long sleep. And it felt good. It felt exciting.

Her fingers curled around the cushion of the seat as she leaned forward to pull the skirt of the dress back over her legs.

'Leave that,' he whispered. 'Let yourself be tempted.'

Her breath quickened. Her heart picked up a strong, thudding beat. She felt herself rooted to the spot, hot and heavy and utterly under his spell. She was in very dangerous territory.

He pushed his chair back too, turned himself round to face her. She was afraid now—but only of herself and the calm, cool exterior that was slipping and sliding and beginning to feel like a puddle of watery ice at her feet.

Kiss me, kiss me, she thought, willing him closer. Her eyes fixed on his lips, her breasts ached under her dress and her back now arched into a curve all by itself, inviting him to savour her and take her.

But he sat there, just watching, drumming his fingers, slowly, slowly.

'I'll make the first move,' he said, and he stood then and closed the two steps to stand beside her. His groin was level with her eyes and her mouth. It was huge and she longed to reach out and touch him.

She was shocked, shocked that these thoughts were in her mind. And it was as if he knew. He stood still as a rock, watching her, then suddenly she felt his hand on the crown of her head, and with a jerk her head was tugged back.

'I bet you've got dark little thoughts and wicked fantasies in that head of yours.'

Her face flamed but she didn't try to deny it.

'I think you want me to forget why you're really here and lift you up and turn you in my arms and let you feel what you are only imagining.

'You want to taste it—it's so close now, Jacquelyn. It's right here. But you're still too afraid to let go.'

Her head was tilted up, her hair caught in a bunch in his hand, her lips were open and his face glowered down at hers, dark and deadly.

'I'm not afraid,' was all she said, her voice hoarse and throaty.

Slowly he raised her to standing, tugging her hair with just the most exquisite mix of pleasure and pain. And she was so close to him now she felt as if she was breathing in the very essence of maleness, the root and power of masculinity, and she was getting drunk on it.

'You want to know what it's like to make love to me.'

She would die rather than admit it, but silence was her confessor.

'And for a reason I still can't quite put my finger on, I am just as curious to know what it's like to make love to you.'

'I'm trying to take that as a compliment,' she said,

rolling her head sensuously as his grip loosened to a caress.

'You should. It's been a very long time since I felt anything like this. A very long time. Maybe never…'

He trailed a finger down her cheek. Her eyes fluttered closed, her lips parted. She felt the finger land on the cushion of her lower lip. She would not give in so easily. She would not grab him the way she wanted to.

Seconds ticked by. His finger followed the lines of her lips, lightly dusted the edges of her cheekbones, the arcs of her eyebrows and with every passing moment she yearned for his lips.

'You know if we do this, Jacquelyn…you know what that means.'

Her head had fallen back and his arms scooped against her back, holding her steady as her neck lengthened in a gentle stretch. His fingers slid up to rest on her collarbone. And then she was closer still and she knew she was past the point of no return, that she had to feel his lips now…

'What does it mean?' she breathed.

Instead of answering, he now followed where his fingers had trailed from the base of her neck, with tiny feverish little kisses, brands. Up her neck to the apex where her jaw began, the most tender spot, so weakening her that her knees buckled.

'It means nothing. Just an amazing night, one amazing night. And tomorrow we go back to where we were.'

She heard his words and she felt his kisses, at her cheekbones, and she knew if she only waited, if she had the patience, if the seconds could only stop stretching for hours, days, weeks, that his lips would finally land on hers, that she would feel his kiss and taste him and know him.

And it was as if every moment of her life had been building to this. As if every single moment she'd ever spent as a girl, learning about her femininity, the way she walked and talked and held herself, the way she put on lipstick and painted her toenails, every moment was building into this, the essence of who she was as a woman.

Kiss me, she gasped, maybe aloud this time…

Her eyes were still closed but she knew he was hovering over her face. She knew he was staring at her, at her opened lips. She felt her body throb with longing, she felt her nipples harden and ache for his hands. She arched her back and pressed closer to him, sinking into his maleness.

'I will kiss you. I'll kiss every part of you. But first… open your eyes, Jacquelyn.'

The rough rasping burr of his voice demanded and received. Her eyes flew open and she stared into his face. His eyes sparkled, points of light in the darkness, the black night sky behind.

'You understand what I am saying? This means nothing beyond pleasure. I don't owe you anything and you don't owe me. Your company and my company are nothing to do with this.'

'I understand,' she breathed, impatient for the sensations to return. If he had given her a contract to sign in blood she would have done it.

She stared at him, and when he didn't move she twisted out of his grasp and put her hands on his face, framing his mouth. She registered the surprise in his eyes, and heard the burst of black laughter that spilled from his throat.

'You are impatient, aren't you?'

But as she opened her mouth to speak he grabbed

her wrists and tugged them down to her sides. Her back arched and her breasts protruded and he growled and then finally, finally he placed his hot harsh kiss on her mouth. And his lips were hard and soft and wet and warm and she began to drown in each moment as the tug to have more and more began to tear at her. Then his tongue teased her lips apart, and now they duelled, and she gasped as another sharp tug built at her core. One of his hands now held her wrists, the other he trailed to her jaw, holding her steady.

'So we're clear—you'll not set this pace. That's not how things roll.'

She had never done anything more than kiss or caress a man. And she knew that none of the kisses or caresses had ever felt like this. Being close to him, the anticipation, each single moment was like a lifetime love affair in itself. The pleasure and pain of waiting, the exquisite heat that was building and building. She was emboldened. She was sexually confident in a way she'd never been before, she'd never known this language, these words and phrases, and she was desperate to start to converse.

'You don't really believe that,' she said, finding her voice. 'We both know who's really in control here.'

'You're deluded, Jacquelyn. You're mine. And I will do anything I want with you.'

'Anything?' she laughed.

She could barely keep the shivering desire from her voice. In the fleeting seconds she saw that she was in a new world. She'd never given away control of her body before, never fully relaxed.

Sex had once seemed part of a wonderful world that she would one day be given a map to arrive at. Then, it became this giant immovable structure that dominated everything, everywhere she looked, everyone was part of it and she was locked out.

She was tired of being the one on the outside. She wanted to know. She wanted to know so badly and she wanted to know now, tonight, with Nikos.

She didn't want to think about tomorrow, there was only now.

'I think you'd succumb to pretty much anything I asked.'

But still he did nothing other than glaze her with his eyes. Her spine felt bent as a bow, strung out, and his body was going to be the instrument that she played. She was almost reverberating with the tension of holding back. She longed to sing and throb and climb the heights with him. But she wasn't going to break and beg.

'You think very highly of yourself, don't you?' she asked, her voice tremulous and she knew he heard it too, because he smiled even more devilishly.

'When it comes to lovemaking? I think we both know the answer to that. You wouldn't be here if you didn't think the same.'

'Well, what are you waiting for?' she said.

'Good question.'

Then he bent his head low, to the exposed column of her neck. And she could see the crown of his head, the thick, dark crop of his hair. He released her wrist and she sank her fingers into his hair, holding him to her neck, her décolletage, her breasts. He growled as he nuzzled first one nipple, then the other. She heard a song in her own throat, a call from her heart.

Hungry, thirsty, greedy for every last bit of this man, she ran her hands over his head and down to his shoulders. She filled her palms with his muscle and drank deeply of the very air around him, the hot, humid night, the sky now bands of orange and mauve and the sun a tiny ball of gold sinking out of sight.

And like an addict craving more and more, she could not seem to get enough of his tongue, his lips, the pleasure he brought. She marvelled at the solid mass of muscle across his shoulders, ached to touch the skin beneath and slid her fingers to the buttons to begin her greedy exploration.

'Let's get comfortable,' he said, standing and scooping her up in his arms in one smooth movement.

Her laptop slid from the seat, from the corner of her eye she saw it land and fold, and as it hit the ground her heart sank with a moment of dread, as she remembered why she was really here and thought of what was still to come—the unfinished presentation, the half-baked plan...

But it was only a moment, a fleeting grey cloud of worry in this dazzling sky, and was gone, because she was up in his arms, her vision now his solid chest and the retreating terrace with all the ornaments of their brewing passion, the whisky bottle, the dining table, the half-drunk glasses of wine, the coffee pot, untouched, the candles flickering in the late evening breeze, to the billowing curtains of the daybed...

And then down she was placed. Soft mattress, cream curtains all around, tiny lights within the canopy like some fairy-tale chamber and there, proud and male and staring down at her like the warrior returned, Nikos.

She sat up on her elbows as he leaned over her and their lips found each other in a new familiarity. His tongue claimed hers, hot breath and wet mouths, his scent, his skin, his utterly irresistible Nikos-ness had her scrabbling up, holding him while he pulled off his shirt.

And then she saw what she had needed to see, and he

was magnificent and marvellous and she felt as if she was reeling at the sight. His shoulders, broad and golden, and biceps, inked and hard, and his chest, wide and dark, and his nipples, small and flat and beaded, and it was there her tongue went, as her hands touched and stroked and grabbed and she filled all of her senses with this man.

What on earth had she been imagining? Not this! This was so much more, so wonderful. The more male he was, the more she felt her own femininity, the more emboldened she was. So this was making love. She was awake and alive for the first time in her life.

She felt his arms slide under her shoulders; her legs wrapped around his waist as if they had a hundred times before.

'Take your dress off,' he said in a growl.

His words splashed water on her fever, and she slid back from the discovery of his body to look up into his face. For a moment he looked distant, his eyes dark and impassioned, as if the fire that burned was darker now, and the light behind his eyes was almost out.

For one horrible second a laser point of fear burned in her heart. She was on fire with lust, dishevelled, her dress around her waist, her breasts soaked with his mouth, her nipples taut, but the sweetness had gone, the sense that something uniquely special was building between them. Now she could be anyone lying here in this chamber.

She could still stop this now. She could roll over, fix her clothes, run back to the terrace, collect her laptop and turn back into the person she really was. She had her life, her business, her family name, her little courtyard and her shop. She was never going to be this woman again. She had opened the door but she didn't need to run through it.

But then he moved. Back. He stepped back as if he sensed what she was thinking. He pulled out of the fiery circle that had been burning around them and she felt the chill of that. Was he having second thoughts? His eyes were trained on her but it was concern she saw there; she saw it and she scorned it. She didn't want his concern, or anybody else's.

She was sick of being Jacquelyn Jones. She was sick of being the devoted daughter whose only goal in life was to replicate the goals of all the people who came before her. She was sick of waiting for a fantasy that hadn't come true. This was her fantasy now—here in Greece, in the villa of one of Europe's best lovers, and she would never be here again...

In a moment she was up on her knees. She threw her arms around his neck and she found his mouth and she kissed him with everything she had.

He paused, he stilled, and then the fire erupted in seconds, the roar of his voice and the cry from her throat as he, one-handed, laid her down, and unfastened his belt and flies and she scrambled out of her dress.

Her eyes and hands started to grab for him, the huge silken-tipped beautiful manly thrust of him, but he grabbed her wrists and shook his head.

'Ladies always come first,' he said, and then he dropped to his knees, and eased hers apart and placed his head where she longed to see it, and instead of re- jecting, because she knew in her heart that there would never be another touch like his, she lay back and let him call the song from her heart with every lap of his tongue.

The bloom of her orgasm built from every pore of her body to her core, one huge wave of pleasure, and she screamed his name as pulse after pulse rocked her.

And as she sank back he was there, naked, sheathing himself masterfully, his eyes boring into her face, his own desire as boldly painted as the inked designs on his chest. His arm was now under her back, her chest lifted, her neck stretched and her head falling back, and then she was down again and he was sliding his shaft inside her body, and as it closed around him, inch by inch, the flash of pain was buried by the last moments of her beautiful, heart-melting orgasm.

But her eyes opened into his face, watching, and she killed his questioning look with a smile and a kiss and a silent prayer of thanks for making her first time better than her wildest dreams.

She squeezed her thighs and urged him on, and he pushed himself inside her, his body sliding over hers, the weight and warmth, the strength and power rubbing against her soft tender flesh and nothing in the world had ever felt as good as this. She relished it like the best food and wine, the best sunset, the softest silk. Nothing was as good now, nothing would ever be as good again.

Her lips kissed and tasted, her hands roamed everywhere—his hair, his muscled back; she grabbed for the sheets of the daybed, then back to him again, as he thrust and built it up all over again.

Then a cry came from his throat, the start of a noise that built—he pushed himself back from her and, bereft of his body, she reached forward and licked at his nipple, flat and hard—and he opened his eyes and smiled, sweetly—he smiled and she licked again and then he started to thrust hard and fast and he was going to orgasm, she could feel the moment swirl and swell between them.

It was all she needed to join him. Like two animals writhing, loving under the light of the stars, lost in passion.

And then it was over. He rolled onto his back, threw his arm above his head. She rolled with him, as if tugged by a magnet, and watched as he blew out a long sigh. He shook his head, first with a kind of incredulity and then as if to settle everything back down to normal.

She lay back beside him, gazing up at the tented roof of the daybed, the tiny lights twinkling down, witnessing their heartbeats slowing, and the cool realisation of each second ticking by, knowing that what was once hidden was now known.

'Are you OK?' he asked, but without moving.

She waited a moment before replying as the images flashed through her mind.

'Perfectly well, thanks,' she said.

He leaned up on one elbow, stared at her.

'For a moment I thought you were a virgin.'

'No. I'm not a virgin,' she said. *Not any more.*

Because technically it was true, and he didn't need to know her truth—not right now. She'd tell him later, because all she wanted to feel now was the relief, the joy of being part of a world that she'd never been able to visit before. She wasn't a little girl any more, she was a woman. A healthy, happy, normal and free woman.

What a truly beautiful experience. What an amazing man…

'My mistake,' he said.

His eyes were soft, his mouth in a smile, his face mere inches away; that special moment bloomed again, that calling to her that this was all OK, that she hadn't been crazy to do this, that she was safe.

Yes, that she was safe…

'Shall we see if we can feel any better than "perfectly well"? Based on first impressions, I think we might just manage it.'

He was leaning even closer and now mingled in with the man was the scent of them and, like a switch, on it went—her lust and longing. Her body turned towards him, complicit and willing, and she was welcomed back into his arms with a smile that turned into a kiss, that turned into an embrace and, with a laugh in her throat that startled her, she was swept up in his arms, and on through the night, to the house.

And with every step she felt a tremor of anxiety, and with every breath she batted it away. This was one night. One night. And all her tomorrows were ahead of her. Nothing was going to change how they passed. Nothing she could do now was going to change a single thing, other than her memories.

CHAPTER SEVEN

GHOSTS. HE HAD never believed in them. It didn't make sense that the dead were still among the living. When your time was up, that was it. Life was bearable if he thought of it that way. But being back here in Greece, he had suddenly started to see them.

Not spectres as such, but the ghosts of his past—images and feelings that had been hanging around, just out of sight. In the corner of a room, the curl of a smile, the heat of day.

Memories—that was all they were, but there was nothing sweet about them. Nothing sweet about that feeling of fear that a hand, or worse, was about to come down on the back of your head, or that the path towards the light had suddenly turned rocky and unsafe, that the love you had once had turned sick—a shiny red apple, bored through and turned rotten by the ravenous worm of addiction and greed.

That was the way it had become with Maria. Now that he knew that love was simply lust, a rush of hormones, temporary blindness, like staring into the sun for too long. His crazy reaction to Maria had been no more than two lost souls finding one another, the bigger the holes inside them, the bigger the fall. Thinking she could fill the hole in him had been the biggest mistake of his life.

Nobody could fill that gaping wound except his House, his world. House was his wife and child, his family.

Nikos stood on the clifftop terrace and braced his hands on the screen that separated him from the deep, still Aegean Sea. How many times had he stood here, staring out across the blues of daybreak and dusk, broken only by the scattering of islands and boats, slowly skating past?

He'd loved this place once. He hadn't realised just how much until he was back here, feeling peace settling slowly around him, enjoying those last few minutes before the world started to waken and decisions had to be made.

He should be sleeping now, he should have squeezed the last balm of rest before starting the day, because he was going to need to stand firm and not allow himself to be swayed by his incredibly strong attraction to Jacquelyn Jones.

His one rule, his North Star, for years had been: will this make money? Will this make the board and my shareholders happy? If not, there was no space for it. No dead weights, no millstones, nothing but relentless progress forward. It was his mark as a leader—shedding the brands and products that didn't fit, even if they were profitable in the short term, for the sake of House.

Ariana Bridal was a company of the past, not the future. He could give Jacquelyn business advice, but he couldn't take her on. Not now. Especially not now.

He'd known this yesterday, he'd known it before he'd even agreed to this stupid idea and he cursed his own weakness in indulging his sexual side at the expense of cold-blooded business.

But it wasn't just that, was it? There was something

sick inside him. Something that he kept buried with every eighteen-hour working day, and every scholarship he funded, and every woman he took to his bed. He buried the evil that was there—smothered it—but last night it had surfaced.

He glanced over to the smooth blue pool, its quiet surface untouched and flat. Beyond it, half-obscured by the thick hedge, sat the hot tub. He didn't shudder now when he thought of it. He could walk past it and he didn't see his father sitting back in it, his shaved head, his tough muscular shoulders, the incongruous tattoos of a rose on one bicep and a mermaid on the other, on arms that had literally choked the life from people who got in his way...

The hot tub had been drained but its empty blue shell still sat, right beside the daybed. Its tented roof poked now above the hedge, innocently concealing the scene of their crazy lovemaking.

He'd almost lost control. He'd been all the way to hell and back with every sip of whisky—the memories of his father and finding him with Maria, right there, in that tub. His taunts, her screaming, begging...

He hung his head in shame.

His hatred and his guilt had sprung back last night like a black geyser, forced through the earth. It was as if none of the five years since had made one blind bit of difference. The plaster was ripped back off and nothing could stop the pain but a beautiful blonde with soft curves and a sweet smile.

And it *had* stopped it for those brief, sweet hours. The pain had gone, the memories faded away in that woman's arms and the world had paused while he found solace. It was as if he were making love again for the first time, it was new and fresh and it felt—right? It felt as if he was with someone pure; there was no other way of putting it.

But she wasn't here for him. She was here to save her business. Everyone had their reasons and those were hers. He didn't despise her for it, but he wasn't going to hang on to the fantasy he'd built up that she was some kind of Goody-Two-Shoes and he was her knight in shining armour. She was as happy as he was to share a warm bed, but the bottom line was that she was here for her business, not for anything else.

He turned to look through the glass, a glimpse of the bed through the split in the curtains. The bed where she lay, naked, tangled in a sheet, where even the thought of her made him once again react. Any other time than this he'd be happy to slide into that warm bed. But he'd been round the block too many times. Business first. Then pleasure.

He gripped the railing and shook his head.

He had to put a stop to this. He had to gather the papers and deliver them to Mark.

At a sound behind him, he turned to look back over his shoulder. The curtains wafted in the breeze, lifting to show the bed, now empty, the imprint of their bodies clear on the sheets. He stepped into the room, sensing her, following the invisible trail through the air. A door closed further inside. The sound of the shower...

The party was over. They'd made the deal, had their fun, and now they had to get on with it.

He made his way to the other end of the house, showered and dressed and sent a maid to Jacquelyn with a message—breakfast would be served on her terrace, in the guest room. He would meet her in the boardroom at eight-thirty.

Half an hour to hear her pitch and then they'd fly

back to London. It wouldn't be a pleasant flight but she was a big girl. She'd get over it.

Then on to New York where he'd take the papers to Mark himself. They'd have to sit down together, go through everything, find the trail and deal with it.

What would happen next would happen. It was out of his control. The last thing he wanted to do was involve the police but if it came to it—well, if it came to it, all hell would have been already unleashed.

And much as it pained him to leave this little corner of Greece, there was nothing here for him now. His mother would never see it again, and there was no one left who even remembered her. He'd sell this house and everything in it and he would close, hopefully once and for all, this chapter in his life.

Jacquelyn's head pounded as if she had a bass drum for a brain. Her stomach flipped butterflies up into her chest and her body ached in a thousand different places.

She dried her hair and put on make-up and looked at the reflection in the mirror. Nothing to see. No cracks showing. Her hair was sleek, her skin was smooth, her eye sockets were camouflaged and she had smudged highlighter where shadows lurked. She looked… OK.

She looked OK, but no matter how long she'd stood in the shower she still couldn't wash away the dirty sense of guilt, the feeling that she had let herself down, and that feeling had clung to every sweep of her mascara wand, every smoothing brush of her hair. No matter how many tricks she played, the face that stared back at her was wretched and desperate and…sad.

So she had waited, her whole life long she had been the one who was saving herself for her wedding day. She put so much store on love and marriage, and sex was the expression of a lifetime promise to the man she would spend her whole life with.

She could laugh out loud but it really wasn't funny. The one time she'd decided to let herself go was the one time she should have been keeping it all together.

The saving grace was that unlike the last time she'd made such a monumental fool of herself, no one was here to witness her stupidity.

No one who knew her would ever think she'd throw her whole existence up in the air, especially when it involved jumping into bed with a man she'd only just met. And she clearly hadn't made that great an impression. Even though she had felt so close to him, so sure that he was feeling what she was feeling, that this passion was surely unique, that their lovemaking couldn't possibly end after one night—other thoughts entirely must have been running through his mind. So much so that he'd left in the middle of the night, leaving her to awaken cold and alone in an empty bed.

She'd slid her hands across the sheets to feel for warmth but there was none; he must have been gone for ages. She'd sat up, looked around in the darkness at the unfamiliar shapes of his room. She tried to remember what had happened. Should she try to find him? Should she be worried? In the end she had buried herself in the bed and curled into a ball, her mind whirling with the awful realisation that she'd been abandoned, not held lovingly, not caressed or kissed.

It's fine, it's fine, she told herself in between forcing slow, deep breaths. *It's just the shock. You're overreacting. It's because of what happened with Tim and this isn't the same at all. This is all OK. It was just sex. He's just a man.*

Why was she so unlucky?

Why couldn't she choose someone who would really care for her? Her mother had found her father. Other people found happy, faithful partners. Why not her? What was she doing wrong?

Well, there was nothing else for it now. All that she could do was make the best of it. She had to pick herself up all over again and get on with it.

You're better than this. You have to do what you came here to do and go down to this meeting, head held high.

She had better stand there in front of him and sell this business and forget those hours writhing naked in bed with him, screaming his name and feeling him lose himself in her, over and over again. She couldn't possibly come all this way and go home with nothing—nothing other than the memory of one night of passion.

But still she sat, staring, numb. Behind her the bed she should have slept in, smooth and intact, a monument to her guilt. She checked her watch. Eight-fifteen. Any minute now she was going to get up from this stool and slip into yesterday's crushed sundress. She was going to walk through this sprawling villa, not thinking all her excited, girlish thoughts, and become the stony-faced businesswoman she had to be.

She wasn't going to use facts and figures and numbers and charts. That wasn't her best language and right now she didn't have the head for it at all. She was going to speak from the heart. She would tell him the real story of Ariana Bridal and how her grandmother had built it from nothing, sewing her own dreams with the dreams of the women whose wedding gowns she'd stitched. She was going to tell him of the tiny shop and how it smelled of flowers and how, as a child, she'd longed to touch the white and creamy silks, and had loved to see the faces of the women who'd tried on dresses, expectant, puzzled and then finally the beaming smiles as each of them had looked like the bride they would be.

She wasn't going to tell him that she had wished with all her heart that she would be one of those brides one day, dressed in white, making her *nonna* proud.

No, what she would tell him was that the tiny shop had become two then three, then more, each of them uniquely, expertly caring for each bride. How could that tiny empire wither and die now when it had so much of what women really wanted? That personal touch… women who understood other women?

That little shop held her dreams safe inside, like an egg in a nest: her dreams, her mother's health, her father's income—everything she held dear was caught up in Ariana Bridal.

How clearly she could still see her grandmother's tiny hands, one buried in silk, the other busily hand-stitching pearls.

A tear formed in her eye. She tipped her head back, desperately holding it in place. She would not cry again. *Please not now…*

She stood up tall, she breathed, and just as she heard the footsteps of the maid she smiled a tiny smile and turned, ready.

On they walked to the boardroom. With every step along the hallway, her heels echoed in the marbled void but her thundering, anxious heartbeat all but smothered her sense of hearing.

She saw a door ahead, and she knew this was it. The maid paused, Jacquelyn rounded the corner of the room and he looked up at her, their eyes meeting in a flash of recognition and acknowledgement. And—damn it to hell—shame.

He waited until the maid closed the door behind them.

'Good morning, Jacquelyn. I hope you found everything you needed this morning.'

'Yes, thanks,' she repeated, automatically.

'Great, well, let's do this. I'm sure you are as desperate to get back to England as I am to get across the Atlantic. I've got meetings set up for the rest of the day so, shall we?'

Complete denial that they had spent the night making love? She had expected a businesslike approach but this was callous even beyond that.

'I've had your laptop hooked up over there.'

He bowed his head to his own machine, cast a hand to the end of the long shiny table where a screen blinked down from the wall.

She looked back to see his dark head bent, his brow furrowed, his hands flying over the keyboard, sending emails as she stood there. He didn't even have the grace to pay her any attention.

'I'm not going to use technology,' she said.

He looked up, his brow furrowed even more. Standing there, she felt like a schoolgirl with unfinished homework.

'You're not? I thought you were working on something yesterday.'

'That was yesterday,' she said. She heard the wobble in her voice but it wasn't grief. It was anger. Pure, cold anger.

'Look, before you begin... Jacquelyn,' he said, pushing back from the desk and sitting up straight in his chair. 'What happened last night was just sex. It has nothing to do with this. I hope I made it clear that the two things are totally unconnected.'

She hadn't expected him to be so *cold*, so brutal. It

was as if he were putting oceans of distance between them before she had even begun. He wasn't even giving her a chance. Dragging her here and then all that they had done, and now he was rejecting not only her body but her business too…?

'You said it didn't count,' she heard her voice say. 'You didn't say it would disadvantage me.'

'I didn't exactly say that.'

'You didn't have to. It's written all over your face.'

'Fair enough,' he conceded, after a long pause. A pause in which she felt as if her whole world were contaminated. But damn him, damn his dark mood and his thin-lipped smile, damn his broad shoulders and washboard-flat abs. Damn his hands that had held her and caressed her and his whole wretched body that had pounded into hers, pounding as her heart was now pounding in her own ears.

'Fair enough,' he said again, but it was without enthusiasm. It was a concession to her boldness, a momentary victory.

'So, can you at least tell me if I'm wasting my time?' she asked. 'I'd rather know now. I don't really want to be here any more than you do. I am very well aware that you've filed what happened last night under "No Further Action".'

He smiled now, to himself, clearly amused at her imagining that anything else was ever likely to have happened.

'Go on,' she said. 'Deny it.'

Her voice was shrill with anger. She couldn't quite believe what was happening, but it seemed to be out of her hands now. Words were pouring out of her mouth.

'Who are you angry with, Jacquelyn? Me, for making the first move, or yourself for thinking I'd fall into line.'

'I'm not angry with myself. I'm not the one with double standards.'

'Maybe not. But you wouldn't be the first woman to think that sleeping with me would get you preferential treatment. It's the oldest trick in the book.'

'How dare you?' she said, white rage now slipping over her. 'You have no idea who I am or what I stand for. But it's quite obvious what goes on inside your head.'

She turned around, as if she could grab her coat and make for the nearest exit and hail a black cab on the street, but all she saw was a blinking blank screen and his reflection outlined in it. She kept her face turned there, feeling the tears welling up and her chin wobbling and that dreadful thickening warning of grief in her throat.

Months she had been like this. Months recovering from that rat Tim, and now here she was back again. A gibbering, soft-hearted idiot who couldn't even stand up for herself.

Every single fibre in her body thrummed with fury at herself. She would not turn round and show him. Not one single sign of weakness. Not one.

But the energy in the room shifted and she watched as, like a typhoon cloud crossing the plain, the image in the screen moved and in seconds he was standing there behind her.

She looked down at her fingers curled white around the back of the chair. She concentrated all her strength into that single spot, tried to repel him with the sheer force of her will, just as she had opened herself up to him last night—welcomed his kisses, his touch, his body. Welcomed them and lost herself in them.

How on earth could she have been so completely naive?

'Look,' he said, his voice low and calm. 'I'm sorry.

That came out all wrong. I just don't want you to get your hopes up. I've had a look through your website and it's not going to work for House. That's it. I don't mind giving you a hand, you know. A mentoring partner or something like that. I can advise on various things that you might find useful. But…'

'My family poured everything into this business. My grandmother's fingers were curled with arthritis by the age of fifty but she stitched and made beautiful clothes for the women of our town, and she would be ashamed to see me standing here like this.'

'The last thing I want is for you to feel ashamed. I'm just trying to keep it businesslike from now on.'

Jacquelyn turned around. She swallowed the bitter pill of self-pity and guilt and lifted her head to face him. Tears were welling in her eyes and her throat was burning but she was damned if she was going to take his crumbs. No matter what happened to Ariana now, she would never stand there begging from a man like him.

'I don't need to say any more to you. I just need you to arrange my transport home.'

Beyond his head the day was shimmering into another dreamy Grecian morning. There wasn't a cloud in the sky, not a ripple on the sea, nothing other than heat and light and promise. And somehow that made her feel even worse.

She had no business being here—she should be back home in Lower Linton, opening up the shop, checking the flowers in the hallway, making sure the staff were pristine and smiling welcomes to the clients, checking the work in progress, the fittings and deliveries, the goodness knew what. There was so much to be done. She had to get away, get back to work, immediately.

She went to brush past the solid wall standing in her way, but he didn't step back and she bounced back just as his hand reached out and grasped her arm.

'Look, I apologise.'

His voice was rough, his grip was strong but she jerked her arm away, hating the heat of his hands and the closeness of his body and the wide wall of his shoulders that obscured her view.

'That really isn't going to make any difference now,' she said. 'Your apology doesn't count for very much and I've got too much to do today so, as I said, can you organise my transport?'

And with that she walked out of the room. She didn't know which way she was going, only that she was heading away from him—nowhere was far enough away. She'd damn well keep walking all the way to England if she had to.

She turned around another corner and the tears were coming—she felt them burn and bubble up. Her eyes were glassy and sightless.

'Jacquelyn, wait!' he thundered.

But she wasn't going to wait for his storm. She was going home under her own steam.

She stumbled along the corridors, the forest of doors, wrong turnings, like being lost in a maze of her own anger and shame.

Thank God no one could see her. Thank God her mother and father were safe in Spain. What on earth was she going to tell them about this? She had to get out of here, away, home.

She found the room. She found her bag, keys, phone, passport, purse.

The sea was to her left, the road to her right. She put her head up and followed the shining marble hallways to the front of the house. No one tried to stop her. And just as well for them that they didn't.

There were the two huge wooden doors she'd come in through. She pulled and pulled at one of them until it finally groaned open.

Heat and light hit her first. A car parked in the turning circle, the plants deep and exotic, a driveway, olive groves on either side, a dusty road, and that was where she walked now, her heels stupid and her toes crushed and her mind whirring with desperate scenarios of how she was going to get home…

And then suddenly along the driveway, a car appeared, driving straight past her. She jumped into the side of the road. The window was lowered and a face with dark glasses peered at her. Then it stopped, reversed back, the door opened. A man got out, a bodyguard? Another one got out the other side.

Instinctively she stopped. She could see her reflection in the window. She looked back at the house and then round to the two men. They didn't move.

This didn't feel right. This didn't feel right at all.

CHAPTER EIGHT

NIKOS STOOD, UNBELIEVING. As unable to move as the pillars propping up the roof of the million-dollar home beside him, watching this hideous scene unfold.

Even from here he could make out the scar on the man's face, the glowering brows, the busted left arm and the hunched shoulders.

His father's best friend, Bruno. Fifteen years older but still as menacing and standing right there in his driveway, still oozing venom, the menacing killing machine that terrorised even the dirtiest, darkest criminals in Sydney.

'Jacquelyn, come back here,' he heard himself bark out.

He shifted his gaze from Bruno and stared at her, willing her back with the force of his gaze. She swung her head slowly round to look at him, and he saw fear sweep over her face, but she didn't move.

'Now,' he growled.

And he could see her waver, he could see her falter in her path. She couldn't possibly go forward. No one could walk into that and not feel the danger. And he wouldn't let her face that, in a million years.

His feet started to move, his arms tensed and his hands bunched into fists, worthless he knew against whatever was in the pockets of the jackets they wore. These men didn't fight with fists, they had bars, and knives and guns and anything else that got their message across. He'd seen them. He'd felt them. He'd screamed silently in nightmares remembering.

Time seemed to have stopped. He was aware of his heart, his gut, the swirls of dust in the road. Jacquelyn swung her head again, her golden hair catching every sunbeam, but her eyes were filled with dark, cold fear. Her arms wrapped around her body and she turned to him with a questioning, terrified look on her face.

And it was as if he saw his mother's face, and remembered her fear and his fear, and he would not let this happen again.

He was at her side, reaching for her, tugging her to him, spinning her round behind him.

'Get off my land, Bruno!' he roared. 'Get out of here now and tell whoever sent you that there's nothing here for him.'

'You know who sent me,' said Bruno. 'He wants what he's due.'

He didn't want any of this aired. He didn't want anyone else touched by this evil.

'Get back in the house,' he hissed to her. 'Please don't argue.'

But she didn't move. She had melted against him. He felt the weight of his body shield her, and she let him be that shield, and he was more grateful for that than anything. The closeness was there, back around them, this strange physical intimacy that made him want to roar and beat his chest and kill anything that tried to harm the soft, trusting body that he held now under his arm.

Every second that passed made him swell with anger

that she was exposed to this. That this sewer had once more flooded the brilliant Grecian world, that somehow his past was here, now, facing him down.

'He should be rotting in jail. That's what he's due.'

'That's never going to happen, Nikos. We both know that.'

'One day.'

Bruno shook his head.

'You're making a mistake, Nikos,' he said as he tracked his steps back to the car and got in. 'He'll come and find you. And he won't be as nice as me.'

The doors closed. The engine started, and then slowly the car began to reverse down the driveway, as dust clouds spilled up from the ground and birds circled high overhead.

Nikos and Jacquelyn stood there until it swung round and the blinking red brake lights disappeared. Neither of them spoke. Her body was still pressed close and his arm held her in place, safe. His heart thundered, and then slowed. The morning settled, and sparkled and righted itself again, as if nothing had ever happened.

At the same moment they pulled apart.

'I'm sorry you had to witness that.'

'They had guns, didn't they?'

'Let's talk about this inside.'

He looked around, half expecting to see them coming back, but everything was quiet, just as it should be. Hot, bright and beautiful.

He shook his head, hating every single thing that was happening. Hating that Bruno had polluted his world. Hating his father. But mostly hating his own fear. He should have faced up to him before now. He should have met him, somewhere, anywhere, sorted whatever needed to be done. But he was a coward when it came to his father. No matter how much he wanted to do it, he just couldn't take the steps he needed to take.

'My legs are like jelly,' she said, and he scooped her up into his arms, holding her even more tightly than he needed, expecting her to push him away, but she didn't move, didn't push back, didn't reject him in any way. And that made him even more furious with himself.

No matter that she was barely an acquaintance, a never-to-be-repeated one-night stand, an out-of-her-depth businesswoman—she was his guest, on his land, at his invitation, and she should never, ever have been exposed to this.

Two more strides to the front doors. He kicked them open, walked in and kicked them closed again. She was still buried against his chest.

He stared around wondering where to go, what to do, how to make this better. Tea. She was English and the English had tea to solve everything.

The kitchen was empty of staff, thank God; they had all gone to Agios Stephanos, the little church on the hillside, to celebrate the saint's day. Jacquelyn slipped out of his arms and into a chair, burying her hands in her hair, and he felt the loss of setting her down as if he'd removed a sheepskin coat in the harshest winter.

'Who were they?' she said, looking up at him, and the look on her face crushed him, squeezed his hard, iron heart.

The only thing that would make this better was honesty.

'They were—they are—criminals.'

Jacquelyn didn't look away from his hard, determined gaze, the one he was using to hold himself in check, to tell her that he wasn't lying.

'Gangsters. From Sydney.'

'They're why you ran away,' she said, as if to herself. 'You were mixed up with people like that and you ran away.'

'Something like that,' he conceded.

'I think I deserve a better answer than that,' she said, her voice slicing right through his self-pity.

He swallowed hard. What part of his past could he share with someone like her? His mother's bruises? Her brain haemorrhage? Maria's last few months on this earth, her drinking and drug-taking, siphoning money from every asset she could get her hands on to pay for her habits. She had sold everything she could, all that was left was herself. He could still hear her pleading cries. He could still feel his disgust, his rejection, his father's laughter. The sight of her car. There had been no hope.

'You might not have the stomach for it.'

'Give me some credit, Nikos. I've just come face to face with armed men. I think I can listen to the backstory.'

He turned and looked at her sitting there, one elbow on the table, spine straight and face composed. The woman he'd held in his arms, the woman who had travelled hundreds of miles to save her business. The woman he'd dismissed without so much as a kind word and who'd kept her cool in front of those low-life scum.

But confessing was tantamount to informing. It was drilled in him so deeply, even if he wanted to say it, he didn't think he had the words.

'He was,' he began slowly, trying them out, '…is, my father's lieutenant.'

A frown crossed her brow, like a prompt for him to continue.

'And my father is one of the most notorious gang

leaders—drugs, counterfeit money, that sort of thing. He was selling drugs to Maria the night she died.'

There. He'd said it. And she didn't even flinch.

'I see. So "he wants what he's due" means payment for the drugs?'

'He's also saying that he gave her money to invest.'

'Do you mean money laundering?' she asked, her eyes widening.

He nodded.

'I think so. The Inland Revenue also want what they're due—the whole thing is a mess and we, my accountant and I, can only find bits of the trail. I want to find the clues before they do—it'll look a hell of a lot better. The last thing I want to be accused of is money laundering.'

'No, it's not a good look,' she said, but without any trace of humour.

'None of this is a good look. The whole thing is a mess until I can clear my dad completely out of my life. I'm going to risk this kind of thing happening again if I don't. And I can't have gangsters turning up in Agios Stephanos. I can't bring this sort of trouble here.'

'Well, short of going to the police I don't see what else you can do.'

He walked to the window, a wall of glass that offered the panorama of rocky cliffs and wide, deep blue sea. There was no place on earth like it.

'I love this place so much, but even when I'm not here it's not safe. There was a burglary six months back. I'm sure it was them.'

'You have to go to the police,' she said.

He didn't even answer that. People didn't understand. The police wouldn't solve anything; they'd only create more problems. Gangs had reach far beyond the law, more terrifying ways than a stretch in jail.

'Well, what else can you do? Apart from sell it?'

Sell the house he'd designed himself, hoping he could one day bring his mum back to it, so she could sit on the terrace and stare at the Aegean, hear the cicadas and taste the olives. That was never going to happen now anyway. One more infection and her body would shut down completely.

'I built this place for myself, but it deserves a family,' he said, looking around, suddenly seeing the answer in rooms full of children running, playing, laughing. 'I'd like to give the local people real work to do, instead of looking after a museum.'

He put the steaming cup in front of her. She nodded at it, muttered a thank you.

'I can see it too,' she said, gazing around, as if the ghosts of the future appeared for her too. She smiled and took a sip of the tea, making a slight face as she put it down.

'The tea OK?'

She smiled up at him then.

'It's hot and tastes vaguely of tea.'

'Jacquelyn, I'm sorry.'

'Oh, don't worry. It's perfectly palatable.'

'I'm not talking about the tea.'

'Oh. Well,' she said, flicking her eyes at him. 'I don't hold you responsible. You didn't look any more pleased to see them than I did.'

'For everything. For dragging you here, for getting drunk last night. For taking advantage—'

'I'll stop you right there. You didn't take advantage of me. I didn't do anything I didn't want to do. But your accusation was unforgivable.'

She spoke quietly, shaking her head, and that simple fact twisted his gut even more.

'You're right,' he said, holding up his hands. 'I was angry with the world, with myself—and I took it out on you. You know I had a great night. An amazing night.'

She looked up then, just a flash of those sky-blue eyes. The last time he'd seen that look he'd thought her coy, but not now—this time, there was no smile on her lips, no playful dip of her eyelashes.

He waited for her to speak, to say the words he realised now he wanted to hear back—that she'd loved it too, that it was special for her, that it wasn't just a little bit of action to pave the way for a sweeter deal.

'I made my own bed, so to speak, and now I've got to lie in it.'

'That's an interesting choice of image, if you don't mind me saying.'

He looked again hoping for even a hint of a smile, but there was nothing other than the implacable composure he'd been presented with when he'd first met her. It was the glassy surface of a pond, the swan gliding, but there had to be something going on under there. It just wasn't natural to be so composed. He'd liked it better when she'd let go, in the two times he'd seen her do it...last night in the bedroom, and this morning in the boardroom.

He wasn't the type to pussyfoot around a subject, and this was bothering him now. They had amazing chemistry. The best. It wasn't the sexual World Championships but she was sweet and innocent and incredibly sexy—how many women had he ever met who made him feel the way he'd felt last night?

It was as if the dirt and grime and muck of the past fifteen years had been rinsed off. As if he'd discovered making love all over again. And he assumed she'd felt exactly the same—dammit, at times she'd made him think she'd never made love before, her reactions were so raw, so visceral.

'Are you regretting the fact that we had sex?'

'Bitterly,' she said, as if she had said, *Pass me the milk*.

'OK,' he said, absorbing that like a slap.

She stood up. She walked to the cupboards, opening doors and looking inside, and without any invitation began to make herself another cup of tea.

She looked at home. She looked very much at home, and it startled him out of his dark daydreams. He'd never let any woman have the run of his house since Maria.

'Would you like another tea?' she asked, turning to stare over her shoulder. She was so beautiful, so feminine, so *right*?

The word formed in his mind and something twisted inside him, something uncomfortable.

'No, you go on right ahead yourself though. *Mi casa es su casa*, and all that.'

In the act of pouring the water into the cup, she stopped. Cool, calm sky-blue eyes blinked at him.

'Let's not get carried away. You practically threw me out earlier, remember?'

'Now, hang on, Jacquelyn. I didn't throw you out. I was being honest with you. I might have been a bit brusque but there wasn't any point in having you go through all the pain of a full-blown pitch for me to turn round and say no. My mind was already made up.'

She put the kettle down with a thump and turned right round to face him.

'What point, exactly, in this fantasy trip did you make your mind up? Before or after we had sex?'

She might be feminine but she was fierce! She was

indomitable. She was every bit the boardroom commander and she almost took his breath away. Nobody could hold a candle to her now, standing here like this.

'Answer me,' she said.

'OK. Since you're asking me a direct question, I'll give you a direct answer. I knew before we had sex that I wasn't going to offer you a business deal. I knew it before you got on the plane. I probably knew it before I agreed to the breakfast meeting.'

A flush of roses on her cheeks was all that he could see but he could feel her anger. He wanted to haul her into his arms and kiss her, and it was getting harder and harder to stand with his arms folded across his chest and a cup of tea in his hand.

'You took me all this way, knowing that you were wasting my time—just to have sex?'

'No. I took you all this way, presuming I might be wasting your time, because I made a commitment to my former brother-in-law, who coerced me into meeting with you because he felt sorry for you, and I had no intention of having sex with you at the start of this. None. In fact, it's pretty much the only intention that I have reneged on in the past year.'

'I can't believe this,' she said, turning her back on him. 'You've made me feel like a complete idiot.'

He sighed. 'I wanted to help you. I liked you. I was incredibly attracted to you and last night—there was so much going on...in my life.'

'So it was just a case of right time, right place. She'll do.'

'That's not how it was.'

The roses on her cheeks had bloomed now and her eyes blazed blue. If he'd been aiming for a better understanding he'd completely failed. He could feel himself getting into dangerous waters and he cursed this stupid situation. He cursed his indebtedness to Maria, and the cord that linked him back to his father. He cursed the whole damn lot of them that had now caught this woman up in the mess of his life.

He cursed it because she was a breath of clean air, and now he felt as if even she had been polluted.

'Well, that's how it felt to me, so do you see how it makes me feel? Do you?'

She spoke with pain in her voice and sorrow in her eyes and he felt a sickening lurch in his gut—she wasn't a player. She was pinning everything on him and he'd really hurt her. He'd built this up, she'd been sucked in, and then he'd not even given her the time of day.

Even after five years the Achilles heel still gave him pain, this weeping sore of guilt that never dried up. He should be properly laying down the boundaries with Maria's brother instead of playing along, playing games with people like her.

She was too nice for this. Far too nice. She wasn't Maria…

'I see now,' he said, quietly. 'But it wasn't a case of "she'll do". You're more than that.'

He was saying words, walking down an avenue in the dark, not seeing where he was stepping, feeling his way along, and all of a sudden he'd arrived at a dead end. He had to stop wandering and turn around and say the words that were stoppered in his throat.

'I like you, Jacquelyn.'

It was as much a revelation to him as it was to her, but the moment the words left his lips he realised he meant them. And not just in the way a man commented on the temperature of the water in his whisky, liking it at room temperature, not chilled—he meant properly, thoroughly, the way he liked to taste the peat of the land, or the sherry of the casks, appreciating the layers and textures of the whisky itself.

'You *like* me?'

But he'd called it wrong again. Whatever she'd wanted to hear it wasn't that. Muscles were twitching on her face. Her eyes turned glassy but if she had opened her mouth and raged at him he couldn't have felt worse.

He reached his arms out but she hunched her shoulders.

'I do. I like you,' he said woodenly, confirming it to himself. He wanted to treat her well—not badly. He wanted her to like him too. And if her business was so important to her, he could make it up to her that way. He could step past his own rules and cut her some slack. It wouldn't cost anything other than a bit of back-pedalling and calling in some favours.

'I want to help you and all I was saying before is that Ariana's not right for House, but I know hundreds of other investors who might take you on, mentor schemes. Or work with an ideas agency. Rebrand. I can set that up today. Right now…'

He touched her, the bare skin of her arm above where she clutched herself, holding her elbows round her body like a shell.

'Come on. I know this seems like a disaster—but what have you got to lose?'

'You have no idea,' she whispered back.

Well, it seemed he'd done a lot of damage. A lot more than he'd realised, but he was trying to make up for it by offering her what he'd never offered anyone. He didn't do personal recommendations, and he didn't do pro bono work that was in any way directly related to House. He wanted… Dammit, he was completely determined now that she would benefit in some way from his business connections.

It was the least he could do.

'I have to head to New York. My accountant's waiting for me and I really can't put it off any longer. Come with me.'

As he said the words he was gripped by an enthusiasm that was so totally foreign to him. The thought of spending more time with Jacquelyn now was exactly what he wanted.

'I'll have it set up—we'll get you a day with the best people in New York.'

'No, no. Hang on. You're just saying words now. I'm not going to get on another plane with you for yet another waste of time.'

'It won't be a waste of time, Jacquelyn.'

'Really?' she scoffed. 'You really expect me to believe that?'

She should be biting his hand off instead of standing there stubborn as a mule, shaking her head. Didn't she know what she was being offered? This wasn't just a gimmick. This was real. This, he could deliver for her.

'Yes, I do.'

She almost laughed but he could see her falter a moment, a sliver of doubt reach her eyes, but then she recovered herself and stood there haughtily, regally, and it made him want her even more.

'So what's changed?' she said.

He levelled her a direct stare, he absorbed her face—the lips he'd kissed, the eyes that had flooded with unspilt tears—he saw arms that had held him and he wanted that warmth again. It had been absent for so long, so many years, and he wasn't going to deny himself any longer, not when he'd been offered it by a woman like her.

'I respect you. I respect that you called me on how I treated you. And the fact that you're still standing here. You came face-to-face with some pretty unpleasant people and you didn't flip out and run screaming. That says a lot.'

She stood a little taller. He saw it and it fed the sense that he was right, he could trust her.

'Just because I haven't run screaming doesn't mean I want any more of it. That's not why I signed up for this trip and I absolutely won't sign up for another where I'm likely to meet people like those two guys that were out there.'

'You're absolutely right,' he said quietly. 'And I am going to deal with it. It's been a long time coming but I can't live my life with this shadow hanging over me.'

'What are you going to do?' she asked, her clear blue eyes widening.

'I don't know yet. I can't turn him in. But I can't go on pretending that I don't know what he does. What he did. But don't worry,' he said, suddenly sensing her fear. 'Nothing will happen in New York. Nothing except the start of the next phase of Ariana.'

CHAPTER NINE

THE AIR-CONDITIONING WASHED OVER Jacquelyn's skin like a tide over pebbles as soon as she stepped inside the vast, gleaming Manhattan skyscraper. People bustled everywhere, a blur of confident strides and efficient handshakes, moving through the building and into elevators that flew skywards in glass caskets.

Jacquelyn stood beside Nikos, crushed so close she could see the tiny spiral of navy ink that peeped above his shirt collar, a tendril of the Sanskrit symbol that snaked over the back of his neck. She had been fascinated by it, kissed it, compared it to the others that covered various parts of his magnificent back and chest. But that was then—that night, never to be repeated. And this was now.

This was where she took every single chance that was offered to her and really made something of her business. This was the start of something wonderful. She was in a different league. Just being here made everything feel more possible. It was brighter, sharper, shinier, the people clear-eyed and confident. It was like the pixels of a perfect world, some computer-animated version of what the working week should really be like.

She tugged the cashmere cardigan over her shoulders, grateful for the hastily acquired luxury wardrobe that had been arranged for her—'an investment in your future', Nikos had said, dismissing her initial indignation at anyone offering charity, particularly when it involved making clothing choices on her behalf.

He was right. She couldn't arrive in Manhattan in a crushed sundress or a borrowed bikini. Instead she'd accepted the bags and boxes that were delivered on the plane and trailed her fingers through the best quality silk blouses in every colour. Cashmere cardigans and pencil skirts. Beige and patent heels, scarves and handbags. Lace underwear, lace-trimmed stockings. As someone who normally made her own clothes, she was completely spoilt for choice.

'I've got a lot to catch up on so I'll leave you with Lauren for most of the morning,' said Nikos as they walked along the moonstone carpets of his corporate suite, his eyes landing on everyone and theirs on him as he cut such a handsome dash in his slate-grey suit and pale blue shirt.

'Make every second count. Every person you meet will introduce you to another ten. At the very least you'll meet some people at the top of their game. You'll go back with a new strategy, a new look, a relaunch, and maybe suppliers, a designer, who knows…?'

He paused at a desk where an attractive young woman was sitting, and leaned his fingers on it. She looked up at him with an air of happy familiarity and Jacquelyn took a mental note.

'Any messages?' he said with a raised eyebrow, picking up the tablet the girl handed him and beginning to swipe.

'Oh, nothing really. You were AWOL for four days so, let's see, about four hundred.'

'Well within your capabilities, Lauren. Let me in-

troduce you to Jacquelyn Jones. Your extraordinary or-
ganisational skills will be put to the test setting up her
itinerary for the next few days. And adapting mine. I
want Jacquelyn to come with me to the gala tomorrow
evening and to dinner with Kostas.'

'I've already made a start,' said Lauren, flicking her
eyes to the screen and then up to Jacquelyn. 'We have
time with Monique on Madison Avenue.'

'Good choice,' said Nikos as he continued to absently
flick through the electronic pad. 'What else?'

'This afternoon a VIP preview of the Bridal Exhibition and then a slot with the House Ideas people before dinner…'

Jacquelyn noticed that Lauren's voice trailed up
questioningly and the pause that stilled Nikos's fingers as he swiped the screen.

'The House team? I would prefer Jacquelyn linked
with an external agency. Try Cube. And for dinner, get
a table at Joro—eight o'clock.'

'Of course. And a suite at…?'

He handed her the tablet.

'I've checked these. There's no sign of a meeting
with Mark. Set that up for this morning. And no suite.
Jacquelyn will stay with me, as my guest.'

With that he turned on his heel and walked off.

'Find Mark. I don't care where he is—I need to see
him now.'

Jacquelyn was aware her mouth was open. So this
was the CEO in his home environment, everybody scut-
tling about following his orders. Command and control.
Well, not with her.

She *should* have had a conversation with him about
their sleeping arrangements before now, and she
couldn't very well shout *Separate bedrooms!* down the

hallway after him. But as soon as she could, she'd tell him. There was no way she was going to let herself get into bed with him again.

With every passing hour she'd rued the moment she'd abandoned the principles that had kept her safe her whole life. Yes, she'd experienced pleasure like she'd never known, and she'd felt it deeply, too deeply. But to Nikos? It was just sex.

And maybe he wanted more; then he would have to find it elsewhere. She wasn't going to wring herself out all over again, she thought, turning back round to look at the efficient Lauren.

'Welcome to House,' the young woman said, turning on a megawatt smile and beaming up at her. 'We'll have your itinerary sorted within the hour.' She lifted the phone. 'Mark,' she said. 'Nikos wants to see you immediately.'

Lauren stood up, a perfect little pixie of health and vitality, and Jacquelyn felt an uncharacteristic stab of jealousy, wondering just how much of Nikos's life his personal assistant had access to.

'I'll take you to the Wellbeing Suite to wait.'

The hallway was screened off on one side with a sweep of cherrywood doors into which Nikos had disappeared, and glass on the other, through which she could see people in meetings, at desks, walking and talking, and that air of purposeful, happy busyness—the magic dust she'd longed to sprinkle in Ariana.

She'd already had to call Victor to tell him to focus only on the two made-to-measure orders they had waiting. She'd died inside, hearing the tone of disappointment in his voice when she'd told him she couldn't yet confirm what was going to happen to their collection, or to the team of seamstresses and machinists that worked for them, but they both knew that there was no money to cover their wages, not unless a miracle happened, and happened soon.

'Have you worked for Nikos for long?' Jacquelyn said, heaving herself back to the moment, as they walked back along the moonstone carpet.

'Four years. I met him when I was an undergrad at Athens University. He sponsors ten students every year and I was one of the lucky ones. I was offered an internship here while I got my MBA from Harvard. He's a fantastic boss. I couldn't wish for anyone better to work for.'

They'd stopped at the edge of a wide open lounge, where the shiny white doors of a sparkly kitchen area and large wooden table, beanbags and gym equipment announced themselves as the Wellbeing Suite. Vibrant citrus fruits were piled high in bowls, muffins and pastries sat alongside neat rows of bowls of berries and granola, and coffee filled the space with inviting scent.

'This is amazing,' said Jacquelyn. 'You can all help yourselves to this? Any time you like?'

'Yes—this is just for little breaks during the day. We have a full gym and a juice bar and café too. And of course access to all the perks that the House retail staff have. He thinks of everything.'

Jacquelyn looked around and thought of the poor girls who worked at the cutting factory in the out-of-town warehouse. They were so loyal to Ariana, when the heating had failed in the winter they'd worn fingerless gloves while she'd plugged in old electric fires for them, as they'd waited for the engineer. They'd work double shifts and go the extra mile every time she needed them. And now, if she didn't go home with good news, they wouldn't even have jobs.

'Yes, it is an amazing place to work. Although this is a first. I've never known him to do this kind of thing before. You must have made a very big impression.'

'I'm trying to save my business. I'll take all the help I can get,' she said, with steel in her voice that cut right through the happy little bubble that seemed to pervade every inch of the House International Head Office.

'You'll get the best from Nikos,' replied Lauren, smiling back sweetly. 'He's in a league of his own. It's the fact that he's willing to mentor a friend that's so unique. Honestly, it's great. It's the single thing that's drummed into us. There's personal, and there's business—but there's never both. No relationships, no favours for friends. Nada.'

'I'm not his friend,' she said, wondering herself what she was. 'I'm—'

'Oh, please—that is not my business. It's another line I don't cross.'

Jacquelyn opened her mouth to reply but her phone buzzed, and the call that she had been dreading lit up her screen.

'Hi, Dad,' she said, walking away from Lauren towards the bowl of gleaming oranges. She didn't need to check her watch to know that it was three in the afternoon in Marbella, that he would have been playing golf in the morning and he and Mum would be enjoying a snack on their terrace, reading the English newspapers and chatting about their dinner plans.

'Hello there, sweetheart. Just thought I'd give you a call to see how things are.'

Jacquelyn touched an orange, feeling the bumps of the skin, imagining her father standing at the kitchen bench, her mother right beside him, the high sierra mountains and the bright blue sky behind.

'Oh, that's nice. How are you two? Is it still as hot? It's been weeks since we had a drop of rain. I'm beginning to wish for winter, already.'

She put the orange down and picked up some other fruit she didn't recognise. The fine hairs on its skin were foreign and strange as she rolled it around in her palm.

'Yes, it's hot here too. So how did it go, then? The Wedding Awards?'

'Same as ever. The food was very nice, but the band was different this year. Some new faces, but loads of people still there that you'd remember. I met Martin Lopez. He was asking after you. He's retiring soon too.'

'Is that right? Maybe he'll join me for a round of golf out here.'

'Maybe,' she said. She could hear the edge in his voice. He was biding his time to ask her.

'I heard Tim Brinley got an award. I hope nobody applauded.'

'He got an award and he tried to speak to me—to apologise. It's fine, Dad. I don't bear him any grudges.'

'He never did deserve you,' he said gruffly. 'And the Australian? He was there?'

There it came. His voice had weakened with age but there was no mistaking the sharpness of his intellect and Jacquelyn winced. It was only a matter of time before word got back to them that she had been seen with Nikos, or that she'd called Victor to say she was in New York.

'Yes, Nikos Karellis was there. He presented an award,' she said in a monotone voice, hoping for insouciance. 'Martin Lopez introduced us and we had a chat about the business. He was in the frame as a financier but it wasn't such a good match, Dad.'

When he didn't say anything she knew she wasn't

going to get away with that. They probably knew other stuff too. Somebody could easily have seen her standing outside his suite after he'd had his shower. People were always jumping to conclusions.

'Did Barbara call?' she asked suddenly. She should know what she was up against at least.

'Yesterday afternoon,' he said.

'I see. And did she have anything interesting to say?'

'I think she's worried about you.'

'I wish she would mind her own business,' said Jacquelyn.

Her father didn't answer and the silent moment stretched by. She began to imagine the look on her mother's face as she listened to the gossipy phone call. The worry that would have crept over her brow, how her father would have gathered closer to the phone to try to listen in. How they'd probably talked about it all day wondering what to do, whether to call, whether to leave her alone. And then finally they'd decided.

'People only want the best, but it's your company now. You have all the big decisions to make.'

The first time he'd ever said those words the flush of excitement had made her feel high as a kite, flying in the air, weightless, exhilarated. Right now she felt worn down and weary, as if she were carrying rocks on her shoulders; every step was an effort.

'That's what I'm trying to do, Dad,' she said, injecting the solid, serious note she saved for these conversations into her voice.

She put the strange fruit back in the bowl and moved further to the side as someone came past to pour coffee. Some happy House International intern.

'And where are you now?'

She looked up. The Manhattan skyline could be seen

through the panoramic windows. The industrious staff were all at work, here in their international headquarters. She felt like a goldfish in a bowl, staring at a world she could see but couldn't properly touch.

Her parents would never understand what she was hoping to achieve by being here. Every moment she was on the phone to them felt like air hissing from the punctured balloon of her ambitions. But there was no point in pretending.

'I'm in New York.'

She heard her mother's, 'Where did she say she was?'

And then his repetition, 'She says she's in New York.'

Her father was never angry with her. Never. She couldn't bear it. Letting them down was almost like a physical pain. When Tim had jilted her she'd been as unhappy for them as she'd been for herself—knowing that they were having to face the town and pretend that everything was all right.

It had crushed her, the shame. The guilt.

'Is this a holiday? May we ask who you are with?'

She stared down at her borrowed clothes, the pointed patent toes, at the pencil skirt and the exquisite blue silk shirt. What had seemed like a Cinderella nine-to-five wardrobe on the plane now felt silly and more than a little bit deluded.

What was she thinking, coming here to New York?

She held the phone to her ear as if she could muffle this world that she was standing in and keep it secret from her parents, keep them from knowing that she was here now because she had formed an unholy alliance with Nikos, an alliance that now involved this unwritten contract built on guilt and shame.

'It's not a holiday, no, but it's complicated. I'm on a business trip.'

She nodded, satisfied at that. It sounded feasible.

'You didn't say who you were with, Jacquelyn.'

She bit her lip.

'Is it Karellis?'

She nodded, just as a coffee was placed in front of her, as an arm rested lightly on her shoulder, as heat and strength and courage wrapped round her like a warm wind, but then as quickly were blown away as he lifted his arm and walked off.

'Yes. I'm at the House HQ, Dad,' she said, glancing after Nikos. He'd taken off his jacket. The blue sheen of his shirt glowed in the subtle low lighting of the kitchen. Her heart stuck in her throat as she watched him. The perfect proportions of his body, his long legs and wide shoulders, the cuffs of his shirt turned back once, exposing the strong bones and dark hairs of his wrists.

It was in every part of her—this feeling she felt for him. This was what happened when you slept with someone, she realised. This contract, this bond. He was her first and she would be linked to him for ever, even though he didn't know it. He was walking about oblivious and she was going to carry his face in her heart for ever. She had waited so long, built this up so much, and then in a single night it was gifted to Nikos and she was left with only a memory, not the lifetime of love that she'd always imagined would follow.

'What on earth are you doing there, Jacquelyn? If there wasn't any mileage talking to him at Maybury Hall, why pursue it in New York?'

A tear sprang up out of nowhere and she shook herself. The last thing she could afford to be right now was weak, in anyone's eyes. This was business, pure and simple. She swallowed.

'I'm going to meet some contacts that might be right

for Ariana. House isn't right, as I said, but there are other opportunities that I'm here to chase up.'

Nikos had opened the fridge and stood illuminated in its blue light, as if he was searching for something, but she could tell he was listening. He took out a jug and poured a glass of carrot juice then reached for a muffin, moving with the graceful alertness of a panther.

'You need to go all the way to New York to find opportunities? Seems an awfully long way.'

'It's too good to pass up, Dad. But I'm only going to give it a day or so—if it doesn't feel right I'll be straight back to work.'

She wanted to glance at Nikos, to see how he reacted to those words, but she resisted, stared at her reflection in the glass instead.

'This isn't another wild goose chase, is it, Jacquelyn? Are you in a relationship with this man?'

She heard her mother's voice and then the phone was muffled, then passed over.

'Jacquelyn, it's me. Are you all right, love? Where are you? I'm worried about you.'

She glanced at Nikos. He'd put down the glass and stood facing her, his arms folded, staring at her intently.

'Mum, I'm twenty-five years old and I'm more than capable of looking after myself,' she said.

'But Barbara said you were with him, this Nikos. He's not your type, Jacquelyn. He's a ladykiller. He'll hurt you. I don't want to see you upset again, that's all. And he might promise you the earth but...'

'Oh, for goodness' sake, please stop worrying. I'm not in a relationship with him or anything like it. Nothing could be further from the truth.'

She turned to the glass and tried to say it quietly, throwing the words down to the carpet beside her shoes as if they might land there unheard. But when she looked up she knew that he'd heard them all right. The glass of carrot juice was sitting half-drunk at the counter, the muffin untouched and only the gleam of his shirt was visible as he walked back along the hallway. A shaft of light spilled out for a moment onto the carpet, and then was gone, as he disappeared inside a doorway, and closed it with a sharp click.

CHAPTER TEN

NIKOS DRUMMED HIS fingers on the table and looked up again at the inscrutable Mark.

'You're sure?'

'As I can be. The Inland Revenue still think you're laundering money. I've spoken to my guy and told him that we've got evidence it was Maria who invested in ghost companies, and that those companies have folded, but they're still sniffing. It's not what you want to hear, I know.'

'I want to hear whatever is going to get me out of this and let me get on with the rest of my life. I'd gift the whole damned lot to charity, every last cent of it—'

'If you only knew what there was to gift. I know. I get it.'

Nikos picked up the papers he had found in the safe again and looked at them, then tossed them down.

'So these are worthless? There was no point in me going to Greece to find them after all?'

'I wouldn't say they were worthless, no. But I think that they're probably only the tip of the iceberg. If you don't mind me saying, Mrs Karellis was a complicated lady with a big past. There's every chance she was involved in something like this.'

'But I can't believe I wouldn't spot it,' he said, shaking his head.

'You'd need to have been on her case twenty-four hours a day to keep up with her.'

'And I certainly wasn't doing that,' Nikos muttered to himself. 'If I needed anything to prove to me that business and pleasure don't mix…'

'You get a lot of pleasure from business, my friend. It's just certain types of pleasure that are better bedfellows with business than others.'

'You can say that again.'

Nikos checked his watch and looked up again at the smoky glass front of the restaurant. Jacquelyn was late. Knowing that was just adding to this list of stuff he had to deal with. He felt responsible for her.

He'd had a guard with her all day, and she was perfectly safe, but the nagging doubt at the back of his mind had got louder and louder, nearly drowning out all other thoughts.

Vital thoughts, like trying to pull memories of Maria's businesses, any possible ways she could have hidden money.

When he'd first met her she had played a huge part in her first husband's businesses, because his illness had left her no other option. And she hadn't trusted anyone else.

But she'd been vague. What he'd put down to a lack of interest was more likely to have been a smokescreen. Always suspicious, always looking over her shoulder, and with good reason, because she'd always been up to something.

He racked his brains again. His first steps into business had been to cut through the mess that had been made with her first husband's businesses. She'd reassured him that she'd known what she was doing with her own money and he'd left it at that. He hadn't wanted to poke his nose in. He'd trusted her.

Had he? Had he really trusted her? He'd never checked her phone, followed her, gone through her things. She'd done all of that to him, had been insanely jealous when he'd spoken to other women. The times he'd stood there, absorbing her anger, her fury, sometimes even her blows. Because a man never hit a woman. As long as he lived he would never raise his hand to a woman, he would never be the man his father was.

That momentary flash of his mother's face formed again, the smile. She was so pretty, so Greek.

But it was those nights that he remembered most clearly. The roar of the motorbike engines in the distance, coming closer. Praying that it would go past the house but then hearing it stop; his father's footsteps on the path, the wooden boards that creaked as he listened to him climb, heavy footed, to the porch; straining to hear them over the sound of his own heartbeat.

The little prayers he would say over and over: *'Please don't make him angry...please keep Mum safe...please, God, take my pocket money and all my toys...'*

It always started hopefully, quietly. As if it might not actually happen, but then he'd hear voices, even muffled under his quilt, breathing in his own humid terrified air, he'd hear them, then the sound of her voice calling his name, letting him know she was all right, even as his father hit her.

'Are you OK?'

Nikos looked up.

'I'm sorry I'm so late, but I got a bit held up.'

Jacquelyn was standing right in front of him, a vision

of blonde loveliness. He drank in the sight of her—the sunshine of her smile, the intense blue of her eyes, the roses on her cheeks shining with health and happiness. It was as if prison doors had opened into springtime.

'Hey, no problem. Grab a seat.'

He stood up and pulled out a chair, watching carefully as she slid herself down, pleased to see that she had chosen the blue silk dress that matched her eyes and showed off her slender arms and legs. And with a neckline that draped invitingly over her breasts, casting a shadow that his eye found pleasing. He felt an immediate stab of lust, and he did not, and would not, smother it.

She sat down and tucked her bag and briefcase on the other seat and looked up expectantly.

'Mark, this is Jacquelyn Jones. Mark is my accountant. We've just finished a meeting so you're right on time.'

'Oh, aren't you joining us for dinner?' she said, shaking Mark's hand. 'I'm really happy to sit and go through my notes. I've learned loads today and have been given some homework to do so I wouldn't be in your way.'

'No, Mark's leaving,' cut in Nikos. The last thing he wanted was anyone hanging around. He'd been looking forward to seeing her since he'd left her at the juice bar on the phone, denying that she was having a relationship with him.

It was interesting how hearing a few words could clarify a whole day's worth of doubt. Until that moment he hadn't known he really wanted a relationship with any woman but now he did. Even now when the timing was so off, especially now. And she had stood there denying him.

'Yes, I'd love to stay, but my boss here has other plans for me.'

'Put a team on this. Your best, most discreet people, but keep it in house.'

'It's lined up. I'll let you know how we get on.'

Nikos shook his hand. A hand he trusted.

'Are you sure you're all right?' asked Jacquelyn, sipping on water but looking at him. 'You looked shot when I came in. Was that bad news?'

'It's not great, but it'll be dealt with. It has to be.'

'Was it anything to do with the guys at the villa?'

He sat back and looked over her shoulder.

'You're doing that thing again,' she said. 'When you check out who's about. Like a secret agent. Not that I blame you.'

'Do I do that?'

'Since the day you picked me up to go to the airport.'

'I suppose I do.'

'A man like you, it's only to be expected. I guess there are always people on the make all around you, even if they only want to get their photo taken with you.'

'That's kind of you, but not every man like me has invited so much trouble into his life.'

'You can't help where you were born, or brought up.'

'No, but I can help who I choose or, rather, chose to marry.'

He didn't expect to feel the weight of those words as they landed but he did, and for a moment he was lost in a cloud of confusion. Marriage to Maria—had that really been him? It didn't just feel like a different life, it felt like a different man. He was so far away from there now he couldn't imagine making such a mistake again.

'I'm sure you'll make a very good choice,' she said quietly.

She dipped her eyes then, that sweep of lashes, such lovely lines that he'd grown accustomed to seeing now, that pleased him, and when she looked up at him again, her gaze was steady and sure.

'I can confidently say that I won't be making a choice like that again. Not when I see the mess it's got me into. Even five years after her death I'm having to pick up the pieces—if I can find the pieces.'

'I see,' she said.

'I'm talking in riddles, I know.'

'It's not my business.'

'Well, no, but you already know a lot of it. I was in Greece trying to find papers from an investment I knew she had, but it turns out she had some more. And we're not sure how she afforded some of the investments she made. Money has been going everywhere and the tax people want their share.'

'It can't be that hard to find. Somebody must know that there's money coming in and nobody is claiming it?'

'You'd think,' he said, musing on that idea for a minute. Somebody must be happily processing dividends into some bank account somewhere. It wasn't feasible that nobody knew what was going on.

'Is that why the guys were there? Have they got something to do with it?'

'That's what's worrying me. It isn't just blackmail.'

'Aren't you worried? Don't you think you should let the police know?'

'Involving the police is no guarantee this will get fixed. It might even get worse.'

'But you can't possibly think you can deal with all this on your own?'

Of course he was worried, of course he knew this was getting out of control. But letting the police know?

It wasn't as simple as that. Things could backfire spec-
tacularly. He had his dying mother to think about, his
staff, even Jacquelyn. Innocent people became casual-
ties in these kinds of wars.

The whole thing was so messed up.

'Anyway,' he said, keen to change the subject. 'How
did you get on today? Tell me about your day.'

He tried to keep the tone light, tried to keep upbeat
and interested. He was determined that Jacquelyn would
feel that the trip was worthwhile, but he must not, would
not, in any way get involved in this business, no matter
how tiny, no matter how tempting it might be to make
that face light up.

Because she was worth a lot of effort. He looked at
her again and crushed down the urge to reach across the
table for her, hold her hand and tug her towards him,
and take a kiss from those lips.

'So yes, I couldn't believe it. The others were great
but when I met Brody and he made me that offer, honestly I was blown away. I still am. I couldn't wait to get
here and tell you.'

She was babbling with excitement, words pouring
from her mouth, and he was just beginning to realise
what she was saying.

'So Brody made you an offer? My friend Brody from
Cube? Cube the digital marketing agency?'

He could feel something rise in his chest and he
knew it was anger.

'Yes.'

She beamed. Her face was glowing and her eyes
shining and it was some other guy who had done that.
Brody—that creep from Cube.

'Literally less than an hour ago. It's—oh, my goodness—it is honestly the best. I couldn't have dreamed

it. We'd met earlier in the afternoon at the Wedding Expo. He looked me out. Lauren had already told him that I would be coming later and he took such trouble to come and find me and talk to me.'

'I'll bet he did,' said Nikos, pouring water even though the waiter had just topped up their glasses. But he had to find something to do with his hands or he might rip something up, like the table.

'Yes. You know him? Of course you do. You set this up. I can't thank you enough.'

She moved as if she was going to reach across the table and kiss him, but then she stopped herself. It was awkward, and he was now even more furious because it was as if Brody were sitting right there between them, on the table.

'You can thank me later—once I've heard what this amazing offer is.'

'He's going to be a backer. He has pots of money himself and funds people like me. I'm getting a million sterling and for that he only wants ten per cent.'

'Ten per cent of what? The business or the profits or both?'

'Well, the business, I think.'

'You haven't signed anything yet?' he said, suddenly aware that his anger was about to pour into curses just thinking about Brody. He should be happy for her, but he was in a rage that was hissing from his skin like steam. He had to keep a lid on himself, but he couldn't seem to dial it back down.

'Have you?' he repeated, unable to stifle the derision in his voice, which made him angrier again at himself.

'No. No, I haven't. Why?'

She sat back in the seat. Her shoulders slumped

down. Her face sank and her eyes filled with concern.
He felt like a piece of garbage.

'Do you think this is a bad move? It sounded so good.
He was so positive.'

'Tell me exactly what happened.'

She looked around as if the answer were somewhere
in the room full of people eating ridiculously expensive
seafood, as if one of them were her witness and might
help her out of this problem that had suddenly appeared,
the storm cloud in her sunny sky.

'I met him at the expo. I told him why I was here…'

'Which was what? What did you tell him? Did you
tell him that you and I…?'

She put her hand to her chest and looked hurt and
horrified, and he caved, he honestly caved. He would
do anything for this woman now, he realised. He would
do anything and that idiotic creep Brody would be dust
before he'd finished.

'No! Of course not. I would never tell anyone what
happened.'

Her eyes had filled up. Silvery tears wobbling on the
lids of her eyes, pools he could dive into and not care if
he drowned in them.

This time he reached for her hand, and held it in
his own. He rubbed his fingers over hers, feeling the
fine bones, the silken skin. He squeezed her hand. She
didn't pull it away but she didn't meet his eyes and that
hurt him.

'I already told you I regretted it so why would I tell
anyone about it?'

She tugged her fingers away but he wouldn't let her.
He leaned forward, touched her chin.

'I don't. I don't regret a single moment. I loved what

we did. I only wish things were different between us, because I'd very much like to take you out. Properly.'

She looked up.

'I don't quite see how that can happen.'

'Things have a funny way of working out. I admit that I haven't covered myself in glory, but that doesn't mean I don't want to do better. I'm always trying to do better—in everything I do.'

'We all are,' she said. 'That's the reason I came here.'

He nodded. Part of him wanted to think that she'd come because of him but he'd blown it with his callous treatment of her. And he had a lot of making up to do.

'So, your new backer. Let's hear the rest of it.'

She sat back, composed again, but much less excited.

'I simply told him the story of Ariana. My grand-mother, Dad, the Jones cut, how hard things are now. The competition from China. The made-to-measure clients that are so hard to come by, and how I'd called that wrong, expanding too quickly...'

She shrugged and his eyes swooned watching her. She was utterly perfect.

'And he offered you a million just like that?'

She sipped the wine that had just been poured.

'No. I told him I had been struggling to design. Since Tim.'

'You told Brody about your ex?'

Why is this hurting you? he chided himself.

Why should it bother him that she had confided in Brody about her ex when she would barely even ac-knowledge the guy's name when he'd raised it?

'Yes. I told him. I told him that my heart had been broken and that I lost control of what I was supposed to be doing. I had fallen in love with the idea of get-ting married and when it didn't work out I was stuck.

I was stuck in a business where I was reminded every day that I'd failed. It was all I had wanted and I couldn't lift myself out. The business got into difficulties and I had to take over design again.'

'You told Brody all of that? And what did this look like? Was he taking advantage of you?'

The black rage was within him now. The angry, jealous beast. The one that he had never allowed to so much as breathe inside him was now a dragon. The thought of sharp, brilliant, handsome Brody with his arm around Jacquelyn, patting her hair and soothing her with his *'There, there'* and waiting for his moment, the fox in the chicken coop.

Nikos had to get a grip of himself, he realised. He had to get back to couldn't-give-a-damn. Because he couldn't, or at least he shouldn't. Giving a damn was what had got him married to Maria in the first place.

Jacquelyn Jones was not his wife. She wasn't even his girlfriend. If she wanted to tell her sob story to some sharp-suited ex-lawyer-cum-financier, then tell it she should.

'He was a gentleman,' she said, with quite a heavy dose of indignation in her voice.

'Was he indeed? Good. Good that your new backer is a gentleman.'

She sat back properly now. 'You're jealous. I've just figured it out. You didn't want to get into business with me but you really don't want anyone else to either. Why are you doing this? Why can't you be happy for me? You were the one who set it up.'

'Jacquelyn, there is nobody happier for you than me right now. I am delighted for you. I just want to be sure that what you see with Brody is what you get. I don't want you walking into a disaster and him walking away with half your business.'

She threw her napkin down now.

'You really have such a low opinion of me. I didn't realise it until now.'

He shook his head. 'No. I have a very high opinion of you. I just don't think that your business is…going the right direction.'

'Brody saw my problem straight away. He saw what I was trying to do and told me to focus on my designs.'

'Sure. Well, we already discussed that it was a designer that you needed only you couldn't afford one. You said yourself that your designs were your Achilles heel.'

'Not any more. Brody saw my new sketches. He thinks they're amazing.'

Now he knew he was on sure ground. The designs she had shown him were sterile, desperate, just not on the money at all.

'OK.' He put his hands up. 'If you're hearing what you want to hear and you don't want my advice…'

'My *new* sketches. I've done another four designs,' she said and her eyes were blazing again. Confidence dripped from the curl of her lashes, the ends of her fingers, the slant of her jaw as she sat back and tilted her head over the plate of crayfish that had just been served.

'I'd love to see them.'

She put her cutlery down and reached in her bag and pulled out her tablet without taking her eyes off him. The screen flashed to light and she quickly opened up a drawing app. Images popped onto the screen he immediately recognised as electronic sketches of wedding dresses. Vibrant, bold strokes, curving to create voluptuous, feminine figures. These were not at all like the ones he'd seen before.

'That's quite a departure from what you showed me last time.'

She nodded.

He flicked through the pages of each design, his eyes lighting up.

These were not the sterile aloof brides he'd expected. These brides were proud, and there was a confidence to the way they stood, hands on hips, facing fully forward.

'Wow, Jacquelyn. I'm impressed. You've taken this to a whole new level. These aren't talking "wedding day". These are talking "wedding night…honeymoon suite". Was that what you were after? Because that's what they're saying to me.'

He looked up. He could tell she was pleased, but pink dusted her cheeks.

'I didn't think so at the time but I see what you're saying.'

He was saying it all right. And he wanted to say it again, in person, now. He wanted to say it with every masculine part of his body. He wanted to imprint on her that he was the man who had made her sigh and cry and scream her passion in his arms. He was the best lover she had ever had, and, dammit, he was not going to give that crown to any other man.

It was no good. He threw down his napkin. He couldn't hold back any more.

'Have you had enough to eat?'

He was hungry—for her. He had to have her. His loins were full and aching and he was only going to get release one way.

She looked startled. He was going to have to manage this better, but somehow all his charm had walked out on him and all he had left was red-hot passion.

He put out his hand and urged her to her feet.

'Come on.'

'Don't you want to hear more about Brody and the deal?'

'That's the last thing I want to hear about. I want to talk about something else entirely.'

He was aware he was touching her, her elbow, her back, her waist, her hand. Possessive and unremitting, all the way through the crowded restaurant where people turned to stare, some of whom he knew, none of whom he wanted to speak to.

Out on the pavement and into the heat of the uptown evening, he stopped, arm around her waist now, checking up and down the street. The urgency with which he wanted to have her in private was tugging at him, it was the only thing he could think about, but he had to make sure there was no one around.

People milled past them, cars cruised and stopped, everything sluggish and hot, the day's heat still hanging over the city like a blanket.

'Let's walk. It's only three blocks.'

'To where?' she said, falling into step beside him. His hand tugged her closer, slid to her hip, felt the movement of muscle and bone through satin, felt his own lust kick in response.

She didn't pull away, she leant in closer and he knew with that single move that she was right there with him. She hooked her arm round his waist too and somehow a path appeared through the busy pavements. As if the universe and everyone in it seemed to know that they were lovers on their way to a night of passion and they were going to be rewarded, because it was beautiful. It was lovely. It was making love.

CHAPTER ELEVEN

THE RAILINGS OF what could only be Central Park stretched out ahead, a forest of iron slicing through grass and trees on one side, and dull grey concrete on the other.

Jacquelyn's heels clicked on the pavement, rattling faster than her heartbeat, signalling each new step on this whirlwind journey.

What on earth was going to happen next today? She'd woken up on a luxury jet, slipped into luxury clothes and cars, then meetings, dinner and now Nikos was steering her towards his apartment block, holding her to his side as if he was afraid the warm, gusty wind might blow her away.

All her wishes seemed to have been granted. Her dreams were coming true, one by one. Brody's offer was beyond anything she'd expected—it would solve everything. Salaries, rent, the lag time until next summer when the new orders would start paying. And he was legitimate, she was sure of it. She didn't sense anything wrong, or creepy, just an honest-to-goodness interest in a traditional wedding dress design company and a belief in her ability, and her new sketches.

They were her best ever. That was the thing. Her hand had flown about as if possessed, as if somehow disconnected from her head, as if her heart or some other part of her was in control.

For the first time in her life her drawings felt alive.

Wedding night. Well, yes, maybe it was that. She knew now what it would have been like. She knew what other women knew, how their bodies would sing and their sensuality would be awakened by the touch of their lover, their husband. They wouldn't have awakened in the night alone and confused.

Nikos tightened his grip, holding her even closer, and her treacherous body swooned in response. She had to be careful. She couldn't let this get out of hand again. They could kiss, but she had to stop at that. She had to tell him.

'In here,' he said, guiding them into a tall apartment block, studded with elegant green awnings and guarded by a smart concierge, who doffed his cap as they strode right on through, past huge displays of white lilies and roses, a pretty East Asian receptionist, and into a plush, velvet-lined elevator.

Inside, and the doors slid slowly closed. Nikos reached across and pressed his thumb to the keypad. Immediately an artificial voice welcomed him by name. He ignored it, and stood back, stared straight ahead, expressionlessly. His arm was still around her but other than that he made no move to touch her.

'Are you all right?' she asked.

'Never better,' he said. 'Cameras.'

He nodded to the corner. The lift glided to a slow stop. A bell tinkled and the doors slid open into a light-flooded, parquet-floored vestibule.

'But there are none here,' he said and he tugged her hand and led her through the space.

She tried to see where she was, absorb her surroundings, this Park Avenue penthouse apartment, but Nikos spun her round in his arms. She felt his body, his strength, and her desire rose up like a flower hungry for sunshine and rain.

'Nikos, hang on. We need to talk about this,' she said, pushing herself out of his arms.

She put her hand up and walked backwards, stopping at a circular table that sat directly underneath a round cupola that flooded the space with light. Doors opened off in all directions, leading on through hallways dark with cherry reds and golds. She put her bag down on the smooth mahogany table, fumbling for the words she should say.

'Jacquelyn—you know I'm sorry about how I handled it. But I can't get you out of my mind.'

He walked up behind her and put his hands on her shoulders. She didn't pull away.

'You feel the same about me. I know you do,' he said, his voice quiet.

Slowly he let his arms slide around her, just holding her, cradled inside his embrace. He gently rocked her and she held his arms in place, loving the feeling, loving the way their bodies seemed to be so in tune.

Isn't this what you really want? To be in his arms again? Would it be so bad to have a kiss...?

He was so close, she let herself fall further back into his arms. Her body tentatively trusting that he was completely there, and he was.

'You know we have something special. This sort of thing doesn't happen very often. And I know I upset you but this time we'll play by your rules. Come on, Jacquelyn. Hmm?'

He bent forward, he nuzzled her neck, and just like that her body sang. She was almost ready to jump again.

She could kiss him, she had to kiss him. She had to kiss him and then she had to stop…

'OK.' She turned around in his arms. 'But I'm not going to sleep with you,' she said. 'I want to make that clear.'

He pulled back, looked at her, his dark eyes glittering, his mouth curled into a smile.

'That's clear,' he said.

And then she grabbed his face, she cupped his jaw and pulled his mouth towards her. And for a moment they kissed, slowly, softly, but as soon as his tongue slid into her mouth she was lost. She knew that all she wanted was to go to that place where pleasure and love seemed to find each other.

'I've been aching to do this,' he said as they frantically grabbed at one another, his hands sliding over her dress, lifting her skirt, and she hooking her leg over his hip. He ground into her, crashing them back against a wall, as she held onto his shirt, laughing as she lost her footing, being scooped up and held fast.

'I haven't stopped thinking about you all day,' he said, and he slid his hands to her breasts, kneading them, weighing them, tugging at her nipples, already painfully hard, desperately proud and aching for his mouth. He tugged the neck of her dress down, ripping the fabric, exposing her nakedness underneath.

'You wore this dress knowing I was going to take it off you, didn't you?'

She threw her head back, clutched his head to her chest and held him there as he laved her with his tongue and teeth.

She had dressed with him in mind, of course she had. Everything she did was with him in mind. He lived in her mind, in her heart. He had got under her skin; every step she'd taken in this town she'd imagined sharing with him. It was hard to remember that she'd known a world empty of Nikos, when he filled it now so completely.

'I've never wanted a woman so much. Touch me,' he said. Her fingers flew to his belt, his zip, the hard, hot force of his erection. She longed to see and touch and taste and feel him inside her.

His breath was coming in short panting bursts, between each clever touch.

'We are going to have another night to remember, Jacquelyn.'

He pulled her closer still.

Another night like her first. The discovery of love, the heights of passion and the novelty of masculinity, but not just anyone's masculinity—Nikos, her first ever lover. The man whom she'd always hold in her heart.

'All night long.'

'You won't get up and leave me in the middle of the night this time?'

'No. You're my guest here. I'm not going to do that,' he said.

His guest.

Was that all she was to him? A house guest, here today, gone tomorrow?

What if there was no tomorrow? What if she was just filling his nights the way Lauren filled his days? Was she just the disposable blonde from England who happened to fall into bed with him whenever he clicked his fingers? No matter how she looked at it, she wasn't his equal in this. It was his apartment, and these were his terms.

And she was worth more than this. She was from a family where love was not throwaway. It was for ever— and she wanted a for-ever love.

With strength that came from somewhere deep inside, she pulled herself out of his arms.

'No,' she whispered. 'No, no, no. I don't want to be your *guest*.'

He stood there, exposed, his erection straining forward, his shirt tugged open, his face stained with lipstick and his eyes wild with disbelief.

'What's the problem?' he said.

'I want to know what I am to you,' she said, quietly.

'Jacquelyn,' he said, but she couldn't look at him. 'What do you want me to say? You're staying here with me for a few days, as my guest. I don't get what the problem is.'

'I'm sorry, no. I can't do this.'

'Why? What's happened?'

She straightened her dress, and turned away from him, fixing herself as best she could, stopping the tears with sheer willpower as they pooled in her eyes. She breathed deeply and, with a sigh that came from the pit of her stomach, she shook her head and walked away.

'I'm sorry, but no. This isn't right. It's not who I am.'

How did she explain this to him? How could she tell him that she felt so strongly that making love was so much more than a fun way to spend an evening?

It was huge, bigger even than she had ever suspected. Since she'd taken Nikos to her bed, she'd given away part of herself and she felt the weight of her decision so deeply.

She looked back but he was still standing where she'd left him, his face a mask of disbelief. How could she say any of this to him when she was just another woman in his bed?

'Would you mind telling me what's going on?'

She looked blankly around. The apartment was exactly as she had imagined it. The walls a dark burgundy, vintage furniture, brass and mirrors from a more elegant age. Statuettes of long-limbed women with short hair holding glass shades, twenties icons, art deco, beautiful.

She clutched her arms around her body, protecting herself from the fierce blast of his maleness, in case she succumbed again, because she did so want to. She had to distance herself from this, put some space between them, calm it all down, pour ice on the heat.

'I shouldn't have come here,' she said.

He stared, incredulous.

'Look, I know it looks as if I've led you on, but I—I can't explain.'

'I wish you'd try, Jacquelyn. I really thought we were on the same page here.'

Why was this so unfair? Why couldn't Nikos be hers? Why, when she had finally found him, was he so unavailable in the way that really mattered? He was everything to her, she would never meet another like him, and it broke her heart that there was no future for them.

She felt tears form and her head hung and then he was there as his arms slid back around her. Close and closer they stood, hugging and holding one another under the cool stares of his art deco sculptures. Through the damp linen of his shirt she scented him, learned the slow steady beat of his heart, let the rhythms of her body and breath settle and synchronise with his.

He was a rock, a solid, kind, stable man. A good man. But he wasn't her husband and he wasn't even her lover. She was just one of many and then she'd be gone, and he'd always have a part of her and she'd only have this part of him, and it hurt her so badly to know it.

It was a bond that was deep, vast, endless. She felt it

with every steady beat of their hearts, but he was miles away from where she was.

'I'm the one who is sorry now,' she said finally, peeling herself back from him. 'I owe you an explanation. But it's hard for me. I don't think like other people.'

'Let's sit down and talk about this.'

In the sleek, modern kitchen he made tea as she eased herself onto a chair. The reassuring sights of water filling a kettle, cupboards being opened, mugs produced, soothed and settled her. It was lovely to watch Nikos's masculinity in such simple, domestic tasks.

He would have been a good husband, she thought. There was no bitterness in her heart; she wouldn't allow it.

'You know your way around this place a lot better than the last kitchen we were in.'

'I can make tea in any country. Bear that in mind,' he said, brandishing a teaspoon. He was trying to lighten the mood, she could tell that, but it was an empty laugh she returned and it echoed around the kitchen, hollow and cold.

'How long have you lived here?' she asked, noting the collection of books that were piled on the table, management and leadership titles, bookmarks poking out. Under a shaft of light in the hallway, photographs of Nikos with some of his very famous and less famous friends. She strained her eyes, noting that Brody was among them.

'Seven years,' he said, wearily, as he settled a mug of tea down in front of her. She clasped her fingers around it, glad of the heat it brought. 'I bought it when I was going through a rough patch with Maria. That's not to say that every other patch was smooth—they were all bumpy one way or another. That time was one of the worst.'

'Was she unfaithful?'

She asked it carefully. Her opinion of the woman wasn't great, but to think she could have deliberately hurt Nikos was awful. Infidelity was as painful as being jilted, she supposed.

He raised his eyebrows and laughed mirthlessly, and she knew she was right.

'Let's keep tonight to the present. You were going to tell me what happened back there.'

'I…' she began. How to find the words? How to say this without looking like a complete fraud? She should have told him before now. She should have told him that she had once believed in something so deeply that she had cherished it until the safety of it had become more important than what it stood for. How she had never, ever before been so swept away that her lifetime promise had felt meaningless. How she had let it go like opening her hand on a breezy day and letting a precious flower be blown away by a gust of wind.

She knew he wouldn't understand her either; nobody did. But she had no other truth to tell.

'I don't believe in sex before marriage.'

He was leaning against the kitchen worktop, handsome, virile and strong, looking godlike, as he always did. The only sign that he'd even heard her was the surprised hitch of one jet-black eyebrow.

'OK. That's not what I expected to hear. So if that's what you believe, why did you sleep with me?' he said. 'You can't honestly think it was going to lead directly to a proposal?'

'Of course not,' she said, blushing furiously.

'Just checking,' he said. 'It's different, but it wouldn't be the first time a woman has asked me to marry her.'

'You're completely misinterpreting what I said,' she said, putting her tea down a little too vigorously.

'Tell me, what does us having great sex have to do with a lifetime commitment? I've lived that particular nightmare already, remember? I've lived it and I'm still reliving it. It's still haunting me. She might be dead but the ties are still choking me. And there's no way, none, that I'm ever going near that again.'

'I'm not asking you to marry me!' she said as anger bubbled right up and over. He was insulting her, choosing to totally misunderstand her, just because he didn't want to lose face.

'Maybe not, but I'm feeling manipulated here. We had a great night together. Why do we need to wrap it up as something it's not? I barely even know you, Jacquelyn. I promised myself I was never going to get into one of these scenes again so, trust me, I'm not the marrying type. Not any more.'

She stood up, pushed herself back from the table, stared at him.

'I—'

'I,' he said, silencing her, 'was asking you to go on a date, with a view to going on another, you know, the way people do, gradually getting to know one another.'

Yes, she wanted to yell, and that was the problem. They should never have done what they'd done. She should never have succumbed.

'Why don't you take that as a compliment? Or are you planning to give me the "bitterly regret it" line again? It only works once. Or at least, it only works once with me. How many other times have you used it?'

'I've never used it,' she said, her voice shaking over the huge hot lump that formed in her throat. The thought of being wrongly accused was always awful, but to be wrongly accused over something like this was beyond the pale. It pierced her, it cut her, and she had no weapon to fight back with, other than the truth.

'I was a virgin. You are the first man I ever slept with. And you have no idea how deep my bitterness goes. None.'

She couldn't see his face because she was staring at the pile of his stupid books, straining so hard not to bleed from the hurt of this awful conversation.

'A virgin?' he repeated, as if she'd said 'an alien' or 'a unicorn' or something equally unusual. 'A virgin? But I asked you. I knew there was something going on and I asked you.'

She didn't look up from the mug of tea in front of her, now glassy and opaque with unshed tears, but she could tell he was walking about the kitchen and she waited to hear him, waited to hear what he would say.

'What am I supposed to do now?'

She shook her head and crushed her eyes through the glassy tears, forcing them to disappear. So that was it. That was how he took the news. The secret and all that it meant to her was just a 'thing' to him. This was even worse than she'd imagined. He was so callous. What a fool she'd been.

She shook her head and pushed herself up from the table. She didn't need to prolong this. The faintest tiny flicker of hope that something might linger and grow was completely doused, ashes cold in a grate.

Everybody does it these days. There is no shame— none...zero—in having sex. There is much more shame in not having it.

She'd thought about that so many times. Her needs were romantic and spiritual. They were lifelong, en- during and deep as the widest, bluest ocean. There was nothing throwaway about anything she offered and nothing she could do would ever change that.

The awful thing was she'd traded that one single night for all the nights that would come after.

'Where are you going?'

'Away from here.'

'I'm sorry if you're not getting the reaction you want but if you'd told me at the time I would have handled things differently.'

'It's not the kind of thing I go around broadcasting.'

'Maybe you should. Because any man taking a virgin to bed needs to know that stuff.'

'My body is my business.'

'You're smarter than that, Jacquelyn. You're the one who's held on for twenty-five years. You were engaged to some guy, for God's sake. What the hell happened there that you chose to sleep with me and not him?'

'Just leave me alone. The last thing I want is a postmortem.'

'No, but I do. You're the one who's been holding all the cards and you've just landed this on me. Look, sit down. I'm not going to let you go anywhere so let's get that straight.'

She stopped in the doorway, her back to him; the beaming smiles of politicians and movie stars gazed at her from photographs on the wall. She searched for the photograph of Brody and wondered with a lurch of panic if Nikos would get in touch with him over this, if it would somehow sour things.

'OK,' she said, lifting her jaw and turning around. 'Maybe I should have told you, but I didn't. I didn't think it was anyone's business but mine, so if I have upset you I apologise.'

'You don't look or sound the slightest bit sorry. Actually, you look angry. With me. As if I'm the one who's done something wrong.'

'I'm not angry. I'm just so disappointed,' she said. 'I had my own rules and I broke them, and I've got to live with myself.'

'Hang on, I think I'm working this out—you actually think that there are rules around this sort of stuff? You need to sign a licence or wear a piece of metal on your finger? Making love isn't about rules, it's about people. It's about chemistry. The fact that you didn't make love until you were twenty-five is because you didn't meet anyone that turned you on enough.

'And then I came along. And suddenly you felt real chemistry. Just like I did. And just like I did you gave in, you followed your instincts. And your instincts were proved right because we fit. We work. On a physical level we work. But that doesn't fit with your plan because in your world of unicorns and fairies, your handsome prince is supposed to marry you first and then you have babies and live happily ever after.

'But life isn't like that. Marriage isn't like that. Marriage is hard work. It's making the best of a goddamned terrible life. It's waking up one morning and seeing your glamorous new wife for what she really is. It's coming home from work one night and finding her naked in the hot tub with another man.'

He threw his head back, bunched his hands in fists and shook them at the ceiling, hissed curses. Then he spun round, and the look blazing from his eyes was awful. He looked tortured, a soul bound in some dark, desperate hell that he could never escape.

'*That's* marriage. And that's what I will never do again. OK?'

'I'm so sorry for you,' she said, hearing those words

as if they were rocks he'd flung at her, flinching with every blow. 'I don't know what you lived through and I'm glad I never will, but your experience is unique to you. It doesn't mean that mine or anyone else's will be the same.'

He shook his head; he'd turned away, defeat in every muscle, every movement of his magnificent body. She sensed it from him and she wanted to wring it out of him like water from a cloth, but there was no point any more—he had moved so far away from her, so far from that place where they'd shared something and could build on it, to a place buried beneath walls of guilt and shame and his own dreadful past.

'Yeah, well, your experience is a bit limited, if you don't mind me saying.'

He poured a glass of water and drank thirstily.

'Not every experience has to be lived first-hand. I saw the marriage of my parents, every day until they moved to Spain. And it wasn't perfect, but it was good. They were solid. Not everyone lies and cheats, Nikos.'

'No, and I don't suppose every wife has to be beaten until she haemorrhages either, but some do, and there's nothing anyone can do about that either,' he said, walking past her back into the hallway. 'I need a drink.'

She stood watching him disappear through a huge doorway. The Beast in his castle, howling with pain and unable to see the light in the world.

She had known pain, but not like his. Not pain so deep it had seeped into the air in his lungs, the blood in his veins. Nobody could leave any creature in pain like that, no matter what he had done or how he had treated her. No matter that she was alone in an unfamiliar apartment in an unfamiliar city with no friends and nowhere to go, completely beholden to this man for his kindness, and dependent on him for a roof over her head, and business contacts and a way out of debt to save her business.

No matter that he was so far gone he'd forgotten she was even here.

She had to do something.

Clicking fiercely along the parquet, she followed him, rounding the massive doorway and entering the room. For a moment she struggled to see him, so vast was the space.

Huge gilt mirrors towered over sleek furniture, all of it way out of her income bracket. A marble fireplace as big as her shopfront, its grate like the mouth of a cave, sat centrally under an oil painting that was surely a Picasso. Windows like skyscrapers opened onto the darkest night sky and the myriad lights of the New York skyline.

It was breathtaking, and there was Nikos, in the corner, turning on lamps and lifting a bottle of amber liquid from a silvery tray. She heard the soft pop of a cork as he started to pour it into a glass. He filled it half-full and lifted it straight to his mouth.

It was an act of self-destruction and it frightened her.

'Not even going to add water?' she heard herself cry.

He paused, but only for a second before he threw it down his throat.

'Oh, I bet that feels better now. Just what you need. Get yourself legless. Anything to drown out the drama that this pain in the backside has brought to your door. Poor you.'

He poured another and put it to his lips, but then turned and stared at her.

'You've got a problem with my drinking now?'

'No. You're the one with all the problems, remember?'

He swilled the whisky around his glass, looking at it as if it was his enemy and he was going to take it head-on.

'That's right, sweetheart, they just keep on coming.'

'You're not the only one in pain around here,' she cried. 'Plenty of people have difficult marriages and hurt each other. But I thought more of you than this.'

'Save the sermon. You don't know what you're talking about.'

'Look at what you've built. Look around you. This was all you. House is your creation, and you're…kind, you're a good man. You were a great husband. And you've given me a chance here—and I know I won't have been the first one. Nikos, stop doing this to yourself and listen.'

His eyes had darted from the glass to a mirror where she could see in the reflection that he was watching her. A hall of mirrors, all reflecting this same dreadful scene.

'Forget it. You're wasting your breath.'

He lifted the glass to his mouth again but this time she couldn't stand it.

'Stop all this self-pity. Just stop it!'

She stormed across the room, her heels sinking into the heavy oriental rug, slowing her down, but she wouldn't be put off and she reached him, reached the glass and yanked it out of his hand.

As quickly he grabbed her arm and the whisky sloshed over her hand and down her arm. Drops landed on her face, her lips, and some on her chest.

His face was blazing, and his grip was unremitting. They stood, like a still life, a cartoon scene of power and anger and beauty, completely still apart from their panting chests and the hard, fast breaths that sounded from their noses and mouths.

He was magnificent, and intimidating, but she would not back down. She stood tall and faced him toe to toe, focusing on his blazing dark eyes, his high stained cheekbones, and tense, square jaw. His lips, when she looked there, had softened, parted.

But it was his presence that undid her. His brooding, masculine presence, close, so close and so magnetic she was utterly compelled to let her guard drop and sink into his space.

And then desire flooded her whole body. She felt it rise like a tide, flushing into her most sensitive parts, weakening her mind, her resolve, her fight.

'What do you suggest we do now, Jacquelyn?' he hissed. 'Are you going to give me another lecture on self-love or do we rip each other's clothes off and make love? Do I take your body the way I did the last time? My God, you're so ready for me, look at you.'

He dropped her arm but he spun her round until they were both facing one of the mirrors. He stood right behind her, holding her arms down by her sides, the splashes of the whisky clearly marked on her dress, one nipple bold like a stud under the damp satin. Her cheeks were pink, her lips were open, her hair was tousled and trailing her shoulders.

She looked wanton.

Behind her, she saw his dark jaw and short dark hair, the inked tattoos of his muscled arm and bare chest exposed, the sheer breadth of him surrounding her, and behind them the opulence of the room, huge, lofty, elegant, immutable.

'Tell me and I'll do it.'

Her head fell back, she longed for his touch, she willed his hands to move, to mould her, his lips to kiss

her, his tongue to lick her. She yearned with every fibre
of her being to have that night again.

She could feel the heat, the strength, the force of him,
hard and desperate, and she knew that he was her lover,
she could be his lover again, rolling in his arms, show-
ering him with her kisses, feeling those strong limbs
entwined with hers, feeling complete, and whole. Feeling that she was a *woman*.

'Mmm… Jacquelyn,' he whispered, softening, drawing her further into his space. Her neck was extended
now, her whole body throbbing with desire. In the mirror she saw his head bend towards her, his lips close to
her ear, and a shudder loosened itself and reverberated
from her neck to her core to her very fingertips and the
sensitive buds of her nipples.

She opened her eyes wide, watching. How wonderful they looked together, she in the sleeveless blue satin
and he in his slate-grey trousers and pale blue shirt.
She was the woman in her sketches. He, the groom of
her dreams.

Almost. But that wasn't real; they weren't that couple. They were two single people alone in New York.
And tonight there would be love but what would there
be tomorrow?

Regret. Pain. Guilt, when she finally, in however
many months or years, stood next to her real husband,
whoever he may be, promising that she would love him
for ever, but knowing that she hadn't waited for him,
that she had given in to temptation and bedded Nikos
again, broken her vow, not just once, but twice.

He wasn't going to change. He'd been as plain as he
could be. He was never going to settle down, or fall in
love with anyone again, not in the way she needed to be
loved. If she slept with him now, she'd lose him for ever.

And she'd been as plain as she could be. There was no compromise. No winner or loser. Nothing for either of them to gain but another night of memories.

How could she live with herself?

She closed her eyes, and shook her head, and with a force of will that felt as if she were moving the earth itself she pushed herself away.

'No,' she said.

Yes, screamed her body. But she shook her head and prayed that he would listen.

'No,' she said again. 'It's not who I am. I can't do this again.'

He moved away, just a fraction of an inch, and in the chasm of silence that stretched now between them she bowed her head and heard the steady tick of a clock, each second moving on in time, past this moment.

It hit the hour and chimed ten long beats.

Like a spell broken, she stepped back onto the rug, sank down on the silk cushions of a hard, high sofa. She was safe. She was back on solid ground.

He sat opposite her, his head in his hands. The long, strong fingers cradled his head, tufts of black hair poking through and the snake of ink disappearing down his forearm.

She stared at him, and such a pain, a physical pain of loss and longing, pierced her that tears sprang in her eyes and she wiped them away. If she stayed a moment longer she would want him so badly that she wouldn't be able to stop. She had to get away.

'Nikos. Can you call me a cab?'

After a few moments he sat up, shook his head. His eyes were dark, unfocused.

'Sure. Whatever you want. Where do you want to go?'

She didn't know. She truly didn't know.

'Home,' was all she could think of to say.

He looked sharply at her now.

'When you've come all this way? You're nearly there. Stay on. Finalise things with Brody.'

'You won't pull the plug on that?'

'I'm a bastard, Jacquelyn, but I'm not that much of a bastard.'

He sighed, long and slow, and in every particle she could hear how exhausted he was.

'I've got things to take care of. I'll be heading back to Greece tonight. I'll make arrangements for a hotel; my car's downstairs. Lauren will take care of everything for you.'

'I can't go to a hotel. I don't have any money.'

A look passed over his eyes, fleeting and final. He nodded. 'You won't need any. You're here now. You've arrived. Things are going to work out for you. I'll take care of the short term.'

He stood up, and she stood up.

They faced each other for the second time, and she stretched out her hand to shake his, businesslike, just how it should be.

'Come on,' he said, shaking his head. 'We're more than that. Way more than that. You don't need to worry. You've drawn your line and I'll respect that.'

He nodded behind him to the space they'd just stood in.

'That won't ever happen again.'

She glanced there and it was as if she could still see that version of Nikos and Jacquelyn, crushed together and loving one another. The way her life would have unfolded if she'd only let it happen.

'Jacquelyn, I would never put you in a position you didn't want to be in, you can be sure of that.'

'Maybe we could date?'

She heard the words escape her mouth—desperate, begging, a last-ditch attempt at staying in his life—and cursed herself.

'We could. But you want to be married. And I don't want to feel responsible for anyone else for the rest of my life. I'm not very good at it.'

He turned on his heel, and walked back through the vast room, picking up his keys and his jacket. He lifted her bag where she'd dropped it and handed it to her, walked to the elevator and it opened immediately.

'I'll see you downstairs.'

She didn't argue, because these were the last few moments she would have with him, possibly ever. Her last supper, those gulps of air, the intoxicating joy of being with Nikos were soon to be gone, and she knew that more and more painfully with each passing second.

As if she were walking to her own execution she followed him downstairs and back through the cavernous lobby. The concierge lifted her face in a smile and dipped it back to her screen. The lilies, proud and beautiful in their square vase, the gleam of the cherry-wood table and the wide cold mouth of the fireplace— all still there, as they had been less than an hour earlier.

Nothing had changed except them. Life moved on.

On the pavement outside, his car waited just beyond the green carpet, its windows reflecting this man and this woman, and this parting.

Nikos smiled and put out his hand to her, then stepped towards her and wrapped his arms around her, surely and confidently, and she felt the tremors of terror build. Panic began to creep over her. She wrapped herself around him, tighter and tighter.

Please don't go, don't leave me, she whispered to herself.

He held her, unmoving, solid and still.

'Shh…' he whispered. 'You'll be fine.'

He knew.

There in the power of his body she slowly began to quieten and they held each other, like friends, like long-lost friends who'd found each other and who knew they must say goodbye again. For ever.

CHAPTER TWELVE

SUMMER ROLLED BRIGHT and warm, like a cheerful carpet of colour, all the way down Fifth Avenue. Here and there yellow cabs and cars cruised and paused patiently at lights. It was early, it was quiet, but Jacquelyn could feel the energy build, like an audience taking its place in a theatre, just before curtain up.

She had three more blocks to walk in heels that were better suited to office floors than pavements. She eyed the trainers of other women who were already making their way to work, fast, efficient, appropriate.

If she stayed on here that would be what she would do, but in two days' time she would be heading back to Lower Linton, back to her studio and to Victor, to the girls in the workshop, finally able to share the good news.

It was the best present of all, and had managed to eclipse some of her sorrow. Her morning mask was truly in place but her eyes were puffy and her mouth pinched. She'd positioned it over and over into the deceitful smile, trying so hard to stop her mind drifting off into hopelessness.

Her business was her husband. That was how it would be. She had been offered this union and she would make it work, for all of them, and she would force her face into that smile all day long if she had to. Because she had the nights to cry into her pillow.

Her heels rubbed again and part of her was glad of the extra pain. It seemed to amplify her suffering even more. But she couldn't afford to get a blister, not with a full day of meetings, lunch and dinner. Brody had taken her schedule from Lauren now and between them they had remodelled it into another series of amazing opportunities. In two days every single worry had been obliterated. Everything except Nikos.

As well as the investment, her new designs were incredible. More than Brody had taken notice; she was in talks to make couture and occasionwear too, with the buyer from one of Nikos's biggest rivals. They were going to run her designs in the biggest stores in the States, Canada and Australia.

And she couldn't stop designing. Her Achilles heel had been repaired and become her engine. Her pen was flying, her designs improving, refining. These women that she sketched now had bodies and felt pleasure behind their blank faces. There was a completeness that had never been there before, an understanding of what it was to be a woman.

She knew she was drawing herself. She wasn't that stupid. She knew it was her way of pretending that her fairy tale was still unravelling to its joyful conclusion, the woman she was now, the bride she was going to be. The last thing she could do was stop to remind herself that the major part of her fairy tale missing was the handsome prince.

No, those thoughts were for the darkness of night, the pillow soaked with tears and the emptiness of her bed, the misery of another day dawning, cold and all alone. The woman who designed wedding dresses she knew she would never wear. Because she couldn't have Nikos.

Her eyes burned again. There was no time for this now. She had to keep on this treadmill, keep focused, keep going, until she got back to Lower Linton and could finally close the door on the world for a while.

She paused at a junction. Her heel throbbed as she waited with the other pedestrians for the Walk sign to change. At the corner of her eye, a limo rolled by, more slowly than the others. So much money in this part of the world, on this street. Luxury everywhere she looked.

The crossing sign changed and she stepped out, caught in the crush of people moving. She checked the street signs, noting the numbers, counting where she should be. Two more blocks to go. Brody would be waiting. He'd offered to send his car but she'd wanted to walk. Another stupid mistake. This blister was sending darts of pain along her foot; every step hurt.

And it was getting busier now. A woman stepped out in front, she adjusted her path; a man appeared at the side, a car parked right next to the kerb, she had no room to move and was bumped, stumbling into someone else's path.

'Sorry,' she muttered, trying to right her steps, but somehow she couldn't rebalance, somehow she was heading further off to the side, dragged by the flow of people.

But then a car door opened and she seemed to be falling towards it.

'No,' she tried to say, 'this isn't my car,' but hands grabbed her and she was shoved right inside, falling on her knees. Her shoe loosened, the door closed, the car moved.

'No!' she said again, pulling herself up from the carpet to the leather seat. The car turned sharply, throwing her across it to the other door. She lunged for the handle, desperately feeling for a button to click, but there was none—just smooth plastic. Panic doubled with every missing lever on the door, the window, but no matter how much she grasped, there were no buttons, no escape.

Frantically she battered her fists against the smoky glass. People passed by, legs moving, heads forward, oblivious.

'No, you don't,' came a voice behind her. Gruff, Australian.

Arms circled her waist and heaved her onto the seat. She tried to push back up but huge fingers curled round her shoulders, shoving her down.

'Sit down. And shut up.'

She sank back in the seat, shrinking away from him, this dark malevolent presence, this strong, terrifying man, but she knew who he was, even as her mind tried to make sense of this, and grasped for reasons why, and how wrong this was, what a mistake.

'You're Nikos's father.' She gasped, daring to look at him.

'Ten out of ten.'

He sat back beside her and she scuttled along the seat, away from him to the door, staring out of the corner of her eye. He didn't move, stared straight ahead. His face weathered, and coarse, his head shaved, he was every bit as brutal as she'd imagined.

'I'm nothing to do with him. I'm not his girlfriend.'

'I told you to shut up, Blondie.'

And then he reached over and grabbed her hair, tugging her neck back, and a sharp pain lanced her. She cried out but he tugged tighter.

'How much further, Bruno?' he said, over her

scream. Then he tugged again until she realised that
with every sound he tightened his grip. She had to swallow the pain, and her scream, and then when she was
silent, save for her breath and her feet scraping on the
floor, he let her go with a shove.

'It works like this. Quiet—no pain. Noise—pain.
You got it?'

He lifted his hand as if he was going to strike her.
She flinched, then nodded and scuttled even further into
the corner, pulling her legs up and hugging herself into
as tiny a ball as she could. There was a driver in front,
the doors were locked, the car was rolling through Manhattan, and she was terrified for her life.

Central Park appeared. The railings, the awnings,
Nikos's apartment block.

'That's it,' he said, leaning forward to the driver.
'Circle the block and then pull up.'

He looked over at Jacquelyn and there in that look
she saw Nikos. She saw his eyes and his jaw. She saw
the shape of his head and the stretch of his shoulders.
She saw his power and might and the strength that had
driven him to greatness, but here in his father all that
power had turned into evil and terror, and she shuddered to think what he would have been like as a father. How brutal.

Poor Nikos. And his poor mother. Her heart broke
to think of them.

'How much longer?' he asked the driver, who
shrugged his shoulders.

The car had rounded the block and now rolled to a
stop and parked, well back from the entrance.

'I don't know. Ten, maybe.'

'OK, Blondie. Your turn. Time to call your little
sweetheart.'

* * *

Nikos tossed his mobile phone down on the sofa and walked out onto the terrace. The magnificent panorama across the park and beyond had been one of this apartment's selling points. It wasn't unique. There were loads of great spaces on Fifth Avenue that he could have had, still could, but this place had grandeur and elegance, and it was isolated. It was impossible to break into and after the burglary at the villa it had been a weight off his mind to know that, no matter where he was in the world, this little slice of Manhattan was safe.

But now that the dragon was out of his lair, nowhere was safe any more.

He was still coming to terms with what he'd found out these past days. The investigators had tracked down Maria's old maid, and, just as he'd predicted, she had delivered up the news.

He was shocked, but not that shocked. Maybe because he'd always suspected his old man had been behind the break-in at the villa, and maybe that was why he had refused the police offers of help. Any path that led back to Arthur was a path he wasn't prepared to take. Even if his father was stealing from him. Even if he'd been naked in a tub with his wife. Nikos had walked away that night, too full of dread at starting something he couldn't control. It was easier to 'turn the other cheek'. Or be a *pathetic little girl*. Those words had been flung at his back, his father's daggers hitting home.

He hung his head, sickened at the thought, but it was the truth. The ugly truth that his father was untouchable, protected by his own wall of fear, his henchmen like gargoyles on the ramparts; no one got near, no charges ever brought against him, so no justice would ever be done.

And anyone who turned informant would have a fate worse than death. That had been drummed into him even as a child. Fear. His whole life had been defined by it and he had gone on the run because of it.

The fear was real. No matter that he was thirty-five now. A widower. Had a multibillion-dollar-turnover business and a place on the *Forbes* list. It was still there, right down there on the streets of Manhattan, brewing. He could feel it. He could feel Arthur's wrath, could feel him coming for him.

Lauren had been the last one on the list to suffer the poison. He'd known as soon as he'd stepped out of his office and had seen her ashen face. At first he'd thought something had happened to Jacquelyn. Panic had grabbed his heart with both hands and squeezed the air from his lungs. Was that the moment he'd realised he loved her?

Lauren handed him the notepad where her shaky hand had written two sentences.

Daddy's home and he wants his money back.
Three p.m. Central Park West.

For a split second he thought about getting the jet ready, heading to Italy or London, anywhere but here. But there was iron in his blood now. There was lead in his spine. He could crush his fear, and he would not run any more. He would use every weapon he could and do the right thing.

Nikos gripped the barrier that encircled the top floor of his terrace and gazed at the park. Somewhere down there he was waiting. He and Bruno.

This was it. Time to finally grow up. He was not going to be the frightened boy hiding under his bedclothes any more. He was going to meet him here, get him to admit what he could with the police listening in, give him money if he had to and let the cops do the rest.

He was doing this for his mother, for Maria, but most of all for Jacquelyn. There would never be another chance, and there would definitely never be another Jacquelyn.

She was one in a million and worth every second of this. She was fighting for her business, her family, her reputation. She had more honesty and integrity than any other human being he had ever met, and she had stayed true to her principles until he had dragged her to his bed.

And he would never forgive himself for hurting her. She had trusted him and look what he had done. Trying to seduce her again and then sending her on her way because she wouldn't get into bed with him.

As soon as this was over he was going to find her. Maybe she would give him another chance. He put his hands together and bowed his head and prayed.

'Hello, Nikos. I'm… I'm outside with your father.'

The second she said the words, he grabbed the phone.

'You hear that. I've got your little friend. So let us up.'

Whatever Nikos said, Arthur's face lit up, then he nodded as the car moved forward like a tank, and then stopped at the carpet.

'This doesn't feel right,' said Bruno from the front.

'Relax. He'd never double-cross me. He hasn't got it in him. Here, sort yourself out,' he said, grabbing up her fallen shoes and bag and shoving them at her.

Jacquelyn slowly uncurled herself from the corner of the seat and tried to make her shaking limbs work. She stuffed her feet into the shoes, the pain of the blister not even registering as she forced her heels down and tried to smooth her dress with trembling hands.

The doorman seemed to hesitate before he stepped towards the vehicle.

'Right, Blondie, you're going to get out and smile at the nice man. Then walk inside. I'll be right beside you. And I don't need to tell you what will happen if you try anything stupid.'

The door opened. Sunlight danced on the green carpet. Her beige patent shoe struck the ground and she tried to stand, and round her waist the hateful hands of Nikos's father—a warning.

She climbed out and he came out right behind her, his hot breath at her ear, chilling and deadly. Bruno followed. She thought about running but her legs were useless, her mind was useless. All she could think about was Nikos and how he'd think she was part of this. How they might hurt him. What she could do to stop it happening.

The door to the building was opened, the concierge looked up and smiled, holding her eyes for an extra second, but then dipped her head back down to her screen.

Help! screamed Jacquelyn silently but there was nobody there to see the panic in her eyes.

The lift flew up, and bumped to a gentle halt at the penthouse. The doors slid open…

And there was Nikos and her heart soared. He looked right at her. His eyes telegraphed shock then anger in quick succession. She tried to mouth *It's OK* to him, but her lips wouldn't work. She felt a jab in her back, urging her forward.

'Long time no see,' sneered Arthur.

'This wasn't the deal,' he answered hoarsely.

'What…no hug for your old dad? After all this time?'

'Adding kidnapping to your list of crimes? I didn't think you'd be that stupid.'

'You can thank Bruno for that. He clocked her on the street. I hear she made quite an impression the first time they met—and here she is: the added insurance in case you decided to pretend you didn't know me again.'

He squeezed Jacquelyn's hand, making her shudder.

'Imagine being disowned by your own son. You'd think I brought him up better than that. All his fancy houses and cars and his money and no respect. What would you do with a son like that?'

Nikos stood still, eyes blazing furiously. Jacquelyn desperately wanted to run to him but she faltered, too afraid to move.

'You didn't bring me up. I owe everything to my mother. You're no better than a cheap little drug dealer.'

'Your wife didn't mind that I was a dealer. Shame you didn't join the party. That was some party,' he said, turning to smile at Bruno.

'You low-life piece of scum. Just tell me what you want and get out of here.'

'You're the same scum as I am, underneath your suits and all your fancy stuff, you're still my son. You make money just like I make money. You get your needs met, you like your women…'

He trailed a finger down the back of Jacquelyn's arm and she shuddered and stiffened in one sickening moment.

Nikos opened his mouth and then closed it again. She saw a flicker pass over his eyes like an icy wind blowing through a stormy sky, but then his face was hard like granite.

'Come here, Jacquelyn.'

She heard the words, her heart flew to her chest and she leapt forward.

'Oh, no. Not so fast, *Jacquelyn*.'

Arthur's fingers curled round her upper arm, crushing it, but she didn't move or make a sound. She looked at Nikos, but the rage in his eyes chilled her and she looked away, too afraid to think of what he would do. It was like being between two bulls, their hooves stomping, breath thrusting from their noses, bull rings shining in the sun.

'Touch her and I swear I will rip your head off.'

Nikos stepped forward; he seemed to broaden, growing in stature, more terrifying by the moment. Jacquelyn sensed something weaken in Arthur behind her, and startled like a deer ready to run. At the same moment Nikos lunged for her, thrust his fist right past her head as he did so, bone meeting the flesh of Arthur's face and her body swung neatly behind his, shielded by him.

Arthur yelped in pain and stumbled off to the side, clutching his face.

'Bruno. Take care of this,' he said, through his hands cradling his head.

Bruno hesitated.

'We know the Feds are all over the Cayman investments. We'll settle for the Picasso.'

'You're getting nothing of mine.'

'Easy for you to say with all your millions. What do you think paid for the shirt on your back when you were a kid?'

'I'd rather have had nothing than anything involved

in crime. You're the lowest of the low, making money from people who can't help themselves. Bullying the weak. I thank God every day that Mum got away from you.'

'She can't run far now though, can she?'

Loathing reared in Nikos like a monster and he lunged forward, trying to land another punch, but Bruno blocked his arm. Maddened, he swung again and shoved him crashing into one of the bronze art deco statues.

'Get out of my home. Get out before I rip your head off too.'

'Bruno. Get the painting…let's get out of here,' Arthur gasped.

Nikos lurched forward, heading straight for his father, who was now reeling, the bull finally charging the matador, the force of his movement huge and brutal and deadly.

And it broke Jacquelyn's heart to see him. This strong, gentle man, this man who had shown her such kindness, who had shown her how to make love and cherished her as much as his broken spirit could allow.

'No,' she called out and tried to pull him back. Her fingers landed on his back. 'Please don't be like him. You're better than that.'

Nikos stopped and reached for her, blindly grabbing at the air, as if he were stopping himself from falling off a cliff, and she found him and held him and hugged him close, pulling him back from the edge.

He looked into her eyes with such pain, and love. Just a moment, but it stretched there like a path to eternity and she knew she would go to the ends of the earth for this man.

'I'm sorry,' he whispered.

Then it all happened. Noises in the hallway, feet thundered on the parquet floor, the doors flew open, figures in dark uniforms. Guns.

Arthur roared, Nikos shielded her. Bruno stood, shoulders slumped, as if he had finally given in.

CHAPTER THIRTEEN

'SO THAT IS HOW I see us taking the intimate, highly personal experience that has been Ariana's trademark for generations, and translating it within each concession, and, even more importantly, online.'

Jacquelyn clicked the final slide on her deck and smiled round at the board. The faces were stony but she glanced up at Brody and saw him wink and give a discreet thumbs-up.

'Questions, anyone?' he said, as she sat beside him at the top of the table.

In the seconds that followed, Jacquelyn knew that her fate was being decided. Not just hers, but Victor's, the seamstresses' and machinists', her father's, her mother's. This was the deal of a lifetime and she had presented it with every ounce of skill she possessed.

'No questions. Just a guarantee of exclusivity. You come to us and you trade in the UK, but that's it.'

'If the price is right, yes,' said Jacquelyn, swinging her chair round slowly to face the CEO of Nikos's biggest rival. Her heart raced faster than the dollar signs she could see spinning in Brody's eyes. But she crossed her legs, steepled her fingers and kept her cool.

'And the stock is owned currently by whom?'

'I own ninety per cent and my business partner—' she nodded to Brody '—owns the other ten per cent.'

'Any plans for that to change? Or let me put it another way—any plans for Nikos Karellis to get involved?'

At the mention of Nikos's name, Jacquelyn's heart skipped a momentary beat. Brody opened his mouth to talk but she put her hand up, silencing him.

'I don't imagine anyone has asked you if your wife has bought stock recently, so you'll understand my surprise at your question.'

'House is our prime competitor. I have to ask.'

'My business affairs are wholly my own. As are my personal affairs.'

She stood up and the faces round the table all rose to watch her.

'If you feel that you need to know more than the quality of my work, or the health of my accounts, then perhaps our chemistry isn't going to work, after all.'

The room held its breath as she reached for her tablet and began to slide it into the leather pocket in her tote bag.

'Now, now, Miss Jones. Please don't be too hasty.'

She kept her eyes down but she could almost taste the buzz in the room.

'I think we're ready to make you an offer.'

She looked up into the eyes of every person round the table, checking for nodders or dissenters, and then, satisfied, she sat back in the sumptuous leather chair and smiled.

'Good. I'm ready to hear it,' she said.

Two hours later Jacquelyn stepped from her car onto the pavement outside her new favourite restaurant in Manhattan.

She stared up at the soaring glass and glimpses of bright blue sky above her head. She was completely in love with this city already, after only five days here. A city that welcomed, and spread out its possibilities like tempting canapés for her to try. Here, she *was* Ariana, unapologetically the CEO of a business that was contemporary and had legacy. She wasn't defined by her father or her grandmother, or by a failed relationship.

She was writing her own history one step at a time.

She stared in through the glass to see if she could see Nikos but the swirl of servers and lunchtime customers was too dense.

She stepped under the glass canopy just as she felt arms wrap around her.

'Nikos,' she sighed, sinking into his warm, strong body.

'Hello,' he said, tugging her towards him, and then he turned her slowly in his arms, and held her face. Then when he had smiled at her, and she had smiled at him, he kissed her slowly and thoroughly.

'I was beginning to think you'd stood me up. Where have you been?' he said, linking his fingers through hers and leading her off down the street.

'With my new best friends,' she said as they waited at the intersection to cross.

'Are you going to tell me who they are or do I have to guess?' said Nikos as he tucked his arm around her and walked them over the street.

'I'll give you a clue. They've got stores in every major city in northern USA and Australia. They've got an online platform to rival the best. And even better, they've just launched in China.'

'You signed with Blue?'

He stopped dead on the pavement, his hands on her

shoulders. She smiled so broadly it felt as if she'd run out of face.

'My biggest rival? You signed with my biggest rival?'

'It was beautiful, Nikos. They were looking for bespoke bridal. The store within the store. Ariana in Blue. Doesn't that just roll off the tongue? Authentic. Italian. They loved my new designs and they can give me the resources to scale everything up. And with the digital team that Brody has hired, we can convert the whole experience to the Internet too. Brides can upload their photos and measurements and we can dress the whole wedding party before they set a foot inside.'

'Wow,' he said as they started to walk again.

'But nothing will ever beat the personal touch. And that's what I'm going to get the most pleasure from creating. We're going to launch in Australia first.'

She'd kept that bit to the end, but he didn't pick up the cue.

'Jacquelyn, you're amazing. Look what you've done. In less than two weeks you've transformed your business. You've walked into New York and owned this city. You've gone further than I ever did.'

'Oh, come on, Nikos, you know that's not true. You built House from the dust.'

She threaded her fingers through his and stared happily at every passer-by, every shop window, every car.

'You and Mark are the only ones who truly know that. Everybody else thinks that I got it handed to me on a plate. But never mind me and House. Tell me how you handled the crusty old chief exec.'

Jacquelyn laughed and looked up. They were nearing the park. Their lunchtime place to stroll and talk, this past week.

'He asked about you.'

'What about me?' he said, pausing a moment to look at her. And just that sideways glimpse made her heart race. Those eyes that captured everything, those lips she ached to kiss, the inky trail of his tattoo snaking down under his Fifth Avenue shirt collar.

'He wanted to know if you would be getting involved further down the line.'

'And what did you tell him?'

'That it was none of his business. And if he wanted to make it his business then we wouldn't be taking this any further.'

They walked along together, her pointed patent toes and his black leather, totally in step. Bright sunshine bounced all around; they were nearing the park.

'*And* I pointed out that he wouldn't like it if I asked about his significant other.'

He was silent, but their feet stepped forward together, left, right, left, right, and she felt the press of his hip against hers, and the strength of his arm holding her close.

'Well. Good for you. Sounds like you handled the whole thing brilliantly. Brody is just as happy with the terms you got?'

She squeezed her arm against his side. Her little way of telling him to wind his jealous neck in.

'He's over the moon. Just like I am. I can go back to Lower Linton with my head held high. I can pay off all my debts and give everyone a pay rise. We can have our own Wellbeing Suite, and I can sponsor kids or start-ups, or do everything I ever dreamed of. Honestly, I've got everything now. And I can't thank you enough, Nikos. You were the first person I wanted to tell.'

'You've done it all yourself, Jacquelyn,' he said quietly. 'I just gave you a shove in the right direction.'

They were outside the gates of the park now, close to the Boathouse.

'So how do you want to celebrate?' he asked.

'This is all that I need,' she said simply, looking at the green water, the trees and paths, the people milling around. 'I don't need to drink champagne or eat a fancy dinner. I don't need any of that stuff. I've never been happier in my life.'

Nikos smiled at her, and trailed his fingers down her cheek. He was holding something back. She knew it. From the moment she'd met him she could tell he had something he wanted to say. She couldn't bear to get her hopes up though.

'How was your day? How did it go?'

'It's getting there,' he said, but there was exhaustion in his voice. 'I'm in the clear, but it'll take months to get through all the investigations and the court case. I'm going to be pretty tied up working with them for the next few weeks, but at least it feels as if we're getting somewhere.'

'And your mum? How is she?'

He bowed his head and when he looked up she could see the worry that leaked through at the mention of his mother.

'I need to take a trip out there next week.'

'Ah, yes, of course, I understand. I'm sure even if she doesn't seem to understand you, the universe will have a way of telling her that everything is going to be OK. That she's safe now. And that nobody else will suffer like she did.'

He tucked her close to his chest and breathed a deep, soulful breath. Under her cheek, his heart pounded a strong, slow beat, a sound she relished, more than any other.

'You're a sweet, wonderful woman, Jacquelyn. You say exactly the right things. I wish she could have met you. I'd love for you two to get to know one another.'

They were right at the Boathouse now. He'd led them into the queue for a rowing boat. Then they were stepping into a boat, steadying and balancing as Nikos took the oars and paddled them out through the smooth green water.

'I should visit my own parents,' she said, enjoying the slow steady glide and the sound of the oars slipping through the water. 'It's been such a long time since I saw them. And now I've got something amazing to tell them, I really want to do it in person.'

Nikos nodded slowly as he rowed them further out, the heavy canopy of the trees screening them from the world.

'Yep. We need to look after our folks. What goes around, comes around.'

She sat back, watching his muscles flex and extend under the sheen of his shirt. There was nowhere more romantic in the whole of Manhattan. There was no one she would rather be with.

'Where are we going?' she asked.

He looked behind.

'Oh, not much further.'

Her heart was beginning to thunder in her chest.

He smiled and winked, and she smiled back. Tears began to form in her eyes, but she mustn't, she mustn't let herself believe it until it was true. They'd never spoken again about marriage, he hadn't pressed her to sleep with him and she'd spent every night in her own suite at the hotel, awake or asleep, dreaming of Nikos.

But it swirled around them. Those unsaid words, their deep desires. She felt her love for him so strongly, but he'd been resolutely silent, occupied completely by his father's arrest and the investigations.

She looked at him now, his dark head bent to check if anyone was close by, then a smile flashed over his lips as there, in the centre of the pond he tucked the oars up into the boat.

They drifted for a moment, caught in each other's eyes.

'Are you happy, Jacquelyn?' he said, smiling softly.

She felt her lip tremble. She nodded, unable to speak.

'Is there anything that would make you even happier?'

She swallowed, she opened her mouth, but no words could come out. She felt her face pucker up with tears of joy, ready to be shed.

'If I told you that I can't live without you, would that make you happy?'

She sat up straight in the little boat, perched on the edge of the little seat, her eyes fixed on his as he reached into the pocket of his trousers.

'Because it's true. I can't. I don't want to. I want you in my life. I didn't think I would ever say these words, but I didn't know love until I knew you, and that's the truth.'

'I want you in mine too, for ever,' she whispered. And the hugeness of what she had just said struck her. She meant for ever and ever.

'For the rest of our lives,' said Nikos and she nodded because it was true. 'So that means getting married. I know how much it means to you, and there's nothing I ever want to deny you.'

'It's meant to be, Nikos.'

He held her close.

'I know. I know you understand it, and you understand me. There's no one else for me and there never will be. So let's get married. For love. For ever. For the children we'll have and the love we'll show them.'

He opened his fist and there was a small blue velvet box. She clasped her hands and he opened it. And there inside was the most beautiful ring she had ever seen. It had one large, brilliant diamond and two smaller ones at either side set on a slim gold band. It sparkled in the sunlight, as he lifted it carefully from its velvet nest.

As if they had practised a thousand times, she extended her hand into his and he lifted it and kissed it.

'Will you marry me, Jacquelyn? Will you make me the happiest man alive?' he said, holding her hand and sliding the ring down to rest in its new home.

And then she nodded, and he kissed her.

There were no words, there were just the two lovers drifting in a boat on the lake in Central Park, lost in each other's arms, each other's kisses and each other's dreams.

EPILOGUE

SUNSET BATHED A gentle pastel palette over the terracotta roofs and whitewashed walls of the village. Shades of lilac, peach and pink lay in overlapping bands of colour from sky to horizon to sea. In the warm evening air, a swoop of swallows darted here and there, looking for insects, before resting in the villa's eaves in their tiny muddy nests.

Jacquelyn watched from the guest bedroom, as she had watched every sunset for the past week. It lifted her heart to see them, and all the other flora and fauna of this beautiful island, things one could only see standing patiently still and quiet. It was a tonic, after New York and everything that had happened. The frantic bustle of the city, the arrests of Arthur and Bruno, the newly launched Ariana in Blue.

Standing here now, staring at the slow, peaceful world falling asleep every night, she knew that this was all that really mattered, the movement of the earth and nature upon it, this little island and its people, the birds and the flowers, and the man who had laid it all at her feet.

She stepped forward onto the terrace and breathed deeply, feeling a smile gild her face. She was so lucky, so happy, so astonished that she was here at all, about to take the next steps in her life. Ariana was safe, probably for ever. Her parents could live out their lives in Spain. She had sewn everything up as neatly as the stitches on the wedding dress that now hung in the next room, the dress she would wear tomorrow.

A knock sounded at the door.

'Can I come in?'

She turned, the smile expanding into a grin at the sound of Nikos's voice, and then as he walked into the room she ran into his open arms, burying herself in his chest, holding on and absorbing him without the slightest shame.

'Everybody is settled in their suites and your mum seems to have stopped crying for the time being.'

'She's so happy for me, everyone is.' She sighed as he swung her gently backwards and forward. 'But I'm going to miss you again tonight.'

'You know where I'll be. Just along the hallway,' he said, with a smile in his voice. 'You wouldn't get lost.'

'I know, I know,' she said. 'But it's only one more night.'

'And then our wedding, finally,' he said, smiling.

'We've got our whole lives ahead, Nikos. Nothing but these beautiful skies and whatever we want to do, underneath them.'

He nodded.

'I only wish Mum could have made it here. It would have made her so happy.'

A tiny tear sprang into his eye and he tightened his jaw, holding himself in check. She wished he would let it go, but he'd been resolutely strong through it all and there would be more to come. She would do everything to help him heal. Everything.

She touched his cheek, feeling the rough stubble

under her palm, the bone of his jaw and cheek, hard and yielding as he was himself.

'She's in a happier place now, Nikos. No more suffering.'

He closed his eyes, and tried to smile, but she knew now of the pain that had risen to the surface. It broke her heart to think of anyone living as he had lived, watching his mother beaten, running away and then learning that she had been so badly injured she had nearly died.

What guilt he carried. And none of it deserved.

'You're an amazing woman, Jacquelyn. I never thought I would find anyone like you.'

She nodded and smoothed her hands over his solid, strong back. Her silence said everything. The past was the past...those ghosts didn't matter any more. This was real, because she knew she would do anything for Nikos, and he her. It felt that the world was safe now; no matter what, they would be there for each other.

'We've found each other, Nikos. We were always going to happen. We just didn't know how or when or where.'

'And tomorrow we make it legal.'

She nodded as the tears now filled her own eyes.

'Tomorrow I finally see the dress I inspired. How many men can say that they inspired a collection of wedding dresses?'

'Sex out of wedlock has its advantages. But you'll never get me to admit it in public.'

'All I want you to admit is that you'll be my wife. In Agios Stephanos in front of your family and my friends. And I promise I'll make a polite, respectful speech about the night we met. And the night after that...'

'You won't whisper a word about the night after that.' She laughed, punching his rock-hard abs. 'I'd never

live it down! A woman with my reputation, for goodness' sake.'

He stretched out his arms, and stared down at her,
and the love that was in his eyes turned fiery and flames
of desire lit all over her body.

'And then?' she whispered.

'And then we'll dance our first dance.'

'And I'll throw my bouquet.'

'And *then*…?'

She breathed in deeply, her chest rising and falling,
thinking of the pleasure they had already shared and
the pleasure they would share for evermore. How could
life ever be any better than that?

'Then we'll make love. Husband and wife.'

'And live happily ever after.'

He kissed her lips, and held her close for the final
time.

'Goodnight, Miss Jones,' he said, and she turned
to see him standing in the doorway, his handsome sil-
houette outlined in the lamplight. 'Sleep well. I'll see
you tomorrow.'

'Goodnight, Nikos,' she said.

She closed the door and walked to the dressing room,
where her white dress shimmered and danced in the
moonlight. And she wept tears of joy, knowing that tomorrow she would wear her beautiful dress to be married to the man she truly loved.

* * * * *

SHEIKH'S
ROYAL BABY
REVELATION

ANNIE WEST

For the late-night laughter and plotting
just when I needed it!
Thank you, AA, Bron, Kandy, Shaz,
Denise, Rachel and Reeze.

CHAPTER ONE

ASHRAF WOKE TO the sound of a door slamming and the taste of blood in his mouth. Blood and dust.

He lay facedown, head and ribs burning with pain, the rest of him merely battered. Slowly he forced his eyelids open. He was in a dark room, lightened only by a spill of moonlight through a small, high window.

Then came rough voices using an obscure local dialect. Three men, he counted, walking away. He strained to hear over the merciless hammering in his head.

They'd kill him tomorrow. After Qadri arrived to enjoy the spectacle and pay them for the successful kidnap.

Ashraf gritted his jaw, ignoring the spike of pain in the back of his skull.

Of course Qadri was behind this. Who else would dare? The bandit leader had even begun to style himself as a provincial chief in the last years of Ashraf's father's rule.

The old Sheikh had moved slowly when dealing with problems in this remote province, the poorest and most backward in the country. He'd left Qadri alone as long as the bandit preyed only on his own people.

But Ashraf wasn't cut from the same cloth as his father. The old Sheikh was dead and Ashraf had introduced changes that would see Qadri dispossessed.

He could expect no mercy from his captors.

Ashraf wasn't naïve enough to believe Qadri would negotiate his release. The man would fight for his fiefdom the only way he knew: with violence.

What better way to intimidate poor villagers than to execute the new Sheikh? To prove that modernisation and the rule of law had no place in the mountains that had only known Qadri's authority for two decades?

Ashraf cursed his eagerness to see a new irrigation project, accepting the invitation to ride out with just a local guide and a single bodyguard into an area that was supposedly now completely safe.

Safe!

His belly clenched as he thought of his bodyguard, Basim, thrown from his horse by a tripwire rigged between two boulders.

Ashraf had vaulted from his horse to go to him, only to be felled by attackers. There was little satisfaction in knowing they hadn't overpowered him easily.

Was Basim alive? Ashraf's gut clenched at the thought of his faithful guard abandoned where he'd fallen.

Fury scoured his belly. But fury wouldn't help now. Only cold calculation. He had to find a way out. Or a way to convey his location to those searching for him.

His father had always said he had the devil's own luck. It had been a sneering accusation, not a fond appraisal, but for the first time Ashraf found himself hoping the old man had been right. He could do with some luck. And the energy to move.

A slight scuffling broke his train of thought.

He wasn't alone.

Ashraf refused to lie there waiting for another knockout blow.

Ignoring the pain that exploded through him at the movement, he rolled over and up onto his feet, only to stop abruptly, his right arm yanked back.

Spinning round, Ashraf discovered he was chained to a wall. Another turn, so swift his bruised head swam and pain seared his ribs. But with his back to the wall, his feet wide, he was ready to take on any assailant.

'Come on. Show yourself.'

Nothing. No movement. No sound.

Then, out of the darkness, something gleamed. Something pale that shone in the faint moonlight.

His guard was *blond*?

Ashraf blinked. It wasn't an hallucination.

Whoever it was, he wasn't local.

'Who are you?' He switched to French, then English, and heard an answering hiss of breath.

English, then.

The silence grew, ratcheting his tension higher.

'You don't know?' It was a whisper, as if the speaker feared being overheard.

Ashraf frowned. Had the blow to his head damaged his hearing? It couldn't be, yet it sounded like—

'You're a *woman*?'

'You're not one of them, then.' Her voice was flat, yet taut, as if produced by vocal cords under stress.

Stress he could understand.

'By "one of them" you mean…?'

'The men who brought me here. The men who…' Ashraf heard a shudder in her voice '…kidnapped me.'

'Definitely not one of them. They kidnapped me too.'

For which they'd pay. Ashraf had no intention of dying in what he guessed was a shepherd's hut, from the smell of livestock. Though the sturdy chain and handcuff indicated that the place was used for other, sinister purposes. He'd heard whispers that Qadri was involved in people-smuggling. That women in particular sometimes vanished without a trace, sold to unscrupulous buyers across the border.

The pale glow came closer. Ashraf saw her now. Silvery hair, pale skin and eyes that looked hollow in the shadows. She swallowed and he made out the convulsive movement of her throat. Calm overlying panic. At least she wasn't hysterical.

'Are you hurt?' he asked.

A tiny huff of amusement greeted his question. 'That's my line. You're the one who's bleeding.'

Ashraf looked down. Parting his torn shirt, he discovered a long cut, no longer bleeding. A knife wound, he guessed, but not deep.

'I'll live.'

Despite the playboy reputation Ashraf had once acquired, he'd done his time in the army. A stint which his father had ensured was tougher and more dangerous than usual. Ashraf knew enough about wounds to be sure he'd be alive when his executioner arrived tomorrow.

'How about you?'

Tori stared at him, wanting to laugh and cry at the same time.

Except tears wouldn't help. And she feared if she laughed it would turn into hysteria.

'Just scrapes and bruises.' She was lucky and she knew it. Her jaw ached where she'd been backhanded across the face but that was the worst. Despite the hungry gleam she'd seen in her captors' eyes as they'd inspected her, they hadn't touched her except to subdue her and throw her in here.

Looking at this injured man, she trembled, thinking she'd got off lightly. So far.

He'd been unconscious when they'd dumped him on the dirt floor. Either he'd put up a mighty fight or they had a grudge against him to beat him up like that.

She hadn't had time to investigate how badly he was injured. His shirt was torn and stained and his head was bloody on one side. Even so, he stood tall. His ragged shirt hung from wide, straight shoulders and his dusty trousers clung to a horseman's thighs. He looked fit and powerful despite his injuries. Under the grime he had strong-boned features that she guessed might be handsome, or at least arresting.

Would she see him in daylight or would they come for her before that? Terror shuddered down her spine and turned her knees to jelly. Panic bit her insides as she imagined what was in store for her.

'Where are we?' Like her, the stranger kept his voice low, yet something about the smooth, deep note eased a fraction of the tension pinching her.

'Somewhere in the foothills. I couldn't see from the back of the van.' She wrapped her arms around her middle, remembering that trip, facing a grim stranger with a knife in his hand.

'There's a road?' The man before her pounced on that.

'Part of the way. I walked the last part blindfolded.' Which was why her knees were rubbed raw after she'd stumbled and fallen time and again over uneven ground.

'Is there a guard at the door?'

'I don't think so.'

She'd heard the men talking as they walked away. Even so she crept to the door, peeking through the gap between it and the wall. No one. She moved along the wall but it was surprisingly solid, with no chinks to peer through.

As if it had been used as a prison before.

Tori thought of the heavy chain that secured her companion and her stomach curdled.

'There's a light further away. A campfire, I think. But no one here as far as I can tell.'

Why would they bother? The door was bolted. Her companion was chained and she didn't have as much as a pocket knife to use as a tool.

What wouldn't she give for her geologist's hammer right now? Designed for cracking rocks, the sharp end might prise open the chain and it would make an effective weapon.

'What are you doing?' He'd turned his back on her and she heard the rattle of metal links.

'Testing this chain.' There was a grunt, then a muffled oath.

She crossed to stand behind him. 'You won't pull it out,' she whispered. 'It's fixed securely. Believe me.'

'You've checked?' His hunched shoulders straightened as he lifted his head and turned around.

Suddenly he was closer than she'd expected, towering above her. Her hissed breath cut the thick silence.

Only hours ago she'd been grabbed by strangers: big men who'd overpowered her despite her frantic struggle. Fear curdled her belly anew and adrenaline pumped hard in her blood, freezing her to the spot.

Yet as she stiffened the man stepped back towards the wall. Giving her space.

Logic said he wasn't the enemy. Her abductors had kidnapped him too.

Tori sucked in oxygen and tried to steady her breathing. In the gloom she met his eyes. It was too dark to be sure but she'd swear she read sympathy in his face. And something else. Pity?

Because the fate of a woman abducted by violent men would be truly pitiful.

Tori stiffened her knees against the images she'd tried so hard not to picture. She couldn't afford to crack up now.

'Of course I checked.' She made herself concentrate on the conversation, not her fear. 'I thought if I could pry it loose I might use it as a weapon when they came back.'

'One against three?'

Despite their desperate situation, Tori felt a throb of satisfaction at surprising him. 'I won't go down without a fight.'

'It would be safer if you don't resist.'

Tori opened her mouth to protest but he went on.

'Three to one aren't good odds. Wait till you're alone with one of them. Someone will probably transport you elsewhere tomorrow.'

'How do you know? What did they say about me?' Her voice was harsh with fear.

He shook his head, then winced. The soft whisper that followed might have been in a language she didn't know, but she knew a curse when she heard one.

'I didn't hear them mention you,' he said finally. 'But their leader arrives tomorrow. They're expecting payment for their efforts then. They'll leave us be until he arrives.'

Tori sagged, her knees giving way suddenly. She stumbled to the wall, propping herself against it. For hours she'd been on tenterhooks, expecting at any moment—

'Are you okay?' He moved closer before stopping, as if recalling her earlier recoil.

She nodded. When she opened her mouth to reply a jagged, out-of-control laugh escaped. She clapped a hand to her lips, hating the hot tears behind her eyes and the sensation that she was on the verge of collapse.

It was ridiculous to feel relief, hearing she was safe for tonight. She was still in terrible danger. Even so, her exhausted body reacted to the news by slumping abruptly.

Firm hands caught her upper arms as she sank, taking her weight and easing her descent to the floor.

His hands were big and hard, yet surprisingly gentle. Tori heard the clank of metal as he withdrew, hunkering before her.

'Sorry.' The word wobbled and she tried again. 'I just…' She looked up into dark eyes. 'What else did they say? What are they going to do with us?'

Did she imagine that his expression turned blank? In this light it was impossible to tell.

'Nothing about you.' He paused, then continued slowly. 'I have no proof, but I suspect they'll take you over the border.'

Like a smuggled commodity? Tori bit her bottom lip. She'd heard stories of the illegal slave trade, particularly in women. Nausea rose as she contemplated where she might end up.

'If that's so there might be a chance to escape. Maybe some of them will stay here.' Tori knew she was grasping at straws but it was better than giving up hope.

'I can guarantee it.' His tone grabbed her attention.

'Why? What else did you hear?'

He shrugged those wide shoulders and sank cross-legged before her. Despite the heavy chain and his injuries he looked at ease. Strange how his air of confidence reassured her.

'Their leader is my enemy. I think it fair to assume he'll be more focused on me than you.' There was a note in that deep voice that sounded almost like wry humour. Grim lines bracketed his mouth.

Suddenly Tori remembered the gesture one of their captors had made as he'd chained this man to the wall. One man had asked a question and another had laughed, a sound that had sent a chill skittering down her backbone. He'd said something sharp and dragged his finger across his throat in a gesture that crossed all languages. Death.

They were going to kill this man.

She should warn him.

Except even as she thought it she realised he knew. Tori read it in that stern face, a chiaroscuro masterpiece of male strength, and knew he wouldn't surrender to fate. Not with that pugnacious set to his jaw.

Instinctively she reached out, her hand fleetingly touching his, feeling living warmth flow into her chilled fingers. 'What can we do?'

For long seconds he surveyed her. Then gave another infinitesimal shrug. 'Check for a way out.'

'I've done that. It's *all* I've done for the last five hours or so.' That and try not to panic.

'I don't suppose you've got a hairpin?'

'For picking the lock on your handcuff?' Tori shook her head. 'I don't need hairpins with a ponytail.'

He watched the swish of her hair around her shoulders and something unexpected zipped through her. Something other than fear and despair.

Tori stilled.

'And I unfortunately didn't think to bring bolt cutters for the chain.'

She choked down a laugh. It was only mildly amusing, but in her emotional state any humour was a welcome break from constant fear.

'The windows are too small even for you.' He paused. 'The roof?'

He rose in a single fluid motion that revealed enviable core strength and left Tori gawping. A short time ago he'd been unconscious.

'Come.' He extended his hand.

She didn't know if it was the command in his tone or not, but a second later her hand was in his and he was drawing her up. They stood so close that she identified the tang of cinnamon and male, and the comforting smell of horse, before he stepped away, surveying the roof.

'Here.' He turned and beckoned.

'What do you have in mind?'

'Hands on my shoulders. I'll lift you so you can check for a way out.'

'But *you* can't get out.' Her gaze dropped to the mana-cle on his wrist.

'That's no reason for you not to try.'

That voice, as smooth and rich as her favourite coffee, warmed her as his gaze captured hers. Tori's racing thoughts stilled. She felt a moment of communion, as if this stranger understood the guilt that made her protest even as the idea of escape made her thrill with excitement.

'What's your name?'

The question made her pause. What would it be like to hear him ask that in different circumstances? There was something about this man...the resonance of his deep voice, his inner strength in the face of adversity, his sureness... that drew her.

Her heart beat hard against her ribs.

'Tori. And you?'

'You may call me Ash.'

Before she could wonder at his phrasing, he continued.

'If you can get onto the roof and away, there's a chance you can raise the alert before daybreak.'

He didn't have to spell out what would happen when day came. That captor's slicing gesture was vivid in her mind.

'But I don't know where I am. Or where to go.'

Long fingers folded around her hand, steadying her. 'You don't have to know. Get away from the hut and the campfire. Stay low. When you're a safe distance out, circle the camp. You'll eventually come across the trail where you entered. Keep out of sight and follow the trail.'

'And hope to find the road or a village?'

'You have a better idea?'

Tori shook her head. It was their best chance. Possibly Ash's *only* chance.

'Let's do this.' She planted her palms on his shoulders, then sucked in a breath as he bent, wrapped his big hands around her and lifted.

It was probably only fifteen minutes before they admitted defeat. To Ashraf it felt like hours.

Frustrating hours, with that cursed chain curtailing his movements. They had only been able to explore one end of the roof and it was disappointingly sturdy.

The slashing pain across his ribs had become a sear of agony. His head pounded. Stiff muscles ached from boosting his companion high, then holding her up while she strained and twisted, trying to find a weakness in the roof structure she could exploit.

Physical exertion compounded with frustration at his helplessness. But it was another sort of torture, holding Tori.

Trying to ignore her rounded breasts and buttocks. Standing solid, holding her high, his face pressed to her soft belly as she heaved and twisted, trying to force her way through the roof. Feeling the narrowness of her waist, inhaling her female essence, fresh and inviting, despite the overlay of dust and fear.

Beneath the loose trousers and long-sleeved shirt she was all woman. Firmly toned, supple and fragrantly feminine.

By the time he lowered her for the last time and sagged against the wall his body shook all over. From reaction to his wounds. From fury at himself for allowing Qadri to get the better of him.

And from arousal. Flagrant and flaming hot.

Ashraf told himself it was the adrenaline high—a response to life-or-death danger. Naturally his reactions were heightened. His need to fight his way free. His primal urge was to defy death in the same way generations had done since the dawn of time, by losing himself in the comfort of a warm, willing woman. Spilling his seed in the hope of ensuring survival, if not for himself, then for the next generation.

'Are you all right?'

She was so close her breath was a puff of warm air against his face.

'I *knew* it was too much with your wounds. We should have stopped earlier. Are you bleeding again?'

A gentle hand touched his chest just above his wound.

'Don't!' Ashraf grabbed her hand, flattening it against his chest. His eyes snapped wide and he found her staring up at him, clearly concerned. This close, he saw her eyes were pale. Blue? Grey? Maybe amber?

Realisation slammed into him.

She feels it too.

The tug of need. The connection between two people trapped and desperate. The powerful urge to find comfort in the face of impending death. For, even if she wasn't being executed in the morning, Tori's fate was dark.

'Don't fuss. I'm fine.' He pulled her palm away from his body. Yet he couldn't bring himself to relinquish her hand.

Because her touch brought unexpected comfort?

He was furious with himself for getting captured. Frustrated that, after all that had happened, maybe his life would end tomorrow and his father would have been right. The old man had said he'd never amount to anything. If Ashraf died within the first six months of his reign, with none of his changes cemented in place…

He released Tori and turned from her searching stare.

'I'm not fussing.'

She drew herself up so her head topped his chin. Her little sound of frustration reminded him of his favourite falcon, fluffing up her feathers in huffy disapproval when he didn't immediately release her for flight.

'I apologise.' He paused, surprised as the unfamiliar words escaped. 'I'm not bleeding again.' Hopefully. 'It was kind of you to be concerned.'

'Kind?' She choked on the word and it hit Ashraf that she was fighting back tears.

For him? No, she couldn't know that he faced death tomorrow. It was a reaction to her kidnap. She'd been courageous—more courageous than most men he knew—projecting a calm façade, persevering in trying to find a way out when many would have given up.

'Thoughtful,' he amended.

She shook her head and silvery hair flared out from her ponytail. Ashraf's hands curled tight. He knew an urgent desire to see that shimmering hair loose, so he could tunnel his fingers through it.

Temptation was a cruel thing. He couldn't take what he wanted. Or ask for it. Not from this proud woman who still fought panic.

'You'd better get some rest,' he murmured, his voice gruff as he ruthlessly harnessed his baser, selfish instincts. 'That's what I intend to do.'

Ashraf lowered himself to the floor. He felt every muscle, every movement. His wrist had rubbed raw against the manacle and there seemed little hope of escape.

Yet despite the pain he felt a sense of exultation. He was

still alive. He had no intention of meekly submitting to execution for Qadri's pleasure.

Ashraf had spent his life fighting for his place, proving himself, ignoring the jibes. Showing his father that his disdain meant nothing. Thumbing his nose at him by building a public profile as a pleasure-seeking playboy, delighting in scandals that he knew would rock the old man.

Now he was back in Za'daq and everything had changed. Especially given his brother's recent sacrifice. Ashraf's belly contracted at the thought of Karim.

'I'd feel better if you'd let me examine your wounds.'

Tori knelt beside him. So close he barely had to move to touch her face, her rounded breast. Too close for a man so severely tempted.

'There's nothing you can do in this light. Unless you have a torch and a first aid kit hidden somewhere?'

She pursed her lips and looked away, that silvery mane sliding over one shoulder.

Instantly he regretted his harsh response. He felt ashamed. It wasn't concern for Karim that had made him snap, but his visceral sexual response to her. He wanted things he shouldn't.

'I'm sorry.' It was the second time he'd apologised. 'That was uncalled-for. You're right, there's some pain, but it's not as bad as it looks.' What were bruises and cuts in comparison to what tomorrow held for him? 'But there's something you *could* do.'

'What's that?'

'Rest. We need to conserve our strength.' He stretched out, stifling a groan as abused muscles throbbed.

After a long silence she finally followed his example, lying down nearby.

Ashraf didn't sleep. Instead he focused on tomorrow, wondering if his security detail would find him before it was too late. Wondering if Basim was alive.

Finally a tiny sound caught his attention. Were Tori's teeth chattering? The desert night had turned chill.

'Come here, Tori. We'll be warmer together.'

She lifted her head. 'But your injuries…'

He reached out his untethered arm. 'Snuggle against this side.'

When she did Ashraf bit his tongue against a sigh of satisfaction.

'Put your head on my shoulder.' She complied and he felt the gentle whisper of her breath through his torn shirt. Soft curves cushioned his side, silky strands of hair tickled his neck and her hand rested warm at his waist.

Ashraf lifted his hand to stroke her hair. It was silken. Like the softest cushions in the royal harem, spun in the days when the Sheikhs of Za'daq had had a bevy of concubines devoted to their pleasure.

Pressed against him from shoulder to knee, she felt…

His breath clogged in his lungs and a tremor started low in his body, vibrating out.

'Am I too heavy?'

She shifted as if to move away and Ashraf rolled a little towards her, capturing her knee between his.

'Just relax. You're not hurting me.'

It wasn't strictly true. He was definitely in pain. But the ache of his wounds and the indignity of the chain were eclipsed by another sort of pain. The taut stretch of a body fighting luscious temptation.

Ashraf's mouth stretched in a mirthless smile. He'd spent years giving in to temptation. He wished he had more experience at resisting it. Perhaps that was why the tension he felt was so acute, the tug of war between honour and desire so fierce.

But honour won.

Finally he felt her breathing slow. She shifted, shimmying her hips as if to get more comfortable, and the friction was exquisite torture. But it was a torture he willingly bore.

Till she moved her arm and her hand accidentally brushed the evidence of his arousal straining against his trousers.

She froze.

Everything inside him stilled.

Ashraf swore they both stopped breathing.

Then his blood pumped again—harder, more urgent. His groin tightened. He had to force himself not to tilt his pelvis, seeking the feel of her palm against him.

'It's okay. You're safe with me, Tori.' Could she tell he spoke through gritted teeth? 'Nothing's going to happen.'

Silence. He waited for her to scurry away.

Then he knew he was hearing things when she said, 'Maybe I don't want to be safe with you.'

CHAPTER TWO

TORI HEARD THE words spill out and then Ash's swift intake of breath. But she refused to play coy. Not when this might be her last night alive.

All afternoon she'd fought not to imagine what awaited her at the mercy of her kidnappers. Pain. Forced sex. Slavery.

A few hours ago she'd have said experiencing desire in her current situation was impossible. But that was before Ash. Before they worked together. Before his matter-of-fact courage bolstered her own flagging determination to be strong. Before the touch of his hand and his understanding made her feel connected to him. Before the undeniable flare of arousal ignited in her belly and saturated her skin till she burned up with it.

She knew their excruciatingly intense circumstances created the connection. Yet it wasn't quite so simple. There was something about this man that spoke to her at a primal, instinctive level. Tori knew with a resolute certainty that defied explanation that this was more than a simple response to danger.

She'd never known such a potent link. As if they'd weathered a lifetime's emotions in a couple of hours.

Never felt such an urgent need for a man.

Never felt so reckless or so absolutely sure of what she wanted.

'Tori?'

His voice was deep and gravelly, his smooth tone banished by shock. Or, she hoped, by matching desire.

She moved her hand tentatively across his flat abdomen, resisting the urge to slip it lower and explore him more intimately. Iron-hard muscles clenched at her touch and a tremor racked his big body.

Tori's heart clenched in sympathy. He was so vibrantly, emphatically alive. She couldn't bear the thought that tomorrow—

Long fingers brushed the hair back from her face, the gesture achingly tender. Then, to her horror, he stroked his thumb across her cheek and smeared the hot track of a tear she hadn't even felt fall.

'Ah, *habibti*.'

She heard the clink of metal as he wrapped his arms around her and pulled her up against him. Soft words fell into her ears as his lips moved against her eyelids, cheeks and hair. The ribbon of words was lilting and beautiful, like the unexpected sound of a spring, bubbling up clear and life-giving in a desert.

Greedily Tori drank in the sound as she absorbed his tender caresses. Blindly she tilted her head, seeking his lips, letting her leg fall across his thighs as she sought purchase to climb up his tall body.

'You have my word, Tori. If there's a way to save—'

Opening her eyes, she pressed her hand to his lips. 'Don't.'

She breathed deep, feeling her breasts push against him. Was she too heavy? But when she made to pull back the warm steel of his embrace held her.

'Don't talk about tomorrow. Please. I only want to think about tonight.'

She was so close that even in the gloom she saw the shift of muscles as he clenched his jaw. His face was strongly made, with bold lines against which the sensuous curve of his lips seemed shockingly desirable. Through the blood and dust she thought she imagined laughter lines near his eyes, but the grooves around his mouth spoke of weighty concerns.

The man's injured. He's likely to die tomorrow. Despite

*that, he's done his best to stop you falling apart. Of course
he has more on his mind than gratifying your selfish desires.*

Tori's heart contracted. He might be aroused, but that
was a simple physical response to proximity and, perhaps,
to danger. It didn't mean he wanted her. Perhaps he had a
woman. A wife, even.

Choking back an exclamation of self-loathing, she pulled
back, determined to put distance between them.

But his arms stopped her. She wriggled, trying to escape, but couldn't find purchase to resist his strength—not
without elbowing his injured side.

'Let me go,' she whispered. 'I need to—'

'I know what you need, *habibti*. I need it too. So very
badly.'

His voice ground low through her body, awakening those
few dormant female nerve centres not already attuned to
his closeness.

Tori felt herself quicken and soften, warmth spreading
in a wave of anticipation for his big, hard body. Her legs
splayed around his, her pelvis pressed needily against his
hipbone.

Flame scorched her cheeks as one large hand slid down
to cup her bottom and pull her closer. Thoughts splintered
at the dazzle of carnal pleasure erupting through her.

'I…'

She fought to find a coherent chain of thought when her
body was already immersed in an intimate conversation
with his. What did she want to say? The important thing?

He tilted her chin so she looked into hooded eyes. 'Talk
to me, Tori. Are you certain you want this?'

She wanted it, *him*, so badly she shook with the force
of her desire.

'Are you married?' The words sounded strange, in
a breathless voice she hardly recognised, but now the
thought had entered her head she couldn't ignore it. 'Is
there anyone—?'

'No one.' His tone was grave. 'And you?'

Tori shook her head.

She felt his chest rise beneath her on a sighing breath.

Even so, what had seemed so natural, so easy, moments before, now felt difficult. She felt gauche, unsure how to proceed. Till his mouth curved slowly into a smile that stole her breath and set her heart fluttering up in her throat.

She'd had an impression of Ash as strong, ultra-masculine and handsome in a severe way. But when he bestowed that smile on her Tori discovered he was far, far more. Attractive didn't cover it. Sexy was closer. Her befuddled brain grappled for a second to find a word that did him justice. Then she gave up and simply *felt*.

His hand rose to the back of her head, pulling her closer. She went eagerly, sinking into a kiss that was devastating for all its gentle persuasiveness. Fire sizzled and sparked from her toes to her ears. From her lips to her breasts and her womb.

Her mouth softened on his, opening automatically around his tongue. She didn't even try to prevent the mew of delight as he delved deeper, inviting her to let go on the wave of wellbeing that swept her up.

The kiss went on and on, deliberate and slow, stoking the blaze between them. Till his hand cupped her breast and Tori seized up. Not in rejection, but because the sensation of that hard hand so gentle on her was exquisite.

She pulled her head back, sucking in a dizzying draught of air, meeting eyes that gleamed like obsidian in the shadowy light.

His hand froze. Clearly he'd misinterpreted her withdrawal.

Once more Tori felt a surge of respect for this man who even now let scruples override potent need.

In another place, another time, she'd want to discover everything she could about him. But they had so little time. The thought brought a desperate sob to her throat. She swallowed it and pressed his hand to her breast, revelling in the delicious sensations.

She leaned down so her lips grazed his ear. 'I want you, Ash. But I'm afraid of hurting you.' He'd stopped bleeding, but she didn't want to reopen his wounds.

She felt a rumbling beneath her that, remarkably, she identified as laughter. 'Let me worry about that.'

While she was still catching her breath he rolled her onto her back, only to freeze mid-movement. It took her a second to realise his arm was stretched out behind him, caught by the chain.

The reminder of their dire circumstances should have splintered the brief comfort of the moment. Except Ash sounded merely rueful as he murmured, 'Not my smoothest move.'

His humour made this once more about *them*, not what lay beyond these walls, and Tori bit down a smile as together they shuffled awkwardly across the floor till Ash had the freedom to move both arms.

'Better,' he whispered, gathering her close. 'Much better.'

Broad shoulders blocked out the moonlight as he bent and kissed her hard on the lips. Then, as everything in her clamoured for more, he pulled back, propping himself on his good arm as he fumbled for the zip of her trousers.

'Let me. It will be quicker.' Excitement fizzed in her blood.

When he moved back to deal with his own trousers Tori stripped off her boots, trousers and knickers. She'd never had a one-night stand but she felt no embarrassment, just an urgency that grew with every passing moment.

'Leave your shirt.' Ash's hand on her shoulder pushed her gently down onto her back. 'It will protect you from the floor.'

His own shirt hung open to reveal a wide expanse of muscled chest. Her hungry gaze began to rove him, only to stop at the dark line across a couple of ribs. Her stomach clenched.

Suddenly it wasn't sex on her mind but the fate that awaited Ash tomorrow. The thought of what they'd do to him and what they might do to her—

'Changed your mind?'

His voice held no inflection other than curiosity—as if he had no qualms about stopping. Yet even in the gloom there was no mistaking the tension in his tall frame or the sight of his arousal straining towards her.

He wanted this, needed it, as much as she.

The sight of him made her wet between the legs, her muscles tightening in anticipation. Tori drew a shuddery breath, shoving away all thoughts of tomorrow.

Live for the moment had never held such profound meaning.

'Wouldn't it be safer if I was on top? With your injuries?'

His chuckle was liquid chocolate, or perhaps a shot of malt whisky, heating her blood. 'Probably. Call me a traditionalist, but I want to lie between your beautiful thighs and take us both to Paradise.'

His words ratcheted her level of arousal from fierce to ballistic. As did the nimble way he flicked open her shirt buttons, then made short work of her front-opening bra, pulling it wide to survey her in silence.

Tori's heart battered her ribs as she felt the cold night air drift across her puckering nipples and waited for his next move. Then he smiled. Another of those charismatic smiles that drove a spike of sharp emotion straight through her rib cage and stopped her breath.

When he spoke again it was in a language she didn't understand. A fluid ripple of sound that wrapped itself around her, caressing her as effectively as those callused hands stroking her breasts, waist and hips. Drawing her into a world of seductive urgency.

Then Ash lowered himself over her and she almost cried

out at how right it felt. Strong, hair-roughened thighs be-tween hers. The weight of him heavy against her. The jut of his hipbones. Broad shoulders above her and heat…heat everywhere.

Tori drew her knees up above his hips and heard a grunt of masculine pleasure. Then long fingers slid low, past her abdomen, down to her hot, slick, swollen centre. She jolted as a shock of pleasure raced through her. His fingers moved again, circling and teasing.

Her hand on his wrist stopped him. 'No. Don't. I just want *you*.'

She was strung so tight, on an unbearable edge of arousal, that she feared one more touch might fling her into rapture. But she needed something more profound than the touch of his hand. She craved the ultimate connection, the intimacy of their two bodies linked as one.

Tori sighed her relief when he nodded. Even so Ash took his time, surveying her face as if memorising it. Tori *felt* his gaze cross her cheeks, lips and forehead. And when his hand brushed the hair back from her face it was a gesture that spoke of tenderness and restraint, for she felt the tini-est tremor in those long fingers.

'Your hair is like silk,' he murmured.

Tori wanted to say something profound, to offer this strong, gentle man something to match the gift of his ten-derness. But there were no easy words.

Instead she lifted her own hand, cupping the stubble-roughened jaw, hard and warm. She felt his slow pounding pulse, then skimmed her hand higher into dark hair that felt thick yet soft. His eyes closed as she massaged the un-injured side of his scalp.

He positioned himself against her. Instinctively she lifted her pelvis, feeling that velvet weight nudge her. Tori held her breath as he pushed, long and slow and further, surely, than any previous possession. Her eyes widened and his grew more heavy-lidded as they held their breaths at the perfection of their joining. The moment went on and on till finally Ash was lodged deep within, vital and impossibly, lavishly male.

A quiver ran through Tori, starting at the muscles surrounding him and spreading till she trembled all over. A matching shiver rippled across his wide shoulders and muscled arms.

Then he withdrew, and the movement was so exquisitely arousing that Tori had to bite her lip to stop from crying out. Ash's lips pulled back in a grimace that looked like pain, but she knew it was a sign of pleasure and his battle for control.

The sight of him fighting for restraint and the generous pleasure of his returning thrust sent Tori spiralling over the edge.

'Please.' Her hands dug into his shoulders as she struggled to keep her voice to a whisper. 'I need you now.'

Ash's mouth covered hers, blotting out the scream rising within. Strong arms held her close as he abandoned restraint and pounded fast, hard and satisfying, filling her so that it seemed there was no longer Tori and Ash but only one being, straining after pleasure. Rapture exploded in a shuddering conflagration so powerful that the very air vibrated with it.

Together they rocked and shuddered. She was overwhelmed by sensations so intense they defied description. Except that at their heart was a delight so profound Tori half expected to die from it.

The world shook. Senses swam. Blood roared in her ears loud as a helicopter coming in to land. And through it all they stayed locked together, mouths and bodies fused.

Finally, when sanity began to creep back in, Ash rolled onto his side and then his back, taking Tori with him. Aftershocks ripped through her as overloaded pleasure receptors reacted again and again.

A rough gasp of pain reminded her of Ash's wounds. Instantly she tried to shift from his grasp. He didn't need her weight on his injuries.

'Stay.' His voice was hoarse, a rough wisp of sound that Tori found it impossible to resist.

She kissed him open-mouthed in the hot, male-scented curve where his shoulder met his neck. He shivered, hauling her closer.

Never had Tori felt this profound oneness. It was shared physical pleasure but surely something more. Something inexplicable that had swept them up and cradled them together.

Tori gave in to the protective urge to spread her arms as wide as she could around his brawny shoulders. She rested her head on his chest, absorbing the reassuring heavy thud of his heartbeat. She'd wait till she caught her breath. Then she'd try to define the change she sensed with every cell yet couldn't name.

It was her last cogent thought for hours.

'Tori.'

The luscious deep voice was warm and seductive in her ear. Ash's hands moved over her body and she stretched sinuously, arching to meet them.

She frowned, for he wasn't caressing her, he was—

'It's time to wake up.' His hands were deftly doing up her shirt buttons, right to the collar.

'Ash?' She opened her eyes to discover pale light filtering through the small windows.

He was dressed, she realised, his torn shirt buttoned and tucked into dusty trousers. Then she recalled him insisting in the night that they dress again. For warmth, he'd said.

Now she felt a chill that was only partly due to the temperature. Grey dawn light revealed a clearer view of Ash than she'd had so far. His features were starkly sculpted and compelling. His face would turn any woman's head. But now she saw clearly the blood caked in his hair. His torn clothes were liberally marked with dark stains and the chain securing him looked brutally heavy.

Tori's stomach turned as dread reality hit her full-force. Nausea rose. Her pulse accelerated to a panicky rhythm. Impossibly, in Ash's arms the peril they were in had been pushed to the back of her mind. Now realisation slammed into her.

She clutched his hands and he paused. His eyes met hers and something passed between them. Then Ash took hold of her hands. In this light she still couldn't make out the colour of his eyes, yet the warmth she read in them counteracted the chill crackling across her bones.

Slowly, as if he had all the time in the world, he raised her left hand and kissed her palm, his warm lips soft on her flesh. He repeated the gesture with her other hand, sending a squiggle of heat from her palms to her breasts and lower, arrowing to her core.

He murmured something against her palm that she couldn't catch. But his eyes as they met hers glowed with a message that made her chest clamp.

'Thank you, *habibti*.' He inclined his head, sketching a quick, graceful movement with his hand that spoke of respect and admiration. 'You did me great honour last night. Your gift is one I'll carry with me.'

Tori was about to respond when Ash's expression changed. His head whipped towards the door, his features intent, as if he heard something she couldn't.

'Quickly.' He grabbed her boots and shoved her feet into them.

'What is it?'

But she guessed the cause of his urgency. Someone was coming.

The thought of their captors made her fingers shake, and she watched Ash push her hands aside to do up the laces with swift efficiency.

'Remember what I said.' His voice was urgent and low.

'Don't fight back till you're alone with one of them. You'll stand a better chance.'

Tori looked into that stern, handsome face and nodded. She swallowed hard. 'You—?'

'I'll be fine. Now the sun's rising the search party will find it easier to locate the camp.'

Neither admitted that the search party might be too late for him.

His hands tightened on hers as they heard voices outside. Leaning in, he whispered, 'When you escape—' *when*, not *if*... Tori's heart leapt with hope '—keep low and—'

His words were cut off by the door banging open to rattle against the wall. Tori blinked against the light, realising belatedly that Ash no longer held her hands but was on his feet, facing the three men who had entered.

What came next was the stuff of nightmares. Brutal, pawing hands and leering faces. A slap that made her head ring as she struggled to free herself. But far worse was the sight of Ash, pulling one of the men off her and then being set upon by two of them. Hampered by the chain, he was eventually overwhelmed by vicious blows to his injured head and ribs.

The last she saw of him he'd crumpled to his knees and then pitched sideways, a scarlet bloom spilling from his wounds across the dirt floor.

The rusty tang of fresh blood was sharp in Tori's nostrils as she was shoved, stumbling, into the chill morning.

CHAPTER THREE

TORI STARED AT the data before her, wishing she could blame her lack of concentration on a post-lunch slump. Stretching, she leaned back in her chair and took in the view of Perth's Swan River, sparkling in the sunlight.

It had been tough, moving from Sydney to Western Australia. She'd had to find a new home, start a new job, create a new life, all on top of the trauma that still haunted her.

If her father had been at all supportive she'd have settled in Sydney. Family was supposed to be there for you during difficult times, after all.

Tori shuddered, remembering the last time she and her father had spoken. It was pointless wishing for the impossible—like a caring father—but his icy disapproval on top of recent events had made Tori miss her mother more than ever. She'd been warm, practical and supportive. Tori could have done with the unconditional love that had died years before, with her mother.

Yet it wasn't any of those things distracting her now. Or even last night's broken sleep. She was used now to perennial tiredness.

It was the date. Fifteen months to the day since she'd been kidnapped in Za'daq.

She'd been about to leave Assara, her geological survey complete and her companions already gone. She'd spent her final afternoon investigating an outcrop that hadn't been in her survey zone but had looked promising.

Until she'd found herself surrounded by armed men.

Fifteen months since she'd last seen Ash.

Fifteen months since the sharp rattle of gunfire had

echoed across the arid landscape, raising the hairs on her arms and neck and devastating her.

She'd never forget that sound.

Or the gloating chuckle of the leader of the small party that had left the bandit camp to make its way across the foothills.

He was the one Ash had knocked aside after the man had grabbed her, his hands insinuating themselves under her shirt. When gunfire had sounded from the camp the man had leered, slicing his hand across his throat in a violent gesture. He'd spat out words she hadn't understood but his meaning had been clear. Ash was dead.

Even now the nightmare reality was almost too much to take in.

The fruit smoothie she'd had for lunch curdled in Tori's stomach and she swallowed hard, trying to keep it down.

Traumatic memories were normal, her counsellor said. And, what with having been up half the night, it was no surprise that Tori was susceptible today to distressing flashes of memory.

They'd pass. They always did.

Meanwhile she had a report to sort out.

Breathing deep, she turned back to her computer.

She was frowning over an anomaly when a waft of pungent aftershave reached her.

'Head down, Victoria? Good to see you making the most of the time you're actually in the office.'

Tori repressed a sigh. It *would* be Steve Bates—leader of the other team on this floor. He always carped about her part-time hours, implying that she took advantage of the company instead of actually working harder than some of her full-time colleagues. And that never stopped him staring at her as if he could see through her clothes.

She needed to tackle him about his attitude. But not today, when she felt so low. Besides, she'd survived far worse than Steve could dish out.

The thought steadied her.

Tori swung around in her chair to meet his stare. Naturally it wasn't her face he was looking at. She sat straighter and his eyes lifted.

'This new survey data is intriguing. Is that why you're here? I'll have the report ready by—'

He stopped her with a dismissive wave. 'I'm not here for that.' He paused, his X-ray stare focused on her face, his gaze sharply assessing. 'You're full of surprises, aren't you?'

Tori frowned. 'Sorry?'

Steve smiled, but instead of putting her at ease his calculating expression made disquiet flicker.

'I had no idea you had such…connections. No wonder the bosses were eager to snap you up. But then it's always who you know, isn't it? Not how good your work is.'

'Now, look here!' She shot to her feet, fury rising. She had no patience for people who thought she'd got where she was through her father's influence. 'I won this job on merit. Simple as that.'

The idea of her father interfering on her behalf wasn't just wrong, it was risible. Despite what he said in public, Jack Nilsson didn't approve of her career. As for exerting himself on her behalf… Not unless it would win him positive publicity.

'If you say so.' Steve raised his hands but his knowing smirk lingered. 'Don't be so touchy and emotional.'

Tori raised one eyebrow at the typical putdown. When she spoke again she used the clear, carrying tones she'd learned when her father had insisted she take up debating at school. 'Was there a work matter you wanted to discuss? Or did you just interrupt me to shoot the breeze?'

Steve slanted a glance towards the open-plan office behind him. His expression grew ugly. 'You're wanted in the boardroom.' His tone was as hard as the diamonds the company mined. 'Immediately.'

He turned on his heel and disappeared, leaving Tori relieved and confused. She hated Steve's snarky sexism. He deserved far more than the mild rebuke she'd given him. But she had no idea who wanted to see her and why. She knew where the boardroom was, but she wasn't significant enough in the company to be invited to meetings there.

She tried to remember if she'd heard anything about an executive meeting today but nothing registered.

Tori smoothed her hair then reached for her phone, her tablet and the not yet finished survey report. Taking a deep breath, she marched across the office, feeling curious glances as she pushed the lift button for the executive level.

Minutes later she stepped into the rarefied atmosphere of extreme wealth. The company was one of the most successful of its type and the executive suite was all plush carpet, expensive artworks and bespoke wood panelling. The views up here were dizzyingly spectacular.

Tori was staring about her when a young man in a pinstriped suit approached.

'Ms Nilsson?'

His manner was friendly, but there was no mistaking his curiosity. She resisted the urge to check her hair or straighten her collar. She'd learned never to fidget in public. Her father hated it because it spoiled the perfect press shot.

'Yes. I understand I'm wanted in the boardroom?' She let her voice rise at the end of the sentence, hinting at a question. But he didn't offer an explanation.

'That's right. This way, please.'

He led the way past a beautifully appointed lounge with panoramic windows. As they approached a set of double doors Tori noticed a man in a dark suit nearby. His feet were planted wide and his hands clasped.

A bodyguard. She'd seen enough of them to recognise the demeanour.

This one met her eyes calmly, no doubt sizing her up. He looked sturdy and, despite his impassive expression, intimidating.

Tori gripped her belongings tighter. Unusual that one of the company's executives should bring a bodyguard into the building. Then she remembered Steve's snide challenge. *'It's always who you know.'*

Which meant it was her father in the boardroom. Though why he'd brought a bodyguard… And why he'd chosen to meet her at work… He hadn't mentioned coming to Western Australia and he never made paternal visits.

'Here you are, Ms Nilsson.' Her guide pushed open one of the doors.

She stepped in to find the room empty. There was no meeting. The long polished table was bare.

Tori blinked and hesitated. She was about to go out again and ask what was going on when a shadow at the far end of the room detached itself from the wall.

A man. A tall man, spine straight and shoulders wide. He was silhouetted against a wall of glass. For an instant all she had was an impression of strength and the loose-limbed saunter of an athlete as he approached. She didn't recognise the walk, but there was something familiar about him.

Tori's skin tightened as premonition swept through her. A split-second certainty that she knew him.

She opened her mouth to say hello, but then he drew close enough that she could make out his features instead of just the shape of his head.

Tori heard a hissed breath. Her hands slackened. Something hard grazed her shin as it dropped with a thud onto the carpeted floor. But her gaze was glued to the man who had stopped just an arm's length away.

Bronzed skin pulled tight over a bone structure that would have made Michelangelo weep. A sensual mouth set above a determined jaw. Eyes that even from here looked black rather than dark brown. Black eyebrows. A forceful nose that transformed his face from an ideal of masculine beauty to one of power. Black hair that Tori knew was soft to the touch.

Her nerveless hands twitched as memory flooded through her. Of channelling her fingers through hair so soft and thick it felt like a pelt. Of being careful to avoid the clotted blood of his head injury.

The twitch in her hands became a tremor. A shudder thundered through her as her heart crashed into her ribs.

Heat suffused her as she met gleaming eyes. Then a wash of icy cold as other memories battered her brain.

Kidnappers. Gunfire.

Her eyes prickled and she blinked rapidly. Tears came easily now—another thing her counsellor said was normal. Yet instinctively Tori tried to dam them.

She swayed. The floor seemed to ripple and the walls appeared to close around the man watching her so intently. Tori grabbed the back of a leather conference chair for support, fingers clawing.

There was no scarring on his face. Nothing to indicate he'd ever been brutalised or shot at. He wore a dark grey suit tailored by an expert. It rivalled anything in her father's expensive wardrobe, and on this man's rangy, powerful frame looked spectacular. A white shirt complemented his burnished skin and a perfectly knotted silk tie completed the image of urbane sophistication.

It couldn't be. It was impossible. And yet…

'I thought you were dead.'

It didn't sound like her voice, so husky and uneven. Yet he understood. His eyes widened and something passed across his face.

'Ah, that explains a lot.'

That voice! That deep, rich voice. She'd only heard him whisper before. They'd both kept their voices low so as not to attract the guards' attention. His whispers had threaded through her dreams for over a year. How often had she woken from a nightmare or the occasional erotic dream with the sound of his voice in her head?

'It *is* you?'

Tori wanted to touch him, to check for herself he was no mirage. But her limbs felt like blocks of basalt. All she could do was stand and stare.

'It's me, Tori.'

Ashraf stared down into her oval face and felt a wave of emotion tumble through him.

He'd searched for her so long, against impossible odds, when even the best investigators had advised him to give up. He recalled the moment he'd received news that she was alive. Alive and safe. Relief had been so intense, so powerful, that for a moment he'd found it difficult to breathe.

He'd been fully prepared for this meeting, and still reality was nothing like his expectation.

Seeing Tori in the flesh unsettled him profoundly.

Maybe it was her eyes. He'd wondered about their colour. Now he knew. Soft blue. The colour of the dainty yet hardy forget-me-nots that grew in Za'daq's mountain valleys. Her gaze held his and he felt the bite of need, of hunger, of regret and a hundred emotions he wasn't in the habit of feeling. Those lovely eyes shone over-bright and her lip quivered.

Deep inside something responded with an intensity that rocked him back on his heels. As if his feelings were engaged in a way that was totally unfamiliar.

He'd admired her in Za'daq. She'd been courageous and strong, hiding her fears. He'd found comfort and welcome oblivion in her lithe body.

But he hadn't expected such a visceral reaction after all this time. He'd told himself danger had heightened their responses.

Ashraf registered the thunder of his pulse and the tingling in his blood that betrayed a surge of adrenaline. He wanted to touch her. More than touch her. He wanted—

He slammed a door on such thoughts. His reason for being here was too important for distraction. Despite other unexpected urges. To comfort and assure her. To protect her as he hadn't been able to fifteen months ago.

Guilt sliced at the memory. But it was blunted by other emotions. Desire. Possessiveness, rampant and untrammelled.

Ashraf tunnelled his fists into his pockets and forced himself to stand his ground rather than close the space between them.

'You need to sit. You've had a shock.'

She blinked up, eyes round and lips open as if she couldn't get enough oxygen.

He knew the feeling. His lungs were labouring as if he were the one surprised. He hadn't expected to feel—

Ashraf leaned past her, pulling out a high-backed chair from the table, and gestured for her to sit. She did, and he saw that even in extremity there was a familiar grace about her movements. He'd thought he'd imagined that, embellished his recollections of this woman with qualities she hadn't actually possessed. He'd told himself guilt and regret had turned her in his mind into someone more remarkable than she really was.

Striving for emotional distance, he catalogued what he saw. She was the same as in the photos his investigators had sent. Yet she was *more*.

Regular features in a face that was long rather than round. Fine lips. Even finer eyes. Eyes that watched his every move with an intensity he felt as a sizzle in his veins. Even the faint shadows of tiredness didn't mar her attractiveness. The hair he'd remembered as pale was platinum-blonde, pulled back and up in a chignon that left her face clear. But why would she hide those cheekbones? She wasn't classically beautiful, yet he defied any man not to take a second look.

Even in a plain white blouse and black trousers Tori Nilsson drew the eye.

That explained his racing pulse. That and the intimate secret they shared.

For a second his attention lingered on those breasts, quickly rising and falling against her blouse. They seemed plumper than he remembered—

'Can you sit, instead of towering over me?'

Ashraf huffed back laughter. *There* was the woman he remembered. Indomitable and practical. How lucky he'd been not to be stuck with a hysterical companion that night.

He pulled out a chair and sat knee to knee with her.

'You're really real.'

Slim fingers skimmed shakily over his cheek, down his freshly shaved jaw, and two things struck him.

First, no one these days ever touched him. He'd been busy in the last two years and it had been a long time since he'd had a lover. Plus his position meant that casual touching was out of the question.

Second, her hand shook. Perhaps he'd been unfair, confronting her like this with no warning. But he hadn't known she'd believed him dead. If he'd realised…

No, even if he'd known he'd still have wanted to see her in person.

'Yes. I'm real.'

He captured her hand, feeling the quick pulse throb at her wrist. At the same time he registered a hint of scent. Something sweet and enticing, slightly citrusy. It transported him to that night they'd been captives together. He couldn't recall noticing it then, but at some subliminal level he must have. It both enticed and disturbed him, reminding him of how close they'd come to death, and how he'd allowed himself to weaken in this woman's arms.

He released her hand and brushed her cheek with his knuckles. Satiny skin trembled at his touch and made his blood fizz.

He'd assumed his physical response to Tori had been fuelled by danger, by the knowledge that he might die. Was this just a hangover from that night? That had to be it.

But he wasn't here for sex.

Ashraf dropped his hand and sat back.

'How did you get away? I heard gunfire. I thought—'

Tori bit her lip, hearing the wobble in her voice. Clearly she'd thought wrong—so why was she upset? Seeing Ash again was a miracle. One she'd never dared hope for. Her reaction had to be due to shock.

'You thought they'd shot me?' His eyebrows rose and then he nodded. 'I'm sure they wish they had. You heard security forces storming the camp. Qadri, the bandits' leader, had just arrived. He was killed in the raid with several of his followers. The rest are serving time for various offences—including kidnap.'

The words sounded matter-of-fact. Like a news report of some distant, almost unreal incident. But the sound of those guns had been brutal reality for Tori for too long. She strove to absorb Ash's news but couldn't prevent a tremor of reaction.

'I thought you were dead. I—' She searched his face, even now finding it hard to believe he was there and whole. 'What are you *doing* here? It's an incredible coincidence.'

'No coincidence, Tori. I've been looking for you.' His voice was deep and assured.

'You have?'

Ash sat straighter. 'Of course! Did you imagine I'd forget about you? That I'd leave you to the mercy of people-smugglers?'

'But it's been fifteen months!'

His dark eyes flashed. 'I'm not in the habit of forgetting my friends.'

Was that what they'd been? Friends? Allies, for sure. Lovers too. And now…?

'I regret it took so long. I'd imagined…'

He shook his head, as if his imaginings weren't important, but the grim set of his mouth told its own story. If she'd been tormented by the thought of him dead, he'd had the burden of thinking her at the mercy of men like those who'd kidnapped her.

Tori closed her hand over his fist where it rested on his thigh. 'I'm not blaming you, Ash. That wasn't a rebuke. I'm just…surprised.' Make that astounded. She'd never in her wildest dreams believed she'd see him again. 'How did you locate me?'

He shrugged. 'A team of top investigators, persistence and in the end one lucky break.'

Investigators working for fifteen months? That must have cost a fortune.

Tori's gaze skittered across that beautifully made suit. Ash wasn't ostentatiously dressed but he projected an aura of authority and wealth, like a man used to wielding power. A little like her father, except in Ash it seemed innate, less cultivated for public consumption. Her father revelled in the importance his position gave him. Ash, on the other hand, wasn't showy or obvious.

'You're a determined man.'

If there'd been an easy trail to follow he'd have found her ages ago. The fact that he'd persevered all this time spoke of a doggedness she could only admire. If she'd still been at the mercy of people-smugglers she was sure he'd have found a way to free her. The knowledge made her heart lurch.

'How did you get away? Month after month my people scoured Za'daq and the border territory for you. They found nothing.'

My people. He made it sound as if he had his own personal army.

Belatedly Tori realised she still held his hand. She forced her fingers open and sat back, folding her hands together and telling herself the throb of heat she felt had nothing to do with touching Ash.

But hearing he'd made it his quest to find her unravelled something she'd kept locked up tight since the horror of the kidnap. And looking into those dark eyes was messing with her head. She squeezed her eyes closed and drew a breath.

This was so complicated. So profoundly difficult. What on earth was she going to do?

'Tori?'

She snapped her eyes open. 'Sorry. I'm still a little stunned.'

The implications of Ash being here were only just seeping into her whirling brain. There was so much to consider. So many variables and, yes, worries. Her skin prickled with anxiety and it wasn't from reliving the past.

But for now she owed him her story.

'Three of us rode away from the camp. Me, the guard you knocked down and a boy—barely a teenager. When we heard the gunshots the older man was happy. He thought you were dead.' Tori snatched a fortifying breath, remembering the sour tang of fear and horror she'd felt at his gleeful triumph. 'But after the first couple of shots he said something to the boy and then headed back the way we'd come.'

'Probably realised there was too much gunfire for an execution.'

Slowly Tori nodded. She hadn't considered that. She'd thought the firing squad had been overly enthusiastic, or perhaps celebrating.

'The pair of us kept riding, but the boy wasn't happy. He began to look scared. Maybe he understood some English, because I told him what would happen to him when he was caught. I might have exaggerated...'

'Good for you!' Ash looked admiring and Tori was amazed at how good that felt.

'What did I have to lose? Besides, I was upset.'

An understatement for the raw rage and fear that had consumed her as they'd trekked through the wilderness. Hearing that gunfire and believing Ash dead had been a living nightmare. Even remembering that moment—

'Go on.'

Tori spread her hands. 'It wasn't really hard to get away. I realised later he let me escape.'

Ash nodded. 'He must have realised something had gone wrong and he'd be in trouble if he was found with you.'

'I ran away during a rest stop. The rope was a little loose and I eventually got it undone. I was terrified he'd come after me but I never saw him again.'

Tori flexed her hands, remembering the burn of dust against red raw flesh.

'Hours later I stumbled into the path of a four-wheel drive. A couple of foreigners were returning to their private yacht after a trip inland.'

Foreigners who had been sympathetic but, for reasons of their own, avoiding the authorities. She'd wondered if they were smuggling contraband.

'They were on their way to the Maldives and took me with them. Once there I made contact with the Australian authorities.'

'You crossed the border from Za'daq into Assara,' Ash said. 'We made enquiries in neighbouring countries, but using official channels it was a slow process with no leads. It was only recently that a witness came forward. A driver passing through on his way to a family wedding. Recently he returned to visit his village again and heard about the search for you. He remembered three foreigners boarding a yacht in a deserted cove.'

Tori digested that. 'And from something so vague you located me?' It was remarkable! She could barely imagine the resources, or sheer luck, required to find her.

'Eventually. Fortunately the yacht was distinctive, so it could be tracked. Your trail was easy from the Maldives, after I knew you'd escaped and where you were headed.' His mouth twisted ruefully. 'If we'd exchanged full names and addresses it would have saved time.'

Heat tickled Tori's throat. Despite their physical intimacy they'd never got past first names. It seemed strange now.

'Well, you found me. I'm glad.' She smiled up at him. Despite the complications she'd now have to face, it was wonderful to know he'd survived. 'It's good to see you alive.'

'And you, Tori.'

His look seared her and she shifted in her seat. It wasn't just relief she felt. Her emotions were complex and she found herself growing nervous all over again.

The longer she sat with him, the more she realised how little she knew about Ash, despite the way her body hummed with awareness. He seemed light-years away from the stoic man with whom she'd shared intimacies in the desert.

She couldn't imagine—

No, that was wrong. She *could* imagine all too easily the urge to be with him again. The realisation sent heat spiralling through her middle and surging up her throat to scald her cheeks.

Yet it wasn't sexual awareness stretching her nerves tight. It was apprehension. For she knew next to nothing about him. His life, hopes, expectations. How he'd react when faced with what she had to tell him.

For a craven moment she wondered if she could avoid that. It would be taking a giant step into the unknown. But it had to be done.

She moistened her lips, ready to speak, but he was too fast for her.

'So, Tori. Or should I call you Victoria?' He leaned closer, his black-as-night gaze pinioning her to the seat. 'Are you going to tell me about my son?'

CHAPTER FOUR

IF ASHRAF HAD had any doubts about the child being his, they were banished by Tori's reaction.

The flush colouring her face disappeared completely, leaving those high-cut cheeks blanched like porcelain. Her gasp filled the silent room.

His investigators had provided a photo—part of a slim dossier on Victoria Miranda Nilsson. A photo of a tiny child with dark hair and what might be dark eyes, though the shot had been taken from too far away to be sure.

Now he was sure. She'd had his baby.

Another surge of adrenaline shot into his blood, catapulting around his body. It took everything he had to sit there, holding her gaze, instead of erupting to his feet and pacing the length of the room.

But Ashraf had learned in childhood to control his impulses, even if later he'd made his name by giving in to them. No, that wasn't quite right. Even when he'd gone out of his way to provoke with scandal and headlines his actions hadn't been impulsive, even if they'd seemed so. They'd been carefully considered for maximum impact.

But now wasn't the time to think of his father and how they'd always been on opposing sides. Now *he* was a father.

Ashraf registered awe as the reality of it sideswiped him. As he thought of this slim, self-possessed woman fruitful with his child. How had she looked, her belly rounded with his baby? Did that explain the urge he now battled to feel her pliant body against his again? Because she'd borne his child? He wished he'd been there, seeing her body change, attending the birth. So much he'd missed out on. So much she'd had to face without him.

'I was going to tell you, Ash. I was just…' She waved her hand in a vague gesture at odds with the determined tilt of her chin.

How wrong he'd been—imagining she'd deliberately withheld the news of his son.

Satisfaction eddied in his belly that his first assessment of her appeared right after all. He'd thought her practical, brave and honest. He'd admired her, wanted to believe she'd got away. Yet when finally he'd received proof that she had, doubts had filtered in. Because she hadn't informed him about the baby.

Now he knew why.

What had she gone through, having his child alone? Without, as far as he could tell, family support? She'd believed him dead. Her shock on seeing him had been no charade. Ashraf tried to imagine how she'd felt, struggling with the effects of trauma alone when she'd most needed assistance.

'You're still in shock. You thought me dead.'

'It's true! I did.' She spoke so quickly she must have read something in his expression.

'I believe you.'

'But?'

He lifted his shoulders, spreading his hands. 'In my work I sometimes appear on the television news. It seemed likely you'd see me.' That had been one of the reasons he'd feared for her—feared that she was dead or unable to contact him.

'Do you? You must have an important job.'

When he merely shrugged she laughed, the sound short, almost gruff.

'My father is a politician. Years of being force-fed a diet of politics means I avoid the TV news.'

Cynicism threaded her soft voice. A dislike of politicians or just her father?

'Especially news from Za'daq.' Another wide gesture

with her hand. 'After what happened I've actively avoided reports from that part of the world.'

Now he saw it in her eyes. Not prevarication but a haunted look that spoke of pain and trauma. Her abduction had left scars.

His hand captured hers, reassuring. He was pleased to feel its warmth. She looked so pale he'd imagined her chilled. Yet when they touched there was a definite spark of fire.

'Besides,' she went on, 'new mothers have priorities other than TV current affairs programmes.'

The baby. *His* baby. That had been her priority.

Now it was his too.

Ashraf would do everything necessary to ensure his son had the sort of life he deserved.

'Tell me about him.'

She looked down at his hand enfolding hers, then away. 'He's the most important thing in my life.'

'As he will be in mine,' he vowed.

Startled eyes flashed to his. Ashraf felt the shock of contact, read the flare of…was that *fear*? Then Tori looked away. This time she slipped her hand back into her lap, curving her other hand protectively around it.

Tori looked into those gleaming eyes and her heart stuttered. Had she ever seen a man so intent?

Yes. The night she and Ash had made love, finding solace in each other's arms. Finding rapture.

For so long she'd wondered what it would be like if Ash hadn't died. If he'd been at her side through the pregnancy and birth, and later to care for Oliver. The thought was a secret refuge when the burdens she'd faced grew too heavy.

Now she discovered her fantasy was real—too real, given her response to him. And Tori had to remind herself that he wasn't the embodiment of her exhausted daydreams but a man with his own agenda.

A shuddery sigh began deep in her belly and travelled up through lungs that contracted hard, stealing her breath, making her turn away.

Ash had done that to her fifteen months ago—stolen her breath, her senses, her self-possession. Now he was doing it again, without trying.

She was in deep trouble. If she'd learned one thing about him, it was that he followed through. When he determined to do something he did it.

Now he'd staked a claim on his son.

Her son. Her precious Oliver.

Suddenly, as if she'd taken an unwary step and plunged off a precipice, Tori was out of her depth.

The working part of her brain told her she should be used to that by now. After her kidnap and escape. After childbirth alone and unsupported by anyone except the competent, kind midwives who'd delivered her son. After relocating to the far side of the country to build a life for her darling boy free of her father.

But this time it felt different. Perhaps because what she shared with Ash was so personal. Not merely her body and her passion, but her son.

Did he expect her to give Oliver up? She knew little of Middle Eastern culture but guessed fathers might have more authority there than mothers.

Her gaze slewed back to Ash to find him watching her with a stillness that did nothing to assuage her nerves. It was the stillness of a predator.

Tori dragged in a deep breath. She was overreacting. Ash wasn't a bully. He was...

She didn't know what he was.

'You'll want to see him.'

Even saying it sent a wobble through her middle, as if she was walking a tightrope and one misstep would send her tumbling.

He inclined his head. 'Of course.'

'That's why you came.'

Now it became clear. If he'd hired investigators to find her they would have discovered she'd travelled to Western Australia accompanied by her infant son.

Tori wrapped her arms around herself.

One dark eyebrow climbed that broad forehead. 'I was searching for *you*, Tori. And when I discovered you'd given birth to a child nine months after the night we spent together...' His straight shoulders lifted in a fluid shrug. 'Of course I wanted to come myself. To hear your explanation.'

Explanation. As if she'd done something wrong—namely deprived him of his child. Was he here to punish her for that? Perhaps by taking Oliver from her?

No, that was unfair. Nothing she'd learned about Ash that night indicated he was anything but decent and admirable. Besides, would she have liked him if he'd learned about her baby and ignored the fact? If he'd shied away from responsibility?

The nervous roiling in her stomach settled a little as the thought penetrated. She was allowing fear to build upon fear, when the little she knew about Ash should have reassured her.

The Ash she'd met last year.

This man, in his hand-stitched suit with an air of assurance in the plush executive suite, was someone she had yet to know.

'If I'd known you were alive I'd have told you about Oliver.'

'Oliver...' He said it slowly, rolling the name around his tongue as if testing it.

'Oliver Ashal Nilsson.' Fire climbed her throat and moved higher, making her ears tingle.

'Ashal?' Both eyebrows arched this time. 'That's an Arabic name.'

So his investigators hadn't got as far as checking the birth certificate. For some reason that made her feel better.

'I know. I wanted…' She dropped her gaze to her knot-ted hands. 'I wanted him to have something from you so I gave him your name—or as close to it as I could find. I wasn't sure if Ash was your real name.'

She looked up to see Ash staring at her as if he'd never seen her before. He swallowed and she tracked the move-ment of his strong throat, finding it strangely both arous-ing and endearing, as if it indicated he was affected by the revelation.

Perhaps her imagination worked overtime.

'I found Ashal in a list of baby names. It means light or radiance.'

'I know what it means.'

Ash's voice was so low Tori felt it trawl through her belly.

'It's a fine name.' He paused. 'It was very generous of you to give him a name that honoured my heritage.'

Tori spread her hands. 'It seemed apt. He's the light of my life.'

Awareness pulsed between them. Not sexual this time, but an unprecedented moment of understanding. The sort she imagined parents the world over shared when they dis-cussed their beloved children. It reassured her as nothing else had.

'So what *is* your name? Is it Ash?'

'Ashraf.'

'Ashraf.' She said it slowly, liking the sound.

'It means most honourable or noble.' His mouth kicked up at the corner, lending his expression a fleetingly cyni-cal cast. A second later the impression was gone. 'Ashraf ibn Kahul al Rashid.'

He watched her closely as if expecting a reaction. Some-thing about the name tickled her memory but she couldn't place it.

When she merely nodded he went on, 'Sheikh of Za'daq.'

'Sheikh?' Weren't they just in books?

'Leader.' He paused. 'Prince. Ruler.'

Tori's mouth dried. She swallowed, then swiped her bottom lip with her tongue. 'You're the ruler of Za'daq? Of the whole country?'

For the second time in half an hour the world tilted around her. Hands braced on the chair's cushioned armrests, she fought sudden dizziness.

Oliver's father was a *king*?

'That explains the bodyguard.'

If she'd known what waited for her in this room, would she have entered or turned tail and run?

'Basim? He's head of my close personal protection team.'

No wonder Ash—no, Ashraf—had spoken of *his people* scouring the land, searching for her. His protection team must have been beside themselves when he was abducted.

'Do many people want to kill you?' Tori's thoughts had already veered to her tiny son and his safety.

'Not any more. Za'daq is actually a peaceful, law-abiding country. But it's customary and sensible to take precautions. Besides, it's expected that a visiting head of state will bring a security detail.'

Head of state. There it was again—that horrible slam of shock to her insides, creating a whirl of anxious nausea.

'Breathe.'

Firm hands clasped hers, anchoring them to the arms of the chair. A waft of spice and heat surrounded her, tantalising.

Tori stared up into fathomless eyes that looked like pure ebony even now as Ash... Ashraf...leaned in. Eyes so like Oliver's, and yet their impact was completely different from the feelings evoked when she looked at her son.

'I'm breathing. You can let me go.'

Even so it took one, two, three rapid beats of her heart before he released her. Was she crazy to think she saw regret in his expression?

'It's hard to believe after our abduction, I know, but you could travel in that same area unharmed today.'

'You said he was your enemy?' Tori murmured. 'That man—Qadri. In Australia, even in politics, when you speak of an enemy you don't mean someone who'd have you executed at dawn.' Even if the backstabbing and political manoeuvring in her father's world was violent in its own way.

Ashraf sat back and the tautness in her chest eased. When he'd leaned in, capturing her with his intense regard as much as his touch, she had felt ridiculously overwhelmed.

'Qadri was a relic of the past. A criminal who, because his powerbase was in a remote province, was allowed to remain untouched for too long.' Ashraf's mouth thinned. 'My father, the previous Sheikh, had no appetite for tackling intractable problems like ousting a vicious bandit who preyed on his own people. It was too far away from the capital and too hard when there were other, easier initiatives that would win him praise.'

So Ashraf and his father hadn't seen eye to eye? It was there in his voice and the slight upward tilt of his chin. Tori could relate to that.

'So you sent in your soldiers to kill Qadri?' That would explain his violent retaliation.

Ashraf's mouth curled in a small smile. 'Is that how things are done in Australia? In Za'daq the Sheikh upholds the law, rather than breaks it.'

He was laughing at her naivety, making a point about Za'daq being a country as enlightened as hers.

'But, given your experience, it's not surprising you thought otherwise. And it's true that centuries ago the Sheikh would have ridden in with his warriors and slaughtered such a man.'

'So what *did* you do?'

'Deprived him of his powerbase. Introduced schemes to bring the province out of the Dark Ages with adequate power, water and food. Began establishing schools and employment opportunities.' He shook his head. 'I'd only been Sheikh for half a year when we met, and the initiatives were in their infancy, but still they'd had a powerful effect. So had enforcing the law. I had police stationed locally to arrest Qadri's stand-over men when they tried to intimidate people. Qadri realised that soon the people wouldn't see him as the power in the region. They'd have choices and laws they could rely on.'

'So he had you kidnapped?'

'Unfortunately I made it easy, riding with only Basim and a guide into a deserted location to view a new project. The guide was in Qadri's pay.' Another twist of the lips. 'Clearly the security assessment was flawed, but no doubt some would say I was reckless.'

Tori frowned. That didn't gel with the man she knew. He was strong and astute, a strategic thinker and formidably determined.

And he was here for his son.

The reminder was a crackle of frost along her stiff spine.

'You can be assured that Za'daq is now safe to visit. As safe as your country.'

Was that code? His way of telling her that Oliver would be okay in his father's homeland? *Did* he mean to take Oliver from her?

Firming her lips, Tori beat down rising panic. She was jumping to conclusions. No one was going to take her son. There were laws about that. Hadn't Ashraf just taken time to prove he valued the law?

She wondered what the law in Za'daq said about custody of a child. Especially a male child. Was Oliver the Sheikh's heir?

It was no good. She couldn't sit here, pretending this was some polite catch-up with an old acquaintance. The rising burble of her emotions was too unsettling.

'Excuse me.' Tori shot to her feet and paced shakily to the wall of glass. She sensed rather than heard him come up behind her.

'I realise this is overwhelming.'

Tori nodded. She felt as if she'd stepped into a different reality. One where people came back from the dead and where handsome princes mingled with ordinary people.

'Imagine how I felt when I discovered you'd survived. And that you'd had my child.'

Ashraf's voice was low, a caress that tickled her flesh and tightened her nipples. Even after the reality of childbirth and six months of single motherhood, there was something seductively intimate about the way he spoke about her having his baby.

In the window she saw his reflection over her shoulder. His face was sombre, and it struck her for the first time that she wasn't the only one dealing with shock.

She turned to him. 'So where does that leave us?'

He didn't hesitate. 'I want to see Oliver. As soon as possible.'

Naturally. She looked at her watch. It was getting late. 'There's a report I have to complete today. It should only take me another hour.'

Ashraf considered her assessingly. Was he insulted because she didn't instantly jump to do his bidding? Did royal sheikhs ever have to wait for anything?

But he merely nodded. 'An hour, then.'

Two hours later Ashraf paced the sitting room of Tori's small villa, battling impatience and what felt remarkably like nerves.

After sleeping on their way home from the crèche Oliver, his son, had begun to fidget as soon as they'd entered. Ashraf had been torn between the need to reach for the child and wariness because he knew nothing about babies. Except that they were tiny, fragile and totally foreign to his world.

Oliver—the more he used the name, the more he'd get used to it—made him feel too big and clumsy to be trusted with a fragile new life.

Yet none of that had prevented the immediate visceral

connection he'd felt. He'd seen a tiny fist wave, caught the gleam of bright dark eyes, and felt emotion pound through his diaphragm strong as a knockout punch.

His son. His flesh and blood.

He'd missed seeing Tori grow big with his baby. He'd missed six months of his child's life. Precious months he could never get back. He had so much to catch up on. So much to learn and experience. And to give. Ashraf would ensure Oliver had the things he'd never had. Paternal love. Tenderness. Trust. Encouragement.

Ashraf would be involved in his son's life. In a positive way.

For a fleeting few seconds it hit him how much his own father had missed by distancing himself from his younger son. By choosing hate and distrust.

But he'd had Ashraf's other brother, Karim. Not that the old man had loved Karim either. Ashraf doubted their father had been capable of love. But he'd taken an interest, encouraged Karim and crowed over his elder son's successes.

A high-pitched grizzle cut into Ashraf's thoughts like an alarm signal resonating through his body. Was something wrong with Oliver?

Fifteen minutes ago Tori had led the way to a small white and yellow room with a cot, a rocking chair and a low bookcase littered with toy animals and little books made of boards. A mat on the floor looked like a farm, with more friendly-faced animals.

Ashraf had never felt so out of place. Especially when Tori had lifted their son high and he'd seen how tiny the mite was without his covering blanket. She'd cast a harried glance at him over her shoulder and suggested he make himself comfortable in the other room while she changed Oliver.

Reluctantly Ashraf had complied. He was curious about the boy but he knew he'd have to give Tori space. He'd thrown a live grenade into her world with his appearance today. He guessed she'd battled traumatic memories since the moment she saw him.

Ashraf frowned. Was it too much to expect her to be pleased to see him? He was used to delighted women... eager women.

For his part, he'd seen her and instantly been swamped with the need for more. The attraction between them might have started as the product of mortal danger, but it was there still, stronger by the moment.

Then he recalled her breathless reaction when he'd held her hand, the tell-tale tremble and the flutter of long lashes over soft blue eyes. She might not have wanted to feel it but she'd been attracted.

He glanced at his watch. How long did it take to change a nappy? They had things to discuss. He wanted to know his son. He'd allowed her time, even permitted her to stay at work and finish off the project she was so worried about. As if he, Ashraf al Rashid, was of negligible importance.

Ashraf strode down the corridor, knocked once and stepped into the nursery.

Wide eyes brilliant as starlight met his. Then he took in the rest of the scene. Tori in the rocking chair, the baby in her arms. His throat thickened. Her blouse was undone, hanging wide open on one side. A tiny dark head nuzzled at her bare breast.

Ashraf's gaze focused on the voluptuous curve of that breast, on his son's tiny starfish hand patting Tori's alabaster flesh, and heat drenched him from head to toe. The heat of arousal, fierce and primal. A surge of lust erupting with dizzying intensity.

Breastfeeding wasn't something he'd ever thought about. If he had it wouldn't have been in terms of eroticism. Yet, watching the woman he'd made pregnant feed his son, Ashraf had never felt such hungry possessiveness.

'We won't be long.' Tori's voice was husky as she twitched her blouse across to cover herself.

Ashraf nodded.

'He's almost finished.' She looked down, her gaze softening instantaneously on her baby.

Ashraf realised that for all the experience he'd gained in the royal court, in the rigours of army life and in the deliberate hedonism of his globetrotting playboy years, he'd never come across anything as real and fundamental as this.

His son.

His woman.

There wasn't even astonishment. Just calm acceptance. Ashraf hadn't got as far as considering a future wife. He'd been too busy cementing his role in a country that had never expected or wanted the younger, scandalous royal son to inherit.

Besides, this wasn't a matter of logic, but instinct.

He smiled as a glow of satisfaction spread out from his belly.

Tentatively Tori smiled back.

Ashraf felt that smile in places he couldn't even name. He'd never seen her smile before—not properly. He wanted to see her grin, he realised. Hear her laugh. Watch her as their bodies joined and she lost herself to ecstasy. In broad daylight. Not in the murky darkness of a desperate hovel that smelled of terror and pain.

'Ashraf…?' She frowned.

Was she picking up on the anger that simmered in his blood at the memory of what she'd suffered? Or was she frowning from embarrassment at him seeing her feed their child?

He smoothed his expression and leaned against the doorjamb, shoving his hands into his trouser pockets. Tori needed to get used to him being around.

'It's okay. There's no rush. Let him feed.'

Whether it was coincidence, or the sound of his voice, Oliver chose that moment to stop feeding. Ashraf saw a glazed pink nipple before Tori quickly drew her blouse further across. A tiny head turned, dark eyes meeting his.

Ashraf crossed the room in a couple of strides. Oliver tracked the movement. Was that usual for a six-month-old? Or was his son inordinately clever? It was nonsense to think he sensed the link between them. Of course it was.

'Would you like to hold him?' Tori's voice was different, as if she couldn't catch her breath.

'Show me how.'

She demonstrated, supporting the baby and then lifting Oliver up to her shoulder, gently rubbing his back. 'When he's hungry sometimes he gulps down air as well as milk. This helps.'

'I didn't think you'd be breastfeeding when you're working.'

Not that he knew a thing about it. Just that he'd been rooted to the spot by the sight of Tori nursing his child.

'I express milk for him to drink when I'm at work.'

Her cheeks grew pink and Ash stifled the urge to ask exactly what that meant. Time enough later.

'Here.'

She lifted Oliver towards him and suddenly, looking down at the tiny form, Ashraf wasn't so sure about holding him.

Tori read Ashraf's uncertainty and bit back a smile. It was the first time she'd seen him anything but confident. Even facing execution he'd been resolute. And there'd been no mistaking his eagerness when he'd seen Oliver.

That had simultaneously reassured and worried her. She had yet to discover what he intended to do about their son.

Now she read consternation in his bold features as well as…hunger? Her amusement died. Why should their son be any less of a wonder to Ashraf than he was to her? Gently she placed the baby in his arms, holding on longer than necessary while he grew familiar with Oliver's weight.

'Gah,' Oliver said, looking up into the dark, serious face above him. 'Gah-gah.'

'Hello to you too, Oliver Ashal.'

Ashraf's voice held a rough gravelly note that made her insides flutter. When he switched to husky Arabic Tori sank back in the rocker, spellbound by both the lilting sound and the sight of the two males staring into each other's faces.

Ashraf stood stiffly, as if wary of dropping his burden. But gradually he shifted Oliver into a more comfortable hold and Tori's chest squeezed at the contrast between the powerful man and the tiny child. The sight of them tugged at some primitive maternal instinct.

But there was more. Something to do with her feelings for Ashraf. Something that had been there from the start and which, remarkably, was growing stronger.

Tori looked away and focused on doing up her bra and shirt. There was a lot to discuss. Ashraf's appearance from the dead changed so much.

She glanced towards him, her busy hands stilling. Ashraf had Oliver tucked close, as if he'd held him since the day he was born, and the smile he gave his son made Tori's heart wobble. It was radiant.

It made her voice what she'd avoided till now. 'What do you want, Ashraf?'

'Want?'

'From me—us?'

'To be a father to my son.'

'It will take some planning since we live in Australia.' Caution told her not to push this now. But she was on tenterhooks. She needed to know his expectations.

Dark eyes meshed with hers. 'But you don't need to. You could live in Za'daq. Marry me and give our son the life he deserves.'

CHAPTER FIVE

ASHRAF LAY ON his back, staring through the gloom at the bedroom ceiling, and berated himself for his impatience. Being Sheikh often meant holding his tongue and waiting for the right moment to act, persuading people to accept his plans rather than forcing them to follow. Especially since in Za'daq his reputation as both a profligate playboy and his father's all but ignored son meant he battled prejudice and mistrust.

He was used to that. Was used to exerting patience as well as an iron will that stopped his father's old cronies from undermining him too blatantly.

But when Tori had asked what he wanted he hadn't been his usual composed self. He'd been holding his child in his arms for the first time, had felt the uprush of an emotion that nothing had prepared him for. In that moment he'd wanted never to let Oliver go. To ensure his life was better than Ashraf's had been.

Plus there'd been the sight of Tori in her plain white blouse, the buttons done up askew in her haste, tendrils of moonlight-pale hair drifting loose to frame her beguiling face. His heart had whacked his ribs in a rhythm of need, want and determination.

He'd realised his error in the split second it had taken her expression to close at the idea of marriage and Za'daq.

Now, here he lay, sleepless, seeking the winning argument to overcome her doubts and persuade her to accept what he offered. What was clearly best for their son.

Tori's refusal was a salutary lesson against complacency. He was accustomed to eager women, not women regarding him with suspicion. She probably thought marriage to a sheikh meant she'd be walled up in an old-fashioned harem.

His mouth rucked up at one side. The idea had some appeal. Tori available at his beck and call, reclining with an inviting smile on silk sheets… Heat threaded through his veins and gathered in his groin.

He shifted restlessly. Right now he could be lying in a king-sized bed in the exclusive suite that took up the top floor of Perth's most prestigious hotel. Instead he lay on the carpeted floor of Oliver's room.

Ashraf grunted and rolled onto his side. It was his fault for not treading carefully. For spooking Tori with his abrupt announcement. They'd discussed the matter through the dinner he'd had delivered to her home, and afterwards. But despite her attempt to appear calm he'd read her tension, and the fear he'd done his best to diffuse.

Finally, seeing tiredness in her slumping shoulders, he'd insisted she sleep. But he hadn't been able to leave for his luxury accommodation. It was too soon. He'd just found Oliver, and Tori, and something inside had screeched a protest at the idea of leaving them.

So he'd suggested sleeping on the sofa and Tori had eventually agreed, perhaps because she'd realised she hadn't a hope of shifting him. Apparently Oliver was teething—something Ashraf hadn't even known was a thing—and Tori had admitted broken sleep was taking its toll.

Another reason for him to remain. Tori's refusal to accept the logic of his plan was a nuisance, but seeing her exhausted had made him protective.

As soon as she'd checked on Oliver and gone to her own room Ashraf had taken the bedding she'd put on the too-short sofa and spread it on the floor beside the cot. He'd slept in worse places on army manoeuvres. Besides, this might remind him to think before he spoke.

A cry sounded from the cot and Ashraf shot to his feet.

Flicking on the lamp, he peered down to find Oliver's face screwed up and turning red.

Ashraf slipped his hand beneath his squirming son and lifted him to his chest. The baby felt almost familiar this time, his nestling warmth both comforting and a reminder of how scarily fragile he was.

Ashraf inhaled the smell of talc and baby that in a few short hours had become so satisfying. He stilled his thoughts, focusing on the moment. On the wonder of his child, flesh of his flesh. The promise of a fulfilling long life ahead. A life Ashraf was determined to share.

A couple of hours earlier he'd persuaded Oliver back to sleep with gentle words, rocking and a pain-relieving gel rubbed onto his gums. This time he suspected Oliver wouldn't be so easily settled.

Ashraf paced the room, gentling the fractious baby, murmuring soothing words in his own tongue. He wanted to win Tori a little more sleep. The sight of the smudges of tiredness beneath her eyes had made him feel wrong-footed, steaming in and demanding she upend her life to move to Za'daq.

Except that Tori marrying him, creating a family for Oliver and allowing their child to grow up in the country he'd one day rule, was the most important thing. Ashraf's experience as an unwanted child, ostracised by his own father, made him determined to ensure Oliver *belonged*. That he was accepted and given every opportunity to shine.

He'd do whatever it took to persuade Tori, for Oliver's sake.

Tori opened the door and felt her jaw drop. She'd been barely thinking as she'd pushed back the covers and climbed out of bed, blearily acting on instinct when she'd heard Oliver cry. Now she was fully awake, and staring.

Ash… Ashraf…filled the room, tall, athletically built and almost naked. His wide shoulders and bare back gleamed, a symphony of muscle overlaid with burnished satin skin.

Tori's throat closed as her gaze tracked his spine, moved down long, powerful legs, then up to navy underwear that clung to rounded buttocks. Near his feet lay the pillow and bedding she'd put on the sofa.

He'd slept on Oliver's floor.

The idea stunned her as much as the sight of Ashraf, overwhelmingly virile and masculine, in her private space.

Then there was the way he rocked from side to side, cradling Oliver against his shoulder. Ashraf's voice was a soft, deep hum as he sang a lullaby in a language she didn't understand. It didn't seem to be working on Oliver, who still fretted. But it worked on her. Tori swayed and reached for the doorjamb to prop herself up, her insides turning to mush at the combination of supercharged sexy male and breath-stealing tenderness.

For a dangerous moment she let herself imagine what it would be like if they were a real family—not as Ashraf suggested, for convenience, but because they loved—

No. She wasn't going there. She'd got this far as a single mother and knew she could manage it. Dreams were all well and good but she couldn't confuse them with reality.

'I think you'd better give him to me.'

Ashraf swung round and Tori was hit by another pulse of—okay, she'd admit it—arousal. He was a truly magnificent man, and the sight of her little son secure against that broad bare chest sent emotion curvetting through her.

Tori blamed overactive hormones. And weariness. But then she read Ashraf's expression and thoughts of herself faded. In those strong features and glittering eyes was a reflection of her own feelings when she surveyed Oliver. Wonder, love and protectiveness.

Ashraf might be new to fatherhood, but that didn't mean his feelings for Oliver were less real. Or that he had a smaller claim to parenthood.

The knowledge rushed at her like a biting wind, piercing the mental armour with which she'd shielded her fears.

She'd told herself Oliver was *hers*. That because she barely knew Ashraf, that he came from a faraway place and a time in her life best forgotten, his claim on the baby was less.

How untrue that was. This man, who ruled a country and probably slept in a gilded bed with silk sheets, surrounded by every luxury, had bunked down on the hard floor beside his son. That hadn't been done to make a point.

'Tori! Are you okay?' Ashraf stepped close in a couple of long strides, one warm hand closing around her elbow. 'You look unsteady on your feet.'

She shook her head, pushing her hair back from her face, and stood straighter. 'I'm all right.' As all right as she could be when her life had suffered a sudden seismic shift.

As if from a huge distance she saw her plans for a new life in Perth fracture. Whatever the future held, it wasn't going to be as straightforward as she'd expected.

Ashraf led her to the rocking chair, his hold supportive and expression serious. When Tori experienced another jolt of awareness she felt like a fraud. Then, when he leaned close to pass Oliver over, the warm, evocative scent of spiced cinnamon and male flesh surrounded her. Her nipples tingled, and it wasn't just reaction to Oliver's hungry cry. It was connected to the pulsing throb low in her body.

She shivered and tightened her hold on her baby.

'You're cold?'

The words trawled over her bare arms like a velvet ribbon.

No, she was burning up.

How could she react so viscerally to a man she barely knew? She wasn't by nature promiscuous. Yet with Ashraf…

She'd told herself that what had happened that night in Za'daq had happened because they'd been in mortal danger. That they'd been driven by a primal impulse to procreate and ensure the survival of another generation. What excuse did she have now?

It was as if she was wired to respond instantly and catastrophically to Ashraf.

'No, not cold. Just tired.'

'I'll get you a hot drink. You need to replace fluids.'

Then, before she could stop him, he strode out of the room.

Ashraf spent as long as he could in the kitchen. Anything to stay away from Tori and regroup.

She'd stood in the doorway, looking dazed and delicate, and he'd been torn between concern and fascination at how the hall light behind her outlined her tantalising shape through her nightdress. Pouting breasts, narrow waist, long, slender legs and gently rounded hips.

He'd wanted to grab her hard against him. Need had clawed, urgent and unstoppable.

Her hair was a messy halo, her cheeks flushed. Her lemon-yellow nightgown had a row of buttons down the front, presumably to make breastfeeding easier. Only a couple of those prim buttons had been fastened, allowing him tantalising glimpses of pearly skin.

Memories of losing himself in Tori's sweet body bombarded him, of her soft cries of encouragement and the incredible bliss of a coupling that had far transcended the brutal reality of that foul kidnappers' hut.

He frowned and moved to the kettle, filling it with water. His years of scandalous indulgence might have been designed to infuriate his father, but they hadn't been a complete sham—even if his sexual exploits *had* been exaggerated. He was used to sophisticated women well versed in seductive wiles. He was used to silk, satin and lace, or complete nudity. Not dainty cotton with embroidered flowers. Not nursing mothers.

Ashraf shook his head and straightened. Nothing about this trip was going to plan. But he was adaptable. He had no intention of leaving without his son. Or Tori.

* * *

Tori had finished feeding Oliver but Ashraf still hadn't returned. Had he thought better of spending the night there? The possibility made her feel curiously bereft. But sneaking off without declaring his intentions wasn't Ashraf's style.

'Shall we swap?'

At the sound of his low voice she swung round, hugging Oliver close.

Far from planning to leave, Ashraf hadn't even bothered to dress. Tori's skin tingled with a blush as she fought to stop her gaze going lower than the mug he held.

She'd never been particularly bashful, and until today rarely blushed. Maybe that was due to her father's demands that she accompany him to public events from an early age. Or because female geologists were still outnumbered by men. As a result she'd learned to hide anything that might be viewed as feminine weakness.

Ashraf put the steaming mug down on a chest of drawers and reached for Oliver.

'He's almost asleep.' Tori hugged him closer, as if the baby could protect her from unwanted feelings.

'Good. I'll hold him for a little, then put him down while you have your drink.'

Remembering the look on Ashraf's face as he'd watched Oliver, how could she resist? Tori passed the baby to him, supremely conscious of her nakedness under her nightie and Ashraf's bare arms brushing hers.

Not that Ashraf noticed. His attention was all on Oliver as he paced to the window, stroking the baby's head with one big hand. Something dipped hard in Tori's chest and she turned away, picking up the mug and taking a sip as she sat down.

'This is good!'

'No need to sound surprised. Even kings can boil water.'

She liked the teasing lilt in his voice too much.

'I expected tea.'

Dark eyebrows lifted as he caught her eye then turned away, rocking Oliver. 'I didn't know how you took it, and I didn't want to interrupt, so I made my own favourite.'

'Lemon, honey and...' she paused, taking another sip '... fresh ginger?' So simple yet so delicious.

He nodded, but kept his gaze on their son.

Tori drew a shaky breath and confronted the reality she'd fought from the moment Ashraf had told her his intentions.

'I've been thinking.'

'Yes?'

His head lifted, gleaming eyes pinioning her. It didn't matter that Ashraf was more than half naked and holding a sleeping baby. He looked as powerful as any sovereign in full royal regalia.

Anxiety feathered her spine but she kept her gaze on his, refusing to be intimidated.

'I can't marry you.' She watched the corners of his mouth fold in, as if he was holding back an objection. 'But I understand your desire, your *right* to be involved in Oliver's life.' Her heart pattered faster as she made herself continue. 'I'm still not sure about him being a prince, though. Surely when you eventually marry your legitimate children will inherit?'

'I told you I can legitimise Oliver. I intend to. And I have no intention of taking any other wife.'

Heat flashed through her like a channel of lava, incinerating more of her defences. It shouldn't make a difference, but when Ashraf spoke like that part of her enjoyed it—though it was ludicrous to believe he cared about her as anything other than Oliver's mother.

Of course he'd marry. Some glamorous princess who'd charm his people and give him a bevy of children.

Something sharp lodged in Tori's ribs and she had to breathe slowly to ease the spike of discomfort.

'I'm not entirely convinced becoming Crown Prince of Za'daq is what I want for him.'

Ashraf's brow corrugated and his mouth tightened. Tori

wondered what he wasn't saying. That it wasn't up to her to decide such things?

'Because you believe my country is unsafe? That's understandable, given your abduction, but believe me, that's not the case now.'

'That's part of it, but not all.'

How did she even begin to express her horror at the idea of her precious boy being thrust into such a public role with no choice? She'd spent her childhood and teenage years as a handy asset in her father's politicking. She'd hated it—especially as she'd got old enough to understand his cynical use of a good photo opportunity and his focus on self-aggrandisement rather than public service.

'I want Oliver to have the opportunity to be a child just like any other.' Not shunted around to smile for the press when the polls looked bad or family values were a hot issue for voters.

'Oliver will have that. You have my word.'

'You've said he's destined to become Sheikh. What if he doesn't want to be?'

The idea of her little baby inheriting seemed impossible. Ashraf was so vital and strong. Tori's insides squeezed at the idea of him dying. But he'd come close just last year.

'That's what you're worried about?' He shook his head and the lamplight caught indigo shadows in his inky hair. 'Most women would be thrilled at the idea of their child inheriting riches and power.'

'Most women don't have a politician for a father. Power shouldn't be an end in itself.' She paused, weighing her words. 'It can have a negative effect on a person and on those around them.'

Her father would say he did what he did for the public good. Tori knew he was driven instead by the need for acclaim and power. He was self-serving, and as a father...

'You're right. Power is an obligation.' Ashraf studied her intently as if fascinated by a new insight.

Tori wished she had more than her nightie and a hot drink to shield her from that penetrating gaze.

Conditioned by a lifetime's training, she found it hard to admit aloud her negative feelings about her father and his profession. But this was about Oliver. Nothing, not even the ingrained habit of old loyalty, took precedence.

'Yet you want to tie our child to that before he's even old enough to understand!' She wanted to grab the now sleeping baby and tuck him close. Her fingers clamped hard around the warm mug.

Ashraf's features tightened, the proud lines of nose and forehead growing more defined. 'I will give Oliver the opportunity to inherit what is his right as my son. To lead the people of Za'daq is an honour as well as a responsibility. I won't deprive him of his birthright.'

For a long, pulsing moment Ashraf's eyes bored into hers and she felt her breath clog in her lungs. He was formidable. Daunting. Yet still she felt the fizz of attraction like effervescence in her blood.

Biased by seeing her father and his cronies at close quarters, Tori had told herself she disliked powerful men. But strength was intrinsic to Ashraf and still she was drawn, fascinated, even as her saner self warned her to keep her distance.

'There's always a choice, Tori. No one will force Oliver if he truly doesn't want to become Sheikh. My brother, Karim, was heir to the throne. Yet when my father died Karim declined his inheritance. I was proclaimed Sheikh instead.'

Tori wanted to ask *why* Karim had chosen not to inherit. What he was doing now. Had Ashraf wanted the throne? But the stern set of his mouth warned against questions.

'Surely it's not too much to give our son the opportunity to learn the ways of his forebears? To have access to both cultures—Za'daqi and Australian.'

'I agree.'

'You do?' The fierce glitter in his eyes softened.

'I told you I'd been thinking.'

She swallowed, her stomach churning at what she'd decided. But she had to follow through. It would be cowardly and selfish not to.

'I have serious doubts about the Sheikh thing…' Ashraf's eyebrows rose, yet he didn't interrupt. 'But I'm willing to accept your suggestion. *Not* to marry,' she hurried to clarify, 'but to take Oliver to Za'daq for a visit.'

She read no change in Ashraf's features. No smile, no lessening in the intensity of that stare. But the next breath he drew was so deep it lifted that mighty chest like a cresting ocean wave.

'Thank you, Tori.' He stepped close, one arm effortlessly holding Oliver, the other reaching for her.

She stumbled to her feet, feeling at a disadvantage in the low rocking chair.

Ashraf took her hand, and the hard, enveloping warmth reminded her of the physical differences between them. Differences that, to her dismay, made her body hum and soften.

Instead of shaking her hand, he lifted it. 'You are generous as well as wise and beautiful.'

Tori blinked, and would have tugged free of his grasp except, still holding her gaze, he pressed his lips to the back of her hand. Instantly energy arced from the spot, shooting to her breasts, her pelvis, right down to her toes.

'There's no need to soft-soap me.'

'Soft-soap?'

For the first time Ashraf looked out of his depth. Tori enjoyed that puzzled expression. It was rather endearing. For once she didn't feel as if she were the one playing catch up.

'Flatter me,' she explained.

'I never flatter. I simply speak the truth.'

Which trashed her fleeting sense of superiority.

She stood, her hand in his, staring up into liquid dark eyes and wishing—

What? Wishing that they'd met under different circumstances? Ashraf would still be a king and therefore not the man for her. Wishing that he was someone altogether different? Some guy she'd met at a weekend barbecue? But she couldn't imagine that. Ashraf's identity was part of what made him intriguing.

But it wasn't the forceful, charismatic side of his personality that had made her change her mind. It was his genuine interest in Oliver. His determination to be a meaningful part of his son's life even if that meant waking in the night and walking the floor with a teething baby. One thing she was sure of: Ashraf wouldn't be a father who only showed up for the fun stuff. He'd be there through thick and thin.

Oliver deserved no less. Therefore Ashraf deserved more.

Belatedly she realised he still held her hand. She slipped it free. 'Don't get too excited. It will take me a while to organise. I've only recently begun this job and—'

'Getting leave from your work will be no problem.'

Tori's hackles rose. 'You haven't already asked without consulting me, have you?'

She saw him register her rising indignation. *Good.* She had no intention of being railroaded.

Ashraf shook his head. 'I know the CEO of your company. He's interested in exploring for diamonds in Za'daq.'

Tori wasn't surprised. The possibility of finding diamonds and other gems in the region was what had taken her to the survey team in neighbouring Assara. That experience was part of the reason she'd won her current position.

'He knows it was you I came to meet. I'm sure, if I indicate that his company can bid for the upcoming exploration contract, he'd believe it worthwhile to give you leave of absence.'

Tori opened her mouth, then shut it again. Of course he

would. The company would probably pay her airfare and keep her on full pay indefinitely!

She felt cornered. She'd counted on having more time before taking Oliver to Za'daq. A year, perhaps.

'I need to sort out a passport for Oliver.'

'No problem. I can expedite that.'

Tori stared up at the big man holding their son and unease slipped down her spine. She reached out and took Oliver, hugging him close before putting him in his cot. The comfort of his tiny body against hers eased her nerves. No one would steal her son. Yet she took her time, trailing her knuckle over his satiny cheek, feeling her heart lurch as he turned towards her touch.

Breathing deep, she straightened. 'You've already made enquiries, haven't you?'

Ashraf's expression confirmed it.

'You haven't got him a passport already?'

'I cannot without your consent. But my staff have checked with the Australian authorities and there's no problem.' He paused. 'I cancelled my schedule to come here but I need to return soon. We can leave tomorrow.'

'Tomorrow!' Tori crossed her arms over her body, holding in rising panic. 'That's impossible.'

He spread his hands in a gesture that might have seemed apologetic if not for the look of satisfaction on his face. 'One of the perks of being a visiting head of state…' His expression grew sombre. 'You don't appear happy to have these impediments removed. Didn't you mean it about bringing Oliver to Za'daq?'

'Of course I did.' She rubbed her hands up her arms. 'I just didn't expect things to move so fast. And…' She chewed her lip.

'And…? Something's bothering you? What is it?' His gaze probed. 'Tell me, Tori. I can't deal with the problem if I don't know what it is.'

She hitched a breath. 'I feel you're taking control. As if

I have no say. That makes me wonder how much power I'll have in Za'daq.' She angled her chin. 'Whether you'll have the power to take Oliver from me there.'

Ashraf read Tori's fear and guilt scrolled like an unwinding roll of calligraphy through his belly.

Of course she was concerned. She'd be crazy not to worry. It was true. In Za'daq, once he'd claimed Oliver as his heir, Ashraf would have the authority to keep his son permanently. Just as he'd have the ability to keep Tori within his borders or, alternatively, have her deported.

Ashraf refused to countenance Oliver living half a world away. He'd do whatever it took to have his son with him, where he belonged. Marrying Tori would ensure that. But their future together would be most successful if Tori *chose* to marry. If she *wanted* it.

Oh, she wanted him. He'd read her physical response. But persuading a woman like Tori into marriage would take patience and finesse.

Or an all-out assault on her senses.

Ashraf considered seducing her here and now. Till he remembered her concern to do the right thing by him and Oliver. He owed her more than that. Even though he was impatient for their physical union.

She spoke of a visit to his country, whereas he intended to keep Tori and Oliver with him in Za'daq. Permanently. That would require a concerted attack on Tori's doubts and defences. Showing her how much his homeland had to offer, how much *he* could offer.

'You have my word. On my family name and my country's honour I won't keep you or Oliver in Za'daq if you wish to leave.'

Ashraf's mouth curved. He looked forward to convincing her to stay.

CHAPTER SIX

TWO DAYS LATER Tori peered through the window of Ashraf's private jet, taking in tawny desert plains far below and misty blue-smudged mountains in the distance.

If it wasn't for the high ridge of mountains this might be central Australia's vast arid zone. But the tension prickling her skin belied the comparison.

This was where she'd been kidnapped.

Where those men—

Ashraf's hand covered hers where it gripped the armrest. His touch quelled the shudder ripping through her.

'Okay, Tori?'

She wasn't. She'd told herself she could do this, that it was right to do this. But at the sight of the desert she felt terrifying memories stir. Distress prickled the back of her eyes and she feared she'd lose the exquisitely prepared meal she'd just eaten.

'Of course.' She blinked, keeping her focus on the view as the shudder reduced to a rippling undercurrent of unease. 'It can't be long till we land.'

Ashraf said nothing. He must have registered her anxiety, yet instead of pulling back and following her lead in the change of subject he leaned closer, his warmth penetrating through her jacket and shirt.

Tori caught her bottom lip, stunned at how needy she felt for more. Even now, when fraught memories threatened her fragile composure.

Ashraf's breath caressed her cheek as he pointed to the mountains in the distance. 'Those foothills mark the border territory between Za'daq and Assara. You were abducted there, then brought to the encampment on this side of the border.'

Tori didn't want to think about it. Yet she craned towards the window.

'Then you crossed back into Assara. No wonder we couldn't find a trace of you. If you'd worked in Za'daq we'd at least have been able to identify you through your work visa.'

Tori wasn't interested in unmarked borders or the state of record-keeping in the neighbouring country of Assara. She stared at the sharply folded hills and her stomach swooped.

'The people there are very poor,' he went on. 'That's one of the reasons I'm considering allowing mineral exploration in the region.'

'Mining doesn't necessarily lead to money for the locals. Some are employed for minimum wages but most companies bring in their own expertise.'

She worked in the industry but that didn't mean she was blind to its flaws.

'It depends on the terms negotiated,' Ashraf responded. 'Nothing will be endorsed unless it provides decent local employment and infrastructure. Profits will be channelled into regional initiatives.'

Tori blinked. In her experience profits went to wealthy investors, making them wealthier.

'That's very admirable.'

His fingers tightened, reminding her that he still held her hand. Then he withdrew, leaving her feeling ridiculously bereft.

'You thought my interest was for personal gain?' Ashraf's lovely deep voice sounded different. Distant. Or perhaps affronted.

'No.' She swung round to meet his stare. 'I—'

'It's fine, Tori.'

Though when he said her name it wasn't with the warmth she'd become accustomed to.

'It's what many will think—that I'm looking for riches to spend on myself rather than the public good.'

No mistaking his bitterness.

'But contrary to popular opinion my focus is my people, not myself.'

She was intrigued—not only by his words but also by the hint of vulnerability she'd sensed at his withdrawal. It belied the haughty cast of his expression.

'Your people believe you're not interested in them?'

He shrugged, those wide shoulders spreading. 'Many do. Or at least…' He paused, as if choosing his words. 'I spent several years scandalising polite society with my "reckless, self-absorbed, self-indulgent lifestyle". Some find it hard to believe that's over.'

Anxiety forgotten, Tori twisted towards him. 'That sounds like a quote.'

'Sorry?' His eyebrows crinkled in confusion.

'The bit about being reckless and self-indulgent. It sounded like someone else's words.'

Ashraf's eyes widened and she read his surprise. Then his gaze became shuttered. Clearly this wasn't something he'd allow her to pursue. But whose words had made such an impression?

'You're not reckless and self-indulgent now.'

It wasn't a question. How could it be when Tori had first-hand experience of Ashraf's character? He'd tried to protect her in the desert. He'd searched for her for over a year, never giving up. He'd accepted his role as Oliver's father without question, without even hinting about the need for a paternity test. No avoidance or denial, just unflinching acceptance of the circumstances and a determination to do the best he could.

One black eyebrow rose as if he doubted her assessment.

'Well, you're not.'

It was true that he'd been notorious—as Tori had discovered when she trawled the Internet. But for the last two years he'd barely been out of Za'daq. Every photo showed a serious, almost grim man, usually surrounded by a flock of courtiers or regional leaders. News reports about him focused on social and political issues, regional trade discussions, health improvements and so on.

However, older reports revealed that the younger Ashraf had lived a lifestyle that kept the paparazzi on its toes.

Skiing at the trendiest resorts, escaping to fabled islands in the Pacific and the Caribbean, frequenting exclusive clubs, casinos and the sort of parties that fuelled the media's insatiable appetite for gossip.

She'd found photos that had made her stare. Prince Ashraf stumbling out of a casino in the early hours, accompanied by not one glamorous model but three, all looking as if they'd like to eat him for breakfast. A long-distance shot of him diving, naked, off a billionaire's yacht after a week-long party. Even the grainy quality of the shot hadn't disguised his taut, powerful frame, and Tori's pulse had tripped to a rackety beat.

'You sound very sure of my character,' he murmured, and she couldn't work out if he was annoyed, intrigued or merely making an observation.

Tori shrugged, turning to the view. This time those rugged hills didn't fill her with quite the same dread, though she still found herself clasping her hands tight.

'There's a lot I don't know about you, Ashraf, but we've shared some intense experiences. Self-absorbed isn't how I'd describe you.'

'How *would* you describe me?' he asked after a heartbeat's silence.

Tori sucked in a breath.

Magnetic. Sexy. Disturbing.

And one step ahead of her since the moment he'd confronted her in Perth. Tori felt she was playing catch-up with someone who knew the rules in a game she had yet to learn. And yet…

'Decisive. Obstinate, but with a well-developed sense of responsibility. Used to getting your own way.'

Tori heard a crack of laughter but refused to look at him. She'd seen him smile, felt the full force of his attractiveness, and wasn't ready to face it again. Not when she was so out of her depth.

'If only that were true. Being Sheikh means tempering my impatience for change so I can persuade others to see my vision for the future.'

Curious, unable to resist, she finally turned, noting the tiny lines bracketing his firm mouth. Lines that spoke of weariness and restraint.

'I thought the Sheikh of Za'daq had absolute power? Can't you just make a decree?'

'You've done your homework.'

'A little. I haven't had time to discover much.'

Again Tori experienced that plunging sensation in her stomach. Everything had happened so quickly.

'There's plenty of time to learn all you want to.' He paused, ebony eyes resting on her in a way that made the blood sizzle under her skin. 'And you're right. Technically I have the power to do as I wish. But in practice the Sheikh works with the Royal Council, which is made up of powerful provincial leaders. It would be madness to institute major change without bringing the Council on board.'

His tone was easy but Tori sensed strong emotion ruthlessly repressed. Or perhaps she was making something from nothing. Essentially he was a stranger. Surely it was crazy to believe she could read him.

Tori tugged her gaze back to the view.

'It's true, you know…'

His voice dropped, holding a low, resonant note that ran through her like warm treacle.

'The border province is peaceful now. You have nothing to fear in Za'daq. You and Oliver are safe in my country.'

Safe? Protected from marauding bandits, perhaps. But

Tori knew with a shiver of premonition that the most peril-
ous threat came from the man beside her. The man determined to raise Oliver as a Za'daqi prince. The man who'd
turned her world on its head and undermined all her cer-
tainties.

She was glad of Ashraf's supporting hand as the plane's
door was opened to reveal steps down to the Tarmac. For
as they emerged bright sunlight engulfed them, and with it
the scent of the desert.

A tremor of panic racked her, making her shake all
over, gluing her soles to the top of the steps. Rough fingers
seemed to scrabble up her nape then curl around her windpipe, crushing the flow of air.

It should be impossible to smell anything other than avi-
ation fuel and the warm cinnamon notes of Ashraf's skin
as he stood close. Yet her nostrils twitched, inhaling the
faint scents of dry earth and indefinable spice she associ-
ated with the desert.

Instead of hurrying her down the stairs Ashraf stood
unmoving, his hand firm at her elbow, giving her time to
take it all in. The airport building to one side. Cars at the
foot of the steps, where a knot of people waited. Hangars,
aircraft. And beyond that, just visible over a collection of
modern buildings, arid brown earth.

Tori inhaled sharply, fear stabbing her chest. Her arms
tightened around her sleeping son and the pulse of her blood
became a panicked flurry in her ears.

Ashraf spoke. She heard the reassuring murmur of his
voice, felt his gaze on her face, and finally managed another
breath, steadier this time.

Eventually his words began to penetrate. A gentle flow
describing the new airport building, finished last year. The
recent economic boost as Za'daq had capitalised on its location to become a regional transport hub. The businesses
clustered around the airport as a result.

Another listener would have heard a sheikh proud of his country. But Tori, catching his eye as her body finally unfroze, saw concern glimmer in those black eyes. A whump of emotion hit her. Like the invisible force-field of an explosion that would have knocked her off her feet if he hadn't held her.

He knows. He understands.

There was no impatience in those strong features. Just reassurance to counter the chill that defied the blaze of sunlight and turned her bones brittle.

Had he expected her to panic? Tori had been nervous, but nothing had prepared her for the sudden freezing dread.

She took a breath, then another. This time Ashraf's warm scent filled her nostrils, and Oliver's comforting clean baby smell. Tori licked her lips, moistening her mouth. Ashraf followed the movement and heat of another kind flared.

'So much development in such a short space of time,' she murmured, her voice husky. 'It must have taken a lot of work.'

It wasn't an insightful observation but it was the best she could do. Ashraf nodded. He appeared relaxed, yet Tori felt the tension in his tall frame, as if he was ready at any moment to gather up both her and Oliver. His eyes flickered to the baby and Tori read his unspoken question.

But with his help her panic had passed. Her knees had stopped wobbling and her hold on Oliver was firm. She inclined her head and Ashraf turned towards the steps and the group of people watching.

He led the way, taking his time as he spoke about the long-term vision to make Za'daq a centre for communications and information technology.

Neither the aircraft crew nor the people by the limousines would have guessed at Tori's sickening wave of fear. Gratitude filled her for Ashraf's support. Especially when they finally reached the Tarmac and she read the barely veiled disapproval on some of the faces turned her way.

An older man approached and bowed. The bow spoke of deference, but the dismissive glance he cast her and Oliver spoke volumes. It shored up her determination to stand tall.

Ashraf frowned as the man spoke. His voice was no longer mellifluous and reassuring as he asked the man a question, then another, in the same language.

A short time later, after a few brisk words from Ashraf, the entourage retreated to the limousines.

'I'm sorry,' he said, turning to her. 'Something has come up which requires my attention. I won't accompany you to the palace. But you'll be well looked after.' He gestured towards a slight gangly figure in a pale grey robe who, instead of retreating with the others, stepped forward. 'Bram will see you settled.'

This man also bowed to Ashraf, but then turned and bowed to her too. 'Ms Nilsson.'

He straightened and Tori looked into a pair of blue eyes, startling against swarthy skin.

'It's a pleasure to meet you.'

'And you... Bram.' Had she heard that right? She'd thought it an Irish name.

He smiled, his mouth hitching higher at one side because of a long scar cleaving his cheek. 'This way, please.'

Tori peered up at Ashraf. He was her only anchor in this foreign place. She battled the impulse to clutch him. That impulse was far too strong.

Ashraf opened his mouth to speak again but she forestalled him. 'It will be good to get Oliver settled.' Their son was awake now, waving one tiny hand. Soon he'd be demanding a feed.

The predictability of his needs helped ground her. Nothing was more important than Oliver. So, within minutes of arriving in Za'daq, she and her son were on their way to the capital while Ashraf attended to his important business.

Bram, in the front beside the driver, turned with that lopsided smile. 'There's our destination. The royal palace.'

Tori's nerves jangled as she stared. Of *course* a king would live in a palace. She'd had so much on her mind she hadn't considered that.

The palace sprawled magnificently across a hill above the city. Its acres of white stone gleamed in the sun, making it visible well beyond the city fringe.

From a distance its size and pristine colour caught the eye, and then its fairy-tale towers and gilded domes. Eventually, as the limousine climbed a road lined with public parks, Tori felt her breath catch at the palace's sheer beauty. There was carved marble, patterns of lustrous tiles worked in deep blues, greens and golds. Even the intricate ironwork of the tall fence pleased the eye.

Yet Tori's skin turned clammy. *This* was Ashraf's home? The place he wanted her and Oliver to live? This was a palace for a potentate, proclaiming wealth and power. Despite its beauty, it sent a shudder through her.

It didn't matter that they were only visiting, or that he hadn't mentioned marriage again. She suspected Ashraf wasn't a man who'd easily give up when he had his mind fixed on an idea. If they were to agree on some way of sharing Oliver this place would become a significant part of her son's life and therefore hers.

As the daughter of a senior politician she'd attended functions at luxury hotels and private venues, but never anywhere like this.

She looked down at the slate-blue trousers and jacket she'd thought so perfect for travelling and felt completely out of her depth. But how *did* one dress for a palace straight out of a fairy tale?

A bubble of panicked laughter rose as she tried to imagine herself bedecked in glittering gems or ermine or whatever it was that royals wore in places like this.

If Ashraf were here beside her it would be easier.

Even thinking that felt like a betrayal. Tori had always stood up for herself and it was especially important that she do so now. Ashraf and his managing ways had swept her back to a country where she'd never wanted to venture again.

Once more icy fingers played up her spine. Had she made the biggest mistake ever, coming here? She'd agreed to come when she'd been tired and stressed, thrown by seeing Ashraf again when she'd believed him dead.

She'd experienced a destabilising uprush of emotions on seeing him so caring of Oliver, so charismatic that her heart had fluttered in a ridiculous butterfly beat high in her throat. That toned, muscle-packed body, those incredible eyes that seemed to see more of her private self than anyone ever had. Even the thin scar along his ribs that told the story of their near-death experience made her feel close to him. As if they shared something profound.

Tori huffed a silent laugh. They did share something significant. Oliver.

Of course she'd done right in coming here. This was a first step in coming to an agreement about how their son would be raised.

Tori's gaze slewed back to the dazzling white edifice taking up the whole hilltop, her hands clenching. She needed some space after days and nights in Ashraf's company. Yet…*she missed him.*

Tori's eyes widened.

How long since Ashraf had prowled the length of the Perth boardroom and her heart had taken off like a rocket? A mere couple of days since he'd blasted her life to smithereens.

The limousine swung past the palace's monumental main gates and followed a road around the perimeter, eventually pulling in to a more utilitarian entrance.

A uniformed servant opened her door. By the time she'd picked up Oliver and stepped out Bram was urging her inside.

Out of the air-conditioned car, with Oliver warm in her

arms, she felt flushed and crumpled. But pride made her stand straight as she was introduced to the palace chamberlain, a tall man in snowy robes.

Gathering her wits, she did what she'd failed to do on meeting Bram, exchanging greetings in Arabic. She knew just enough to understand his wish that she would be comfortable during her stay and to thank him in the same language.

Was that surprise in his eyes? She didn't have time to find out, for Bram was ushering her into a cool, beautifully tiled hall.

'Your apartment is here, at the rear of the palace.'

After turning into another hallway, even more lavishly decorated, and through a courtyard filled with the scent of lilies, he opened a door and invited her to precede him.

Tori stopped dead a few paces in.

'A maid has been assigned to you, and a nanny to help—' Bram's words halted as he saw her face. 'Is the suite not suitable? If not I—'

'It's perfectly suitable, thank you.'

Tori dragged her eyes from the domed ceiling with its mosaic tiles depicting an idyllic garden filled with flowers. The glittering background tiles couldn't be real gold, she told herself. As for the elegant sofas and the beautiful, delicately carved side tables and the pots of colourful orchids… It was impossibly luxurious and gorgeous.

Tori felt simultaneously out of place and desperate to flop down on one of those pale couches and close her eyes.

The sound of water caught her ears and she turned. Tall, arched windows gave on to another courtyard where water sprayed in jets beside a long, inviting pool.

'There's a cot in the second bedroom and a range of baby supplies. If anything is missing you just need to ask the maid or pick up the phone. I can personally—'

Tori roused herself from her daze. 'I'm sure we'll have

everything we need. Thank you, Bram. You've been most kind.'

Twenty minutes later she was feeding Oliver, seated in a deeply upholstered chair so comfortable it felt as if her bones melted into it. Her luggage had been unpacked for her. At her side was a frosted glass of juice and an array of mouthwatering pastries brought by a friendly maid.

She was surrounded by luxury, by people eager to please. And yet as she surveyed her sumptuous surroundings Tori wondered if she'd walked into a trap.

A trap devised by a man intent on securing his son at any cost.

CHAPTER SEVEN

'THERE'S ALREADY CONJECTURE about Ms Nilsson.'

'So soon?' Ashraf met Bram's eyes. The rumour mill around the royal court was more efficient than any modern communication software. 'I should have expected it.' Yet he'd convinced himself they had more time.

He rolled his head from side to side, feeling the ache in his neck from too many sleepless hours. They faced a full-blown public scandal when the truth of Tori's and Oliver's identities were known. Yet he had no regrets. How could he have done anything other than bring Oliver and his mother here?

Bram spread his hands. 'Once the Minister for the Interior heard you had a female companion—'

'He manufactured a reason to meet the plane.' The Minister had been a friend of Ashraf's father. He'd absorbed the old Sheikh's disdain for Ashraf and now waited—daily, it seemed—for his new King to take a false step.

Ashraf wasn't naïve. He knew the powerful men who'd formed his father's innermost clique still harboured hopes that something would go wrong. That *he'd* go wrong and then his brother, Karim, would return to take the crown.

That would never happen.

Karim's reason for rejecting the crown was insurmountable. Karim would return to Za'daq one day, but only to visit. He'd made that clear. Only the two brothers knew the real reason for his refusal to become Sheikh, and Ashraf cared for Karim too much ever to betray that secret. Not even to squash the machinations of those trying to destabilise his rule.

He was more than capable of dealing with them. Life had

made him more resilient and determined than those waiting for him to fail. As for being underestimated...they'd learn. Ashraf wouldn't countenance failure. He'd never been good enough for his old man but he was determined to be the Sheikh his country needed, no matter what the political establishment thought.

'If it's any consolation,' Bram went on, 'we discovered who leaked the news that you had a travel companion. Someone in the palace administrative team. He's been dismissed.'

Bram paused, frowning, presumably at the knowledge that it was someone in his own unit who'd breached confidentiality.

'But this morning I offered him an alternative job, in the outer provinces, coordinating the infant immunisation campaign. It will give him a chance to put his talent for disseminating information to good use.'

Ashraf felt a smile tug his mouth. 'You think he'll do well there?' The rural location would challenge someone used to city life.

Bram spread his hands. 'I said if he did an outstanding job, meeting all our targets for immunisation over the next three years, I *might* be able to persuade you not to prosecute him for breach of privacy.'

Ashraf's smile became a grin. 'Trust you to turn a problem into an opportunity.'

His old friend was an expert at that—possibly because he'd had so much experience at picking himself up and moving on, no matter what life threw at him.

Bram shrugged. 'He's got talent. It would be a shame to waste it. As for fixing problems—that's what you pay me for.'

'We need to change your job title from Royal Secretary to Chief Troubleshooter!'

Ashraf would have sacked the palace employee and

washed his hands of the man. But then, as his father had enjoyed pointing out, Ashraf was his impulsive son.

Over the years he'd changed that, learning in the military to think strategically as well as quickly. But sometimes his desire for swift action led to complications. Like taking a too-quick security assessment at face value, riding into bandit territory and getting kidnapped…

He rubbed a palm around the back of his neck.

'The news is contained for now,' said Bram. 'No one knows the truth about Ms Nilsson or the boy. Just that they're here.'

Ashraf nodded. 'I want it to stay that way as long as possible.' And it wasn't just that he needed time to persuade Tori into marriage. 'We need to suppress the story of how we met. Permanently.'

'Of course. Admitting you were kidnapped within our borders—'

'It's not just that.' Though such news wouldn't do his standing any good. 'She'd be horribly embarrassed if all the world knew just when and where our son was conceived.'

Ashraf's time with Tori had been a pure blessing in the midst of what he'd imagined would be his final painful hours on earth. He didn't want the press or his father's cronies discovering the details and turning them into salacious gossip, so the world could picture Tori giving herself to him in that foul prison filled with the stink of past torture and brutality.

A shiver scudded down his spine and Ashraf's mouth firmed. If nothing else, he'd save her that.

'When the time comes the world can know that we met and I fathered a child. But as for anything else—' He sliced the possibility off with a swift lopping motion.

'You're shielding her?'

'Of course.'

Bram nodded, but Ashraf knew from the speculative

gleam in his eyes that he was processing his friend's protectiveness.

'We should be able to manage that. The rescue team never saw Ms Nilsson at the camp.'

'Excellent.' Ashraf looked at his watch. 'Have we finished?' He'd already been delayed for hours. He wanted to see how Tori and Oliver were settling in. Make sure she wasn't planning to get the next plane out of there.

Not that she'd succeed.

But it wasn't merely that concerning him. The look she'd sent him at the airport when he'd told her to go with Bram had revealed how much he'd asked of her. For a second she'd looked beseeching. The sight had stunned him as even her moment of panic on the plane hadn't.

Before today he'd seen Tori shocked, struggling to process the news that he was alive, and he'd seen her battling to hide terror during their kidnap. But her vulnerability in that split second when her gaze had clung had curdled his gut.

It had taken more determination than he'd imagined to watch her walk away before turning calmly to the officials awaiting him.

Ashraf had wanted to lash out at the politician whose judgemental gaze had rested so dismissively on Tori. Who'd inserted himself into the royal schedule solely, Ashraf knew, to make mischief. He'd wanted to turn his back on the high-level meeting that had been arranged in his absence.

But instead Ashraf had quashed the impulse to ignore his regal responsibility and go with Tori and Oliver—his family.

The word snagged the breath in his lungs.

Given his utterly dysfunctional family background, Ashraf had never dwelled on the idea of creating a family of his own. Now he had one. The realisation was arresting, satisfying and disturbing.

The sound of Bram clearing his throat jerked Ashraf's attention back. 'Yes? Is there something else?'

'Nothing.'

For second he could have sworn he saw amusement in his friend's eyes. But the next moment Bram was frowning at the royal schedule.

'We're finished for today, but tomorrow's timetable is packed. Suddenly half the Cabinet Ministers need to see you urgently.'

Ashraf lifted one eyebrow. 'I'm sure they do.' He shook his head, resisting the urge to massage those tight neck muscles again. 'If only they spent as much energy on public policy as they do trying to undermine me.'

'Actually, on that… It's too soon to tell, but you may have had a couple more wins. Two provincial governors have been in contact privately this week, full of enthusiasm about the results of your latest initiatives. They're hoping to meet you to discuss ideas they have for further implementation.' Bram paused. 'It could be that the tide is turning.'

Or it could be that you'll never be accepted, no matter how hard you work or how sound your policies. You're an outsider. You always have been. Nothing will change that.

The voice in Ashraf's head wasn't new. It had always been there, undercutting his early attempts to be a son his father could be proud of.

With the ease of long practice he ignored it. 'Let's hope.'

And he hoped, too, that he could win Tori over. She'd agreed to this visit but persuading her to stay, to accept his proposition, would take all his persuasive skills and more.

Tori hadn't answered his knock so he entered her suite, taking in the silence and lengthening shadows. A quick investigation revealed no sign of her or Oliver.

Ashraf frowned. Had she turned tail and left the palace? But that wasn't like Tori. Nevertheless he felt better seeing her clothes in the wardrobe.

He retraced his steps to the sitting room, then went out into the suite's private courtyard. A slow smile curved his lips and warmed his belly.

Tori lay on a sun lounger set in dappled shade beside the long pool. A portable cot where Oliver dozed was positioned beside her.

Heat thwacked Ashraf's chest as he looked at his tiny son. And as for Tori...

His gaze trailed over her silver gilt hair, enticingly loose across her narrow shoulders. Over the open shirt and slinky scarlet bikini that revealed full breasts and a narrow waist. Down lissom bare legs.

His groin stirred as desire smoked across his skin. He wanted Victoria Nilsson. Wanted her naked and eager. Wanted so much more. Everything he discovered about this woman attracted him. Plus, he wanted all that maternal love for his son.

Ashraf drew a deep breath, relieved at the reason for these unusually intense feelings. The need to provide for his son. That explained his determination to have Tori permanently. Ashraf wanted the very best for his boy. That meant Oliver's mother to love and care for their son. As Ashraf's mother hadn't been around to love and care for him.

As if she sensed his scrutiny Tori's eyelids fluttered open. For a second Ashraf read pleasure in those forget-me-not-blue eyes. Pleasure and welcome. But only for a second.

Too soon she was scrambling to sit up, hauling her shirt closed with one hand, eyes wary.

'Relax.'

Ashraf sank onto a nearby chair, looking around the courtyard. He needed to concentrate on something other than Tori. He refused to betray the urgency that sang in his blood when she was near.

Yet even with his gaze elsewhere he was aware of her. The soft hitch of her breath, the creak of her chair as she moved, her sweet, tantalising scent.

He forced himself to focus on his surroundings. He hadn't been in here before. The royal family's rooms were on the other side of the palace and he'd never investigated the guest apartments. Bram had chosen well. The courtyard was restful and private.

'Does the apartment suit you? If it's lacking anything...'

'Lacking?' Tori shook her head and that stunning hair spilled around her shoulders. 'It's beautiful. More than we need.'

Ashraf dragged his attention back to her face, to the frown lines between her brows. As if she was worried she'd been allocated something to which she wasn't entitled.

Didn't Tori realise how much more she'd be entitled to as his wife? Or was she really not concerned with wealth?

Another reminder that she wasn't like the women he'd known.

'I'm glad to see you resting. It's been a turbulent time for you.'

Ashraf congratulated himself on his tact. Far better than blurting out that she looked tired. How she'd managed those months alone with Oliver and starting a new, demanding job...

'Now, *there's* an understatement.'

A ghost of a smile curved her lips and Ashraf felt his tension lessen.

Once more he sensed a fragile understanding and acceptance between them. It was rare. He'd only experienced it before with his brother and Bram, the two men who really knew him and rather than just his reputation.

Deliberately Ashraf settled back and let his eyes rove the tranquil garden. Sweet blossom perfumed the air and from nearby came the chitter of a bird.

How long since he'd taken an evening off?

His gaze turned to the small table beside Tori. A newspaper lay there, and a book. He tilted his head to read the title.

'You're learning my language?' Satisfaction glowed. This was a good sign.

Tori made a deprecating gesture. 'Trying. A little. It seemed like a good idea.'

'It's an excellent idea.' He beamed and watched her eyes widen. 'But you don't need to use a book. I'll arrange a tutor.'

Instead of thanking him, she frowned. 'That's not necessary. I'm only here on a visit.'

So much for seeing this as an indication that she'd decided to stay. Ashraf schooled his features not to reveal emotion, but that didn't stop the bite of disappointment.

'You can't *really* expect marriage, Ashraf,' she said when he didn't respond.

Her voice was low but he heard the echo of the arguments she'd put up before. Arguments she thought were reasonable but which meant nothing in the face of his all-consuming need to protect his child.

Impatience grated. How did he make her understand? Make her see the damage that threatened little Oliver if they didn't work together to protect him?

Ashraf knew Tori's relationship with her father wasn't close now, but surely she'd grown up with a mother and father, a sense of belonging. She'd been nurtured and, he guessed, loved.

Oliver would survive with the love of both his parents even if those parents weren't together. Yet that wasn't enough for Ashraf. Not when he knew first-hand the isolation of being different. The poisonous rumours. The continual battle to be accepted.

Ashraf would do anything to ensure his son didn't face that. He didn't want Oliver merely to survive. He wanted him to thrive.

Ashraf expelled a slow breath, realising there was only one way to convince Tori. He'd planned to seduce her into agreement. But, while that might help, Tori was a woman who thought things through. Who weighed up options and responsibilities. Sexual pleasure wouldn't be enough. She needed concrete reasons.

The thought of baring those reasons filled him with cold

nausea. Even with Bram and Karim the past was a territory he didn't visit.

'Family is very important,' he began.

'Of course. But Oliver can have that without us marrying.'

'Not the sort of family he'll need.'

'Sorry?'

'Za'daq is a modern country but it still has traditional roots. Traditional values.'

'You're saying we should marry because you're worried about what people will *think*?' Her mouth tightened. 'You believe public opinion is worth an unhappy marriage?'

'You assume it will be unhappy?'

Tori spread her hands. 'We don't know each other. We probably don't have anything in common—'

'We have Oliver.' That made her pause. 'And we have more too. Respect.' Ashraf held her eyes. 'Liking. Attraction.'

White-hot desire was a better description, but he sensed she'd baulk at such straight talking. He'd seen her nervous reaction to the craving they both felt.

'That's not enough.'

'You want romantic love?' He searched her face, watching her gaze skitter away.

'It's usually the basis of marriage.'

'In your country, but not mine. Here love often comes with time, with respect, with liking and shared experience. All of which we have.'

'We shared one night of captivity!'

'An intense experience. You can't deny the connection between us is strong because of it. Far stronger than if we'd met on an online site and begun dating.'

Tori pursed her lips but said nothing.

'We have what it takes to make a good marriage. For Oliver's sake we need to try.'

Ashraf paused but she refused to admit his point. He ignored the churning in his belly and plunged on.

'I want our son to have what I didn't. Two parents who care for him. Who are there for him every day.' He watched her brow knot. 'Every child deserves a supportive environment. Without that life can be tough.' His lips curled as a sour tang filled his mouth. 'I don't want that for Oliver.'

'I didn't know your childhood was difficult.' There was curiosity and sympathy in Tori's look, but instead of pressing for details she went on. 'But I don't see how that applies to Oliver.'

Ashraf shook his head. 'I want Oliver to have the best in every way. I can declare him legitimate, and that will give him legal status, but I want him to be part of a *real* family. To give meaning to the bare legality and make it something more.' He paused and turned to look at the innocent child who, he knew, would suffer if Ashraf wasn't careful.

Suddenly his lungs ached, pain searing deep.

'I want him protected from scorn and prejudice.' He took another slow breath that still didn't fill his chest. 'Above all I don't want him to believe, for a moment, that I'm not committed to him or don't want him here. I won't have him growing up in the shadows, unsure where he fits.'

Tori's arguments stilled on her tongue as she read the lines of tension wrapping around Ashraf's mouth and pleating his forehead. An icy wave washed over her, despite the balmy evening.

Here was something she didn't understand. Something important. Ashraf wasn't posturing. Whatever the problem was, it was deep-seated. She felt the ache of it just watching his still frame as he stared at Oliver.

'What do you mean, growing up in the shadows?'

Ashraf turned and for the first time she could recall, his dark eyes looked utterly bleak. But only for a moment. Just as she was registering what looked like anguish, his expression became unreadable.

He lifted wide shoulders and spread his hands. 'I wasn't meant to be Sheikh, you know.'

Slowly Tori nodded. 'You said your older brother was supposed to inherit. Is this something to do with him?

'No.' The word was emphatic. 'Karim's reasons for rejecting the throne are his own and private.' He paused as if to make sure she got the 'no trespassing' message.

Tori got it, all right, but that didn't stifle her curiosity. She watched as Ashraf swung his legs off the lounger to sit facing her, elbows on his thighs. The stance emphasised the power in his athletic frame and awareness fluttered through her, making her hurry into speech.

'So you weren't first in line to the throne… What's that saying? Having an heir and a spare lined up?'

Ashraf's huff of laughter was humourless. 'Good in theory, but I was never the spare—not as far as my father was concerned. He hated me because I wasn't his.'

'Not his?' Astonishment gripped her.

'My mother left him for another man when I was tiny. The official story in Za'daq is that she died. My father couldn't bear the thought of the public knowing the truth. In those days the press was carefully controlled. Nothing went public that would offend the Sheikh.'

Tori shook her head, still grappling with the first part of what he'd said. 'She left to be with another man? The man who'd fathered you? Yet she didn't take you?'

She couldn't imagine leaving her baby behind.

'She knew the Sheikh wouldn't denounce me as illegitimate because his pride wouldn't permit a public scandal. She was right. Publicly, he didn't.'

Ashraf's expression, as hard as cast bronze, confirmed that in private things had been different.

'Surely she could have taken you?'

'You didn't know his pride.' Ashraf shook his head.

'Once he'd acknowledged me as his son he'd never release me. Anyway, she probably thought I'd be better off here. Her lover wasn't wealthy.'

Tori stared, her mind racing. 'You never *asked* her why she left you behind?'

His mouth tightened. 'I didn't get a chance. She died of complications from influenza when I was a child. I only discovered that later—when I set out to locate her.'

Tori sank back, stunned. Ashraf an unloved child... abandoned by his mother and left to the mercy of a proud, arrogant man for whom he was a reminder of his wife's desertion. Her skin crawled.

'I never had what you'd call a family life.'

Ashraf's voice was uninflected. He might have been talking about the weather.

'Except for my brother, Karim, no one cared about me.'

He drew a breath that made his chest rise, then turned to lock his gaze with hers.

'My father never told anyone about my parentage but he made his disapproval clear to me in every possible way. There was no warmth or encouragement. He constantly found fault and his attitude rubbed off. The courtiers, all the people who mattered in Za'daq, took their cue from him. Everyone viewed me as useless, shallow, lacking the virtues my brother possessed. Whispers and innuendo followed me no matter how hard I tried.'

'So you acted up?'

She thought of those press reports about the Playboy Prince, spending his time flitting between scandalous parties and shockingly dangerous sports. Because he'd had nothing better to do with his time? Or because he too had believed he had nothing better to offer?

Tori's hand went to her throat. It was hard to imagine Ashraf, of all people, so vulnerable.

His mouth twisted. 'As a kid I tried hard to please my father. But nothing was good enough. Later...' He shrugged.

'Later it seemed a fine revenge to make him squirm a little by living down to the reputation he'd built for me.'

She didn't know what to say. Finally she asked, 'Did you ever meet your real father?'

Ashraf's expression had been wry before, his features taut. Now, though, it was as if an iron shutter slammed down, blocking out even the cynical amusement that had gleamed in that half-smile a moment before.

'That's the ultimate irony. When the old Sheikh was taken ill he needed a bone marrow donor. Even though he was so sick he still couldn't bring himself to countermand the suggestion that I get tested for compatibility. That's when we discovered I *was* his son after all. He'd spent years despising me on the basis of unfounded suspicion. Just because he'd found an old letter that predated my birth, sent to my mother by the man she later ran off with. He assumed—wrongly—that she'd slept with him and conceived me as a result.'

'Oh, Ashraf.'

She sat up, instinctively covering his clasped hands with one of hers. It was like touching warm but unforgiving steel. All that hate. All that distance between father and son for nothing but pride.

One of those large hands moved and covered hers. Eyes dark as a stormy night captured hers.

'I want Oliver to have what I never did. A family. Parents together in one place, loving him, caring for him—'

He broke off and Tori wondered with a wobble of distress if Ashraf's throat had closed as convulsively as hers had. She swallowed, trying to dislodge the choking knot of emotion blocking her larynx as she imagined his childhood.

'I don't give a damn what people think of me. But I don't want him subjected to prejudice because he's not in my life full-time. Because he's not seen to belong.'

Her gaze slewed to their precious boy, who'd woken and

was now staring at them with lustrous eyes so like Ashraf's that her chest squeezed.

'He *does* belong. He's ours.'

But as she spoke Tori's heart sank. Ashraf was right. Oliver could be legitimised, but to some his birth out of wedlock would for ever leave a taint of scandal.

'Whether he's in Australia or Za'daq he'll attract public interest. It's inevitable. I want to do everything to protect him from the negatives of that. I want to support him. I want him to feel safe and secure, proud of who he is. Sure right from the start that we're united and on his side.'

Ashraf's voice rang with sincerity. Tori wanted that too. She could understand Ashraf's reasoning now, and her heart ached for the boy he'd been, a victim of circumstances beyond his control, abandoned by both parents.

Part of her wanted to nod and say of course she'd do anything for her son. Yet even as she opened her mouth her own survival instinct kicked in. Everything rebelled at the thought of marrying for appearances' sake.

Flashes of memory filled her brain. Of her parents' marriage where whatever tenderness there might once have been had died. All that had remained was a sham, a pretence of a happy family constructed to salvage pride and win votes.

Tori had vowed never to have a marriage like that. Since childhood she'd known she wanted more. She'd promised herself she'd never settle for anything less than love.

'I…' She met Ashraf's gaze and her throat dried. She was torn between determination to do what was best for Oliver and fear that she'd become like her mother, living an unhappy half-life. 'I need time.'

After what seemed like a full minute he nodded. 'Of course. I understand.'

But that wasn't what his eyes said, or the pressure of his hand on hers. He was a determined man. A king. How far would his patience stretch?

CHAPTER EIGHT

FOUR DAYS LATER Tori knew Ashraf's patience was far stronger than hers.

Heat climbed her cheeks as she realised she almost *wanted* him to break the impasse between them. She lived on tenterhooks, feeling the tension screwing tighter with each hour.

Despite her reservations about marriage, Tori couldn't switch off her intense response to Ashraf's magnetism. The yearning for his touch, his tenderness, his body, just wouldn't fade. She remembered being in his arms, lost in a sensual abandon so profound the world had fallen away. The memories were fresher than ever and more tempting.

Late each day he came to her rooms to share a meal and spend time with Oliver. From that they'd begun to develop a new type of intimacy which was simultaneously challenging and precious.

Despite the unanswered question hanging over them, those hours were relaxing and companionable. Ashraf never mentioned marriage. He was an easy, amusing companion, sharing anecdotes and asking about her day, fascinated by what she and Oliver had done.

Nor did he shy from answering her questions. His frankness intrigued her, especially when she discovered areas of common ground or subjects in which their differing views led to stimulating debate.

Debate, not argument.

Unlike her father, Ashraf never tried to browbeat her into accepting his views.

It was her favourite time of the day. A time she recalled

late at night, long after Ashraf had left and she'd retired to her lonely bed.

Tori shivered and stared absently at the tiny shop's display of bright fabrics. She lifted the filigreed glass of tea to her lips. The scalding liquid warmed her and might even explain the flush she felt in her cheeks.

What she recalled most often, and in excruciating detail, was how Ashraf, after kissing Oliver on the brow, always took her hand and pressed a lingering kiss there as he said goodnight. His eyes shone like polished onyx and he held her hand so long she was sure he must feel the throb of her pulse racing out of control.

Every night she wondered if *this* would be the moment he'd break his self-imposed distance and pull her close, giving in to the ever-present spark of desire between them.

And every night, just as she decided she couldn't stand the suspense or the longing any more, he'd say goodnight and leave her alone in her sumptuous apartment.

'I won't be much longer, Tori. I promise.'

Azia's voice interrupted her thoughts. Tori looked towards the crimson curtain that hid the small shop's changing room and smiled.

'Take your time. I'm enjoying all these fabulous silks. It's like being in Aladdin's cave.' She nodded to the shop owner, who beamed and pulled down a bolt of sea-green silk threaded with silver before taking it to Azia.

It was a treat to be on a girls' shopping expedition with Bram's wife, while a nanny looked after Azia's little daughter and Oliver. Two days ago, when Bram had introduced her to his wife, Tori had been reluctant to accept Azia's invitation to coffee in the city. She knew all about duty visits, having done her share while supporting her father.

But Azia's smile had been warm and Tori had longed to get away from the palace's gilded luxury. She loved her apartment, with its pretty courtyard and pool, but she didn't know her way around the massive building and didn't feel comfortable wandering through it.

To her surprise, their coffee date had been fun and Tori had laughed more than she had in ages. Azia had an irreverent sense of humour and a kind heart. The next day they went to lunch and visited an exhibition of exquisite beadwork by an upcoming designer.

Today they were at the silk shops in the bazaar, where Azia was determined to find fabric for a special outfit.

'How about this?' The curtains swished back to reveal Tori's new friend draped in green and silver.

Tori tilted her head. 'It's very beautiful...'

'But...? Come on, tell me.'

'Personally, I loved that bright lime-green. This one is pretty, but that bright pop of colour really complemented your colouring.'

Azia laughed, but her expression was uncertain. 'I liked that one too but it might be a bit too bright.'

'Too bright?' Tori frowned. 'Why shouldn't you wear bright colours? You look fantastic in them.'

Her friend shrugged. 'It's for a royal event and...' She glanced at the shop owner, who took the hint and moved towards the front of the shop, giving them some privacy.

Azia shrugged. 'I don't really fit in there. I'm not highborn and nor is Bram. Last time I went to a reception I overheard comments—' She shook her head. 'It doesn't matter. I just want to fit in.'

Her words echoed Ashraf's, jolting Tori's composure. Who *were* these people who busied themselves making others feel out of place? What gave them the right to judge? Because they were rich or born into powerful families?

Tori knew about the flaws hidden in many powerful and 'perfect' families.

'Which colour makes you happy?'

'The lime,' Azia answered instantly.

'Then buy the lime. You look beautiful in it.'

Azia wavered, then nodded. 'You're right. I will. Thank you.'

With a rattle of curtain rings she stepped back into the changing cubicle, leaving Tori alone with her thoughts. Inevitably they returned to Ashraf. He'd spoken of not being accepted. How had that moulded him into the man he was? He wasn't uncertain or insecure. In fact he was one of the most determined people she knew.

But what if Oliver wasn't strong enough to endure the censure of others so easily? Her spirits plunged. Was she selfish, refusing to marry Ashraf and give Oliver a conventional family? Not all conventional families were like hers, where only one parent had loved and supported her.

Her father had been too wrapped up in his career to care for anyone but himself. He'd married Tori's mother because she came from a family with money and political influence. Tori had always thought if she married it would be to someone who wanted *her*, not what she represented.

She sighed and put down her tea. At least she and her mother had been close. How Tori wished she were here now, to talk over this enormous decision.

For the first time she understood why her mother had stayed with her father. For the security he offered while she raised Tori. A woman would put up with a lot for her child.

Not that Ashraf would be a hands-off father, like her dad. On the contrary, he'd be very hands-on—

'You look flushed.' Azia emerged with a bolt of bright silk under her arm. 'I'm sorry, I shouldn't have taken so long.' She paused. 'Do you already have something for the reception or should we look now?'

'I'm not going.' Tori got up from the visitor's chair.

'You're not? But...' Azia looked confused. 'It's a very special event, hosted by the Sheikh himself. You'd enjoy it. There's music and traditional dancing as well as a spectacular feast.'

Tori shrugged, suppressing a pang of regret. It did sound interesting. 'I don't have an invitation.'

Azia's brow knotted. 'That's impossible. Bram wouldn't forget your invitation. He *never* forgets—' She broke off as the shop owner bustled forward to complete the sale.

Hours later, as the sun paused above the horizon, making the sky ribbons of scarlet and tangerine, Tori entered her private courtyard. It was beautiful, with its delicate marble arches and fragrant garden.

Her gaze strayed to the long green-tiled pool. Ashraf had been delayed. She had time to swim before he arrived. She liked swimming, but hadn't done much since Oliver's birth—partly from lack of time and partly because of babysitting costs. This was a wonderful luxury.

Tori was grateful to Ashraf. If nothing else, she welcomed this break from solo parenting. She felt better for more sleep and proper exercise. Nor did she miss the early starts, getting herself and Oliver ready each day, or dealing with Steve Bates and office politics. Her job was good, but not the workplace.

She reached the end of the pool and turned, the rhythmic strokes inviting her mind to drift to the upcoming royal reception.

It was curious that Ashraf hadn't mentioned it. According to Azia, there'd be hundreds of guests. But not Tori. Silly to feel left out. She didn't *want* to attend stuffy official events. She'd done enough of that for her father.

Except this didn't sound stuffy. Invitees would enjoy displays by acrobats, swordsmen, riders and archers, including a feat where galloping horsemen shot flaming arrows into impossibly tiny targets.

Strange… Wouldn't Ashraf see this as a chance to showcase his culture? To introduce her to his friends? Instead he kept her secluded like a woman in an old-fashioned harem.

Or an embarrassment he didn't want anyone to discover.

The thought slammed into her and she swallowed water. An embarrassment? Was that how he saw her and Oliver?

Tori flicked her hair from her eyes and gasped in a lungful of air. No, Ashraf wasn't like that.

Except the day they'd arrived he'd spoken to her like a casual acquaintance, not a lover. Anyone watching wouldn't guess they'd been intimate. At the time she'd been grateful to him for helping her to save face before strangers. But what if he had another reason?

He'd sent her off immediately, not even introducing her to the man who'd met them. Plus he hadn't accompanied her to the palace as she'd expected.

Despite refusing him, you still want his attention, don't you? You want to be with him. Want him to want you.

The truth taunted her and she shied away from it.

Ashraf—hiding her?

She recalled that first day. The limo avoiding the palace's main entrance to use the back gate. Bram hurrying her inside—to avoid curious eyes? Bram telling her that this apartment was at the rear of the palace and quiet. She'd thought that considerate, but maybe it was because she and Oliver were an embarrassment.

It fitted with what Ashraf had said about prejudice. And with what Azia had hinted.

Bile was sour on Tori's tongue as she swam to the poolside and levered herself out. She shivered and turned to grab her towel—only to see it being held out for her.

'Ashraf!'

Tori's voice was harsh, as if he was the last person she'd expected. No, it was more than that. She didn't sound surprised as much as put out. As if she didn't *wish* to see him.

Impatience stirred. And a trickle of annoyance. He'd looked forward to the end of an interminable yet necessary meeting so he could enjoy a few hours with her. Didn't he deserve a warmer welcome?

Tori should be used to his presence. Yet the pool's underwater lights and the antique lanterns around the colonnaded courtyard revealed a face set in severe lines. And a body as arousing as ever.

Usually she smiled when he appeared, though it took her a while to relax fully. Ashraf had told himself that she needed time to adjust. But part of him—the part that had always taken for granted his ability to attract any woman he wanted—felt it like an insult.

He'd been patient. Beyond patient. He'd ignored his own needs to put hers and Oliver's first.

Since his accession he'd put the needs of his people and his country before his own and he didn't regret a second of it. But with Tori his altruism faltered when he looked into her wide blue eyes and felt the tug of desire in his loins. And when she stood before him in a skimpy scarlet bikini he had to pretend not to notice her sumptuous sexiness.

'Sorry I'm late.' The day had been difficult and he'd looked forward to her company. Clearly she didn't feel the same. 'I've already checked on Oliver. He's fast asleep.'

Tori took the towel and hurriedly wound it round her body. Annoyance jagged him again. Didn't she trust him? He had treated her as his honoured guest. He'd put no pressure on her for intimacy. He'd been scrupulous about giving her time and space to consider the arguments in favour of marriage.

For a man used to quick decisions and immediate follow-through his restraint had been remarkable. Yet did she appreciate it?

His mouth tightened. 'Is something wrong?'

She tucked in the end of the towel firmly, as if daring it to slip.

Ashraf forced down his irritation. It would achieve nothing. 'You're frowning.'

'Am I? No, nothing's wrong.'

One stubborn woman resisted him. One woman whose

fears he understood, which was why he'd held back rather than forcing the issue between them.

'Shall we go in? Supper has been laid out inside.' Hunger for food was one appetite he *could* satisfy.

'Not yet.'

Tori's tone was over-loud, her words quick. Her jaw had firmed, the way it did when she argued and when she'd masked her fear during their abduction.

Ashraf's frustration dissipated. How could he blame her for being cautious? She was facing such major changes.

'I have a question,' she said.

Maybe it was about what her life would be like in Za'daq. Pleased, Ashraf nodded. 'Go on.'

Tori crossed her arms over her chest and fire kindled in her eyes. 'Are you *ashamed* of me and Oliver?'

'Ashamed?' The idea was outrageous.

'Or just a little embarrassed?'

Tori's expression morphed into a searing disapproval that would have done his father proud. Even with her moonlight-pale hair dripping rivulets down her shoulders and chest she looked strong, compelling. And angry.

She wasn't the only one. 'Where did you get such an idea?'

'You're not answering the question.'

Her hands went to her hips, pulling the towel down to reveal more of her breasts. Ashraf dragged his attention back to her face and her perplexing words.

'That's ridiculous. Who suggested that?' If one of his political enemies had been bothering Tori he'd—

'No one. I'm able to think for myself.'

Ashraf frowned. 'But you *can't* think that.'

Surely his actions showed that he respected her? He'd gone out of his way to ease her into this new world. It was true he'd rushed her back to Za'daq because he couldn't afford more time out of the country right now, and because instinct had demanded he keep her and his son close. But otherwise he'd been the acme of consideration.

'You haven't answered me.'

That rounded chin tilted and Ashraf felt an urge to angle it even higher, so he could slam his mouth down on hers. He'd stop her insults and take out his frustrations as he ravished her mouth, then moved on to ravishing her body.

'I'm neither ashamed nor embarrassed about you and Oliver.' He held her haughty stare with one of his own and watched her eyebrows twitch in confusion. 'What gave you such an idea?'

Tori held herself stiffly. She clearly didn't believe him.

The realisation ground through him like glass grating beneath his heel. Except he felt it inside—as if his windpipe and belly were lined with shards. No one, not even those vultures waiting for him to fail as Sheikh, had ever accused him of untruth. Ashraf's hackles rose.

'It's the way we live here in the palace...alone, not mixing with other people.'

'I understood that you and Azia had been out together for the last three days?'

The fire in Tori's eyes flickered. She hadn't expected him to know about that. He breathed deep, biting back the impulse to tell her it had been *his* suggestion that Bram's wife visit her.

'Yes, we have. But if it weren't for her Oliver and I would be isolated here. Except for your visits late in the day.'

Ashraf stared. In other words, his presence counted for nothing. The hours he carved out of his packed schedule weren't appreciated. *He* wasn't appreciated.

Fleetingly Ashraf felt something dark and hurtful—a whispered memory of all those times when he'd tried to please his father and failed. But that boy was long gone. Ashraf had moulded himself into a man who would *never* be needy.

'Is that all?'

She must have heard a trace of suppressed anger in his tone for her hands slipped from her waist and she wrapped her arms around herself. Yet still she held his gaze.

'No. There are other things. The way we were hurried off from the airport without being introduced to anyone except Bram. Even when we got here Bram hurried us inside so fast that I wonder if he was worried we'd be seen. We always use the back entrance, and this apartment is at the rear of the palace. Is it because you don't want anyone knowing about us?'

Ashraf opened his mouth to respond but she hurried on.

'You spoke about marrying because of people's prejudice when your father believed you were illegitimate. You're worried about what other people think. And…' she sucked in a quick breath '… I'm obviously not good enough to attend your big celebration next week.'

He stared down into her flushed face, torn between fury at the insult and regret that Tori should believe that for a second. His hands clenched so tight the blood was restricted and his fingers tingled. He flexed them and shoved them in his pockets.

'First, Bram probably hurried you inside because he was worried about you coping with the heat—especially when you were tired from a long journey. Second, I didn't introduce you to the man who met our plane because his sole purpose in being there was to find out about you so he could make trouble. He's the Minister for the Interior, one of my father's oldest cronies, and he's devoted to the idea of unseating me from the throne. Call me prejudiced, but I didn't want him to be the first Za'daqi you met.'

Ashraf rocked back on his feet, forcing further explanations through clenched teeth.

'As for you being at the rear of the palace—that *was* intentional. Because I believed you needed rest. And I thought you'd appreciate some peace while you acclimatised and thought through your options for the future.'

So much for her appreciating his efforts on her behalf!

'You haven't been isolated. I moved out of the royal suite to be near you and Oliver.' He nodded to the windows on the side of the courtyard adjoining her rooms. 'I've spent every night since you arrived right next door. If you care to check, there's a concealed door between the suites. The staff have instructions to wake me if you call for assistance in the night.'

'I… I had no idea!' Tori's eyes rounded. 'Why didn't you say?'

'Foolishly, I thought you might feel pressured. As if I were encroaching by wanting to help out if Oliver had teething pains.'

Strange how he missed those night-time sessions, pacing the floor with a fractious baby. But holding his son in his arms, knowing he was building a bond that would last a lifetime, had stirred new and incredibly strong emotions.

Those hours in Tori's home, watching her feed Oliver, doing what he could to ease the burden, had held an intimacy and significance against which everything else paled. Even his royal responsibilities couldn't eclipse that.

Tori unwrapped her arms and the towel slid off, revealing her bikini-clad body, but she didn't notice. She stared as if she'd never seen him before.

'And I haven't introduced you to people at court yet because I respect your wish for privacy. You insisted this was a private visit, to test the waters. You *know*—' his voice ground low '—that I want to introduce you as my future bride.'

Ashraf's lungs tightened again at all her unjust accusations.

'I am not and never will be ashamed of either you or our son.' He paused, giving her time to absorb that. 'Yes, I've faced prejudice because of my father's attitude. No, I don't want Oliver to suffer anything like that. But I'm not *afraid* of public opinion.' He barely restrained his bitter laughter.

'I've lived with scandal so long I'm used to it. Most of the time it's in the minds of others rather than based on something I've actually done.'

Deliberately he moved into her personal space, leaning so close that her evocative scent blurred his senses.

'I want to marry you to give Oliver the best start in life. Not because I'm scared of tittle-tattle.'

'Ashraf, I—'

'And you haven't received a written invitation to the reception because I wanted to invite you myself. It's a perfect chance for you to see something of my culture, meet people and enjoy yourself. I wanted to give you time to rest and acclimatise before mentioning it.'

He'd been sure his painfully patient approach would bear fruit. That Tori would see the wisdom of his proposal and accept. It appeared patience wasn't working.

Tori blinked up at him. Finally she cleared her throat, moistening her lips in an unconsciously provocative movement that, to Ashraf's annoyance, shot a bolt of lust through him.

Even angry, he wanted this woman. Even after she'd questioned his honour and tested his patience to the limit.

Eyes the colour of a soft spring sky met his. 'I'm sorry, Ashraf. I got it completely wrong.'

'You did.'

Indignation still ran like a living current under his skin, heating his blood. This woman drove him crazy. She fought him over things that were, in his opinion, patently obvious, yet at other times was so reasonable it surprised him. Like accepting his need to see Oliver immediately and to be involved in his life.

And it wasn't just her contrary reasoning that exasperated him. Her ability to ignore the rampant attraction between them was unprecedented and provoking. While *he*, damn it, was distracted by the sight of those lush breasts rising and falling beneath the skimpy triangles of fabric. And the gleaming abundance of slick, pale skin.

'I should be thanking you, not accusing you.'

She lifted her hand to his sleeve. Ashraf stilled. Her touch was light, barely there, yet he felt it acutely.

'It's no excuse but, nice as it is to relax, I feel dislocated, cut off from work and home. I've overreacted. Can you forgive me?'

A huff of laughter escaped Ashraf. 'I don't suppose you feel chastened enough to marry me?'

Her eyes widened, as if he'd suggested something shockingly debauched instead of honouring her with a proposal that would make her a queen and the envy of half the women in Za'daq.

The anger that her apology had quenched spiked anew. Impatience surged.

'Is that a no?'

He turned his hand, capturing hers. His fingers encircled her wrist and he detected the wild pulse hammering there. Was she really so timid? Or was that arousal?

Ashraf was tired of tiptoeing around Tori's doubts. Tired of waiting. Tired of holding back.

'In that case, this will have to do.'

He tugged her close and she fell flush against him, her breasts to his torso, her other palm on his chest. To steady herself or to push him away?

Ashraf didn't wait to find out. In the same instant he roped his other arm around her slick body, lowered his head and kissed her full on the lips.

CHAPTER NINE

TORI SAW THOSE mesmerising eyes glitter and knew a moment of sharp, shocking anticipation.

Not dismay. Not even a second of doubt. Just anticipation.

It thrilled through her like an electric current, making all the fine hairs on her body lift and her breath seize. Then Ashraf's mouth was on hers, hard and demanding rather than coaxing.

She didn't need coaxing. Tori was primed and ready for his kiss. Had been from the moment he'd walked back into her life and some primitive part of her had hummed with excitement and want.

She wanted him so badly.

Relief was profound as she finally gave in to what she'd secretly craved. In this moment she didn't need to reason, or argue, or try to unknot the tangle of her mixed emotions. All she needed to do was feel.

She loved the taste of him, the heat and extraordinary *maleness* of him, hard and unrelenting. From that first instant there'd been no coercion. Just a demand that she was eager to meet. It had always been like this with him.

Her lips softened beneath his, inviting him in, all but begging him for more. He took up her offer and a shudder racked her as his tongue plunged deep, swirling against hers, exploring with a thoroughness that mixed determination and expertise. It was like tumbling through bright starlight, ceding control to this man whom she knew would never let her fall.

Ashraf scooped her closer, his hard frame solid muscle against her wet body. Tori clung tight, one hand clutching his robe, the other slipping from his grasp to slide up the back of his neck.

She heard a muffled grunt of approval as her fingers channelled through thick hair to splay possessively over the back of his head.

Her tongue danced with his, hunger cresting as she went up on her toes, trying to meld herself to him. His taste, his scent, his mouth were achingly familiar, as if it was just a few days since they'd made love.

Had they kissed like this in the desert? Surely not. Then they'd been strangers. Ashraf didn't feel like a stranger now. Remarkable to think they'd been together such a short time, for it seemed they knew each other at some deep level beyond words. He was the man who filled her thoughts and dreams. Who had done so since that night together. He was the one man who'd woken her dormant libido after the rigours and exhaustion of pregnancy and motherhood.

The one man she needed as she'd never before needed anyone.

The realisation made her freeze in his embrace.

Instantly he lifted his head, eyes glinting like black gems as they searched her face.

Tori heard the stertorous rasp of heavy breathing, felt her lungs heave and the push of his chest against her breasts as he too hauled in oxygen. Reaction juddered down her backbone and quivered across her skin. Being so close to him, touching him, undid her carefully cultivated caution. It allowed something wild inside her to take hold.

The air was smoky with desire, thick and scented with arousal. Yet the unspoken question was clear in Ashraf's expression. Did she want to stop?

She was bent back over his arm, plastered to him, so she felt the uneven catch of his breathing and his waiting stillness. They were on the brink of far more than a kiss. It was there in the taut awareness singing between them. But even now Ashraf would release her if she wanted.

Emotion swelled. As strong as the desire emblazoned in

her bones. Tenderness for this man who put her needs before his own. It struck her how remarkable that was, given that Ashraf literally had all the power in this kingdom of his.

Now her earlier doubts about him seemed absurd. She'd never met anyone with such innate integrity.

Tori shivered at the enormity of her feelings. Yet still she shied away from investigating them too closely.

Ashraf straightened and pulled away. He'd misread her.

'No!' She fastened both hands on his shoulders, fingers digging into fine cotton, pads of muscle and beneath that implacable bone. 'Don't.'

'Don't kiss you or—?'

'Don't stop.'

Yet instead of closing the gap Ashraf surveyed her as if he felt none of her urgency. Only the flare of his nostrils betrayed that he'd been affected too.

'So there's at least one thing about me you approve of.'

He wanted to *talk*? Frustration surged—and suspicion. 'Are you fishing for compliments?'

She spied a flicker of movement at the corner of his mouth and a tingle of delight teased her.

'No. But I'll take any you want to throw my way.' His lips firmed. 'You're not a woman easily swept off her feet, Victoria Miranda Nilsson.'

Tori shook her head, a snort of bitter laughter escaping. 'Really? Don't forget I'm the woman who had sex with a stranger in a prison cell after just a couple of hours' acquaintance.'

She shivered, remembering her father's disgust even at the airbrushed version she'd recounted to him.

In the desert what she and Ashraf had done had felt utterly right—a blessing rather than anything else. But after her father's talk of hushing up a dirty secret and Ashraf's talk of illegitimacy—

'And I'm the man who found solace and hope in sharing my body with a stranger in that same prison cell.' Firm fingers cupped her chin, easing it up. 'You're not ashamed of us, are you?' He didn't wait for her answer. 'I'm not. You gave me a precious gift that night. Not just your body but your kindness, your passion and strength. Believe me…' his mouth rucked up in a wry smile '…to a man on Death Row they were a gift from Heaven.'

His words sank deep, warming her. Despite her determination not to relive the past, sometimes she couldn't quite believe she'd had sex with a man she didn't know. A wounded stranger she should have been nursing instead of seducing.

Yet memories of that night held magic as well as trauma.

Tori surveyed him intently. 'You're not on Death Row now.'

Every sense told her he shared the passion she felt. But could she trust her instincts? Was it possible that Ashraf's kiss had been motivated by pique at her questions and her refusal to accept marriage?

Her uncertainty surprised her. Surely the attraction between them was self-evident? Yet adrift from the world she knew, plonked into a fairy-tale palace with a handsome, powerful prince and experiencing an ardour she'd only known once before, it was easy to feel this wasn't real.

Maybe it was wishful thinking.

Her experience of sex was pretty limited. She might work in an industry dominated by men, but that just meant she'd got into the habit of shutting down attempts to engage her interest. Having a relationship with a co-worker was a complication she didn't need.

At her lower back one large hand splayed wide then pulled her close. Closer. Till she felt his arousal. A hot shiver raced through her and internal muscles warmed and softened.

'No.' His voice was rich and low, eddying deep within her. 'And you're not in prison here. You understand that, don't you? You're free to make your own choices.'

Ashraf regarded her steadily. She nodded. The claustrophobia she'd felt in this beautiful building was of her own making. Everyone here had been friendly and helpful. *She'd* been the one imagining she was confined to this part of the citadel. She'd found it easier to stay cloistered in this gorgeous apartment than to learn more about Ashraf's home.

Was she intimidated by his royal status, or by the fact she was being forced to share Oliver?

If Bram hadn't introduced her to Azia she'd probably never even have left this courtyard apartment. She'd have blamed it on tiredness. Or the need to protect her son from possible prejudice. When had she become so timid?

'And so…?'

His hands went to her hips. Tori loved his touch. Pleasure shimmered through her.

She tilted her head. 'And so…?' She refused to admit she'd lost the thread of the conversation.

The gleam in Ashraf's eyes told her he'd guessed, but for once she didn't mind that he found her easy to read.

'And so what would you like now? You're my honoured guest. It's my responsibility to see that your wishes are met.'

'My wish is your command?' Tori couldn't prevent the laugh bursting from her lips. It sounded like an *Arabian Nights* fantasy. Yet Ashraf's hard hands on her bare flesh turned her thoughts away from storybooks into an earthier direction.

'Something like that,' he murmured.

This time there was gravel mixed with the thick treacle of his voice. Tori shivered as it scraped her nerve-endings, drawing shuddery awareness in its wake. This, she realised, was the mesmerising voice of a man with the sexual experience of a playboy and the single-minded determination of the warrior Prince she'd come to know.

Was it any wonder her defences lay in splinters?

What was she defending herself against?

Ash… Ashraf…sought only what she longed to give.

Tori slipped her hands down over his cream robe. Her palms lingered on the swell of defined pectoral muscles and her belly clenched. Ever since that night she'd found him half-naked, cradling Oliver in those strong arms…

'There must be something you want.' His grip on her hips firmed and his warm breath trailed across her brow.

She nodded and licked dry lips. Then sucked in a fortifying breath as she saw the flare in his eyes. That look sent need quaking through her. She'd spent ages grieving this man's death and now he was here, so very alive. Contrary to what she'd told herself, absence hadn't exaggerated her reaction to him.

'I want you, Ash.'

It really was that simple.

Just as well that he held her, for his sudden smile undid her at the knees. She swayed and clutched his shoulders, her pulse sprinting at the sheer glory that was Ashraf's smile.

He leaned so close that Tori thought he was going to kiss her, but he stopped a tantalising breath away.

'Your wish…' his words caressed her face '…is my command.'

Then he swept her up in his arms as easily as if she weighed no more than Oliver. He made her feel small, something she'd never experienced before, being on the tall side of average. And he made her feel treasured which, she realised in a flash of revelation, no man except Ash, her desert lover, had made her feel.

Tori wrapped her hands around his neck and smiled. 'You do that very well. I think you've had practice.'

It was a sign of her infatuation that she didn't care. He might have been a love-them-and-leave-them playboy once. But for this moment he was all hers. She'd given up fighting the inevitable.

* * *

Ashraf stared down into eyes the colour of heaven and thanked all his lucky stars that he hadn't died that day fifteen months ago. One brief taste of this amazing woman was far too little.

Did she realise she'd called him Ash? As if time had peeled away and they'd just met?

In what he thought of as his exile years, deliberately courting scandal, he'd answered to Ash just to fit in more easily with the westerners with whom he partied. He'd automatically used the short form of his name when he met Tori.

But the way she said it, her voice soft with longing, was unique.

No other woman had made his name sound like that.

No other woman had made him feel this way.

He hauled Tori closer, losing himself in her bright smile and inviting eyes. In her scent, alluring and fresh as spring itself. In the sense of utter freedom, of triumph, that was his body's response to her invitation.

His clothes clung to her wet body, but the dampness couldn't douse the heat burning inside. He felt as if he'd waited for this moment half a lifetime.

Dragging his gaze away, he strode into the sitting room. Pillar candles had been lit in ornate lanterns and more candles were clustered on the table, where a feast was spread. The room looked romantic. Had Bram noticed Ashraf's frustration and decided to play Cupid?

Ashraf gave the room one brief, curious glance but kept going. In the bedroom, he was about to kick the door shut when he remembered Oliver. They needed to be able to hear if he cried out.

At the bed he slowly put her down, gratified when her hands stayed locked around his neck. She swayed, and satisfaction stirred at her neediness. It matched his.

Lamps cast the room in a golden glow, yet Tori outshone it. She looked vibrant, delectable.

Ashraf's hands slid up from rounded hips, past the inward sweep of her waist and around to her back. One tug and the back of the bikini top loosened. Her breath hissed but she didn't move, just stood, her fingers clasped at his neck. Her expression notched his ardour even higher.

It was a moment's work to undo the bikini top and drag it away. Now Tori's hands at his neck shook and her breasts wobbled. He felt unsteady himself, his lungs cramping at the sight of the bounty of her pearly flesh. Some small part of him was surprised that he, once reviled by his father as a voluptuary, was undone by the sight of a woman's breasts.

Reverently, greedily, he cupped them, their plump softness perfect in his hands. The rose-pink nipples were hard and trembling under the swipe of his thumbs. Tori bit her lip and he was torn between the need to capture her mouth again, to plunder her breasts or strip off the rest of her bikini and thrust himself deep inside her.

Ashraf bent to skim kisses around one breast. Tori's weight on his shoulders grew as she sagged closer. With one arm he caught her around the waist, pulling her to him. Her breathing roughened, hoarse and aroused, as he closed his lips around her nipple and sucked.

'Ash!'

It was a protest and a plea, possibly even a prayer. And it shot all the blood in his body to his groin. He was buried in her scent, her flesh, her yearning. Needy fingers clamped his skull, pressing him closer as if she feared he might stop.

He did stop, but only to lavish attention on her other breast, drawing a groan from her that tightened his belly. Ashraf's need grew urgent, especially when Tori spread her legs around his and pressed close.

It was an invitation he couldn't resist.

Ashraf pulled back, ignoring her protest, and dropped to his knees. He smelled damp flesh, sweet woman and the musky, smoky scent of arousal.

His gaze fastened on her belly, which had once cradled

his son. Pride, wonder and possessiveness gave added depth to carnal arousal. He stroked the tiny striations running across her skin.

'Stretch marks...' Her voice was breathless.

Wondering, he shook his head. 'You're amazing.'

Tori's laugh was uneven, as if she didn't believe him, but he was lost in wonder at the miracle her body had made and in sheer, blistering lust. He was afraid that if he wasn't careful he'd push her onto the floor and take her with the finesse of a rutting stallion.

Ashraf forced himself to slow, watching the contrast of his dark olive-skinned hand on her pale, satiny skin. But despite his best intentions his patience was negligible. Seconds later his fingers had insinuated beneath the narrow sides of her bikini bottom, sliding it down.

She was blonde there too, the damp V between her legs pale gold.

'I've found treasure,' he murmured, running his hands down her thighs and then back up and around to anchor in her buttocks. Her muscles squeezed beneath his touch.

Tori's hands were in his hair. He grabbed one, nipped the fleshy part of her palm with his teeth, then kissed the spot, feeling a voluptuous shiver race through her. She was deliciously responsive. So responsive that he couldn't resist leaning in and nuzzling the pale golden hair that pointed the way to Paradise.

'Ash!' Her voice was reedy and weak, but her grip spoke of robust feminine need as she tilted her pelvis forward.

Ashraf explored with his tongue in thorough strokes that turned her shivers to deep shudders. Her gasps were the most satisfying music and the perfume of her arousal was heady, beckoning him to delight.

He'd intended to take his time, to seduce her so thoroughly that he'd overcome her scruples about marriage. But now he discovered a flaw in his plans. He wanted her too much to wait. This time, at least. He had never felt so strung out. It shouldn't be possible, but he felt as if he'd spill himself here and now, bringing her to climax.

After a lingering kiss he pulled back and rose to his feet. Unfocussed eyes met his and satisfaction warmed him. He liked her dazed with need for him.

'Undress me, Victoria,' he ordered, enjoying the sound of her full name, an intimacy they alone shared.

His satisfaction cracked as she reached for his long robe and pulled it up his legs with clumsy hands. He liked her touch, but even the brush of her fingers tested his control, teasing him when he was already stretched to breaking point.

He'd left his shoes at the door, so when she lifted his robe off he was bare but for silk boxers. This time Ashraf was the one to shudder as her gaze raked him. He felt it as if she'd stroked her slim fingers across his skin. He stood proud, lifting towards her, hardening still further.

'Your scar healed well,' she said finally.

Her touch slid along his ribs, tracing the knife mark. Where she touched he burned, as if she trailed ice over searing flesh.

'You haven't finished,' he gritted out, capturing her fingers and securing them in the waistband of his boxers.

Amusement flickered in her eyes. 'How remiss of me.'

But instead of pulling the offending garment away she sank to her heels before him. Ashraf's lungs atrophied at the sight of her there, naked and alluring, a carnal fantasy made flesh. His brain and lungs stopped when she tugged his underwear down and leaned in, taking him in her mouth.

Ten thousand volts jolted through him. He felt soft lips, moist heat, the tease of silken hair and then incredible, sweet delight as she drew hard on his flesh.

For a moment that lasted half a lifetime he gave himself up to carnal gratification. The feel of what she did to him, the sight of her there on her knees…it was too much.

Ashraf grabbed her shoulders and gently pushed her away, almost relenting when he saw her heavy-lidded eyes and moist lips.

'Later…' His voice cracked right down the middle.

'You didn't like—?'

'Of course I liked.' He sounded angry—probably from the effort it took not to pull her back. 'But I want to be inside you. *Now.*'

A flush crested her cheekbones. Amazing, given what she'd just been doing. And charming. Utterly charming.

'Come.' Ashraf drew her to her feet.

They stood so close she swayed and he pulled her in against him, revelling in the slide of her body against his. Every part of his flesh was an erogenous zone. One more touch, one more look from this woman, might send him over the edge.

How exactly they got onto the bed he wasn't sure. And that was remarkable to a man used to taking the lead in sexual encounters.

Their legs entwined as they lay facing each other. The way she looked at him made his chest swell. But there was no time to ponder unaccustomed feelings. His need was too strong. Especially with delicate feminine fingers urging him nearer.

It was the work of a moment to roll her onto her back and settle between her splayed thighs. Ashraf's mouth curved in a tense smile. He appreciated her complete lack of coyness now she'd decided to stop fighting.

The only fight now was his own as he battled sensory overload—her silky skin, the beckoning heat teasing his groin, her piquant feminine perfume and the sight of her achingly beautiful breasts jiggling with each breath.

Tori stroked his shoulders restlessly, her eyes brilliant as gems. Ashraf knew he should take his time, savour every second, but he also knew his limits.

'Next time, *habibti*,' he murmured as he captured one of her hands.

'Next time what?'

'Next time we'll take it slow.'

He caught her other wrist and lifted both hands above her head, holding them with firm fingers. He watched her eyebrows lift, but though she could have broken his grasp she didn't try.

'I don't want slow.'

Her words ignited the blaze he'd tried to bank down. She'd barely stopped speaking when he pushed her thighs wider, grinding himself against her core. His gaze fixed on her face and the arrested expression there. Her look, the feel of their bodies together, were delight and torture together. More than flesh and blood could withstand.

'Nor do I.'

He slid his free hand between them, feeling her lush wetness, the hungry pulse of her body as he probed, hearing her swift intake of breath. A second later his hand was beneath her bottom, tilting her towards him as he bore down in one long, steady push that left him centred within her.

Sweat broke out at his nape and his brow. Muscles seized as the full reality of their joining penetrated his brain.

He had waited so long for her. Since that night in the desert he'd taken no lover, telling himself he was too busy. Now he understood with a flash of terrible insight that he hadn't wanted any woman but this one.

The realisation took a millisecond—less time than it took to draw breath. Yet it rocketed through him like the rush of a desert sandstorm, blanketing all thought.

Then primitive instinct took over.

Ashraf's mouth went to her breast, drawing hard, making her cry out and wrap her legs around his waist, rising against him in hungry desperation. A desperation that matched his own.

He erupted in a storm of movement. He withdrew and

thrust harder, deeper than before, setting up a rhythm that matched the hammer beat of blood in his ears and the rough syncopation of their breathing.

It seemed only seconds before he felt the first fluttery tremors deep in her body. Setting his jaw and stiffening his arms, he tried to withstand the drag of delicious sensation as her climax shuddered through her. But the expression in those eyes locked on his, the sound of her desperate gasps, even the way she clutched him, as if he were the only solid point in a swirling universe, amplified the ecstasy he felt as she convulsed into orgasm.

'Ash! Ash, please!'

It was too late. Her pleasure became his. The clench of her muscles blasted him off the edge and into an oblivion so deep he knew nothing but the pleasure-pain of rapture.

When his senses returned he was trembling all over like a newborn foal. His pounding heart filled his ears and his strength was gone, leaving him plastered across her pliant body.

'Victoria...' It was a silent gasp against the fragrant skin of her throat. There was nothing else except this woman and the aftershocks of explosive passion racking a body he was sure would never move again.

She filled his every sense. He nuzzled her throat, needing even now to be connected to her. And then the hands grabbing his shoulders slid down his back. Her arms wrapped tight around his middle as if she, too, needed to be as near as possible.

She planted a kiss on his shoulder and he felt her lips curve. 'Thank you, Ash.'

With a superhuman effort he lifted his head. Forget-me-not eyes met his. They were heavy-lidded and she wore a dreamy smile. This was how he wanted her—sexy, warm and biddable. And the way she used the shortened form of his name pointed to another barrier smashing down between them.

Ashraf's mouth tilted up in an answering smile. 'Thank *you, habibti.*'

They might be together because of the child she'd borne, but he knew in the very marrow of his bones that this was the right thing.

His hold on her tightened.

His woman. Soon to be his wife.

CHAPTER TEN

TORI SIGHED AS pleasure trickled through her. The bed was soft, she'd had the best sleep she could remember and, half-awake, she sensed all was well with the world.

It took her a few moments to realise that the delightful sensation that had roused her was a trailing caress. The brush of fingers across naked skin.

Naked skin.

For a moment her dulled brain couldn't compute that till, in a flurry of excitement, memories swamped her.

Ashraf, even more potent and magnificent in the flesh than in her dreams, powering into her with a single-minded focus that had been almost as arousing as the feel of his hard body.

He'd been strong yet tender, urgent yet considerate. She trembled, recalling how his body had made hers sing. How his touch had reduced her defences to rubble. How the pleasure had gone on and on and—

'Ash!'

Her eyes popped open as that wandering hand strayed across her breast, pausing to circle in ever-diminishing rings towards her eager nipple.

Dark eyes held hers—eyes that danced with devilry and hunger. By the pearly light filling the room she knew it was very early morning and she felt a fillip of delight that Oliver had slept through, leaving her and Ashraf uninterrupted. Soon, she guessed, he'd wake...

Then Ashraf pinched her nipple and her thoughts shattered. Tori all but rose off the bed as arousal shot through her. His leg across hers held her down and even that, she discovered, excited her.

Mouth dry, she licked her lips. His eyes followed the movement. At his throat a tiny pulse flickered hard and the tendons at the base of his neck pulled taut.

Tori breathed in sharply, excited by his arousal. It was a heady thing, discovering she had power over this man she found impossible to resist.

'Good morning, Victoria.'

Even the way he said her name—her full name, that no one but her father used—tugged at unseen cords in her belly. She used the name Tori partly because its less feminine sound fitted her work environment, but mainly because she hated how her father expressed his disapproval by drawing out the syllables.

Now, on Ashraf's tongue, her name sounded sensual and inviting.

'Good morning, Ashraf.'

His hand slid down to circle her navel and feather her belly, drawing a shiver from her and an eager softening of muscles. Her legs quivered.

'Last night it was Ash.'

'Was it?' She remembered, but pretended not to. Because last night he'd flattened every barrier between them.

When they made love it was as if time ripped away and she was with Ash again, the vital, viscerally exciting man she'd known in the desert. The man who tried to protect her, who'd given her the gift of his support when she'd been terrified. Rather than Ashraf, the man whose intentions worried her, despite his attempts to allay her concerns. For nothing could take away the fact that he was supreme ruler in this foreign land and that he wanted her to relinquish her freedom and everything she knew.

If he knew the full extent of his power over her...

She shivered.

His hand paused just inches away from the apex of her thighs and, despite her worrying thoughts, Tori felt the sharp bite of frustration. No matter her concerns for the future, she needed more.

Tori pressed her palm down on the back of his hand, holding it against trembling skin.

Their eyes clashed.

'Why did you stop? You want me to call you Ash?'

Broad shoulders shrugged above her. 'Call me whatever you like.'

Yet he made no move to complete what he had been doing just moments before.

An ache set up inside her, deep in that hollow place he'd filled last night. And in her chest, as if her heart or lungs were bruised.

Tori shook her head, bemused by her imaginings. Yet she wasn't imagining the bone-deep yearning for completion. Or her lover's waiting stillness as he looked down at her.

Her lover. The words washed through her, and with them a kind of relief. Whether she thought of him as Ash the honourable stranger or Ashraf the determined King, she wanted him.

What more did he want from *her*?

She'd already proved she was no match for the desire he ignited in her. It was a mere week since he'd come back into her life and she was amazed she'd withstood his allure so long.

Desire made her limbs tremble as she looked up into eyes that beckoned and challenged at the same time.

Tori's mouth firmed. If he was waiting for her to say she'd changed her mind about marriage he'd have a long wait. Or was it something else he wanted?

She lifted her hand from his and cupped his shoulder, pushing him back. Her pulse accelerated with excitement as he let her, falling back onto the bed.

He lay there, big and bold and utterly still, like a bronzed cat lazily sunning itself in the pale light spilling across the rumpled bed. Yet there was nothing lazy in the eyes that meshed with hers. A frisson ran through her at the invitation she read there.

Shedding any hesitation, Tori rose to straddle powerful thighs. Ashraf was all heavy muscle and heat—incredible heat. His mouth tugged wide in a satisfied smile but otherwise he didn't move. Until Tori leaned forward to lick to one dark nipple and a tremor ran through his supine body. Hard hands grasped her hips. She licked again, then nipped with her teeth, hearing his breath catch as he lifted beneath her.

This time she took the lead. She brushed kisses across his torso, with its scattering of dark hair, then drew on his other nipple and heard what sounded like a low growl. His fingers tightened on her. Lifting her gaze, she found his eyes locked on her and a thrill of empowerment zigzagged through her.

Levering herself higher, Tori stretched up his body, letting her breasts skim his chest. It felt so good she had to stop and stiffen her wobbly arms.

There was no laziness in Ashraf's face now. Watching the convulsive movement of his throat as he swallowed, feeling the swell of his arousal beneath her, Tori knew for the first time that he was at her mercy. It was delightful—if short-lived. For then Ashraf lifted his hips, letting her feel the full force of his appetite for her. Tori's pulse hammered in her throat, her lips firming over a moan of need.

'Ride me, *habibti*.'

So much for being the one setting the pace. But how could she object as he urged her up onto her knees? Besides, his voice was more gravel than velvet, and his hands on her hips betrayed his desperation.

Tori knelt above him, dragging out the moment of anticipation, one hand on that broad chest the colour of old gold. Beneath her palm his heart raced. That was what undid her—feeling Ashraf equally at the mercy of their mutual desire.

Closing her other hand around him, watching his hooded eyes, she lowered herself so slowly that the sensation of him rising to complete her seemed to take for ever.

When, finally, she rested fully against him, Tori experienced again that sense of quiet magic. As if time stood still in the presence of something extraordinary.

But it couldn't last. Already the need to move was unstoppable. Tori rose high, then slid down with an exquisite friction that made everything inside her quiver.

Ashraf's body was fiery hot, his eyes glittering fiercely as she moved again and again, arching in an instinctive dance against him. She set the pace and every movement took her closer to bliss.

The threads inside her body tightened, pulling into a coiling knot where every feeling converged. Then, without warning, a searing white light engulfed her. Tori heard a threadbare voice in the distance calling for Ash. Felt the sudden, cataclysmic wave of ecstasy and could do nothing but ride it out, her eyes locked on his.

She watched as the wave took him too. And the sight swept her from rapture to oblivion.

All Tori knew was the fire-burst of bliss and Ash—everywhere Ash, within her, around her, below her, his hands anchoring her, his body worshipping her, his rough voice praising her.

She didn't even remember falling. Just knew, as Ash's arms roped her to him and she inhaled the familiar cinnamon and spice scent of his skin beneath her cheek, that she never wanted to be anywhere else.

Ash emerged from the shower in Tori's suite wearing a mile-wide smile.

Life was good. The afterglow of spectacular sex filled him, but it was more than that. Everything was falling into place. He'd announce their impending marriage at the upcoming royal reception.

Now he'd cleared up Tori's fears that he'd hidden her and Oliver out of shame all would be well. He'd reassured her that she was free to make her choices and she'd chosen *him*, coming to him utterly of her own volition.

It was good that they'd had that confrontation. It had clarified things, allayed her doubts. And it had showed him another facet of his future wife. She was a woman who would stand for no insults against her son, a woman who'd defy anyone, even Ashraf, to protect Oliver. The way she'd argued her points, standing toe to toe with him, had aroused his admiration.

And his libido.

He grabbed a towel and rubbed his hair, remembering the spark in his belly as she'd faced him. Even his annoyance at her misconceived doubts hadn't quenched that.

Nor, he realised as he towelled his body, had a cold shower. Despite his heavy schedule he'd happily have spent another hour in bed with Tori. Only the sound of little Oliver, awake and hungry, had stopped him.

And even that interruption had its positives. Going to Oliver's room to find his son looking up at him curiously, Ashraf hadn't felt impatience but a surge of tenderness. Getting to know his child, having a real role in his life, meant everything to him.

Ashraf flung the towel away and dressed, his thoughts returning to Tori.

She was a strong mother. She'd make a superb queen, given time. And they had plenty of that—a lifetime.

Satisfaction warmed him—and the familiar pulse of desire. It was still early. There might be time before his first meeting...

No. He had other priorities. Namely, hearing Tori say she'd changed her mind about their future together.

Quickly combing his hair, he strode back to the bedroom—only to pause in the doorway.

Tori sat in bed while Oliver sucked at her alabaster breast.

Lust pierced Ashraf. He recalled the taste of that breast, and the way his mouth on Tori's sensitive skin had catapulted her from languorous acquiescence to raw desperation. He breathed slowly, savouring the memory, and the peaceful picture of his woman and child.

Early sunlight turned her hair into a gilded angel's crown. Against the sumptuous coloured silks and satins her pale beauty shimmered like rare, fragile treasure. But her smile as she met his eyes sent a kick to his belly and told him that Tori was a robust, flesh-and-blood woman.

'I like watching the pair of you.'

The admission surprised him. He hadn't intended to say it aloud. At the sound of his voice Oliver half turned, then resumed feeding. A curious feeling filled Ashraf. Satisfaction? Excitement? And something bittersweet.

It seemed his son responded to him. That he recognised his father's voice.

Whose voice had Ashraf known as a child? Only his mother's, and then only for a short time. Oh, there'd been servants, even some kindly ones, but no adults to whom he was the wellspring of the world.

The only love he'd really known was his brother's. But Karim had been kept busy by their father, learning all that a future sheikh had to know. He'd had little time to spend with his kid brother, especially since he'd had to sneak time with Ashraf behind their disapproving father's back.

Ashraf would like Oliver to have a sibling. Several, if Tori agreed. He wanted Oliver to have the things he'd never enjoyed and would never take for granted.

'How do you feel about large families?'

Tori's brow furrowed, her smile fading. 'Why do you ask?'

Ashraf shrugged and walked to the side of the bed. 'We didn't used protection last night.'

At the time he'd been too busy exulting in how freely Tori gave herself to him. He hadn't paused for contraception. After all, they were to marry and he had no objection to more children.

'We didn't?' Her voice struck a discordant note and she suddenly sat straighter, making Oliver grumble. Her brow crinkled. 'No, we didn't, did we?'

Ashraf read her concern and understood. For Tori's sake a longer gap between children would be better. He'd seen her weariness and understood how pregnancy and single motherhood had taken a toll. There was no rush for more children. They had plenty of time.

'But they say the chances of getting pregnant are less while you're breastfeeding.' It sounded as if she was trying to reassure herself.

Ashraf reached down and touched her leg, stroking satiny skin. 'You're probably right.' Though he knew nothing of such things. 'And even if there is another baby sooner than we expected we'll manage together.'

'Sorry...?' Her eyes shone large and lustrous. But her expression wasn't what he expected.

'Next time you're pregnant...' He paused. 'Whenever that is, you won't have to manage alone. I'll be here to support you.'

Ashraf smiled and was surprised when she didn't reciprocate. Instead her features froze. Abruptly she closed her robe around her and put Oliver against her shoulder. Then she shuffled higher up the bed, sliding her leg away from his hand.

'There won't be a next time.'

'Sorry?'

'There won't be another pregnancy.' Tori paused, her breasts rising on a sharp breath. 'At least...' She shook her head. 'If it ever happens it will be far in the future. If I marry.'

'*If* you marry?' Ashraf saw her tilt her chin high and realised he was on his feet, looking down at her.

She shrugged, but there was nothing easy about the movement. She looked as rigid as he felt.

'Who knows what the future holds? If, later on, I fall in love, I might consider having another child.' She paused and glanced down at Oliver, nestled quietly at her shoulder. 'A brother or sister for Oliver *would* be nice one day...' she mused, as if the idea had just struck her.

Ashraf stared, outraged that she was still apparently rejecting him, even after tacitly accepting him last night. Forget tacitly. She'd been *blatant* in accepting him. Choosing him. Could she have been any more forthright? And that sultry smile she'd given him this morning as she straddled him...

His hands fisted as all his fighting instincts roused.

The idea of Tori, *his woman*, in love with some other man, *giving* herself to that unworthy stranger, filled him with a taste for blood he hadn't felt since he'd been a teenager, facing his father's sneering contempt.

'You gave yourself to me.'

His voice sounded strange, as if it came from a distance. Ashraf felt a constriction in his throat that matched the sudden cramp in his gut.

Her gaze turned to him and he watched understanding dawn.

'That was sex.'

She had the gall to make it sound like nothing.

'You wanted me. You accepted me.'

'Yes, I *wanted* you.' She said it slowly, enunciating each syllable. 'And you wanted me.' That was pure challenge—as was the flash of defiance in her fine eyes. 'But it was sex. It had nothing to do with...' Tori waved her hand, as if struggling to find the words.

Ashraf found them easily enough. 'My marriage proposal?'

Tori shook her head, her pale hair slipping around the deep rose-coloured robe that reflected the colour cresting her cheekbones. She wriggled to the side of the bed, holding Oliver close.

Ashraf caught tantalising glimpses of her slender thighs, then she stood, clutching her robe closed with one hand, the other cuddling Oliver.

'You never *proposed* marriage. You put it forward as a solution to a problem. Oliver isn't a problem.' Her voice rose to a wobbly high note.

Ashraf felt his forehead knot. What had happened to last night's passionate, accommodating woman? The woman who, he was sure, had finally agreed to be his?

Impossible as it seemed, his intended bride was rejecting him. *Again.* He clenched his teeth so hard that pain radiated from his jaw.

Never had a woman rejected him. Yet this woman made a habit of it.

'Is that what you want? Me on bended knee? Or would you prefer a candlelit meal with violins playing and a shower of rose petals? Would that satisfy you?'

Anger tightened every muscle. Disappointment, sharp as acid, blistered and scorched its way through his body.

And there was more.

Hurt.

Ashraf told himself it could only be hurt pride. He'd never considered offering any other woman what he offered Tori. His name, his honour, his loyalty.

'There's no need for sarcasm, Ashraf. I thought men were supposed to be good at separating sex and love or marriage.'

Despite the jibe, and the arrogant angle of her jaw, Tori's voice was brittle, her mouth a crumpled line. And abruptly, despite his roiling emotions, Ashraf realised something his anger had blinded him to.

Tori was scared. He read it in the obstinate thrust of her jaw and those over-wide eyes. In the protective way she held their son and the tremor she couldn't hide.

Scared of committing herself?

Or scared that he'd take Oliver?

That, as absolute ruler, he'd force her into a life that terrified her?

Drawing in air through his nostrils, Ashraf reminded himself that Tori barely knew his homeland except as a place of peril. He hadn't really helped her acclimatise. He'd deliberately left her alone during the day, believing she needed rest. And their evenings together had tested his determination not to seduce her.

How right he'd been. Sex had resolved nothing.

Tori hadn't tried to tease him or mislead him, giving him a night of unfettered passion and then withdrawing. She'd simply surrendered to a force too strong to withstand.

'Say something.' Her voice sounded stretched as if from tight vocal cords. 'What are you going to do?'

That was easy. He'd do whatever was necessary to secure Oliver and Tori.

Marshalling control, he smiled and watched her gaze drift to his mouth. 'I'm going to spend the day with you.'

And the next and the next. However many it took to convince Tori that life in Za'daq, with him, was the right choice. He'd court her till she stopped putting up barriers and surrendered.

CHAPTER ELEVEN

TORI LOOKED AT the vast landscape spread below the chopper and felt a mix of awe, curiosity and unease. The desert plain seemed to wash up to the edge of ragged mountains that fringed the border.

She gulped, tasting remembered fear. It was somewhere there that she and Ashraf had been abducted.

A warm hand closed around hers, making her turn to the man beside her.

'Okay?' The expression in those ebony eyes told her he understood the fear closing her throat.

Tori nodded, refusing to succumb to panic.

'I enjoy travelling by helicopter,' Ashraf added, as if suspecting she needed distraction, 'but I know some find it challenging.'

'I like it,' she finally admitted. She'd often flown to remote locations for work.

Why they were venturing so far from the city, she didn't know. Yet the opportunity to spend time with Ashraf, seeing him in his own environment, had been too precious to pass up. Tori had important decisions to make about Oliver's future. Getting to know Ashraf and his country was part of that.

Even if, after last night, part of her wanted simply to succumb to his demand for marriage.

If she'd known how profoundly making love to him would affect her she'd never have gone to bed with him.

Who did she think she was kidding? It would have taken a far stronger woman than she to say no. From the start he'd been irresistible.

She shivered and Ashraf stroked his thumb across her

hand. Darts of arousal pierced low in her body. It worried her, how easily and how deeply she responded to him.

'Here we are.' He leaned across and pointed to a valley between two trailing spurs, where she saw traces of green and the sinuous curve of a river. 'That's our destination.'

'It's a long way to travel for a picnic.' When he'd suggested leaving Oliver behind for a couple of hours, she'd imagined they'd go to a beauty spot near the city.

His hand squeezed hers. 'I wanted you to see something of Za'daq apart from the capital.'

She turned to meet his eyes, trying to decipher that intent stare. 'And you wanted to show me how safe this part of the country is now?'

It was a guess, but the curling groove at one side of his mouth gave Tori her answer. He *had* chosen this location deliberately. Did he know she was still anxious about returning to the desert? Did he read her so easily?

'I don't want you afraid of shadows, Tori.' His eyes held hers. 'Plus, I want you to meet my people. For a long time this region hasn't had the benefits found in the rest of my country.'

The helicopter descended and he gestured towards what looked like irrigation channels following the contours of the land, and a surprising amount of green vegetation.

'They are proud and hard-working. And things are changing here now Qadri has gone.'

Tori took a slow breath and nodded. She hated the anxiety niggling at her insides. Surely facing her fear would help her overcome that? It would be good to replace those terrifying memories with something else.

'I'll be interested to see them.'

Ashraf's smile as he threaded his fingers through hers made something hard inside her shift. Logic told her to keep some distance between them. He'd so readily assumed she'd changed her mind about marriage because she'd gone to bed with him. But she didn't have the energy to hold herself aloof. Basking in the warmth of his smile, in his company, was too tempting.

It was impossible to switch off the current of connection between them. Just this morning she'd gloried in his body and he in hers. She'd found heady delight and a sense of personal power in their lovemaking. How long since she'd felt powerful, much less mistress of her own destiny?

Since the kidnap she'd felt as if she was at the mercy of forces beyond her control. First her abductors, and then as her body altered to accommodate a new life, and later as she changed her life to put Oliver's needs first. She'd taken her current job so she could work child-friendly hours, not because she especially wanted to work there.

'Tori? Are you all right?'

Ashraf squeezed her hand. She looked around to discover they'd landed.

He leaned close, looking concerned. 'If you'd really rather go back...?'

But a crowd had gathered. A cluster of serious-faced older men in traditional robes, and behind them people of all ages.

'No. They're expecting you.'

From what she could see of the village, with its tumble of mud brick houses, Tori guessed a visit from their Sheikh would be a special event. She couldn't make him leave and disappoint them.

'How will you introduce me? Won't people wonder who I am?'

Ashraf grinned. 'Don't worry about that. Just come and meet them. Be yourself.'

Undoing his seatbelt and headset, he alighted from the chopper.

Tori hesitated, a hand going to her hair when she noticed most of the women wore headscarves.

'I'm not really dressed for this.' She'd worn a bright red

top which usually made her feel good, but now it made her wonder if she should have dressed in a more conservative colour.

'You're perfect.'

His gaze lingered for a second, as if he could see through her loose-fitting top and summer-weight trousers. Instantly Tori's self-consciousness was swamped by awareness. Wind rushed in her ears and her breath snagged at the look in those gleaming eyes.

'Come.'

He reached out, took her hand and helped her down. The dying rotation of the helicopter's blades made her hair whirl around her face, but Ashraf didn't seem concerned that she looked slightly dishevelled. Presumably it didn't matter.

Then Tori had no time for self-consciousness as she was introduced not only to the village elders but it seemed to every adult in the place. Children stared up at her with wide eyes, but she was used to that. When she'd worked across the border in Assara, people had been fascinated by her pale colouring.

While Ashraf was deep in discussion with the elders one little girl, held in her mother's arms, swayed towards Tori, reaching out to her. Rather than pulling back, she let the child tentatively touch her hair.

The mother looked horrified, trying to draw away, apologising. But Tori shrugged and smiled. 'She's just curious. That's a good thing.'

The local schoolteacher, acting as interpreter, translated, and suddenly, instead of hanging back, more women approached. There was no more touching, but there were smiles and shy questions which gradually became a steady flow. Not, Tori was relieved to hear, about her relationship with the Sheikh, but about her homeland, so far away, and what she thought of Za'daq.

'If you'd care to take a seat, my lady?'

The teacher gestured as the small crowd parted and Tori

saw, in the scanty shade of what appeared to be the village's only tree, a striped awning. Spread in the shade beneath it were richly coloured rugs and exquisitely embroidered cushions.

When they were seated a woman arrived with a bowl and a small towel. Another carried a jug of water, offering it to the guests to wash their hands. Then platters of food arrived—dried fruit and nuts, and pastries dripping with syrup. Coffee was prepared with great ceremony and offered in tiny cups.

'Thank you,' Tori said in their language. 'It's delicious.' She stumbled a little over the pronunciation but knew by the smiles around her that she was understood.

Ashraf turned and his expression warmed her even more than the pungent coffee.

'After this I'll inspect the irrigation scheme behind the village but I won't be too long. I promise to get you back to the city in good time.'

Because Oliver would be ready for a feed. It seemed incredible that a king would so readily fit his arrangements around that. As incredible as him changing his schedule at short notice to take her out.

'Would you like to come with me? Or you could stay here and chat? Or maybe see the school?' Tori saw him glance towards the teacher.

'I'll stay.' She turned to the teacher. 'Perhaps you could show me around?'

Her choice was a popular one. While most of the men went with Ashraf, the women and children accompanied her. The children pointed out places of interest like the well, now with a pump powered by a solar generator. And then there was the tower on the hill, which had brought modern communication to the valley for the first time. They also stopped to look inside one of the houses, where a loom was set up for silk weaving, and Tori admired the fine fabric.

The school was a one-roomed stone building. But to Tori's surprise it wasn't the bare little space she'd expected. It was well-stocked with books, colourful posters and a couple of computers.

Seeing her surprise, the teacher explained. 'The government is keen to ensure all Za'daqis have a good education. In remote areas where children can't travel to bigger schools we now have smaller schools, each supporting a village or two. In the old days children here didn't get any formal education.'

'It seems to be working well,' Tori said, watching the children talk to their mothers about the art on one wall. 'They seem very engaged.'

'They are. The difference here in just a couple of years is amazing.'

'Only a couple of years?'

'The school is very new.' He paused, as if choosing his words. 'Until Sheikh Ashraf there was no funding for local schools here. Now even the children in small settlements have access to education. It will give them a brighter future.'

Tori felt pride stir at his words, as if she had a vested interest in Ashraf's achievements. Perhaps she did. She was well past the stage of pretending indifference.

'Sheikh Ashraf tells me there have been a number of changes in the region?'

'There have, indeed.' The teacher said something to the women surrounding them and received nods and eager comments in response. 'Life is better here now, with plenty of food and even visiting doctors. It's peaceful too.' He shot her a sideways look. 'In the past there was a problem with evil men…lawless men who did bad things.'

Despite the warmth of the day ice slid down Tori's spine. 'Yes. I've heard about that.'

The man nodded. 'But now they are gone and we have the Sheikh's law. Things are much better. The people are safe.'

His words stayed with Tori through the rest of their visit, as she watched the boisterous children and the women's smiles. *Safe.* Ashraf made her feel safe too. Except for her doubts about accepting a convenient marriage and living in a country where his word was law.

When she was with him she felt different. Better. *Happier.*

Were those feelings enough to compensate for accepting a loveless marriage? She was surprised even to be considering it.

'Is everything okay?' Ashraf asked as the helicopter took off and they left the waving villagers behind. 'You're very quiet.'

It was because she was distracted by conflicting feelings. The more she learned of Ashraf, the more she understood his idea of marriage was rooted in good intentions. He didn't plan to take advantage of her.

Yet good intentions weren't always enough.

Tori looked down at the silk scarf on her lap, a kaleidoscope of sumptuous colour.

'This present is so beautiful but I didn't have anything to give in return.' It had been pressed into her hands by the woman whose house she'd visited—the silk weaver. 'Weaving is her livelihood and I'm not sure she can afford to give it away.'

Ashraf shook his head. 'Your interest in her life is enough. That is something these people haven't had much of in the past. Besides, they're proud. They brought out their very finest for our visit, but they didn't expect an exchange of gifts. You did the right thing, accepting this.' He paused. 'Don't worry. No one will be worse off because of our visit.'

Tori knew without asking more that he'd be as good as his word. She leaned back in her seat and turned to watch the foothills slide into the distance. This time she felt no nervous tingle of apprehension at the sight.

'It sounds like they're already better off because of you.'

In her peripheral vision she caught his shrug. 'We've had some useful initiatives. They're beginning to bear fruit.'

'Like medical services, education, electricity and reliable clean water.' She ticked them off on her hand. Most men she knew would crow about their personal role in such successes. Her father especially.

Ashraf wasn't like the men she knew.

He caught her gaze and a surge of emotion enveloped her. Tenderness, yearning and something more. All sorts of feelings that she knew made her weak but which she couldn't suppress.

Ashraf captured her hand, setting off whorls of eager sensation just under her skin.

'What are you thinking, *habibti*?'

His voice had dropped to an impossibly deep note on the endearment.

Tori opened her mouth, about to give voice to the tremulous emotions that filled her. But at the last moment caution surfaced. She forced a casual smile. 'Just wondering how Oliver is doing with the nanny.'

Was that disappointment in his eyes?

The impression was gone in an instant, yet Tori couldn't banish the feeling that she'd been cowardly and less than generous with Ashraf.

That suspicion grew as her first week in Za'daq became a second. Instead of seeing Ashraf only in the evening she began to be taken out daily, introduced to his country and his people.

Despite her reservations, Tori looked forward to their outings and his company. She told herself she was relieved that he no longer pressed her to marry. Yet, to her chagrin, nor did he come to her bed.

Torn between pride and fear at how easily he dismantled her defences, she didn't dare initiate sex, not trusting herself. And that left her frustrated with herself and him. If it hadn't been for the smoking hot looks Ashraf sent her when he thought she wasn't watching, and his palpable tension when she stood close, Tori might have imagined him indifferent.

Was he trying to prove they could build a relationship based on more than sex?

She could only admire Ashraf's self-control. Hers frayed dangerously. Each day she fell further under the spell of this place and this man. And while Oliver settled into life in the palace she discovered so much in Za'daq to like.

Ashraf took her to the old parts of the city, with quaint buildings, narrow streets and hidden courtyards. They went to a vast covered market that sold everything from carpets and brassware to jewellery, perfumes and spices in all the colours of a desert sunset. Then to a dazzling art gallery, and a technology park where they visited fascinating new enterprises, and public gardens filled with families enjoying the green space. They drove out to a spectacular gorge where a rare breed of eagles nested and the scenery stole her breath as they watched the sun sink.

Tori met nomads in a desert encampment, traders, teachers and so many others who made her feel welcome. Wherever they went people were respectful but friendly, and gradually her nervousness about being in Ashraf's country eased.

He took her to a horse-trading bazaar on the edge of the city. Breeders had come from throughout the country and beyond, and the event had a holiday atmosphere. There was a great open-air feast and dashing displays of horsemanship. Tori watched in surprise when Ashraf agreed to take part, unable to take her eyes off him. He had the grace of a natural athlete, and when he rode it was like watching a centaur, man and horse moving as one.

It was late as they returned to the palace. The limousine's privacy screen was up, separating them from the driver, and Tori wished Ashraf would reach for her. She missed his touch. Missed the intimacy they'd shared. Her resolve to keep her distance was bleeding away like water in the desert sands and a new sort of tension filled her.

She turned to him, sucking in a sustaining breath as her pulse quickened. 'It was kind of you to give me such a lovely present but I really can't accept—'

'Of course you can. I watched your reaction when you saw that mare. It was love at first sight.'

Tori wrinkled her brow. If she didn't know better she'd say that Ashraf sounded *envious*. It was a bizarre thought that she hurriedly put aside.

'She's beautiful.'

It was true that Tori had fallen for an Arab mare being sold at the bazaar, but if she'd thought for a moment Ashraf would buy it for her she'd never have let her gaze linger on the gorgeous animal. She loved riding, but hadn't had a chance to indulge her passion for years, and it just wasn't practical now.

'But she needs someone who'll care for her full-time. I may not be here—'

Ashraf raised his hand and Tori was struck by the sudden austerity of his features. He looked handsome yet remote. More distant even than a week ago, when they'd argued after that glorious night together. When he'd believed she'd marry him because she'd gone to bed with him.

'She's yours, Tori. No strings attached. If you accept my offer and live here she'll be stabled at the palace. If you return to Australia she'll be shipped to you and I'll arrange stabling.'

It was the first time Ashraf had spoken of her possibly remaining in Australia. Instead of welcoming it as a sign that he'd finally seen reason Tori felt her stomach drop like a weight through a trapdoor.

She swallowed hard, trying to understand her reaction. Surely that wasn't disappointment she felt?

Increasingly she felt she clung to her determination not

to marry out of obstinacy rather than anything else. But to marry without love—

The sound of her phone interrupted her agitated thoughts. Frowning, she fished it from her bag. She'd kept in contact with her friends via social media while in Za'daq. She wasn't expecting any calls.

'Victoria? Are you there?'

The familiar voice cut through her thoughts like shrapnel through flesh. He hadn't even waited for her to speak and that tone, the way he said her name, told her he wasn't happy.

Her lips flattened as she sat straighter. 'Hello, Dad. I'm afraid I can't talk. I'm—'

But it took more than that to stop Jack Nilsson. 'What are you playing at? Why did I find out from a bunch of diplomats that you're living with the King of Za'daq? I had to read it in the diplomatic post reports. The press there are already speculating about you and it won't be long before the media here gets hold of the story. *Then* what am I supposed to say?'

His voice grew more strident with every word and Tori shut her eyes, cringing at his tone despite the years she'd spent telling herself she wasn't responsible for his bad temper. She leaned back into the corner of the wide seat. She knew how her father's voice carried, especially when he was annoyed.

She shot a sideways glance to Ashraf and found him regarding her steadily. No polite fiction that he couldn't hear her every word. For a second she thought of simply hanging up—but her father would ring back, more incensed than ever.

'I told you Oliver and I were coming here.'

'But not to the bloody *palace*! You didn't even mention you knew the King, or that you were in a relationship. Are you *trying* to make me look like a laughing-stock?'

'Hardly.' The word was snapped out and actually succeeded in stopping the acid flow. 'I wasn't thinking about you when I agreed to come here.' She had been thinking of Oliver.

'You should have thought of me! You know there's an election looming. If I'd known you had such *personal* connections there, we could have pressed for exclusive rights in that Za'daqi mining exploration project…'

The rest of his words faded into a blur as nausea rose. Her father had discovered she was the guest of a stranger on the far side of the world and his first thought was what he'd say to the press. His second was whether he could trade on her intimate relationship for commercial and thereby political gain.

Tori swallowed convulsively, fighting back bile. She should be used to her father's ways but sometimes he outdid himself in callous self-interest. There'd been not a word about how she was, or Oliver. How did he still have the power to hurt her even now?

'Dad, I can't talk privately.'

'Why? Aren't you alone? Is *he* there?'

Tori opened her mouth to say goodbye when a hand reached for the phone.

'If I may…?' Ashraf couched it as a question but there was no mistaking it for anything other than a command.

For a second she hovered on the brink of cutting the connection. Then she shrugged. Fine. The two alpha males could battle it out between them.

But as she listened to Ashraf's smooth voice she realised her father had met his match. Ashraf was gracious but firm, making it clear that their relationship was private, assuring her father that she and Oliver were safe and with every amenity at their disposal.

Her father's tone changed from blustering to friendly, almost eager. Tori rolled her eyes. He thought to use this situation for personal advantage. The idea made her queasy.

* * *

Ashraf ended the call and handed her the phone. 'He's concerned about you.'

'*Concerned* about me?' She shook her head, her expression disbelieving. 'He's never been concerned about me—except to make sure I don't embarrass him publicly.'

Ashraf inclined his head. Tori's words confirmed his impression of the man.

'You don't like him?'

Nor did Ashraf. Her blustering father had turned slyly obsequious, talking about building stronger links between their countries. His concern for Tori and Oliver had been surface-deep.

'He's hard to like.'

'Go on.' He'd been curious about her relationship with her father, but hadn't pressed for details since he and Tori had other priorities. Maybe knowing more about it might help him understand her better.

'I'd rather not.'

Ashraf considered her steadily. 'I prefer to be prepared. He mentioned negotiating a marriage settlement.'

She goggled at him. 'He *didn't*? That's outrageous! I never mentioned marriage to him and nor did you.'

Ashraf shrugged. 'Nevertheless... I have a feeling he'll be calling my office again soon.' Not that he anticipated any difficulty in dealing with one whose motives were so transparent.

Tori sank back, rubbing her forehead, the picture of distress. 'I'm sorry.' She shook her head. 'I never—'

He reached out, capturing her hand, relishing its fit against his as he closed his fingers round hers. 'You've nothing to be sorry about, Tori.'

She met his eyes and sighed. She looked so upset Ashraf almost told her it didn't matter, that they didn't need to discuss this, but instinct told him it was important.

He waited patiently as the car drove towards the palace.

'He's completely self-focused,' she said at last. 'He married my mother for money and her family's political leverage. He wasn't interested in us, except to trot us out as the perfect family when it was time to impress the voters or the VIPs.'

Ashraf heard the hurt she tried to hide and vowed that Jack Nilsson would learn to respect his daughter.

'Fortunately my mother was lovely. We were close.'

Presumably it was from her mother that Tori got her sweet, honest character.

'Your father…he hurt you?'

'Not physically.' She paused. 'Really, I was lucky. He wasn't around much. He was away when parliament sat and the rest of the time he had other priorities.'

As if his family wasn't a priority. Ashraf's teeth clenched. He hated the idea of Tori with an uncaring parent. Yet surely that should make her more willing to create a real family for Oliver?

'Everything I did was judged on how it would look. I wanted to play soccer but he thought it more ladylike if I learned piano.' She shook her head. 'As a kid I couldn't get dirty or be seen in public with a hair out of place. It was extreme and unnecessary. I knew other politicians' kids who didn't live like that, but he saw me as an extension of himself. Everything was about appearance, not about being a real family. Our only value was as props to make him look good.'

Tori grimaced.

'I think eventually it destroyed my mother. She stayed with him because of me. She thought any family was better than none. But I *know* we'd have been better just the two of us, without him.'

Now Ashraf began to understand. Did Tori see parallels between his proposal that they marry to create a family for Oliver and her mother sticking at a bad marriage for her child's sake? Worse, did she compare his motivations with her father's?

The idea revolted him.

'And even now he tries to manage your life?'

Tori laughed, the sound sharp. 'Hardly! I rebelled when my mother died and I went to university. He wanted me to study law and follow in his footsteps.'

'But you chose geology.' He smiled. 'An act of rebellion *and* a chance to get your clothes dirty?'

Her chuckle warmed him, expelling the chill he'd felt since they'd begun this conversation.

'You could be right. It also gave me a career that would take me far away from him.'

'When you found yourself pregnant you didn't seek his assistance?'

He found it perplexing that she'd moved to the opposite side of Australia from her father. Without family support things must have been tough.

Her hand twitched in his, as if she'd withdraw it. Ashraf placed his other hand on hers, holding it steady. 'What is it?'

Her gaze met his then slid away. 'I told him what had happened and he told me to abort the baby. He said there was nothing to be gained from having it and that it would make it hard for me to secure the right sort of husband.'

Ashraf's hands tightened around hers. His throat choked closed on a curse. He drew a slow breath, searching for calm. 'Maybe he thought a permanent reminder of what you'd been through—'

'Don't try to excuse him!' Tori's voice rose to a keening note. 'He wasn't interested in me or how I was doing. He didn't even want me to see a counsellor in case my story leaked to the press.' She shook her head. 'He said my behaviour was *sordid*. He washed his hands of me and he has no interest in Oliver.'

Indignation exploded through Ashraf. Tori had been kidnapped and traumatised and the best her father had been able to do was tell her to abort the baby. He knew by her expression that her father had said far more too. Had he blamed Tori for what happened?

For her sake Ashraf had to stifle his incandescent fury. With difficulty he sat, outwardly calm. Yet he imagined getting his hands on the man who'd dared talk of marriage settlements and closer relations when he hadn't the common decency to care for his own flesh and blood.

'In that case you're better off without him. While you're in Za'daq I can make sure you never have to deal with him again.' It was little enough, but he'd take pleasure in doing it for her.

She nodded. 'Thank you.'

It was a good thing for Jack Nilsson that he was on the other side of the globe. Ashraf wasn't a violent man but he'd enjoy making an exception in this case.

No wonder Tori was wary of a pragmatic marriage. He'd mentioned the importance of public perception in Za'daq and maybe she assumed his motives were like her father's. The idea sickened him.

He stroked his fingers down her hot cheek, then lifted her chin so she had no choice but to meet his eyes.

'I give you my word, Tori. I'm not like your father.'

'I know that.'

But her smile was crooked. It cracked his heart to see her look that way. He was used to her being defiant, strong and independent. He hated it that perhaps some of the pain he read on her face was because of *him*.

'I make you a promise, Tori.' He placed one hand over his heart, his expression grave. 'If we marry I will be devoted to you and our children. Always. To be Sheikh is a privilege and an honour, but I know, I *understand* that family is more important than power and prestige.'

How could he not know? He'd grown up unloved and unregarded except by his brother. Ashraf would have given anything to have had an atom of love or even liking from his father. Or a genuine memory of a mother's tenderness.

'My family will be the centre of my life. You have my word on it.'

CHAPTER TWELVE

FOUR DAYS LATER Ashraf's words still echoed in Tori's ears. She recalled each nuance, the deep cadence of his voice, the searing look in those impossibly dark eyes, the feel of his hands, hard and warm but so gentle, clasping hers.

He'd made her feel cared for.

Special.

Tori bit her lip. She'd never been special to anyone except her mother. It was a strange feeling, both wonderful and nerve-racking.

If she believed him.

That wasn't fair. She *did* believe Ashraf. He meant every word. Tori had no doubt his intentions were good. But would good intentions be enough when his heart wasn't engaged? For, despite the shivery excitement his words, his look, his intensity had conjured in her, it was impossible to believe that after spending just a few short weeks together the King of Za'daq had fallen in love with her.

And without love how could she commit to marriage? She knew what a lack of love did to a family.

Yet Ashraf wasn't her father. He'd told her that but she'd known it from the first. Ashraf was—

'What's taking you so long, Tori? Do you need help with the zip?'

Azia's voice came from the bedroom, jerking Tori into the present. She blinked and took in the unfamiliar image in the mirror. It had been so long since she'd dressed up she barely recognised herself. And she'd never looked as she did in this dress.

'Just coming,' she called, smoothing her palms down the

black velvet. It was reassuringly soft…like Ashraf's voice when they made love.

The thought sent another flurry of nerves jittering through her. Instead of making life easier, abstinence from sex had left her a wreck. The wanting hadn't stopped. It grew stronger daily. Especially since she knew Ashraf slept in the room neighbouring her own bedroom, connected to hers by a single closed door.

She caught her wide eyes in the mirror and dragged in air. This wouldn't do. She couldn't think about that if she was going to get through tonight's reception.

Smartly she stepped across the tiled floor and opened the door to the bedroom, sweeping in, her long skirts flaring. Azia waited, looking fabulous in the shimmery lime-green that complemented her sable hair and dark eyes.

'Ah…' Azia drew the syllable out, gesturing for Tori to turn. Obediently she did. When she faced her friend again, Azia nodded. 'Perfect. You'll stun them all.'

'That's what I'm afraid of.' Tori grimaced. 'You're sure it's not too much?'

'Too much?' Azia laughed. 'You're the guest of one of the richest men on the planet. How much is too much?'

'Well, the glitter, for a start. Though I love the silver embroidery. It's exquisite.'

Azia nodded. 'It's some of the best work I've seen, especially given how little time they had to make it.'

The dress had been made by a friend of Azia's, a designer just starting her own business with a couple of seamstresses.

'I wouldn't change a thing.'

'It's not too revealing?'

Tori had wondered about that, but left the detail to the designer, who'd been so excited and grateful to make a gown for a formal court event. Tori had told herself a local designer would know what was appropriate in Za'daq. But the narrow silver straps over her shoulders left a lot of bare flesh.

'Does it *feel* revealing?'

Tori shook her head. It felt wonderful. If she weren't so nervous she'd feel like Cinderella heading for the ball. She'd never possessed a dress so glamorous, or one that made her feel beautiful.

'Of course it doesn't.' Azia's tone was firm. 'The neckline's not too low and though the dress is contoured to your body it's not tight. You look sophisticated and elegant. I can't wait to see the look on Ashraf's face.'

The thought of him washed heat across Tori's cheeks but Azia, bless her, pretended not to notice.

'I'm glad you chose black instead of the deep red. It's perfect with your colouring. Besides,' she added with a twinkle, 'you can wear red for the next one. Or maybe that gorgeous kingfisher-blue we saw.'

Tori smiled automatically but her heart wasn't in it. Would there *be* a next time? She remembered Ashraf talking about having her horse shipped to Australia. And he hadn't pressed her again to accept marriage.

Maybe his offer for her to stay in Za'daq was no longer on the table, with or without marriage. She couldn't expect it to be open-ended. There must be limits to Ashraf's patience.

Yet returning to Australia didn't appeal. Was she getting used to a life of royal luxury? Of ease and comfort?

More likely she was growing used to basking in Ashraf's attention. The more time they spent together, the harder it was to imagine leaving. Even if it was for her own good. Ashraf was more, so much more even than she'd imagined.

A knock sounded on the door and before she could answer Azia was there, curtseying low.

'Your Majesty.'

Ashraf stood framed in the door, looking debonair and so handsome that Tori felt her insides roll over. She'd expected him to wear traditional robes tonight but instead he wore a dinner jacket, superbly cut to his rangy, powerful

frame. The crisp white shirt accentuated the rich bronze of
his throat and his hair shone black as jet.

'Majesty? Why so formal in private, Azia?' He took the
other woman's hand and pulled her upright.

Azia dimpled up at him but her eyes were serious. 'Just
practising my curtsey for tonight. I'm told I still haven't
got it right.'

Ashraf frowned and kept hold of her hand. 'I can imagine who told you that. Just ignore them. I'd rather have your
genuine smile than perfect court etiquette.' He paused. 'Just
as I'd rather have your herbed lamb with lemons and pilaf
than any ten-course royal feast.'

Azia blushed. 'Then you must come to dinner again soon.
I'll talk to Bram about setting a date.' She darted a look
at Tori. 'I'd better go. He'll wonder where I am. See you
there, Tori.'

Then she was gone, surprising Tori, who'd expected to
accompany her to the reception.

The door closed and Ashraf faced her. There it was again.
The throb of sensation as if all the oxygen had rushed out
of the room while heat pooled low in her body. She should
be used to it. Instead of familiarity lessening the impact of
Ashraf's presence, it only heightened her response.

'Victoria.'

His voice was a rough purr, drawing out the syllables of
her name into something exotically beautiful.

'You look magnificent.'

She felt her shoulders push back, her lips curve at the
extravagant compliment. 'Thank you. So do you. Though
I expected to see you in traditional robes.'

He paced towards her. It felt as if the room shrank till
there was nothing beyond Ashraf.

'It's good to mix things up. A change from tradition and
court formality can be useful occasionally.'

Tori read the lines still bracketing his mouth. 'Is this
something to do with Azia? With the people who don't

think she and Bram are good enough to be here?' She'd finally prised that out of her friend and still reeled from what she'd learned.

'Some of the older courtiers look askance at anyone different, or any change. But they'll learn.'

The determined set to Ashraf's jaw told its own story. Tori knew Ashraf would make that change happen. Azia had explained how Ashraf and Bram had become friends—one a prince, the other literally a pauper.

Bram's mother had been a servant and his father a foreigner who'd left her pregnant, unmarried and struggling to feed herself, much less a baby. She'd been shunned and Bram's blue eyes had been a constant reminder of her shame. Doing his military service with Bram, Ashraf had saved him from a vicious whipping by some men who had objected to serving with a clever upstart from the gutter. Bram still bore scars from the attack, but he and Ashraf had been stalwart friends since.

The tale had left Tori seething with outrage. And warmed by Ashraf's actions and the men's friendship.

She blinked now as Ashraf moved into her personal space, pulling something from his pocket. A small leather box.

Tori's heart leapt. Surely he wasn't—?

'For you to wear tonight.'

Once more that low voice curled through her, like smoke caressing her senses. She breathed deep, registering Ashraf's warm cinnamon scent, and knew that soon she'd be begging for more from him. Days of companionship and those searing, unsettling looks had done nothing to satisfy her craving.

Slowly she opened the box and found a pair of stunning earrings. 'Are they…?' She peered more closely.

'Diamonds and obsidian.'

The diamonds were large and exquisitely cut, and be-

neath them the long teardrops of pure black obsidian were
flawless.

'I've never seen anything like them.' She might be a geologist, but she usually saw stones in their raw state. She
estimated that these were unique and incredibly expensive.
Yet it wasn't their monetary value that mattered. It was
Ashraf's expression as he offered them.

Her heart stilled. Could it be…?

'You like them?'

Ashraf cringed inwardly at the neediness of that question. Like a kid seeking validation from an adult, or a love-
sick youngster mooning over a girl he could never have.

Yet he knew Tori would eventually come to him. He'd
seen hints that she'd begun to see the sense of his arguments.
Plus there were clear signs of her sexual frustration. Her
hungry stare as he entered the room had been like an incen-
diary flare. He still felt the sparks in his blood.

'They're stunning. But I can't—'

'Of course you can. And it would please me if you wore
them.' He paused, watching her waver. 'Azia will be disappointed if you don't. She made a point of telling Bram what
colour you were wearing, knowing he'd tell me.'

Tori's mouth rucked up ruefully. She liked Azia, which
pleased him. Azia and Bram had kept him sane these last
couple of years since he'd taken the throne. True friendship
was in scarce supply in the royal court.

'In that case, thank you.'

Colour streaked her cheekbones. Ashraf knew she wasn't
used to accepting gifts. He liked that. Liked knowing she'd
never been beholden to other men. She'd been shocked when
he had procured that horse for her, protesting at length
though it had been clear she adored the mare. His Tori was
very independent but he enjoyed giving her presents.

He watched her replace her plain silver studs with the
new earrings. As she turned the light caught the gems,

drawing attention to the pale pearl lustre of her skin and her slender throat.

Ashraf's pulse quickened.

His. His magnificent Victoria.

She *would* be his—and soon.

Not just because she was the mother of his son. But because he wanted her. He'd never want any other woman but her.

It should have been a shocking revelation. Instead the knowledge was like the final piece of a puzzle slotting into place. Ashraf felt a buzz of excitement and at the same time the peace of acceptance.

His gaze fell past pale skin down to a dress that glittered like the fathomless night sky in the desert, awash with stars. Traceries of delicate silver thread gave way to pure black where the dress skimmed her gorgeous body.

Ashraf swallowed hard. His baser instincts urged him to forget the people already gathered in the royal audience chamber. He'd rather spend the evening here with Tori.

He read her eyes, which had turned misty with awareness. It would take little to persuade her into bed…

But he had a duty to his people. A duty to Tori. To show her what her world would be like in Za'daq. That included events like tonight—not as much fun as visiting a souk or a village. She had to know the worst as well as the best. He just hoped, with a nervousness he hadn't felt in years, that the reality of court life didn't terrify her.

As expected his arrival, with Tori on his arm, caused a ripple. Cronies of his father raised eyebrows and matrons who'd shoved their unmarried daughters in his direction since he'd ascended to the throne barely hid their chagrin.

Ashraf surveyed them undaunted from his superior height. Tori was his personal guest. When she married him people would have to accept his choice.

None of them were courageous enough to say what was

on their minds. That the woman at his side wasn't a Za'daqi aristocrat. That he'd actually *touched* her in public—even if it was just a guiding hand on her elbow. That he'd broken custom by wearing western clothes.

They'd put up with his changes to government policy because even the most hidebound had begun to see the benefits. But alterations to court tradition, and by extension to their own sense of superiority, would be harshly judged by some. There had already been dismay because he'd been seen holding Tori's hand on a rural visit.

However, he sensed change wouldn't be as difficult as it had been when he'd inherited the throne. His nation was altering. Ashraf had enjoyed the evening more than usual. There was a wider mix of social groups and foreigners attending. Plus the atmosphere became more relaxed after the crowd had gone outside to watch feats of horsemanship, archery and acrobatics. He'd seen Tori's delight and viewed it all through new eyes, enjoying her enthusiasm.

Now, late in the reception, he was enjoying a joke with an army officer who'd been a friend in the old days. When he'd believed he'd found his future in the military. Before his father had cut short his career, outraged at the thought of the despised cuckoo in the nest excelling at something.

Ashraf saw Tori, stunning in silver and black, eyes bright as she laughed with Azia, another woman and a man he recognised as a foreign diplomat. Tori was gesturing towards Ashraf, as if pointing him out.

At that moment an older couple broke in on the group. The irascible Minister for the Interior and his haughty wife. They spoke and Azia flushed furiously. Tori's chin lifted. The two foreigners with them looked startled.

Ashraf started forward but a voice in his ear said, 'No. Wait.'

It was Bram.

'Is there a problem?' his army friend asked, craning to look past the crowd.

'Only a little one,' said Bram. 'Not worth worrying about. Besides, I think… Yes, it's taken care of now.'

He was right. Whatever poison the older couple had tried to spread clearly hadn't worked. Tori was speaking now and his nemesis looked discomfited, his wife embarrassed. Then Tori and the foreign woman began chatting again. Colour flushed Tori's cheeks but otherwise she looked serene.

'Nevertheless, I'll make sure,' Ashraf murmured. 'If you'll excuse me?'

He reached the group and all eyes turned to him. The Minister opened his mouth to speak but Tori was faster.

'Your Majesty.'

Tori said it as easily as if she called him by his title daily. Her eyes glittered bright as diamond chips, and the slight flare of her nostrils hinted at displeasure, but otherwise her expression was calm, her smile welcoming.

'I don't believe you've met Ms Alison Drake, the new American ambassador.' She turned to the slim brunette, 'Alison, I'm pleased to introduce you to His Majesty Sheikh Ashraf ibn Kahul al Rashid of Za'daq.'

Not by a flicker did Ashraf betray surprise at her remembering his full name, or at her deft handling of the introduction. Hadn't she spent her youth at her father's side, mingling at official functions?

'Ms Drake, it's a delight to meet you.' He shook her hand, preventing her from curtseying. 'I understood your flight had been delayed? I expected you tomorrow.'

'The pleasure is mine, Your Majesty. Apologies for my very late arrival. I managed to get an alternative flight and was advised…' she glanced at her companion from the embassy '…that it would be okay to attend—though I haven't yet formally presented my credentials.'

The Minister for the Interior cleared his throat but Ashraf silenced him with a look. He had no role in diplomatic matters and he'd tried to stir up trouble for Tori and Azia. Ashraf wouldn't tolerate that.

'Of course. It's a pleasure to welcome you. We'll leave the formalities till tomorrow. In the meantime, I hope you're enjoying yourself?'

'Oh, yes. I've had such a wonderfully warm welcome to your country.'

He didn't miss the way her eyes flickered towards the older man. Or how Azia bit her lip and focused on adjusting her shawl. His curiosity deepened.

'Excellent. Let me introduce you to some more people.' He looked across the crowd to Bram, who was already ushering forward a number of dignitaries to meet the ambassador.

Ashraf turned to the couple standing stiffly to one side. 'Minister, your wife looks very tired.' He offered her a charming smile and watched her swallow nervously. 'You have my permission to leave. We'll talk tomorrow.'

It was hours before Ashraf could be alone with Tori.

The guests had been encouraged to leave and the staff had shut the doors, leaving them the sole possessors of the audience chamber. They stood before the large arched windows looking over a city washed in the national colours of crimson and gold from a final flourish of fireworks.

But Ashraf's eyes were on Tori, not the view. She'd never looked more beautiful. Nor had the connection between them, invisible as spun glass but strong as the desert sun, been more palpable. She'd spent the last part of the evening at his side and it had felt right.

It was where she belonged.

Tonight, for the first time in a week, he dared to hope she felt the same. The way she smiled at him, the sense of understanding, the fizz in his blood when their eyes met, had to mean something.

Any fear he'd felt that she might be scared off by the

pomp of a royal event had been short-lived. She'd shone.
She was charming and interested in people. Those qualities had endeared her to his people on their excursions.
Plus those years of supporting her father had stood her in
good stead.

'You were magnificent tonight.'

He caught and held her hands. Their eyes met and he felt
the impact square in the centre of his chest.

She shook her head, her mouth curving up. 'That was
you, Your Majesty. Magnificent.'

He tugged her closer, almost close enough to kiss. But
there was one matter to clear up first.

'What was that scene with the Minister for the Interior?'

Tori's eyebrows pinched. 'You saw that? I didn't think
anyone had noticed.'

'That he'd been insulting?' Again, Ashraf felt fury burn.
'I don't think anyone else did—only me and Bram.'

Both had been watching their womenfolk. Yet only Bram
had been sure that the women could handle the problem.
Ashraf had underestimated Tori.

'You handled him well. Now, tell me.'

She sighed. 'He had no idea who Alison was. He saw us
laughing and assumed she was simply a friend of mine or
Azia's and therefore unimportant.'

Ashraf had learned tonight that the ambassador had once
been posted to Australia. She was an old friend of Tori's
mother.

Tori lifted her shoulders. 'He made disparaging remarks
about court standards slipping since shopkeepers and…and
others had been invited to such events. He suggested we
leave as we must feel out of place.'

Ashraf understood the reference to shopkeepers. Azia's
parents ran a shop in the main souk. But 'others'…

'Others?' He was sure the colour washing Tori's face
had nothing to do with the fireworks. His jaw clenched.
'Tell me.'

'I've forgotten his exact words.'

Tori wasn't a good liar, but before he could call her on it she continued.

'He lost his air of superiority when I stared him down, mentioning how kind and welcoming most Za'daqis were to guests.'

Ashraf didn't miss the emphasis on *most*.

'I introduced him to the new ambassador and Alison mentioned that her parents had run a grocery store back in the States.'

Despite his anger, Ashraf laughed. Hospitality was something Za'daqis prided themselves on. The Minister would have hated being called out on his rudeness. 'I like your friend Alison more and more. Nevertheless, I want to know—'

Tori put her finger to his mouth, stopping his words. Touching him felt so good. How had she kept her distance this last week?

'I'd rather forget him. He's rude and self-opinionated— but you know that.' She felt Ashraf's surprisingly soft lips against her flesh and longing shivered through her. And something more profound. 'Don't let him spoil what's been a wonderful night.'

'Wonderful?'

Eyes gleaming, Ashraf captured her wrist and kissed her palm, turning that shiver into a pounding torrent of awareness.

Tori gulped, her throat closing as she looked into that strong, dear face.

She prided herself on her honesty and her willingness to face facts, no matter how unpalatable. But tonight she realised she'd hidden from the truth.

Far-fetched as it seemed, if she counted on the calendar the time they'd actually spent together, Tori was in love with Ashraf al Rashid.

In love. Not just in lust. Not just admiring of his determination to do right by Oliver and his people or grateful for his understanding of her doubts.

In love.

Totally.

When he'd given her these fabulous earrings and she'd caught his tender look the truth had struck. She'd wondered if his feelings were more deeply engaged than she'd suspected. Had she resisted his proposal so adamantly because she cared too much for him? Because she didn't want to commit herself till she knew he felt the same way?

The thought of loving Ashraf but never having his love terrified her. It was a roiling wave in her belly whenever she dwelled too long on doubt. But tonight, as she watched him with his people and basked in his attention, she couldn't hide from her feelings any longer.

If her abduction in the desert had taught her one thing it was to live for the moment. You never knew what was around the corner. Whether you'd have another chance to do what really mattered.

What really mattered was Oliver and Ashraf.

'Victoria? You're miles away.'

Ashraf curled an arm around her waist, securing her against him, and everything inside her rejoiced. *This* was where she wanted to be.

She licked her bottom lip and saw his eyes zero in on the movement. Heat drenched her. But as well as physical need she recognised now the deeper sense of contentment that swelled her heart.

Life in Za'daq would have challenges. Life with Ashraf would be a learning experience. But love couldn't be denied. She'd made up her mind.

'I've come to a decision.'

Ashraf's grip tightened, his brows furrowing. 'Don't let one bigoted man—'

'Shh…' She reached up on tiptoe and silenced him, this time with her lips. How she'd longed for his kiss!

He gathered her in with both arms and would have deepened the kiss but Tori leaned back just enough to speak. She felt secure in his embrace—not because she needed protection or looking after but because Ashraf made her feel as no other man had. Because she loved him.

'If the offer is still open, I'll marry you.'

For a moment she thought he hadn't heard. Or that she hadn't said it aloud, just thought the words. He looked down at her, his expression unreadable.

Then, to her amazement, he dropped to his knee. Her hands were in his and he kissed first one and then the other. Not in passion but with a deliberate reverence and a formal courtesy that belonged in a world of warrior knights and beautiful maidens.

'You have my word, Victoria, that you won't regret this.' His voice made it a solemn vow. 'I will do all in my power to make you happy. To support you, honour you and care for you. And our family.'

His words sent a flurry of emotion through her.

Care. That was good. More than good when combined with the rest of his promise.

Tori shut down the querulous inner voice that said care wasn't love. That the chances of Ashraf ever loving her were slim, given how he'd grown up unloved. The fact that he loved Oliver was enough for now. It had to be. And maybe, just maybe, over time—

Her thoughts stopped as Ashraf surged to his feet. That sombre expression had vanished, replaced by a smile so brilliant it undid something inside her.

'Thank you, Tori.'

Then, before she realised what he was about, Ashraf swooped low, scooping her up in his arms, swirling her around and striding across the room.

She laughed. 'Where are we going?'

As if she didn't have a fair idea.

'To bed. To show you how good our marriage will be.'

Because he was afraid she'd change her mind? No. She'd decided. She wouldn't expect the impossible. Tori would accept what was offered and make the most of it.

She didn't believe in fairy tales.

CHAPTER THIRTEEN

ASHRAF SEETHED AS he marched into his office. There'd been satisfaction in sacking the Minister for the Interior, but not enough.

'Meeting didn't go well?' Bram looked up from his desk.

'It went as expected. We now have an opening in the Ministry.' And an offended ex-minister, shocked that his King had actually dismissed him. The old goat had thought himself untouchable.

'Good. The Council will run better without him.'

Ashraf shoved his hands in his pockets. 'I expected you to counsel patience.' That had run out last night.

Bram shrugged. 'You gave him chance after chance, compromising to bring the old guard along with you and allow him some pride. But he's dead wood, holding the government back.'

Ashraf lifted his eyebrows. Bram really was speaking his mind today. 'What's happened?' He knew his friend. Something had prompted his militant attitude.

Bram nodded to his computer. 'The press reports are worse than we first thought. Somehow they've got a photo of Tori and Oliver, taken in Australia. Speculation is rife that he's your son.'

Ashraf ploughed his fingers through his hair. It had been a gamble, waiting to legitimise Oliver. Ashraf had wanted to announce a wedding simultaneously, but he'd respected Tori's need for time.

'The cat's out of the bag, then.' He took a deep breath. 'Arrange a press release. I'll—'

'That's not all.' Bram looked grim. 'I've received a pe-tition from a small group of Council members. They've heard about Oliver and know that you've moved out of your apartments to be with him and Tori. They insist you give them up or abdicate.'

Ashraf snorted. 'As if they have the power to *insist*! Let me guess.' He named three cronies of the sacked Minister and Bram nodded. 'They seem to forget it's only by *my* pleasure that they have a role in government.'

'They threatened to approach Karim and ask him to assume the throne.'

Ashraf gritted his teeth. The last thing Karim wanted or needed was a delegation of old fogeys bothering him. 'Karim rejected the throne. He can't simply change his mind. Even if it were possible, he'd never agree.'

Bram lifted one eyebrow but Ashraf said no more. Only he and his brother knew the reason for his action. A medical test had revealed that Karim, not Ashraf, was the cuckoo in the nest, the son of another man.

Privately Ashraf thought that had precipitated his ailing father's death. The revelation that the son he'd groomed as heir wasn't his while the despised younger child was his true son.

Karim had stayed after the funeral only long enough to see Ashraf crowned and then left Za'daq. He had no plans to return.

'Is that all?'

'One of the latest press reports has a particularly nasty edge. It makes a great deal of Tori's work in isolated areas, often as the only female on a team. It draws conclusions about her morals and insinuates…'

Bile rose in Ashraf's throat. 'I can imagine. Where, precisely, was this from?'

Bram mentioned a media outlet owned by a friend of the sacked Minister. Ashraf nodded. 'Show me, and call the legal office. They can check the libel laws.'

He'd end this *now*, before it came to Tori's ears.

But as the afternoon wore on Ashraf's fiery indignation was overtaken by something far harder to bear. Especially when the lawyers dithered over whether the law had actually been broken. Ironically, if Tori were Za'daqi, or if she'd already married him, the reports could have been taken down and the outlet closed. As a foreigner, her situation was less clear.

Ashraf had grown up being vilified by his father. He was used to people assuming the worst about him. But to see Tori belittled and be unable to stop it tore at something vital within him.

He stalked the offices, trying to find a solution but finding none. He either abided by the laws he'd introduced, allowing more freedom for the press, or he gave up all pretension of being anything other than an autocratic ruler, thus destroying the hard work he'd put into turning Za'daq into a more democratic country.

He was caught by his own insistence on reform, and his inability to sweep the ugly innuendos away and protect his woman ate at him. He'd expected scandal. But seeing the negative focus shift to Tori, with such snide inferences, sickened him.

His wonderful woman had been through so much. Now, generously, she'd finally agreed to marry him for their son's sake. She'd signed on for a marriage without love, though it wasn't what she wanted. She'd agreed to learn a new way of life—not only in a country foreign to her, but as a royal, under constant scrutiny. He'd promised she wouldn't regret her decision.

And now... How could he ask this of her?

The answer was simple and terrible.

He couldn't.

Tori was on the floor with Oliver, watching his eyes grow round with excitement as, wobbling, he managed to stay sitting up before losing his balance and falling onto the cushion she'd put behind him.

Smiling at his achievement, and his delight, she was taken by surprise when Ashraf appeared.

'You're early.'

Pleasure filled her. All day she'd wondered if she'd done the sensible thing, agreeing to marry Ashraf. In the end she'd given up wondering if it was sensible, contenting herself with the fact that it was her only option if she wanted to be with the man she loved.

The glow inside her as she looked up at him told her she'd done right. Better to love than to turn her back on the chance of happiness.

'Gah-gah-gah.' Oliver, on his back, waved his arms and legs as he saw his father.

'Hello, little beetle.' Ashraf bent and scooped him up, lifting him high till Oliver crowed with excitement.

As ever, the sight of them together tugged at the sentimental cord that ran through her middle. It was stronger today, after she'd spent all night making glorious love to Ashraf.

Tori told herself that was why she felt emotional. Lack of sleep. *And finally admitting you're wildly in love with this man.*

'We need to talk.'

Ashraf looked down at her and that warm, squishy feeling solidified into a cold lump of concern. Something was wrong. She read it in the lines bracketing his mouth.

'Of course. I'll ring for the nanny.' Tori scrambled to her feet.

'No need. I've called her. Ah…' He turned at a knock on the door. 'Here she is.'

He took time to buss Oliver's cheek and let his son grab his fingers, all the while murmuring to him in his own language, before handing him to the nanny.

Finally they were alone. But Ashraf didn't pull Tori close. He didn't even take her hand, though when she'd last seen him he'd been reluctant to leave her bed. He'd lingered, stroking her hair, kissing her and murmuring endearments in a voice of rough suede that had made her feel maybe she was wrong. Maybe he might learn to love her one day.

Now, Ashraf didn't even look at her. He seemed fixated on the view from the window. His brow was pleated and his mouth was set so grimly that the back of her neck prickled in anticipation of bad news. Her stomach churned.

'What's wrong?' She came up beside him, put her hand on his arm then dropped it as he instantly stiffened. 'Ashraf?'

Tori had a really bad feeling now. During everything they'd been through never once had Ashraf shied away from her touch. Shock slammed her. It did no good telling herself that it wasn't revulsion she read in his grimace, even if the idea seemed crazy.

He turned but didn't reach for her. Instead he shoved his hands deep in his pockets, broad shoulders hunching. Tori felt his rejection like a punch to the solar plexus that sucked out her breath. What had happened to the tactile man who couldn't get enough of her?

'I'm sorry, Tori. I was distracted. Let's sit, shall we?'

She shook her head and planted her soles more firmly on the silk carpet. 'I'm fine here.' If it was bad news she'd rather have it standing up. 'Is it my father?'

'No, no. Nothing like that. There's no news from Australia.'

Tori's swift breath of relief surprised her. She didn't *like* her father but it seemed she did care for him at some level.

'So it's news from Za'daq?'

She looked into fathomless eyes and wished she knew what Ashraf was thinking.

Just when she thought he wasn't going to speak he took her hand, enfolding it in long fingers. Warmth trickled from his touch but dissipated with his words.

'I'll always treasure your generosity in agreeing to marry me, Victoria.'

For the first time the sound of Ashraf saying her full name sent a cold shiver through her—nothing like the shimmer of lush warmth it usually generated.

'But I'm freeing you from your promise.'

Tori felt his encircling hand tighten as she stumbled back, away from him, till finally she broke his hold.

'You don't want to marry me?'

In another time, another place, she'd have winced at the sound of her ragged voice. But it matched the way she felt. Off balance, as if someone had ripped that beautiful hand-woven rug from beneath her feet.

But the only ripping here was her heart. Her sad, foolish heart, which had opened itself up to Ashraf's kindness, strength and caring.

'I'm sorry.' He held her gaze, his own unwavering. 'It's for the best. I was selfish to ask you to give up your life and home and live in Za'daq. I see that now.'

Tori wanted to protest that living with him in Za'daq was what she craved, but he continued.

'As you wisely pointed out, Oliver will still have a family even if we live apart.'

Live apart.

Tori pressed her hand to the place below her ribs that felt hollow, as if an unseen hand had scraped out her insides. He didn't even want her in his country!

Out of the miasma of shock and hurt, indignation rose. 'That's not good enough.'

'Sorry?'

He'd obviously expected her simply to accept his decree. He wasn't the enlightened man she'd thought. All those generations of absolute rulers had left their mark. She read surprise in the lift of his eyebrows and determination in those haughty features.

'If you're going to jilt a woman you need to do better.'

For a second—a millisecond—she saw something pass across that set face. Then it was gone. If anything he stood straighter, imposing and rigid, like the soldier she'd discovered he'd once been. Or an autocrat looking down on a lesser being.

Yet even in her distress Tori couldn't believe that of Ashraf.

'Of course. I apologise. Again.'

He paused, and if she hadn't known better Tori would have said he was the one struggling for breath, not her.

'I should have started by saying I'm sorry for changing my mind.'

Changing his mind? Tori stared, incredulous. He wanted her to believe he'd simply *changed his mind*?

She shook her head, wrapping her arms around her middle to contain the empty feeling which threatened to spread and engulf her whole.

'Still not good enough, Ashraf. I need to know why.' A thought pierced her whirling brain. 'Is it someone else? Have you found a better bride?'

Someone local who understood Za'daqi ways. Some glamorous princess.

'Of course not!' He actually looked insulted.

'There's no "of course" about it.' Tori's voice grew in strength as anger masked pain. 'This morning, *in my bed*, you were happy with the arrangement. What changed?'

He winced and half turned away. Tori began to wonder if the caring, wonderful man she'd fallen in love with had been an illusion.

'You're right. You deserve to know.' He paused, breathing deep. 'The press, stirred by my opponents, have learned about Oliver. About us. The stories they're printing…' He spread his hands and grimaced. 'They're not to be borne. The filth they're spouting will only continue and I can't allow that. I have to stop it.'

'I see.'

It was clear from Ashraf's expression how important this was to him. Tori recalled his talk of past scandals, how he hadn't been accepted by the political elite, how he'd had to strive to win support for his schemes.

Was his situation so precarious? It seemed so. And so was the crown he wanted to pass to Oliver. Tori wanted to tell him that it didn't matter. That Oliver could make his way in the world without a royal title. But it did matter. This was Ashraf's birthright. He'd worked all his life to prove himself. Since becoming Sheikh he'd worked longer and harder than his predecessors to improve the nation. Tori had had that from Azia, who was forever singing Ashraf's praises.

This was his destiny. His purpose in life.

But that didn't stop her searing anguish as she faced facts. The man she loved was rejecting her because when it came to the crunch he, and his people, believed she wasn't good enough to stand at his side.

CHAPTER FOURTEEN

TORI TURNED AND marched away from the window into the shadows.

Ashraf wanted to follow and haul her close.

He didn't do it. If he touched her his good intentions would collapse and he wouldn't release her.

He swallowed and it felt as if he'd swallowed a desert of sand, his mouth so dry the action tore his throat to shreds.

This was the cost of releasing the one woman he'd ever cared for. *The one woman he could ever love.*

That, above all, gave him the strength to weld his feet to the floor.

He loved Tori. Loved her with such devotion that watching her struggle with his decision felt like the most difficult thing he'd ever done. Harder than facing the threat of death at Qadri's hands.

What would it be like, living the rest of his life without her?

The laceration in his throat became a raw ache that descended to his chest, intensifying to a sharper pain with each breath.

But he had to protect her. In his arrogance he'd assumed they'd face the scandal together. That it would be directed at *him*, with his notorious past, and that Tori would be seen as a victim of his licentious ways. He hadn't bargained on her being represented as some...

He frowned. Was that a sob?

Tori stood with her back to him, facing the courtyard. Her shoulders were straight but her head was bent. As he watched another quiver passed through her.

Seconds later he was behind her, hands lifted but not touching those slim shoulders. 'Tori, are you all right?'

Stupid question. Of course she wasn't. But how could he comfort her?

'Does it matter?'

Her steady voice made him feel, if possible, worse. 'It's my fault. I shouldn't have let this happen.'

'Which? Suggesting marriage or fathering Oliver?' She snorted. 'Don't answer that. Clearly you regret both.'

'No!' His fingers closed on her shoulders and he gritted his teeth, fighting the need to spin her round and into his arms. To hold her properly one last time. 'You can't think that.'

'There are a lot of things you control, Ashraf, but what I think isn't one of them.'

'Parting is for the best.' How he wished there were another way.

'Whose best? Yours? Not Oliver's or mine.' She shrugged from his hold and swung to face him.

Ashraf stared into eyes that glittered with tears she refused to let fall. For the first time he felt himself to be the failure his father had accused him of being.

The one woman in the world he wanted to protect from harm and he'd brought her infamy and scandal. The sight of her, brim-full with pain, knotted his conscience and stole his resolution.

'Don't lie, Ashraf. Just say it. It's too risky for your crown to take on a woman with a bastard son, even if you're his father.'

His breath hissed at the words and her eyes narrowed.

'That's it, isn't it?'

For a second she stood stock-still, eyes wide. He'd seen the victim of an accidental gunshot look exactly the same— that moment of disbelief before he crumpled to the ground. But Tori didn't crumple. She turned and stalked to the bedroom.

'It won't take me long to pack. We'll leave today.'

It was what he wanted. What was best for Tori. Yet Ashraf couldn't let her do it. He was too selfish.

'Wait!'

She kept walking, head up, shoulders back, but she stumbled as if she wasn't watching her step.

His heart twisted. 'Tori.'

'There's nothing to say.'

But there was. So much he barely knew where to start. He inserted himself between her and the bedroom door, frustrating her attempt to shove him aside.

'This isn't about me protecting my position—it's about protecting *you*.'

'You're not protecting me. You're banishing me.'

His heart, the organ he'd so long thought dormant, beat harder at the torment in her voice.

'If you're not here they'll focus on me, like they always have. You won't be a target.'

Silence. Silence that lasted so long he wondered if she were trying to freeze him out. Finally she blinked, like a sleepwalker rousing.

'The stories aren't about you?'

'Partly. But…'

But the most negative ones made it sound as if he'd fallen prey to some avaricious *femme fatale* who went through men like a fish through water.

'They focus on me, then,' she murmured. 'That makes sense. It makes you look bad and you can't afford that.'

Unable to stop himself, Ashraf grabbed her upper arms and pulled her close. 'How many times do I have to say it? I'm used to bad press. It's *you* I want to protect. You shouldn't have to put up with this.'

Her eyes rounded and she stopped trying to pull free. 'Are you serious?'

'Yes, I'm serious!'

He saw her blink and realised he'd raised his voice. It

was something he never did. His father had shouted all the time when he was riled—at him, at servants, at inanimate objects.

Ashraf shuddered. Another sign he was losing control.

'Tell me what they're saying,' she said.

At first he refused, but Tori wore him down. When he'd finished she shook her head sadly and Ashraf knew he was right to send her away. If only he had the courage to do it.

'You'd really banish me so the press won't hound me?'

His chest rose high on a deep breath. 'It's not banishment. It's—'

'Sending me away from the man I love is banishment.' Her soft voice cut across his.

Everything inside Ashraf stilled. Even his pulse slowed, before speeding up to a gallop. He swallowed. This time the sand in his throat had been replaced with a choking knot of tangling emotion.

'You don't love me.'

It was impossible. Even his mother hadn't loved him, choosing instead to run off with her paramour and leave Ashraf to her husband's mercy.

'Why don't I?'

Tori's smile trembled and his heart with it. He shook his head, unwilling to say the words. It was too big a risk. Yet perhaps for the first time in his life he needed to open himself up, though it made him even more vulnerable.

'Because I've never craved anything so much. And life's taught me never to expect such a blessing.'

'You poor, deluded man.'

Her palm covered his cheek and his eyelids drooped as the pent-up tension was expelled from his lungs. One touch, just one, did that.

'I've been in love with you more or less since we met.'

'That's crazy. You didn't know me.'

Yet he greedily hoarded each precious word. His hands firmed around her waist, pulling her closer.

'It was instinctive, and everything I believed about you has turned out to be right.' She frowned. 'Even down to your managing ways. Do you *really* think I'll curl up and die because the gutter press prints lies about me?'

'You shouldn't have to face that.'

Her chin lifted. 'You're right. I shouldn't. And I'm sure you and your lawyers will help me make them stop. But if you think I'm going to be scared away by gossip, think again.' Her mouth tilted at one corner. 'I work in a male-dominated industry. I've faced prejudice and sexual innuendo all my working life. Most of my peers are great, but there are always some who can't cope. I won't put up with it and I certainly won't let it destroy my happiness. Besides, I've learned a thing or two from my father about dealing with the press.'

Ashraf stared, stunned by the pragmatic courage of his beloved. He'd known she was special, yet still she surprised him.

'Ash?'

Her use of the old nickname was even more intimate than the feel of her hand on his flesh.

'You do want me?'

'Of course I do. I never want to let you go.'

He wrapped her tight in his arms. Not kissing her but simply embracing her. Feeling her heart beat against him, her breath a warm caress against his collarbone, her body a perfect fit to his.

Tori's uncertainty made heat prickle at the back of his eyes. His breath shuddered. He had a moment's recollection of feeling this close to tears only once before. He'd been about four and he'd often gone to play in the courtyard that had been his mother's. The garden's fragrance had reminded him of a long-ago comforting presence that he guessed must have been hers. But someone had told his father of his secret visits and he'd arrived to find all the scented roses pulled out. The place was a barren waste.

But Ashraf's palace wasn't barren. He had Tori—his woman, his lover, soon to be his wife. A heroine strong enough to stand beside him through whatever life held. And there was Oliver too.

'You do know,' he murmured, tilting her chin so he could look into her glorious eyes, 'there's no turning back now.' His chest swelled with feelings he'd suppressed too long. 'I love you too much ever to let you go. If you get cold feet before the wedding I'll have the border closed and—'

'What? You'll kidnap me and ride off with me to your secret desert encampment? I like the sound of that.'

Her smile was wide and unshadowed. It seemed his Tori really had moved on from the trauma of their abduction.

Ashraf lowered his head so his mouth hovered above hers. 'I'd planned to honeymoon on my private island off the coast, but if you prefer the desert…'

'I prefer you kiss me and tell me again that you love me.'

He looked down, reading marvellous things in her gentle smile.

This. This was what he craved.

'Your wish,' he said against her lips, 'is my command.'

EPILOGUE

IT WAS A long wedding. Days long. Filled with good wishes, lavish entertainment, music, feasting and enough pomp to convince Tori that she really had married a king.

She returned to the audience chamber after freshening up to find Karim waiting for her, a query in his moss-green eyes. Beyond him the room was filled with guests in their finery, the air buzzing with animated conversation.

Funny to think she'd been wary about meeting Ashraf's brother. Everyone spoke of him in glowing terms and she'd wondered if it was true that he really didn't want Ashraf's crown. Till the brothers had told her their story and Karim had welcomed her into the family with genuine warmth.

His smile had been almost wistful as he'd admitted he'd never seen Ashraf so happy. That neither brother had expected to find true love. Tori's heart had squeezed at his words and she'd hugged him hard, eliciting mock protests from Ashraf and a quaintly clumsy hug from Karim. Clumsy, she suspected, because like Ashraf he wasn't used to emotional displays. It certainly couldn't be from lack of female companionship, for despite Karim being only his half-brother he shared Ashraf's chiselled good-looks and potent appeal.

'How are you holding up?' he asked.

Tori beamed at him. 'I'm doing well. Especially since everyone is so happy for us.'

Contrary to expectations, the ghastly rumours had ceased almost straight away when it turned out that the die-hards who disapproved of Ashraf were completely outnumbered by those who thought him an excellent Sheikh.

As for Oliver being born outside marriage—that didn't seem to be a problem now Ashraf had legitimised him. If anything, many Za'daqis viewed it as proof of their King's masculine potency and thought it natural that Tori had been swept off her feet. She'd discovered a strong romantic streak in his people.

'Ashraf sent me to find you.' Karim offered her his arm and when she curled her hand around it he bent to murmur in her ear. 'Unless you'd rather skip this bit and rest?'

She should be tired but Tori had never felt so energised. 'I wouldn't miss it for anything.'

'You don't even know what it is!'

Karim laughed as he steered her through the throng, his deep chuckle reminding her of Ashraf's. Even after a few days she knew that Karim, like her husband, rarely laughed aloud. Both were so serious, though Ashraf was learning to relax more.

'So tell me.'

They were outside now, on the terrace, looking down at the wide space where she'd previously watched horsemen and archers perform stunning feats of skill and bravery. Now the space was filled with people. More than filled. They spilled down the slope beyond into the public gardens and streets as far as the eye could see.

Tori stumbled to a halt. 'Where have they come from?'

A deep, familiar voice reached her.

'From everywhere—all across the country.'

It was Ashraf, his eyes shining. He looked magnificent in white robes trimmed with gold as he strode up and took her hands.

Tori's insides melted. Her Ashraf. Her husband.

Beside them Karim spoke. 'They're not VIPs, just ordinary people who've made their way here to wish you both well.' He clamped his hand on Ashraf's shoulder, leaning close and lowering his voice. 'You've done well, little brother. They love you.'

Ashraf shrugged, making little of the praise, though Tori saw that it moved him.

He turned to her. 'There's even a delegation from that first village I took you to in the foothills. Where you got that scarf.'

Tori looked down at the deep jewel colours of the scarf she'd teamed with a dress of vibrant teal, embroidered at the hem with silver. Over the last three days it seemed she'd worn every colour of the rainbow, and each time her pleasure in the magnificent wedding clothes was outshone by the appreciation in Ashraf's eyes.

'What are we waiting for? There are a lot of people to greet.'

Ashraf's slow smile made her heart drum faster.

'Thank you, *habibti*. It will mean a lot to them.' He looked at Karim. 'You'll come too, brother?'

Karim shook his head. 'This is your day—yours and Tori's. I'll go and deal with the VIPs.' He turned towards the palace, leaving Ashraf and Tori alone.

As Ashraf led her towards the expectant throng he tucked her close against him. 'I'm afraid this will add extra hours to the wedding celebrations. You'll need to rest when this is over.'

'It's not rest I need. I have other priorities.'

Ashraf stopped and turned to face her. 'Have I told you how very much I love you?'

His deep voice resonated and a ripple ran through the watching crowd.

'Yes.' She knew there were stars in her eyes as she looked up at him. 'But I never tire of hearing it.'

'And you love me.' His declaration was loud and proud. 'I do.'

The crowd cheered, and Ashraf grinned, and Tori knew she'd just embarked on the most remarkable, wonderful adventure of her life.

* * * * *

COMING SOON!

We really hope you enjoyed reading this book. If you're looking for more romance, be sure to head to the shops when new books are available on

Thursday 3rd October

To see which titles are coming soon, please visit
millsandboon.co.uk/nextmonth

MILLS & BOON

Coming next month

A PASSIONATE REUNION IN FIJI
Michelle Smart

'Hiding away?' Livia asked.

'Taking a breather.'

Dark brown eyes studied him, a combination of sympathy and amusement in them. Livia knew well how social situations made him feel.

She caught the barman's attention and ordered herself a bourbon too. 'This is a great party.'

'People are enjoying it?'

'Very much.' She nudged him with her elbow and pointed at one of the sofas. Two of the small children he'd almost tripped over earlier were fast asleep on it. A third, who'd gone a pale green colour, was eating a large scoop of ice cream, utter determination etched on her face. 'Someone needs to get that girl a sick bag.'

He laughed and was immediately thrown back to his sister's wedding again.

He'd approached Livia at the bar. She'd said something inane that had made him laugh. He wished he could remember what it was but it had slipped away the moment she'd said it, his attention too transfixed on her for words to stick.

She'd blown him away.

Those same feelings...

Had they ever really left him?

The music had slowed in tempo. The dance floor had filled, the children making way for the adults.

'We should dance,' he murmured.

Her chest rose, head tilted, teeth grazing over her bottom lip. 'I suppose we should...for appearances' sake.'

He breathed deeply and slowly held his hand out.

Equally slowly, she stretched hers out to meet his. The pads of her fingers pressed into his palm. Tingles shot through his skin. His fingers closed over them.

On the crowded dance floor, he placed his hands loosely on her hips. Her hands rested lightly on his shoulders. A delicate waft of her perfume filtered through his airwaves.

He clenched his jaw and purposely kept his gaze focused above her head.

They moved slowly in tempo with the music, their bodies a whisper away from touching...

'When did you take your tie off?' Livia murmured when she couldn't take the tension that had sprung between them any longer.

She'd been trying very hard not to breathe. Every inhalation sent Massimo's familiar musky heat and the citrus undertones of his cologne darting into her airwaves. Her skin vibrated with awareness, her senses uncoiling, tiny springs straining towards the man whose hands hardly touched her hips. She could feel the weight in them though, piercing through her skin.

Caramel eyes slowly drifted down to meet her gaze.

The music beating around them reduced to a burr.

The breath of space between them closed. The tips of her breasts brushed against the top of his flat stomach. The weight of his hands increased in pressure.

Heat pulsed deep in her pelvis.

Her hands crept without conscious thought over his shoulder blades. Heart beating hard, her fingers found his neck…her palms pressed against it.

His right hand caressed slowly up her back. She shivered at the darts of sensation rippling through her.

Distantly, she was aware the song they were dancing to had finished.

His left hand drew across her lower back and gradually pulled her so close their bodies became flush.

Her cheek pressed into his shoulder. She could feel the heavy thuds of his heart. They matched the beats of hers.

His mouth pressed into the top of her head. The warmth of his ragged breath whispered in the strands of her hair. Her lungs had stopped functioning. Not a hitch of air went into them.

A finger brushed a lock of her hair.

She closed her eyes.

The lock was caught and wound in his fingers.

She turned her cheek and pressed her mouth to his throat…

A body slammed into them. Words, foreign to her drumming ears but unmistakably words of apology, were gabbled.

They pulled apart.

There was a flash of bewilderment in Massimo's eyes she knew must be mirrored in hers before he blinked it away.

A song famous at parties all around the world was now playing. The floor was packed with bodies all joining in with the accompanying dance. Even the passed-out children had woken up to join in with it.

And she'd been oblivious. They both had.

Continue reading
A PASSIONATE REUNION IN FIJI
Michelle Smart

Available next month
www.millsandboon.co.uk

LET'S TALK
Romance

For exclusive extracts, competitions
and special offers, find us online:

 facebook.com/millsandboon

@MillsandBoon

@MillsandBoonUK

Get in touch on 01413 063232

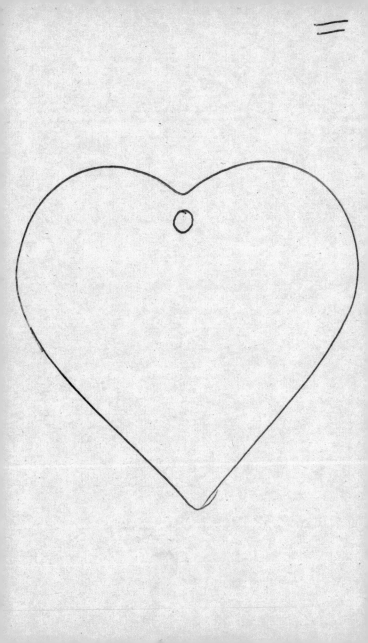